1636

SEAS OF
FORTUNE

THE RING OF FIRE SERIES

1632 by Eric Flint

1633 by Eric Flint & David Weber

1634: The Baltic War by Eric Flint & David Weber

1634: The Galileo Affair by Eric Flint & Andrew Dennis

1634: The Bavarian Crisis by Eric Flint & Virginia DeMarce

1634: The Ram Rebellion by Eric Flint with Virginia DeMarce

1635: The Cannon Law by Eric Flint & Andrew Dennis

1635: The Dreeson Incident by Eric Flint & Virginia DeMarce

1635: The Tangled Web by Virginia DeMarce

1635: The Eastern Front by Eric Flint

1635: The Papal Stakes by Eric Flint & Charles E. Gannon

1636: The Saxon Uprising

1636: The Kremlin Games by Eric Flint & Gorg Huff & Paula Goodlett

1636: The Devil's Opera by Eric Flint & David Carrico

1636: Seas of Fortune by Iver P. Cooper

Grantville Gazette ed. by Eric Flint

Grantville Gazette II ed. by Eric Flint

Grantville Gazette III ed. by Eric Flint

Grantville Gazette IV ed. by Eric Flint

Grantville Gazette V ed. by Eric Flint

Grantville Gazette VI ed. by Eric Flint

Ring of Fire ed. by Eric Flint

Ring of Fire II ed. by Eric Flint

Ring of Fire III ed. by Eric Flint

Time Spike by Eric Flint & Marilyn Kosmatka

For a complete list of Baen books and to purchase all of these titles in e-book format, please go to www.baen.com.

1636

SEAS OF
FORTUNE

IVER P. COOPER

1636: SEAS OF FORTUNE

This is a work of fiction. All the characters and events portrayed in this book are fictional, and any resemblance to real people or incidents is purely coincidental.

Note: Several of the stories in the "Stretching Out" section of this book were published, in slightly different form, in the online magazine *Grantville Gazette*, as follows:

"Stretching Out, Part One: Second Starts," *Grantville Gazette*, Volume 11, © 2007 by Iver P. Cooper; "Stretching Out, Part Two, Amazon Adventure," *Grantville Gazette*, Volume 12, © 2007 by Iver P. Cooper; "Stretching Out, Part Three: Maria's Mission," *Grantville Gazette*, Volume 14 © 2007 by Iver P. Cooper; "Stretching Out, Part Four: Beyond the Line," *Grantville Gazette*, Volume 16; © 2008 by Iver Cooper; "Stretching Out, Part Five: Riding the Tiger," *Grantville Gazette*, Volume 18, © 2008 by Iver P. Cooper; "Stretching Out, Part Six: King of the Jungle," *Grantville Gazette*, Volume 21, © 2009 by Iver P. Cooper.

Map 1 © 2014 by Iver P. Cooper and Gorg Huff, used by permission. Maps 2–6 © 2014 by Iver P. Cooper.

The sources for the epigraphs for the stories in the Rising Sun section of this book are given in footnotes.

A Baen Books Original

Baen Publishing Enterprises
P.O. Box 1403
Riverdale, NY 10471
www.baen.com

ISBN: 978-1-4516-3939-1

Cover art by Tom Kidd

First Baen printing, January 2014

Distributed by Simon & Schuster
1230 Avenue of the Americas
New York, NY 10020

10 9 8 7 6 5 4 3 2 1

Pages by Joy Freeman (www.pagesbyjoy.com)
Printed in the United States of America

To my family: my parents Morris and Lillie Cooper,
my wife Lee, and my children Jason and Louise.

I thank Eric Flint for giving me the opportunity to
participate in the development of the 1632 Universe.

Preface

The stories of *1636: Seas of Fortune* are set in the alternate history universe created by Eric Flint, and introduced in his novel *1632*. These stories reveal that the Ring of Fire, by hurling the town of Grantville from 2000 West Virginia to 1631 Germany, is affecting history in places as far away as Brazil and Japan.

This isn't a novel, and it isn't a traditional short story anthology. It's a braid, or, more precisely, two braids. The first, "Stretching Out," presents seven short stories dealing with characters who find adventure on the other side of the Atlantic, in South America and the Caribbean. The stories are linked by recurring characters and locales, and overarching themes.

The second, "Rising Sun," presents another five linked short stories that reveal how the Japanese respond to the Ring of Fire.

The braided story format allowed me some flexibility that I wouldn't have in a novel; stories can overlap in time, and follow the activities of different lead characters. That works well for covering the branching of events natural to alternate history. On the other hand, braided stories have more of a sense of unity than a mere collection of short stories.

I hope you like reading it as much as I enjoyed writing it!

Iver Cooper

Contents

1636

SEAS OF
FORTUNE

Stretching Out

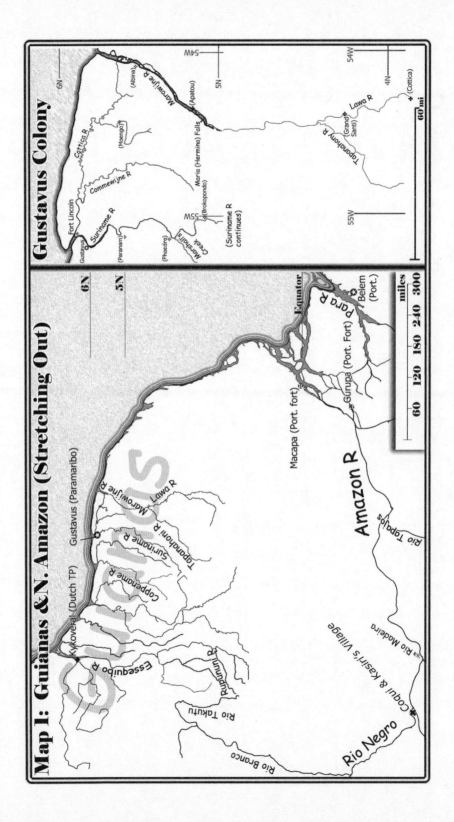

Map 1: Guianas & N. Amazon (Stretching Out)

Gustavus Colony

Amazon Adventure

Late 1632 to Fall 1634

Belém do Pará, Estado do Maranhão (northern Brazil), Late 1632

Like an arrow falling from heaven, the cormorant plunged into the waters of the Pará. For a few seconds it was lost from sight. Then it emerged triumphantly, a fish in its mouth. Two gulls spotted the capture and winged over, no doubt hoping to snatch the meal away. Before they could carry out their designs, the cormorant gave the fish a little toss in the air, and swallowed it. The would-be hijackers swerved and headed out toward the sea.

Henrique Pereira da Costa, watching this drama from the docks of Belém do Pará, hoped that his own dive into the unknown would be as successful.

He heard a cough, and turned. It was his servant, Maurício. "We're packed and ready to go."

"May I see the fabulous map again?" Maurício asked. Wordlessly, Henrique passed it over.

Maurício studied it carefully, then handed it back. "It's got to be a fake, sir. I asked around, and no one has explored beyond where this river"—he pointed to the Rio Negro—"comes into the Amazon."

"M-m-my family has assured me that I can stake my v-v-very life upon its accuracy." Henrique had an unfortunate tendency to

5

stammer under stress. It had been mild at first, but had worsened after his parents' deaths.

"Trouble is, you *will* be staking your life on it . . . while they're home, safe and sound in Lisbon." Henrique was the da Costa family's factor in Belém, which lay near the mouth of the Pará, the river forming the southern edge of the Amazon Delta.

"Bu—um—bu . . ." Henrique's stammer was one of the reasons he was stuck here in Belém, rather than enjoying the high life of a successful plutocrat in the capital. Instead of collecting expensive artwork and mistresses, he was looking for *drogas do sertão*—products of the hinterland—that might one day have a market in Europe. Most recently, he was pursuing a strange material that his relatives called "rubber."

"Speak English, or Dutch, sir, no one here will care." Henrique's stutter disappeared when he spoke a foreign language. Even one of the Indian jawbreakers.

Henrique nodded. "But there are those rumors . . ."

"Right. Like the Seven Cities of Cibola. Or El Dorado and the Lake of Manoa. Or the Kingdom of Prester John. Or—"

"Will you let me finish?" Henrique glowered at Maurício until the servant inclined his head in acquiescence. "Rumors of a town called Grantville, which has visited us from the future."

"If true, showing poor judgment on their part."

"Well, even if the story is false, I have my orders. Find the rubber trees, teach the natives how to tap it."

"And your family knows how to tap it, even though they don't know where the trees are?" Maurício's eyebrows flickered.

"Perhaps they found the trees in the Indies already? Or perhaps it's more knowledge from the future."

"Coming aboard, Maurício?"

Maurício jumped into the canoe. The boat rocked for a moment, then steadied. Maurício nervously checked to make sure that his neck pouch hadn't slipped off in mid-leap. What it held was more precious than gold: his letter of manumission, signed years ago by Henrique.

Maurício had been born into slavery. His mother had been one of the housemaids employed by Henrique's parents, in Bahia. In his childhood, he had been one of Henrique's play-mates. Henrique's handwriting was a disaster—sometimes, even

Henrique couldn't read it—and Maurício had been trained to be his scribe.

Henrique's father, Sérgio, was a physician, the usual choice of occupation for a da Costa who was temperamentally unsuited for the business world. He had one of the largest libraries in Bahia, and it was Maurício's second home. Maurício mastered Latin, and Greek, and even Hebrew. Not that there was much need for any of those languages in the rough-hewn society of Brazil.

Sérgio's will had instructed Henrique to make Maurício a *curtado*, a slave who had the right to earn his freedom by paying a set price. Henrique instead freed Maurício outright. "I hope you can now be my friend, instead of my slave," he had said. The words were burnt into Maurício's memory, as deeply as a slaver's brand had bitten into his mother's skin.

The canoe, perhaps forty feet long, had eight Indian rowers and a "bow man." The middle of the boat was roofed over with palm fronds to provide a somewhat flimsy shelter. Henrique was glad to be on his way. In town, his stuttering was a recurring source of embarrassment. In the wilderness, he could relax.

Henrique knew the Amazon about as well as a white man could. He was a *criollo*, a man born in Brazil but of European descent, and he had been among the first settlers in Belém. Henrique had frequently canoed up or down the main river and its tributaries, and he had lived in some of the native villages for months at a time. Maurício occasionally joined Henrique, but mostly remained in Belém to look after Henrique's interests there.

It started to drizzle. Maurício held out his hand. "I thought you said it was the dry season." It was an old joke between them.

Henrique delivered the customary punchline. "The difference is, in the dry season it rains every day, and in the wet season, all day."

Whether in appreciation or mockery of the witticism, the drizzle became a shower. Henrique dived for the shelter, Maurício following.

"I don't understand," Henrique muttered.

"Huh?" Maurício had been watching a giant river otter playing in the water. He looked up. "Don't understand what?"

"Why none of the Indians we have questioned have heard of

the rubber tree. I would have sworn that they knew every tree within ten miles of their villages." Henrique and Maurício had visited the tribes of the lower Xingu River: the Tacunyape, the Shipaya, the Juruna. The explorers had been shown some trees which produced sap of one kind of another, but none of them matched the description of the rubber trees.

"So it doesn't grow on the Xingu. Perhaps we'll have better luck on the Tapajós."

"We're in the shaded area of the map, where the tree is supposed to be found."

"Perhaps we don't know what to ask for."

"We asked them to show us a tree which weeps when it is cut. Because, uh..."

"I know. Because the first letter from Lisbon said that rubber is also known as *caoutchouc*. From the Quechua words *caa,* 'wood,' and *ochue,* 'tears,' that is—"

Henrique finished the thought. "The 'weeping tree.'"

"A lot of good a Quechua name does you," Maurício said. "It's the language of the Incas, who are, what, two thousand miles west of here?"

"Even if it's a rare tree, you would think that some Indian would try cutting it down," Henrique said. "See if it was good for building a dugout canoe, or at least for firewood. And then see it bleed."

Maurício brushed an inquisitive fly off the document. "Sure, but that might have happened a century ago. And they don't remember it, because they don't use its, what's that word... latex...for anything. The latex is old news."

His expression brightened. "Of course, they might still know of the tree. Maybe they use its leaves to thatch their huts. Or—"

"Um..."

"Or, they eat its seeds. Or—"

"Uh-uummm..."

"I know, it's sacred to their Jaguar God, so it's forbidden to speak to strangers about it."

"Maurício!"

"Yes?"

"Shut up."

Henrique brooded. Clearly, he thought, merely asking for a "weeping tree" wasn't good enough. But Henrique's superiors, or the mysterious up-timers, had provided more than just the map. He also had received drawings of the rubber tree, and its leaves and seeds. And even a sample of rubber. So he had thought he had *some* chance of success.

"Shit!"

Maurício gave him a wary look. "What's wrong?"

"I have been going about this all wrong. The drawings are meaningless to the Indians we've been talking to; their artwork is too different.

"What we need to do is make a model of the leaves and seeds. Out of clay, or mud, or something. Life size, if possible."

Maurício waited for Henrique to continue.

Henrique crossed his arms.

"Oh," said Maurício. "'We' means 'me.'"

It had taken months, but they found the trees, trained and recruited rubber tappers, and went to work. The rubber tapping operation was nothing like a sugar plantation. The rubber trees were widely separated, perhaps one or two in an acre, and paths, often circuitous, had to be hacked out to connect them. Each tapper—*seringueiro*—developed several routes, and walked one route each day. A route might connect fifty to a hundred trees.

Henrique and Maurício made periodic trips to collect the rubber, and bring the *seringueiros* their pay, usually in the form of trade goods. And they also took advantage of the opportunity to spot-check that they were following instructions.

"Are we there yet?" Maurício asked.

"Almost. Yes. Pull in over there." It was a short walk to the trail.

Maurício stood quietly, studying the man-high herringbone pattern carved on the nearest rubber tree.

Henrique joined him. "Something wrong?"

"I was just thinking, it's like the Amazon writ small."

"What do you mean?"

"Look. You have the diagonal cuts. Those are like the tributaries. And they feed into the vertical channel, the main river. First on one side, then on the other."

Henrique considered Maurício's metaphor. "And the cup at the bottom, where the latex collects, that's the ocean." He walked over to the trunk, and felt the cuts. "We have a good tapper, here. He's getting flow, but the cuts are still pretty shallow. We won't know for sure until next year, but I don't think he's harmed the tree significantly."

"We really need something better than knives and hatchets for making the cuts the right depth."

"I agree. In fact I said so in the letter that went home with the last shipment. But I have no idea what sort of tool would do the job."

"Are we done here?"

"Well . . . I want to talk to this *seringueiro*. Perhaps give him a little bonus. Word will get around, and the other tappers will try to emulate him."

They waited for the tapper assigned to this route to appear. Even though they knew the direction from which he would be coming, and were watching and listening for him, they had little warning. One moment, there was nothing but the green of the forest, and the next, he was standing ten feet away, appraising them.

They greeted him, and he relaxed. They offered the Indian some water, and he took a quick swig and set to work. He deftly cut a new set of diagonal grooves, slightly below the ones cut the time before, and rubbed his finger over them.

Henrique complimented him on his work, and handed him a string of glass beads. The *seringueiro* held them up in the sunlight, laughed, and fastened them around his upper arm. He gave the two Belémistas a wave and headed on to the next tree on his route.

The visitors returned to their canoe and paddled on. That evening, they were able to witness the climax of the *seringueiros'* daily routine.

"Here, look," one said, handing them a large gourd. He had made a second round of his trees in the afternoon, collecting the latex from the cups. Henrique dipped his finger in the milk to test its consistency, and passed it on to Maurício. Maurício rolled his eyes, but dutifully accepted the vessel. He made a pretense of drinking from it, which greatly amused the Indian.

It was time for the next step. The Indian dipped a wooden paddle inside, coating it with the "milk." He then held it in the smoke of a fire.

"This is exciting," Maurício said. "Like watching paint dry."

The first coat of latex slowly hardened into rubber, and the tapper put the rubber-coated paddle back in the gourd. He repeated the process, building up the mass, until it had reached the desired thickness for a rubber "biscuit."

He then pried it off the paddle, and handed it to Henrique. Henrique nodded to Maurício, who handed the Indian some brightly dyed cloth.

"Time to call it a night," Henrique said. Maurício agreed.

Henrique pointed. "There's a good place for you to hang up your bed." Maurício walked over, hammock in hand, to the trees that Henrique had marked out. He tied it to one trunk, and was ready to fasten it to the other, when he suddenly stopped short. A moment later, he was hurriedly untying the hammock.

Henrique was laughing.

"Very funny," Maurício commented. "I haven't been in the rainforest as often as you, but I don't fall for the same trick twice." One of the trees in question was notorious because it often served as a nest for a breed of ants of malignant disposition. It was commonly used in practical jokes on greenhorns.

Maurício sniffed haughtily. "As punishment for your crime, I am going to read you the poem I wrote last night."

The men were getting bored. And irritable. There had been two knife fights a day for the past week. Bento Maciel Parente, the Younger, knew something had to be done.

"Time for a *coreira*," he announced. His people were delighted. They so enjoyed hunting. As they readied their canoes, one man accidentally knocked down another. What a few hours earlier would have led to another duel, was laughed off. Clearly, Bento had made the right decision.

Bento had scarred himself like a native warrior, but he was no friend to the Indians. Like his father and his brother, he was a slaver.

It took a bit of time to find a suitable Indian village. At last they found one which, according to his scouts, was in the throes of a festival. The kind that involved imbibing large quantities of fermented drink laced with hallucinogens.

Bento watched as one villager after another collapsed to the ground. At last he waved his men forward. Their first target was the place where the Indians had stacked their bows. They cut the bow strings and threw the weapons into the fire. Then they started shooting. The snores were replaced by screams.

Bento nodded approvingly. "Kill the fathers first, enjoy the virgins afterward," he reminded his band. They didn't need the reminder; and half their work was done already. They laughed as they chased down the women.

The da Costa family had helped finance some of the sugar mills in Bahia, and it made arrangements for the sugar boats, en route to Lisbon, to stop in Belém and see if Henrique had any rubber for pickup. Those ships came up the coast monthly ... assuming they weren't picked off by Dutch privateers near Recife. And the captains didn't mind the stopover too much; it wasn't out of their way and they could take on food and water.

The visits had increased Henrique's popularity in Belém. The town mostly exported tobacco, cotton, and dye wood, but not enough to warrant regular contact. There was some sugarcane grown in the area, but it was used locally to make liquor. So Belém was a backwater compared to Recife. Before rubber tapping began, a whole year could go by without a vessel coming into port.

Henrique was under orders to expand production, but to do that he needed to find more rubber trees, and more Indians to milk them. He hoped that the town leaders, who were mostly plantation owners, would help him now. They had looked down on him for years as a *mateiro*, a woodsman, and a small-time merchant. The stuttering hadn't helped, either.

"Henrique, I am astonished," said Francisco de Sousa. He was the president of the Municipal Chamber of Belém. "I never would have expected a bachelor, in Belém no less, to have such an elegant dinner presentation."

"Th-th-thank you, *Cavaleiro* Francisco. It is in large part my late m-m-mother's legacy."

"I particularly like your centerpiece," his wife added.

"It is a family ... heirloom." The piece in question was a massive flowerpot.

Henrique had hired extra servants for the occasion. They brought in one serving after another. First came a *mingau* porridge, followed by a *farinha*-sprinkled *pirarucu*, caught earlier that day. There were Brazil nuts, palm hearts, and mangoes, too. The meal ended with a sweet tapioca tortilha.

"So what are you doing with those Indians?"

Henrique had known this question would come, and had rehearsed his answer with Maurício, to make sure he could deliver it smoothly.

"There is a tree that produces a milky sap. They tap the tree, a bit as you would a pine tree to collect turpentine. The sap hardens into a substance which is waterproof, and can stretch and . . . bounce."

Grrr, Henrique thought. *I almost made it through my spiel. I hate B's.*

"Bounce?"

"Wait." He left, and returned with a rubber ball. He dropped it, and it returned to his waiting hand, much to their amazement.

"So, there's a market for this?"

"Somewhat. The rubber can be used to make hats and b-b-boots to protect you from the rain. And I understand that it can be applied in some way to ordinary cloth so that the fabric stays dry, but I don't how that's done.

"I could produce and sell more, if only I had enough tappers."

"Perhaps I can help you there. I can demand labor from the Indians at the *aldeia* of Cameta. We just need to agree on a price."

"What are you doing here, B-B-Bento?" Henrique had seen the slaver, followed by several of his buddies, saunter into the village clearing. Henrique kept his hand near the hilt of his *facão*.

"Just paying a friendly visit to these Indian friends of yours, H-H-Henrique," Bento said, imitating Henrique's stutter as usual.

"You've been making life difficult for folks, Henrique. I hear you're paying your tappers ten *varas* of cloth a month. It's making it tough to get Indians to do real work."

"Ten *varas* isn't much, Bento." A *vara* was about thirty-three inches. The largesse had not entirely been of Henrique's choosing, although he was known to be sympathetic to the Indians; he had specific instructions about wages from Lisbon.

"It is when the Indians are accustomed to working for four. Or three. Or two."

"Or none, in your case."

"Yes, well, it's my natural charisma. Anyway, dear Henrique, you want to watch you don't end up like Friar Cristovão de Lisboa." Cristovão had preached a sermon against settlers who abused the Indians, and later someone had shot at him.

"I assure you that I am extremely careful." Henrique's own men had in the meantime flanked Bento's party. Bento affected not to notice, but several of his men were shifting their eyes back and forth, trying to keep track of Henrique's allies.

"So I thought I'd have a palaver with the big chief here. Mebbe he's got some enemies he'd like to ransom." If a Portuguese bought a prisoner condemned to ritual execution, he was entitled to the former captive's life; that is, he had acquired a slave. An "Indian of the cord."

"You know the Tapajós don't ransom. How many times have you tried this?"

"Aw, can't hurt to ask. And look at this bee-yoo-tiful cross I brought the chief, as a present. Hey chief, you want this? It would look real sweet right in the center of your village."

The chief gave Henrique a questioning look. Henrique shook his head, fractionally.

"Sorry, no," said the chief. "It is too beautiful for our poor village, it would make everything else look drab."

Henrique thought, *Good for you*. The cross was a scam. If the cross fell, or was allowed to fall into disrepair, then it was evidence that the tribe opposed the Catholic Church, and war upon it would be just. Leading, of course, to the enslavement of the survivors. The Tapajós were a strong tribe, and the slavers so far had been leery of attacking them, but that could change.

"Well, I can see I'm not welcome here today," said Bento. "I'll go make my own camp. But remember, Henrique, there's always tomorrow."

Whump! Henrique ducked, just in time, and took cover. He looked around, trying to spot the shooter. As he did so, one part of his mind wondered what had been shot at him. The sound hadn't been quite that of a bullet, or an arrow, or even a slingshot. More like a grenade exploding, although that made no sense at all.

It happened again. *Whump!* Suddenly, he realized that the Indian tappers were completely ignoring the sound. With the exception of one, who was laughing his head off.

Henrique rose cautiously. "What's making that sound?" Laughing Boy pointed upward at the fruits hanging from the rubber tree, and then down at the ground. It was thus that Henrique discovered just how the rubber tree spreads its seeds.

His superiors in Lisbon would be very pleased. Henrique had received precise instructions to collect seeds, if he found them. Henrique set the Indians to work.

Belém do Pará, Early 1634 (In Rainy Season)

Henrique fumbled with the door, and stepped into his home. He stumbled. Looking down, he saw that he had tripped over a cracked vase.

It was no ordinary vase. It was Henrique's magnificent flower pot. When it wasn't gracing his dining room, it reposed in a case in his foyer. His housekeeper, apparently, had taken it out to clean it, dropped it, and then fled the house.

Henrique blanched. His reaction had nothing to do with the cost of the piece, or even its sentimental value.

Did she see the secret compartment? he wondered.

He was hopeful that she hadn't. He studied it carefully. What he found wasn't good. The vase wasn't merely cracked; a piece had broken off and been reset. Lifting it off again, he could see into the compartment. Unless the woman were completely devoid of curiosity, she would have looked inside. And what she would have seen would have been far too revealing. A *b'samin* spice box. A small goblet. And, most damning of all, a miniature *hanukkiya*. The housekeeper was a *caboclo*, a half-Indian, and had certainly received enough religious instruction at an *aldeia* to know what that signified.

It was the *hanukkiya*, a silver candelabra, that was missing. And that led to some fevered speculations. Had she taken it as evidence, to show to the authorities? If so, his hours were numbered.

Henrique thrust his *facão* into his belt sheath, and barred the door. He loaded a musket, and set it close by.

The soldiers would be sent to arrest him. There was no inquisitor in Belém, but an inspector would be sent from Lisbon. Henrique would be questioned, tortured. He would be called upon to repent his heresy, and he would refuse. Eventually they would classify him as a recalcitrant, and the Inquisition would recommend his execution. He would don the black *sanbenito*, tastefully decorated with pictures of flames and devils, and be paraded to the place of execution. He would be tied to the stake and—

Wait a moment. Perhaps she was planning to melt it down, knowing that he wouldn't dare report a theft?

Of course, even if cupidity had triumphed over piety, he was in trouble. Unless she could convert it to an innocuous ingot herself, she would have to recruit an assistant, who might alert the Church. And even if she didn't arouse any suspicion, life wouldn't be the same. She might blackmail him, or denounce him if he did something to displease her.

As a secret Jew, Henrique had known that his life might come to this turning point. It was time to get moving.

There was a knock at the door. Henrique put the musket on full cock. "Who's there?"

"Maurício."

"Are you alone?"

"Yes." His voice sounded puzzled, not nervous or fearful.

"Bide a moment." Henrique uncocked the weapon, and set it down again. He unbarred the door, took a quick look at the street past Maurício, and pulled his servant into the room.

"What—"

"Bar the door again," Henrique said. "I am glad you returned in time." Maurício had been off on an errand to Cameta.

Maurício fiddled with the door. "I hope you have a good explanation."

Henrique started throwing provisions into a sack. Cassava bread. Beef jerky. Acai fruit. "I have to flee for my life. Actually, we both do."

"What's wrong?" Maurício asked. Henrique told him.

Maurício raised his eyebrows. "I certainly don't want to see you get burned as a heretic. But why exactly do I have to flee? Can't you just, oh, tie me up so I can swear that I wasn't complicit in your crimes?"

"Sure. But they would probably put you to the torture anyway, you being my long-faithful servant and all.

"Even if they didn't, the Church will seize my assets. And where would that put you?"

Maurício blanched. Under Portuguese law, an ex-slave could be re-enslaved by the creditors if his former master went into debt.

"Is there a ship about to leave for Lisbon?" Maurício asked. "We could board it, and outrun the bad news. Once in the city, we could lose ourselves in the crowd, perhaps sail someplace outside the reach of the Inquisition. France, perhaps."

Henrique shook his head. "A sugar boat came through two weeks ago." They didn't have a regular schedule, but they came up the coast once a month, on average. There was no reason for another to appear within the next week.

Henrique pried up a floorboard, probed underneath with a stick. In Amazonia, you didn't search a dark opening with your hand. Not unless you were fond of snakes. He pulled out a pouch, which held money and jewels. He might need to bribe someone to make good his escape.

"Could we reach Pernambuco? Or Palmares?" There was a Dutch enclave in Pernambuco. And, farther south, in Palmares, there was a *mocambo* of runaway slaves.

"We'd never make it by sea; both the wind and the current would be against us." That was, in fact, why Maranhão had been made a separate state, reporting directly to Lisbon, in 1621; it was too difficult to communicate with Salvador do Bahia in the south. Coasters did go as far south as São Luis, the capital of Maranhão, but taking one would just delay the inevitable. The authorities in Belém would send word to São Luis, and the latter was too small a place to hide for long.

"And the overland route is completely unexplored. Nor would the map from the future aid us there."

Maurício had started collecting his own possessions. Mostly books. "Then why not sail north? There are English, and Dutch and French, in Guiana and the Caribbean. We might even get picked up en route by a Dutch cruiser."

Henrique was sure he was forgetting something important. Ah, yes, a hammock. You didn't want to sleep on the ground in the rainforest. Not if you didn't like things crawling over your skin. Or burrowing into it. Hammocks were a native invention, which the Portuguese had adopted. And that reminded Henrique of a few other native items he needed. He gathered those up, too.

"Henrique, are you going to answer me?"

"Going north is what the garrison would expect us to do. And before you ask, they would be equally on guard against the possibility that friends would hide us, and smuggle us onto the next sugar boat to Lisbon."

"So, what are we going to do? Did the people from the future teach your family how we might turn ourselves invisible?"

"In a way. We will flee into the Amazon, lose ourselves among the trees of the vast rainforest. Go native. At least for a time."

Maurício wailed. "But I'll run out of reading matter!"

Captain Diogo Soares shook his head. His good friend, Henrique Pereira da Costa, a Judaizer! He could scarcely credit it. Perhaps it was a mistake, a dreadful mistake. Although Henrique's flight was certainly evidence of guilt.

Diogo leaned back in his chair. Even an innocent man, if he thought he was to be the target of an accusation of heresy, might flee. Especially one with enemies, who might try to influence the inquisitors. Everyone knew that Henrique had enemies. The younger Bento Maciel Parente, for example.

The captain's superiors thought that Henrique had boarded a southbound coaster. A fishing boat had been commandeered, and was heading down to São Luis already, to stop what boats it found, and also warn the authorities. The governor of Maranhão could also send a *guarda costa* back up the coast, and make sure that Henrique hadn't tried sailing north, to Guiana.

Nonetheless, Diogo's sense of duty demanded that he consider other possibilities. Such as Henrique taking refuge with one of the Indian tribes. One of the Tapajós tribes, perhaps. It was fortunate for Henrique that Bento was off on a slaving expedition, as Bento would be delighted to bring Henrique out of the rainforest, dead or alive. Probably the former.

But Diogo was obligated to cover that avenue of escape. Exercising appropriate discretion as to who he sent, of course. "Sergeant, call in all the soldiers who are on punishment detail."

In due course, the sergeant returned, followed by six soldiers whose principal point of similarity was a hangdog expression.

"Ah, yes, I recognize all of you. And remember your records. Which of you *degredados* is senior?"

One of them slowly raised his hand. The others edged away from him.

"You are Bernaldo, right? I remember you, now." Bernaldo winced. "You will be in command of this little patrol. You are hereby promoted to corporal in token of your good fortune. You are to go out into the Amazon and arrest Henrique Pereira da Costa, who has been accused of heresy."

"But how will we find him, sir?"

"Did your mother drop you on your head when you were an infant? You are looking for a lone white man in a canoe. Or perhaps in one of the Indian villages. Or wandering a trail. It shouldn't take long to locate him. Sail to Forte do Gurupá first, put them on alert." The fort, which guarded the south channel of the Amazon Delta, had been captured from the Dutch in 1623.

"How long should we look for him?"

"If you come back in less than six months, you better have him with you. Or you will be on your way to where Brazil and Maranhãos send *their* undesirables. Angola."

They slowly filed out. "Good," said Diogo to the sergeant. "That solves more problems than one."

"I still think we should make a sail," Maurício said. "It's not easy for the two of us to row upstream. With a sail, we can take advantage of the trade wind." He let go of the paddle for a moment, opened and closed his hands a few times to limber them up, and took hold of the wood once again.

"And you brought the cloth, after all. You can cut some branches and vines for the mast and stays."

Henrique shook his head. "A sail will be visible from a great distance. And the natives don't use sails."

"Not before Europeans came. But a few do."

"Not enough, just those who are in service. It would still draw attention. Even if the searchers didn't think it was our sail, they would approach the canoe, to ask if we had been seen, or perhaps to recruit more rowers. If they got close enough—" Henrique drew his finger across his neck.

"Then why don't we just head upriver with the tide, and lie doggo in a cove the rest of the time. We need to conserve our strength."

"It will be easier soon. We'll leave this channel, then cut across the *várzea*, the flooded forest."

Henrique wiped his forehead. "We're lucky that we had to make our escape during the rainy season. If this had happened a few months later, we would have been limited to the regular channels, and they could catch us more easily.

"And there's less of a current in the *várzea*, too."

"Also, less in the way of anything to eat. The land animals have fled to high ground, and the fish are hiding in the deep water."

"We have enough food to get us to a friendly village."

"And another thing. It's easier to get lost in the *várzea*."

"I never get lost."

"Okay, we're lost."

The good news was that Henrique and Maurício had made it back to the main channel of the Amazon. There, it was hard to get lost; you always knew which direction was upstream.

The bad news was that they had emerged, closer than Henrique had planned, to the fort at Gurupa. They had to worry about being spotted, not just by Portuguese troops, but also by the Indians who traded with the fort. They might pass the word on. And they would be a lot harder to avoid.

"You, there!" shouted Corporal Bernaldo. He was addressing a lanky Indian, sitting in a small canoe, and holding a fishing rod. His companion seemed to be asleep. "Speak-ee Portuguese? Have you seen a white man? About so tall?" He stood up, and gestured, almost losing his balance. The Indian shook his head.

"Ask him if he has any fish to sell?" one of his fellow soldiers prompted.

"You have fish?"

The Indian pulled up the line, showing an empty fishhook.

"Ah, let's stop wasting time, we've got plenty of rowing to do." They continued upstream, and rowed out of sight.

The apparent sleeper opened his eyes. "I thought they'd never leave," Maurício said.

Henrique smiled. "Well, you were a cool one."

"Cool? I'd have shit in my pants ... if you had let me wear my pants, that is."

Henrique and Maurício had hidden their European clothes, and Henrique had painted himself with black *genipapo*. The vegetable dye not only made him look like a native, at least from a distance, but also protected him from insects. Both wore loincloths, which observers would assume was a concession to European morality, but which would in fact conceal that they didn't follow the native custom of having their pubic hair plucked.

Now that the pursuit was in front of them, they could take it easy for a while. But not *too* easy. There were other soldiers, after all.

Corporal Bernaldo and his men, with six impressed Indian rowers, strained at the oars of their longboat, fighting against the current. They had set aside their helmets and cuirasses, so their heads were bare, and their torsos protected only by leather vests. These exposed the sleeves of their shirts, cotton dyed with red *urucum*.

As the western sky darkened, they beached their craft and wandered inland, looking for a suitable campsite. They couldn't see more than fifteen feet or so in front of them, so it wasn't an easy task.

They gradually became aware of a rumbling sound.

"Sounds like rapids," João suggested.

"Perhaps it's an elephant," said António.

"There are no elephants in the Amazon."

"That's what you think."

The Indians became agitated. Bernaldo tried to figure out what they were talking about, but their excitement made them more difficult to understand, and Bernaldo was the sort of person who felt that if you couldn't understand his question, the solution was to repeat it, louder.

After a few verbal exchanges which satisfied no one, the Indians fled.

"What's was that all about?" João asked.

"What do you expect?" Bernaldo shrugged. "They're cowardly savages."

António wondered whether the natives knew something that they didn't. He also knew better than to say anything.

They could now hear a clicking sound.

"Giant crickets?"

"What's that stench? Some kind of skunk?"

Several dozen white-lipped peccaries burst out of the under-growth. They were piglike animals, each about two feet high and about fifty pounds. They weren't happy to discover the Portuguese party. Had they not been clicking their tusks to warn other creatures to get out of their way? The herd included several youngsters, which made the adults especially temperamental.

Peccaries are also known as javelinas, because of their formidable weaponry. They charged. Manuel stumbled, and was gored to death. António and João tried scooting up the same tree. António, already on edge, had made his move earlier, and made it up without difficulty, but João lost his hold, and slid down. An angry male swung its tusks, slicing open his leg. João screamed, but was able to get hold of António's outstretched hand, and was pulled out of the immediate danger. The other three soldiers were on the periphery of the peccaries' stampede, and they simply ran out of the way.

It was hours before they were reunited. The survivors congratulated each other on their narrow escape.

"Where are the Indians?" asked Bernaldo.

António was studying the riverbank. "More importantly, where's the boat?"

"*Dios mio!*" Plainly, the Indians had decided to row off without them. The five survivors were stranded in the rainforest.

Despite his perilous situation, Henrique was happy. According to his reckoning, today was a Friday, and at sunset he intended to celebrate the Sabbath as best he could. He had improvised Sabbath candles from the stems of a resinous plant, and he had allowed a fruit juice to ferment to make wine. He would have to use the concavity of a stone as a kiddush cup.

He had no bread, let alone challah, unfortunately. But he had a *tortilha* made from manioc flour, and that would have to do. The Lord would understand when Henrique uttered the prayer, "Blessed are you, Lord our God, King of the universe, who brings forth bread from the earth."

"So, do I pray, too?" Maurício asked.

"Sure."

"I don't know. Is it a good idea for me to call God's attention to us? You're a heretic, after all."

"Maurício..."

"He might send an angel to tell those idiot soldiers where to find us."

"Maurício..."

"Or perhaps he'll just hurl down a lightning bolt." Maurício darted a quick look at the threatening sky.

"Or—"

Maurício's mouth was open, and Henrique deftly thrust a *tortilha* where it would do the most good.

"Just a little farther," Henrique said.

"Are you sure you know where we're going?"

"Of course I'm sure."

"That's what you said about the 'shortcut' through the *várzea*."

"This is different." Near the mouth of the Maicuru, they had made a detour north, to find a small hill overlooking the Amazon. There, in a patch of upland forest, Henrique had prudently secreted a cache of trade goods and other useful items. Just in case he ever had to make a run for it.

"I wonder if this hill of yours should be considered an outlier of the Serra de Tumucumaque. According to that fabulous map of yours, the source of the Maicuru is there, about one hundred miles to our north.

"You know, perhaps we should backtrack to the Paru. We could cross the mountains over to the Litani, and the Maroni, and end up in what the map called French Guiana. Not that the French are there yet."

Henrique grunted. "Keep walking, I want to reach the cache by nightfall." The sun was just setting. And night came quickly in the tropics.

"Or perhaps," Maurício continued, "we should head up the Trombetas and the Mapuera, cross the Serra do Acarai to the Essequibo, to Dutch territory."

"Serra up, serra down," Henrique muttered. He stopped for a moment to adjust his *warishi*, his backpack. Maurício walked past him; they were on a well-defined game trail.

"According to the maps," Maurício said, "they can't be much more than three thousand feet high. That can't be hard, can it? Hannibal took elephants across the Alps, after all.

"Not that I've ever climbed a mountain, mind you. Unless this hill counts. Have you, Henrique? Climbed a mountain, I mean?" Henrique didn't respond.

"Henrique? Did you hear—"

"Freeze!" Henrique shouted.

Maurício froze.

"Don't move your arms, or your head. Not even a muscle. You

can move your eyes...slowly. Look a little above, and slightly to your left."

Maurício scanned the foreground. Then he saw it, a *jararaca verde*, a leaf-green-colored viper, perhaps two feet long, hanging from a branch nearby. Close enough to grab. Not that grabbing a fer-de-lance of any kind was one of the options Maurício was considering.

"Very slowly, put your left toe back...not so far...now slowly, bring your heel down, without bobbing your head. Good, now, same with the right. Keep your eyes on the snake at all times."

The fer-de-lance, untimely awakened by Maurício, was eyeing him suspiciously.

"Can't you kill the snake?" The words were mumbled; Maurício was trying not to move his jaw as he spoke.

"With a machete? While it's hanging on a tree? Not a chance. Need to club it on the neck, while it's on the ground. With a long club, mind you.

"Keep up your little dance backward, please."

Gradually, Maurício inched away from the serpent.

"Okay, you can relax."

Maurício fainted. Henrique poured a bit of water on his lips and forehead. After a few minutes, Maurício revived. "How did I miss it?"

"In the rainforest, you can see perhaps fifteen feet ahead. But you can cover that distance in ten seconds, even at a walk. You can't afford to relax your vigilance, even for a moment."

Maurício, his spirits somewhat restored, harrumphed. "You're just looking for an excuse to keep me from talking."

Bento grinned. "So dear Henrique is a pig-loving Jew. Well, it is my duty, my *sacred* duty as a son of the Church, to bring him home and teach him the error of his ways. Or perhaps the other way around, yes?"

His fellow thugs laughed. Bento had just returned to Belém from a slaving run down the Tocantins, and in town there was much gossip about Henrique's disappearance, and the stymied search for him.

"We'll take three boats, I think. Might as well do a little enlistment of native labor, while we're up the Amazon. Be ready to leave at the crack of dawn tomorrow."

✧   ✧   ✧

"Sing, Maurício."

"I thought you didn't like my singing."

"I don't. But you have a loud voice, and that's what we need right now."

"How come?"

"We've never been in this part of the *sertão*. This is a well-marked trail, almost certainly leading to a village. We want them to know we're coming."

"But wouldn't the Indians sense us? Being wise in the ways of the bush, and all."

"Let me rephrase that. We want them to know that we know that they know we're coming."

"I am not sure that was an improvement. You are as clear as a philosopher."

"If they think we're trying to sneak up on them, they'll think we are up to no good. And either flee, or prepare an ambush for us. Whereas, if we approach them openly, they'll assume we've come to trade."

A couple of dogs came down the trail and barked at Henrique and Maurício. They stopped, and let the dogs sniff them. Then they continued walking, and the dogs, still barking occasionally, followed.

The village was just a circle of conical huts. Various animals milled about the central clearing, but no people were there. Occasionally, a head would look out of a hut, then pull back in.

"Hey, that was a pretty girl, over there," Maurício exclaimed. "Hope she comes out again."

And, a moment later, "Ugh, look at that crone. Hope she's not the mom, wouldn't want her for a mother-in-law."

Henrique didn't respond; he was studying the village. "Maurício, we need to leave. Now."

"What about trading for food? What about getting better acquainted with the young ladies?"

"Didn't you notice? There are only women in this village."

"Hey, you're right. Wow, *we* found the village of the Amazon women warriors. The ones Father Cristobal de Acuna wrote about. And Sir Walter Raleigh. There are only two of us, so we will certainly enjoy favors of their queens. For a whole month. And—"

Henrique grabbed Maurício by both shoulders and forcibly rotated him about-face. "What it means, Maurício, is that their men are off on the warpath, and we really, really don't want to be here when they come back."

Henrique and Maurício made it safely back to their canoe, and pressed on. They felt safe enough, at this point, to erect a makeshift sail, so they could travel more quickly. It didn't seem likely that they were still being pursued.

A few days later, they saw a large canoe overtaking them from the south. They hastily took down their mast, but it was a false alarm. The canoe was crewed by Manao Indians. The Manao were great traders, criss-crossing the central Amazon. The Portuguese had first encountered them on the Solimoes, the "River of Poisons"—so-called because the tribes there used poison arrows. Rumor had it that the Manao came from far to the north, way up the Rio Negro, but no Portuguese had visited their homeland.

Henrique raised his hands, palms open, signaling peaceful intent. The Manao greeted him, and, politely, asked his business in their region. He said that he was looking to trade and, perhaps find a path to the Great Water in the north. He gave them a few beads, and they offered him some *cachiri* to drink.

This particular trading party was returning from a run up the Madeira, one of the tributaries on the right bank of the Amazon. That night, Henrique, Maurício and the Manao camped together, on an island, and Henrique questioned them about what tribes lived along the Madeira, and what goods they had to offer.

Maurício had other concerns. He eagerly asked them whether they had seen any women warriors there, and they told him that it was a nonsensical idea. "No more *cachiri* for you," one suggested kindly.

Maurício whispered to Henrique. "Perhaps these Manao haven't traveled widely enough. Someone else at the village may have heard of the Amazons. After all, Acuna and Raleigh reported them."

Henrique was unimpressed. "Perhaps Father Cristobal de Acuna and Sir Walter Raleigh were a pair of bald-faced liars."

The Manao invited Henrique and Maurício to follow them to their village. This was located near where the Solimoes joined with the Rio Negro to form the mighty Amazon. The site had been abandoned, for some mystical reason, by the local Taruma Indians. The Manao had first used it as a trading camp and it had gradually evolved into a village. It was definitely a good location for traders.

And for refugees from Portuguese law, it was a place to gather news of pursuit.

Summer 1634

Henrique raised his eyebrows. "You sure you want to go through with this?"

Maurício continued painting himself for the ceremony. "Coqui told me that I have to, if I want to marry Kasiri. Or any other of the village girls, for that matter."

Henrique knew who Kasiri was. Wherever she walked, she was followed by a crowd of admirers. Including, most recently, Maurício. Henrique did have to admit that Maurício seemed to have eclipsed the former favorite. The lure of the exotic perhaps.

As soon as Maurício discovered that Kasiri's name meant "moon," he had started composing poetry in her honor. Fortunately, it was all in Portuguese.

These ruminations only occupied a fraction of a second. "Uh, huh," Henrique said. "Kasiri's older brother really wants to help you get inside her loincloth. Right."

"He's always been polite to me."

"Are you sure you understand what this ritual involves?"

"I just have to let them put a few ants on me. And not complain. No big deal, I've had ants crawl onto my hammock and bite me. Thanks to you. If ants are so bad, why did you try to get me to hang my hammock on that 'greenhorn' tree?"

Henrique decided not to answer with the truth, which was that after years in the wilderness, he had acquired the native taste for practical jokes. "Have it your way. At least you're doing the ant ceremony, not the one which uses wasps. Remember, it's all a waste if you cry out in pain, or flinch away."

Maurício went off the join the other initiates; in other words, to dance and get drunk, not necessarily in that order. The village maidens brought them gourd after gourd of *cachiri*, which was made from fermented manioc root. And encouraged their dancing and drinking with flirtatious looks and gestures. At first Maurício was self-conscious about being in the company of youths little more than half his age. But the *cachiri* soon took care of that problem. Well before the three days of ceremonial boozing were completed.

On the third day, Henrique went off with the party that was to prepare the *marake*. The Indians had picked out, in advance, a likely ant colony, and their first task was to drive the ants out into the open. They blocked all save two tunnels, and blew tobacco smoke into one of them. That did the trick. The ants emerged and were carried, on top of leaves or sticks, to a *calabash*. They were dumped inside, and found themselves awash in an infusion of roucou leaves. This dulled them satisfactorily.

One of the shaman's apprentices used a parrot feather to carefully position each of the two hundred or so somnolent red ants into the mesh at the center of the damp *marake*, their heads all facing the same direction. It dried, tightening the mesh about them, before they recovered. The apprentice gingerly carried the armed *marake* back to the chief's hut, where it would remain until noon.

Maurício felt like he was flying through the air as he danced in the big circle. *I wonder what they put in the* cachiri? "I am a bird," he shouted. "A *kokoi*, a hawk." He looked at Kasiri. "Shall I swoop down on you?" he cried. She giggled. Her brother, Coqui, also seemed amused for some reason.

The initiates were called into a line, standing in front of a great trench with bark stretched across its entire length. They rhythmically beat upon the bark with sticks, summoning the Sun God.

At noon, with the sun at the zenith, the oldest woman in the village tottered forward. She picked up the *marake*, and pointed at Maurício.

"You first. Arms up, feet apart." He complied, still in a hallucinatory daze.

She raised the *marake*, and put the business end against his cheeks for a few seconds. Then his arms. His dreamy expression started to show signs of uncertainty, but fortunately he didn't show any pain. His chest. The outside of his thighs.

"Did they warn you that some initiates die in this ordeal?" she asked. He didn't respond.

She paused. Then, very deliberately, she put the *marake* against the inside of his left thigh. She gave the back a tap, and then held it in place. Ten seconds. Maurício's eyes widened. Twenty seconds. Each ant bite was a lance of fire, mortifying his flesh.

"Kasiri is supposed to marry my grandson, did you know that? Her grandmother and I had it all planned out, when they were both little. You, a stranger, of no great wealth or skill, are trying to spoil our plans."

Maurício's eyes were tearing now.

"I can't help feeling a bit...resentful."

Thirty seconds. His breath was unsteady.

"Of course, if you fail the test, there's no problem."

Forty seconds.

"And I take this *marake* away, and the pain will be over."

Maurício didn't notice it, but there was angry muttering in the background. And suddenly he heard Kasiri's voice, strident with rage, but he couldn't understand what she said.

The old woman pulled the *marake* away. "Passed," she acknowledged regretfully. "Next."

Maurício looked at Henrique. "See, that was nothing," Maurício declared. Then he fainted.

It had taken a week for Maurício to recover from the vicious bites. His only consolation had been the solicitousness with which Kasiri had applied oil to the inflamed areas of his body. Still, he had had to be real careful how he walked until the salves finished their work.

Maurício and Kasiri, arm in arm, strolled down the sandy beach where her people went bathing. They passed a small stand of palm trees and, abruptly, Coqui stepped out in front of them.

They halted. Coqui, his lips compressed, arms akimbo, watched them silently. Maurício waited for Coqui to say something. Kasiri, for once, was also quiet.

Suddenly, Coqui started hopping about, bowlegged, his hands on the inside of his thighs, yelling "ahh, ahh, ahh." After a minute of this, he exclaimed, "You very funny. You now my friend, Ant-Man." He walked off, laughing.

"Wake up, Maurício." Maurício didn't stir. Henrique gave the hammock a push, and it started swinging wildly, to and fro, dumping Maurício to the ground.

"What the hell, Henrique!"

"Time to pack. A trading party came back from downriver. Said that they saw three big canoes tied to trees, and many men camped nearby. Best guess is that they'll be here soon, perhaps tomorrow or the next day."

"An *entrada*?" That was the term for an expedition whose principal purpose was purchasing or capturing slaves.

"They did ask whether the Manao had any captives to sell. But what they were most interested in, was whether any white man, alone or accompanied by a black man, had been seen recently."

"Uh-oh. Did the Indians reveal our presence?"

"They couldn't; this party had left the village way before we left Belém. But there's more. They described the leader."

"And?"

"He's our old pal, Bento Maciel Parente."

"I'll start packing."

Maurício broke the news to Kasiri. "So I have to flee at once. I love you, but I don't want to put you in any danger. So I guess this is goodbye—"

She slapped him. "Don't be stupid. I'm coming. And you're letting me come, or I'll kill you myself." She squirmed out of his embrace and started ordering her family around, collecting the supplies that would do them the most good.

The plan was to go up the Rio Branco and the Takutu. The latter did a hairpin turn, and then ran parallel to a Guianan river, the Rupununi. The markings on the map suggested that the ground there was relatively flat. In fact, the Manao told him that there was a lake that appeared and disappeared there. It sound a bit improbable, but Henrique was willing to grant the possibility that the land between the two rivers flooded during the rainy season. In any event, Henrique hoped to ride the Rupununi down to the Essequibo, and ultimately to the Dutch settlements near the mouth of that waterway.

Somewhat to everyone's surprise, Coqui announced that he would join them. "I don't like any of the local girls. Perhaps I'll have better luck upriver."

The going had been slow. During the rainy season, the water level of the Amazon and its tributaries rose, eroding the banks, and toppling forest giants. When the waters began to recede, the trunks were left behind, hindering navigation.

From time to time, Coqui and Kasiri would leave them and scout their backtrail, to see if they were being pursued.

Henrique and Maurício, left alone once again, held the canoe steady against the current, studying the latest obstruction. They could get out of the canoe, thus lightening its load, and try to push the canoe over or under the log. They could try to shift the log out of their way. Or they could beach the canoe and portage around.

Like the Indians, they didn't much like the idea of getting into the water. There were caimans, electric eels, stingrays and piranha to worry about. Not all in the same place, of course. And when the waters were high, piranhas usually were a problem only if you were bleeding, or acted as if you were in distress.

On the other hand, the vegetation on shore looked especially nasty, with plenty of long thorns. They would have to cut their way through, and that would be extremely slow and arduous. And a giveaway to anyone following them.

"I guess we're going to get wet," Henrique said. They probed the bottom with their paddles, then gingerly lowered themselves into the water. They each grabbed a side of the canoe and started moving forward, shuffling their feet to minimize the stingray hazard. They looked back and forth, studying every ripple to make sure it wasn't the wake of an inquisitive caiman.

At last, they reached the obstruction. They tentatively rocked the offending log, their attention still divided between it and the river surface. The response was an angry drumming sound.

"Down!" Henrique took a quick breath, and submerged himself.

Maurício saw what appeared to be black smoke coming over the log, and heading straight toward them. Wasps. Hundreds. Perhaps thousands. Enough to kill them both, several times over.

"Shit!" he agreed, and followed suit.

Henrique had flipped the canoe, and they both swam underneath, putting their heads in the breathing space it provided. The canoe slowly floated back downstream, away from the angry insects.

After some minutes, Henrique poked his head out of the water. No wasps attacked, so he rose further. Maurício copied him.

"Why did you overturn the canoe? We're going to have a devil of a time finding all our belongings. And some will be ruined, for sure."

"We had to use the canoe so we could just breathe quietly in place. If you swam underwater, in a panic, your flailing about might have attracted piranhas." He paused. "Some things will float down to where we are now, and in an hour or so, it'll be safe to go back and look for the stuff that dropped to the bottom. Provided we don't rock the log, of course."

"How come we didn't hear the buggers? Or see them flying into and out of their nest?"

"Those were *Acaba da noite*, night wasps. We disturbed their beauty sleep."

"Jeesh. They should have a sign, 'Night workers. Day Sleepers. Do Not Disturb.'"

"Trouble," Coqui announced. "Some of the bad people are coming up this river."

"How many?"

"Many."

Henrique cursed the inadequacies of the Manao counting system. "How big is their canoe?"

Coqui thought about this. "It makes two of this canoe."

"Okay, so call it eight of them."

Maurício piped up. "How soon will they be here?"

"One day, perhaps," said Coqui.

"Too close for comfort," Henrique said. "They have a heavier canoe, so the logs will slow them down more than they do us. But they have more oarsmen, so in clear stretches, they'll be faster."

"If they come as far as the wasp nest log, Henrique, they'll see where we cut around. Then they'll be sure we're up here."

"We need to set up an ambush."

"I know," said Maurício. "We can half cut through a tree, then, when they reach the vicinity of the wasp nest, fell it. It drops on the log, and rouses the wasps. And they sting the bastards to death."

Henrique sighed. "Have you ever felled a tree before? Can you imagine how hard it is to control where it falls in a forest like this one, dense, with lianas everywhere? And if the wasps didn't kill them all, then the wasp swarm would be between us and the survivors.

"We'll try to kill them with arrows, not wasps."

✧   ✧   ✧

Henrique, Coqui and Maurício had bows, but Maurício wasn't a particularly good archer. He was a good shot, but the musket which they had carefully preserved over the months and leagues of their flight was now entertaining the local fish life. Kasiri only had a knife, and so she had been cautioned to stay back.

The slavers' canoe came into view. Coqui gave a bird call, to warn the others to engage, and then fired. His arrow took down the rear man, who was steering. Henrique's shot killed the pole-man in front. That threw the crew into disarray. Coqui picked off another.

The slavers were returning fire now, and Henrique's party had to take cover. In the meantime, the slavers beached their canoe on river left. That was Henrique and Maurício's side. There, on the strand, another of Bento's men fell, with one arrow in his chest, and another in his left arm. The others ran into the bush.

Coqui, on the right bank of the river, grunted, and set down his bow and arrows. "Wait here," he warned Kasiri. "Stay out of trouble." Coqui, armed with a blowgun and the steel hatchet Maurício had given him, went downriver, and around a bend, then swam across, out of sight of the pursuers.

Henrique and Maurício had dropped their missile weapons; there were too many leaves and branches in the way. The slavers likewise realized that the time for musketry was passed; they drew their machetes.

The slavers were at a disadvantage; they hadn't walked this ground before. Henrique and Maurício took advantage of their ignorance, making quick attacks and then disappearing. In the slavers' rear, Coqui aimed his blow gun at the rear man, the dart hitting him in the neck. He slapped, thinking it an insect sting. A moment later, he collapsed.

Coqui picked out his second victim, and fired. But the second one cried as he fell, giving warning to the others. One turned, and Coqui had to leap quickly out of the way of a machete swing. There was no longer any question of reloading the blowgun. And the hatchet was a good weapon, but not the equal of a machete. Coqui backed up rapidly, a move that would have been dangerous for anyone lacking his wilderness senses. The machete wielder followed and, in his haste, stepped in an armadillo hole, turning his ankle. Coqui finished him off.

One of the surviving slavers decided he had enough, and fled downriver on foot, running past the boat. Coqui hesitated, then decided he couldn't take the chance that the man would summon reinforcements. He gave chase.

Henrique and his last opponent gradually shifted deeper into the forest, out of sight of the others.

Maurício and his foe wandered onto the beach. Both were tired, and bleeding from small cuts, but neither had been able to strike a decisive blow. They circled each other warily.

One of the slavers struck down on the beach earlier was not dead, as Maurício had assumed. As soon as Maurício's back was to him, the injured man slowly crawled to where his musket had skittered earlier in the action. It was still loaded. He only had one good hand, so he braced the musket on a rock.

Maurício's more obvious foe could see what was happening, and did his best to keep Maurício's attention directed forward.

The musketeer took aim at Maurício's back...then slumped, an arrow in his neck.

Kasiri was holding her brother's bow in her left hand; a fresh arrow was already in her right.

Maurício's other foe was taken aback, and just stood, open-mouthed. Kasiri's second shot killed him.

A few seconds later, Henrique struggled out of the bush and gave Maurício a nod. Henrique grabbed a leaf and wiped his blade clean.

"Where's Coqui?"

Kasiri crossed the river and told them she had caught a glimpse of him heading downriver, pursuing the last of the slavers.

"We better not take chances. Grab a musket, Maurício, and I'll get my bow." They all concealed themselves, not knowing if more slavers might be on their way.

Soon, Coqui returned, smiling. Until he saw Kasiri, still holding the bow.

They were soon screaming bloody murder at each other.

Maurício gave Henrique an anguished look. "What are they saying? They're talking too fast for me to make out more than one word in three."

"He's angry at her, because she used his bow."

"I'm not complaining! She saved my life."

"He says, 'Picking up a man's bow makes a woman sterile, everyone knows that.' And that means that she can never marry, because by Manao law, a man and woman cannot marry until she is pregnant."

"What about Raleigh's Amazons? They use the bow, according to legend." Coqui turned to look at Maurício, his face suddenly a frightening mask. He shouted an insult, and brandished his hatchet. Kasiri shoved him and did some shouting of her own.

"Ouch, you shouldn't have mentioned that. He remembers now that you spoke of them publicly once. He thinks that Kasiri must have overheard, that you put the idea of female archery into her head. Thereby ruining her marital prospects.

"He also says that the Spanish story of the Amazons is complete nonsense, that the Spaniards must have seen one of the tribes whose men wear their hair long."

Henrique paused to listen to Kasiri's response. "And *she* said that she made her own little bow years ago and has been sneaking off and practicing with it for years. And then *he* said that explains why she hasn't ever gotten pregnant, despite, uh, never mind."

Maurício said, "I'll settle this."

He confronted the quarreling siblings.

"So, Coqui, you think she's unable to bear children." The Indian nodded.

"Well, perhaps that means that only with an Indian father. But I'm not Indian."

She ran over and hugged him. Then dragged him off into the bushes.

"Brother, when my tummy comes out, so you know I am right and you are wrong, I expect you to make me a real bow, not the toy I had to sneak around with." The "real bow" was six feet tall, and used eight-foot arrows.

"You mean if your tummy comes out."

"I said, 'when.'"

"Fine. When. In the meantime, I'm going hunting."

"Stop tickling my toe, Kasiri. Kasiri?" Maurício awoke to find a vampire bat feeding happily on the appendage in question. "Get the fuck off my foot," he screamed, and started kicking, to persuade it to move along.

Kicking while in a hammock isn't recommended. Maurício tumbled to the ground, and a well-nourished vampire bat flitted off.

Fall 1634

It was an awkward time to attempt to cross from the Takutu to the Rupununi. A few months earlier, the area was completely flooded, forming Lake Amuku, and Henrique and his companions would have had an easy time canoeing across. A few months later, at the height of the dry season, and they could have abandoned their canoe and just walked across the savannah. Unfortunately, this was the transition period. Paddle and carry; paddle and carry.

Visibility was surprisingly poor, given that they were in flat country outside the rainforest. The Rupununi savannah was pockmarked with "sandpaper trees," each six to ten feet high, and appearing every twenty yards or so.

When they spotted it, they were already too close. What they had seen was a mound, a few feet from the edge of a creek. As Amazon dwellers, they immediately recognized it as a caiman's nest. The question that came first to mind was, where's Mama? Unlike, say, turtles, crocodilians were quite protective of their young.

Very, very softly, they set their canoe down on the ground. Kasiri climbed one of the trees, so she could see over the bank. After a few minutes, she spotted it. "*Jacaré açu*. Big one. Close."

The black caiman. The largest crocodilian of South America. Unlike birds, caiman didn't just sit on their nests. But if they left them, they didn't go far off. Any suspicious movement, or sound, would be investigated. And Mighty Mama's motto was, "bite first, ask questions later."

They signed to Kasiri. "Leave?"

"No. Too close. Wait." She would tell them when the caiman had moved far enough away that they could slip off unnoticed.

The three males kept watch on the mound. If the mother lay down on her nest, and went to sleep, that would work, too. They could pass, at a respectful distance. Even if their passage woke her up, she probably wouldn't charge. Probably not.

What's going on now? thought Henrique. He had seen a disturbance on the side of the mound. *It's too early for them to hatch, I thought.*

A *tegu*, three feet long, emerged in a puff of dirt, a black caiman egg in its mouth. It did a little victory dance.

The last spasm of dirt movement had not gone unheard. Mighty Mama threw herself out of the creek, and saw the dastardly lizard. She—all fifteen feet of her—charged.

The *tegu* fled. Straight toward Henrique and his companions. With Mighty Mama in hot pursuit.

Maurício gallantly, and rapidly, decided to join Kasiri. He started climbing; Kasiri extended a helping hand. Coqui ran, at right angles to the track of the approaching behemoth, and then found himself a tree of his own.

Henrique hesitated for a minute. Could he grab the *tegu* and throw him back toward Mighty Mama? That would make a nice distraction.

It was also an insane idea. Henrique sprinted, picking the direction opposite Coqui's.

The *tegu* ran past Maurício and Kasiri's tree. Mighty Mama, still intent on the thief, ignored the humans' scent and kept running. The *tegu* was normally much faster, but it refused to let go of its prize, and that slowed it down.

Maurício and Kasiri looked at the departing beasts, then at each other. In silent accord, they dropped to the ground and ran forward, in the party's original direction. Mighty Mama, they hoped, was sufficiently distracted at this point.

The following day, the rest of their party showed up. First Coqui, then Henrique. Of course, there was one problem. No canoe. They had to circle back and, very stealthily, carry it off. It helped that they knew where the nest was, and, equally important, where Mighty Mama liked to lurk. This time, Mighty Mama was indeed asleep on her nest, and they took pains not to disturb her.

It wasn't long before they wondered whether it had been worth the effort. The Rupununi fed into the Essequibo, as predicted. What they didn't predict was what the descent of the Essequibo would be like. As the river dropped out of Guiana highlands, there had been a succession of falls and rapids. Most of which had to be portaged. In Kasiri and Coqui's home country, they would have just left their canoe upriver and taken someone else's canoe at the end of the rough water section. They couldn't be sure that this convenient custom applied in the Guianas, unfortunately, so they had to carry their canoe whenever they couldn't just unload it and line it down.

Eventually, they reached the calmer waters of the lower Essequibo and were able to paddle with fewer interruptions.

Soon, Fort Kykoveral came into sight, looming above Cartabo Point. It was really a glorified watchtower, with barracks, a magazine, a storehouse, and a few private rooms. It overlooked the confluence of the Essequibo with the Mazuruni and the Cuyuni.

Henrique's party beached their canoe, and approached the fort. A bored-looking guard called down for him to identify himself. "I am Henrique Pereira da Costa. We come from Belém do Pará, in the Amazon."

The guard's boredom vanished. "Wait here!" He came back a moment later with several other Dutchmen.

"I am Commander Van der Goes of the Zeeland Chamber of the Dutch West India Company. You say you came from upriver, but ultimately from Belém do Pará?"

"Yes, we found the connection from the Amazon to the Essequibo."

He was congratulated on this great achievement. The Dutchmen ignored Maurício, assuming he was a slave. And of course the Indians were equally uninteresting to them.

Maurício fidgeted. Henrique realized, suddenly, that Maurício might be uncertain of how their return to civilization would affect his status. Kasiri also seemed ill at ease, sensing Maurício's discomfort. Coqui, on the other hand, appeared oblivious to their emotional turmoil.

Henrique interrupted the governor. "Forgive me. Allow me to introduce my fellow explorer, Maurício ... my half-brother."

Second Starts

May 1632 to July 1633

Grantville, May 2, 1632

"Race time ten minutes," blared the speaker. The murmur of the fairground crowd rose in volume, then subsided.

"I can't believe you talked me into this," Maria Vorst said. Maria had come to Grantville with her brother Adolph, the curator of the Leiden Botanical Gardens, and a member of the faculty of medicine of Leiden University. They had visited Grantville's greenhouses, and Adolph had met with Dr. Nichols and Dr. Adams. Adolph had returned to Leiden; he had classes to teach and meetings to attend. Maria had stayed in Grantville to study botany and gardening.

Her partner, Lolly Aossey, waved to some of her middle school students. Lolly was their science teacher. She was also a girl scout leader and a gardener. Maria was boarding with her.

"Good luck, Ms. Aossey!" they chorused.

"Thanks, kids!" Lolly turned to Maria. "Don't worry, Buffalo Creek is about as gentle a river as you are going to find anywhere."

"There's that drop," said Maria doubtfully.

"Oh, that? Two feet, maybe three. Now, if we were running Schwarza Falls, upriver, you'd get some real action."

"Buffalo Creek is more than enough for me, today."

39

"One day I'll teach you whitewater kayaking. Then you'll look forward to a drop taller than you are." Lolly taught canoeing, climbing and other wilderness skills at the Girl Scouts' outdoor adventure camp each summer.

Someone bugled the traditional horse-racing "first call." Lolly and Maria stood on either side of the middle of their canoe.

"Welcome, folks, to the fifth running of the Great Buffalo Canoe Race. Sorry we missed last year, but we didn't expect to enter a time warp.

"Contestants, line up according to your entry number. The first team will start at the sound of the starting gun. After that, the teams will enter the water at one-minute intervals. Sorry you can't all start at once, but the creek's a wee bit too narrow for that. We will call you by number.

"Each team must start on the bank, at the starting line. Getting your canoe into the water, and yourselves into the canoe, is part of the fun.

"When you come to a drop, you can portage, but you must carry the boat and get back on board without outside assistance.

"Friends, don't forget that one of our sponsors is Thuringen Gardens. Show them you appreciate their support of this event by drinking lots of beer! Of course, if you're a contestant, you might want to wait until after the race. And if you're underage, forget I said anything.

"Okay, all rise for 'The Star-Spangled Banner.'" The middle school chorus sang the anthem. The ceremonial marshal, standing on the footbridge, waved his staff.

That was the announcer's cue. "Team One, on your mark, get set..." The starter fired his gun. "Go!" The Baker twins, Billy Joe and Jim Bob, grabbed the gunwales of their canoe and ran with it to the bank. One jumped down, painter in hand, and started pulling, while the other went to the stern and pushed. The canoe lurched down the bank, and the canoeists slid it into the water.

"Team Two!" The second pair, Walt Jenkins and his apprentice barber, the down-timer Erhard Matz, headed to the water. The Germans in the audience cheered.

"Team Three! Hey, it's a brother-and-sister team, Phil and Laurel Jenkins. Try not to kill each other."

"Team Four!" That was the cue for Phil's friends, Larry and Gary Rose. They were carrying a garishly painted Chestnut Prospector.

"Team Five!" That was Lewis and Marina Bartolli. Their parents owned Bartolli's Surplus and Outdoor Supplies, so they had a real racing hull, an eighteen-foot-long, three-by-twenty-seven pro boat. "Buy Bartolli's" was painted on both sides.

"Ouch," said Lolly.

Maria flinched. "What's wrong?"

"Oh, look at that canoe. The longer the boat, the faster it can go in the water."

"Ouch, indeed."

"On the other hand, it's a pain in the butt to carry, it turns slowly, and I have my doubts as to how well it will do in whitewater."

"Team Six!" Phil Gerard and "Ikey" Pridmore were upholding the honor of Grantville Sporting Goods, the Bartollis' main competitor. They, too, had a USCA competition cruiser. "Go, Grantville Sporting Goods!" they shouted in unison, and picked up their canoe.

More teams followed. Finally, it was Lolly and Maria's turn. They walked a bit farther than the others, in order to go down to the river where the going was easier. The time they lost up on the bank was regained when they descended rapidly and safely to the water. Lolly held their canoe, a fourteen-foot Mad River Synergy, pointing upstream, and Maria swung herself into the bow position. Then Lolly jumped into the stern, and they came about and edged their way into the main current.

Seeing all the other canoes in the river ahead of them was discouraging, but they knew that contestants' actual running times would determine their placement.

"Buffalo Creek's a bit woollier than it used to be," Lolly remarked. "Faster and deeper. The water from the Upper Schwarza tumbles a few hundred feet down the southwest ring wall, rushes into the Spring Branch and then into the Creek. Which is a real river, nowadays."

A couple of strokes later, Maria did a double-take. "Wait a moment, you said it was gentle."

"A gentle river. Just not a creek anymore."

Walt and Erhard's canoe entered the Hough Park loop, staying on the inside.

"Bad choice," said Lolly. "That may shorten the distance, but the current is strongest on the outside of a curve." The wind carried her voice forward. Maria nodded.

"But you don't want to get too close to the outer bank. That's where the erosion is greatest, and so you tend to get fallen trees there. We call 'em strainers, 'cause they let water through but trap boaters."

The canoes passed under the Hough Street bridge. Its pilings acted a bit like a "rock garden" on a wild river, creating little eddies. But they were easily avoided.

A few minutes later, the contestants were approaching the mouth of Dent's Fork, on river left.

"Be careful here, Maria. If you look closely, you'll see the shear line, where the waters merge. Stay away from it."

The pack swept past Dent's Fork, and under the Clarksburg Street bridge. The bridge was packed with spectators. Maria couldn't help but wonder whether some poor soul would fall off and have to be rescued.

High Street Bridge. Lolly and Maria were fourth from the lead, at this point. Pretty good, considering that they had started last. Phil and Laurel Jenkins were in the boat ahead of them.

A ninety-degree turn. Now they were heading east-southeast. This was a long straightaway, and it gave a bit of an edge to the longer canoes.

Route 11 Bridge. More onlookers. Another ninety-degree turn, bringing them into a nearly southerly course.

High up on the bank, they saw the sign, LEAVING GRANTVILLE.

Some minutes later, they were approaching Rainbow Plaza. The crowd assembled there yelled encouragement (and an occasional jeer).

The high school was the next major landmark, and it signaled that they were approaching the wilder part of the river.

Now came the Drop. This was a broad ledge, two feet high, extending the full width of the river. A large crowd stood nearby, on the low bank. It was a popular vantage point, since the spectators got to see how the contestants would handle the drop.

Walt and Erhard took the easy way out. They ferried over to the side, where the current was weakest. They clambered out, holding their canoe in place, and then walked it over the Drop.

Phil and Laurel paddled up close to the ledge, then set their paddles down, grabbed both bulwarks tightly, and braced themselves. The water carried them to the brink, where they teetered and then crashed into the foam below, with a teeth-jarring crash. But they were upright, and more or less dry, at least.

Billy Joe and Jim Bob tried to copy this move, but with both hands raised in the air, like thrill seekers on a roller coaster. That wasn't a good idea. Their boat rolled to port, and without paddles, there wasn't much they could do to stop it. In a moment, they were taking a swim.

"Count the fish!" a spectator yelled. They righted their canoe and pulled themselves back in. With grim expressions, they resumed paddling downstream.

Lolly and Maria's canoe neared the Drop. As it did so, they increased the power of their strokes, accelerating. As her toes came even with the lip of the drop, Maria planted her paddle where the green water met the white, like an Olympic pole vaulter preparing to jump. She pulled back on the paddle, bringing it past her hips. Lolly's paddle struck the water at the same time and grabbed more water, adding to their forward momentum.

Their canoe went airborne, traveling several feet, over the boil where the waters fell, before pancaking in the quiet water farther downstream.

Phil Jenkins had turned his head back a moment earlier to see what was happening behind him, and had watched the whole boof. "Wow," said Phil. "Who's the pretty girl with Miz Aossey?" Maria was blond and blue-eyed, which was very definitely Phil's "type."

He had also stopped paddling, and the boat had veered a bit. "Keep your mind on your oarwork," Laurel snapped.

Larry and Gary Rose, battling to catch up with Lolly and Maria, were also impressed. "How are we going to top that?" said Larry. "It's not like we're going to win the race, so we have to find some way to impress the girls."

"I dunno. Maybe we can strike a pose?" Gary said sarcastically. "How about we just finish the race?"

"Great idea! Let's strike a pose," Larry said, ignoring his brother's obvious dismay. "The girls will love it. When we're almost at the Drop, back paddle to hold us there. This'll be spectacular."

It was. Although not perhaps the way Larry had in mind.

Gary held the boat against the current, so it jutted out over the Drop. Larry, in the front seat, set his paddle down, and shook his fists in the air. The crowd roared appropriately.

"Bring us back a little, Gary," Larry ordered. "Now lean back, and keep paddling." Gary groaned, but complied. Larry slowly rose up from his seat, extending his arms for balance. The boat trembled as Gary fought the rush of the water. Larry was standing now, and brought his hands together, like a prizefighter after a K.O.

"Can we go yet?" said Gary, through gritted teeth.

"A moment more. I can see someone adjusting a camera."

An inquisitive wasp buzzed Gary's head, and he lost control as he tried to keep an eye on it. With a great lurch, the boat toppled. It first penciled down, throwing Larry into the water, and then its butt dropped with a great thud. Since the falling water had carved a deeper hole at the base of the ledge, this in turn caused the prow to seesaw upward. At some point, Gary also lost his seating, and joined his partner in the drink. The boat bobbed downstream as the Rose boys scrambled, sputtering droplets, out of their little bubble bath.

"So, did we impress the girls yet?" asked Gary.

"That was fun!" said Maria. "I'm glad we did those practice runs, though. I would hate to mess up in front of a crowd like this."

"Practice makes perfect," Lolly acknowledged.

"So what's the next step?"

"In whitewater rafting? You need to learn to handle a kayak. Start on flatwater, then try the lower Schwarza when the power-plant discharges coolant water. Once you have enough experience, you can tackle Schwarza Falls, upriver. Or at least the little falls below it."

"Little falls?"

"Where the Schwarza flows over fallen chunks of the ring wall."

"Sounds good to me."

Grantville, Summer 1632

"So you're the plant ladies."

"That's what people call us," Irma Lawler acknowledged. She studied Maria. "You're the Dutch gal who's boarding with Miriam's daughter?"

"That's right."

"Edna and I know Miriam from the Garden Club. So you want to buy a few seeds?"

"A lot, actually." Maria took a deep breath. "Probably some of every variety you have, if that's possible."

Irma looked at Edna, then back at Maria. "Well, now. That sounds like a lot of business, and we can use the money. But some of the varieties are getting a bit scarce. We give them to you before we grow any more, and other people will have to go without. For a long time; it's not like we can just order more out of a catalog."

"Why do you want so many seeds, girl?" asked Edna.

"It is for the *Hortus Botanicus*, in Leiden. It's the botanical garden of the University of Leiden; my brother Adolph is in charge. As was our father before him. The medical students use the garden to learn the herbs used in medicine, and scholars come from all over Europe to study its many botanical curiosities. Those are exotic plants, sent to us by the Dutch East India Company, or by other gardens."

"And you send plants to the other gardens, too?"

"Yes, we trade."

"Well, why don't we compare inventories? We'd like to expand our own collection."

Maria saw her friend Prudentia Gentileschi leaving the Nobili house, and waved. Prudentia was the daughter of the world-famous artist Artemisia Gentileschi, an up-and-coming artist in her own right, and a part-time assistant in the middle school and high school art classes.

"Prudentia!" Maria crossed the street and joined her. "On your way to class?" Prudentia nodded.

"I'll walk you there, if you don't mind. Shall we take the scenic route?"

They walked a bit, in companionable silence, then Prudentia spoke up. "So what's new, Maria?"

"I got a letter from my brother."

"You don't sound happy about it. Is there bad news?"

Maria sighed. "Nothing like that. He's fine, his wife Catarina is fine..." Her voice trailed off.

"It's just that he's so lazy. So smug. So uncomprehending of all his advantages, denied to those of our sex. So—"

"So *male*."

"A decade ago, he and cousin Gijsbert got to go on a grand tour, see England, France, and Italy. Whereas I thought myself lucky to visit Amsterdam, or Delft. And, in Italy, they studied at the famous University of Padua. While I made do with academy classes and language tutors. And puttered about in the garden with Papa, of course."

Maria shook her head. "Adolph came home in 1623, and, the next year, he was appointed professor extraordinary of medicine, with a salary of six hundred guilders a year. In 1625, when Father died, he became curator of the Hortus Botanicus. Did he continue to recruit departing ship captains to bring home exotic plants, as Papa did? No, he was content to administer potions to rich merchants, and flirt with their daughters."

"Catarina was the last of those daughters, I hope."

Maria nodded. "Then the curators of Leiden University told him he needed to . . . what is the American term? 'Publish or Perish.' So he produced a catalog of the plants in the garden."

"That's the one you illustrated, is it not?"

"Yes. Elzevier will be publishing it. Next year, I hope. Anyway, that was his big chance to honor our father's work. But Adolph did the minimum work possible, contenting himself with the garden inventory. *I* prepared the list of 289 wild plants. Limited to the vicinity of Leiden, of course, because *I* didn't get to travel to anyplace exotic, unlike Adolph."

Prudentia gave Maria a quick hug. "None of what you have told me would have seemed at all surprising before we came to Grantville,"

"That's true."

"So what's in the letter?"

"Complaints. The students are complaining that he doesn't spend enough time with them, don't they realize he is a busy man? Catarina has extravagant tastes, doesn't she realize he is just a scholar, not a wealthy merchant like her father? Why am *I* lingering in Grantville, when I should be home in Leiden, seeing to the cataloging and description of all the seeds I have sent him? And planting them. The gardener quit and so he must do it himself."

"Poor baby."

Grantville, Fall 1632

Maria was standing in front of an easel, a canvas in front of her. On it was a half-finished rendition of one of the "Painted Ladies" of Grantville. This one had a covered porch, a turret, and an attic with a rayed window. It was colored blue and green, and a tall sugar maple, the official tree of West Virginia, stood beside it. At least in Maria's painting. Maria had exercised artistic license and moved the tree to stand beside her favorite Victorian. The tree itself was a brilliant mass of scarlet, its leaves having already turned.

"Hi, Maria. What are you drawing?"

"This is—" Her voice faltered. Looking up, she realized that she didn't recognize the woman addressing her. She was an elderly up-timer, dressed conservatively, but without any concessions to down-time practice.

"You don't know me, but I am one of Lolly's colleagues, Elva Dreeson. I teach art at the middle school." She offered her hand; Maria took it.

Maria smiled apologetically. "I am sorry, she introduced me to so many people, so quickly, when I first came to stay with her."

"Actually, you didn't meet me at that time. I heard about your visit, but I was out sick that day. Another of our colleagues pointed you out to me, when you and Lolly were out paddling in the Great Buffalo Canoe Race. And when I heard that you were an artist, I resolved to look you up. So here I am. Belatedly."

"Well, I'm not really an artist."

"Oh? That looks like art to me." She pointed at Maria's canvas.

"I mean, I'm not a professional artist. For a woman to be a master in the painters' guild, she pretty much has to be born to it. Like Artemisia Gentileschi. Or Giovanna Garzoni."

"And you weren't?"

"Why, no. My late father, Aelius Everhardus Vorstius, was a great scholar. At the University of Leiden, he was Professor Extaordinarius in Natural Philosophy, Professor of Medicine, and Curator of the Botanical Gardens."

"So how did you learn to paint?"

"I attended an academy. They cater to amateurs, especially high-born women who see it as an elegant pastime, like playing the harpsichord."

"And is that how you see it, as a hobby?"

"While I find it relaxing, it isn't just a hobby. When I was young, it was a way to help my father. I could draw specimens that had been loaned to us for study. And my brother, who is the present curator, has written a *Catalogus plantarum*, a description of our entire collection, and I illustrated it."

"You know, I have a book you might like to read. It's about women artists throughout history."

"That sounds fascinating. But I don't know when I am going to find the time. I need to finish my paintings of the West Virginia trees before they all lose their leaves. I have to complete my thirty hours of volunteer work to get my Master Gardener's certificate. And I have so much homework for Lori Fleming's biology class. And the geology class Lolly roped me into."

"Tell you what. I'll give it to Lolly just before winter break. You'll have some time to spare then."

Maria bent down to study a wildflower by the side of Route 250, near the high school. Phil Jenkins came up behind her, and watched her for a few moments. Finally, he coughed. "I hear you've been looking at people's houseplants."

She looked up, and gave him a smile. "Yes, that's right. I am making drawings of them, and sending seeds and cuttings to Adolph."

"Who's Adolph?" he asked sharply.

"My brother."

"Oh.... You know, lots of people here in Grantville have house-plants, but I am something of a specialist."

"How so?"

"I grow trees."

"Your house must have very high ceilings."

Phil laughed. "No, that's not necessary. Although it would be nice. The trees just don't grow as tall as they would in the wild."

"So what trees do you grow? Sugar maple? Sassafras? Pitch pine?"

"Hmm, you've been studying West Virginia trees. But there isn't much point in growing those indoors. I mostly grow tropical trees. Would you like to see them?"

Maria considered the invitation. He was so much younger than she was, he couldn't possibly be courting her, but still, what would people think?

"May I bring a girlfriend?"

Maria and Prudentia arrived at the Jenkins house the next day, arm in arm.

Laurel Jenkins opened the door. "Oh, I recognize you," she said. "You were the star of the canoe race in May."

"You are kind to say so. We are here to see your 'house trees.'"

Laurel turned and yelled upstairs. "Phil, turn off your stupid CD! You have company."

She shrugged her shoulders. "Brothers."

"Hi, Maria! Hi, Prudentia. You came at a good time, my Angel's Trumpet's in bloom. Come along, I'll show you. There, you can see how it gets its name."

Maria admired the plant. The gracefully arching branches were festooned with long white trumpet-shaped flowers. "What lovely curves."

"That's from Brazil. Now, can you guess what this is?" The plant had nondescript green leaves, perhaps six inches long, and many flowers, each a five-pointed white star. There were also a few green cherries. The girls shook their heads. Maria actually recognized the tree—the Leiden Botanical Garden had gotten one from Aden years ago—but Phil was so obviously proud of his specimen that she didn't have the heart to say so.

"This is *Coffea arabica*—the coffee tree. From Ethiopia, originally."

Prudentia pointed to one of the cherries. "I have seen coffee beans here in Grantville. This doesn't look like one."

"It isn't. There are two beans, seeds really, inside each cherry. You wait until the cherries turn red—that means they're ripe—and then you take out the beans, and roast them."

"So, do you supply coffee to Grantville?" asked Maria.

"I wish. You can't get a lot of coffee beans out of one tree, I don't have room for a whole bunch of trees, and it's too cold in Thuringia to grow them outside. The coffee comes from the Turks. When they feel like selling it to us."

"I don't care for the taste myself," said Maria. "Too bitter."

"Okay, here's another tree. Any guesses?"

Maria looked it over closely. "Some kind of fig?"

"Yep." He favored her with a big smile. "This is *Ficus elastica*, the Indian Rubber Tree. East Indian, that is. Cut it, and it bleeds a sap, latex, that hardens into a kind of rubber."

Maria fingered the stem. "So that is where you Americans get the rubber you use in your tires?"

"Uh, uh. Some of that's made from the latex of a different rubber tree, *Hevea brasiliensis*, and the rest is synthesized from chemicals. But if you want to know more about that, you'll have to check the encyclopedias."

"Perhaps I will."

Fort Zwaanandael (modern Lewes, Delaware), Early December, 1632

Bones. They gleamed in the winter sunlight, amid the white sparkling sand, and the chill that Captain David Pieterszoon de Vries felt was not entirely due to the coldness of the air. Here was a femur, there, a skull. David reached down and picked up an arrowhead. It was easy enough to visualize how this particular colonist had met his Maker. David didn't know if he had been fleeing, or had bravely faced his attacker. Certainly, he had not escaped from this beach to the dubious haven of the waters of the Zuidt River Bay.

The dismal find had not been a surprise. In May, the *Kamer Amsterdam* of the West India Company had heard, from its agents in Nieuw Amsterdam, that the Zwaanandael settlement had been wiped out, save for one survivor. David had been about to leave, with two ships, to go a-privateering in the Caribbean. Since the easiest return route to Europe was to go partway up the American coast before heading east, he logically had planned to stop at Zwaanandael along the way. Sell them European manufactures in return for tobacco, grain, and fresh meat. And perhaps do a bit of whaling as well.

The news of the massacre, of course, had been devastating to David and his fellow patroons. And surprising, because the Lenape had been friendly the previous year. But David had hoped that either the ill tidings would prove to have been exaggerated, or that the breach with the natives could somehow be remedied. At the least, that he could trade for furs.

Briefly, David had toyed with the idea of making a quick trip to Grantville, the mysterious town from the future, to see if its fabulous library could tell him whether Zwaanandael had indeed survived. But he couldn't afford the time; it would have delayed him enough so that he would have been sailing in the Caribbean at the height of the hurricane season.

David's longboat was beached just behind him. One sailor had stayed behind, to guard the boat and man its swivel gun. The small cannon was loaded with grapeshot. The yacht *Eikhoorn* stood just offshore, ready to lay down covering fire if need be. David's own ship, the *Walvis*, was anchored in deeper water, closer to Cape Hinlopen. It was a four-hundred-ton fluyt, with eighteen cannon, which likewise were in range.

Still, David couldn't help but feel a little anxious about how exposed he and his landing party were. The dark forest could conceal ten Indians, or a thousand.

The sailors spread out in a ragged line abreast. Ahead of them was Fort Zwaanandael.

David's cousin, Heyndrick de Liefde, put his hand on David's shoulder. "Where are the walls of stone? The moat and draw-bridge? The portcullis?" He had been shown the settlement plans.

"Just what I was wondering," David replied. "Especially since we went to such expense to provide them with everything they needed. And I checked the equipment myself, before it was loaded onto the *Walvis*."

Instead of a granite wall, the settlement had merely a palisade. There was no portcullis, just a wooden gate, now hanging askew from a single hinge. The only part of the fort which was more or less as David expected was the great brick blockhouse, the warehouse and strong point of the colony. Although it was ash-black now.

"They should have given me command of the *Walvis* back then, not that idiot Heyes."

Heyndrick nodded. "Even back home in Rotterdam, people were talking about him. He sent the *Salm* ahead, and lost it?" The *Salm* was a yacht, like the *Eikhoorn*, used for inshore work.

"That's right. Taken by a Dunkirker, with all our harpoon-ers, and their equipment. And he brought the *Walvis* back, nine months later, without a cargo." That was sacrilege, to a Dutch merchant. "We lost a mint."

Despite Heyes' blundering, David and his fellow investors had been confident that the colonists could grow wheat, tobacco and cotton, and hunt the whales that frequented the bay from December to March. Now that seemed a forlorn hope indeed.

David poked around in the debris at the foot of the gate, and found the bones of a large dog. A spiked collar and several more arrowheads lay nearby. David detailed two men to stand guard at the gate, and the rest of his party followed David inside.

All was chaos, both inside the blockhouse and without. The fort, quite clearly, had been looted. All that was left were the items that the savages had no use for. And the skeletons. David had hoped to find a diary, which might reveal the reasons for the attack. If one had once existed, it had burned, along with the furnishings, when the invaders had overturned lamps in their pursuit of the settlers inside. Or in their haste to find loot.

They then checked the fields. There was no sign, there, of any organized resistance. The skeletons of the Dutchmen and their livestock were scattered over the weed-infested fields. If they had been carrying arms, these were now in the hands of the Indians. The Lenape, David assumed, although it was possible that some other tribe, perhaps the Minquas, had been the enemy.

By now the sun was low in the horizon. This was no time to linger in hostile territory. "Back to the ship," David ordered. David and his search party returned to the longboat, and rowed over to the *Eikhoorn*.

Jan Tiepkeszoon Schellinger, the yacht's captain, greeted him. "What news?"

"The colony of Zwaanandael was wiped out, as we were told." *Some thirty men had sought a new life at Zwaanendael*, David mused, *where there was land for the taking. And their lives, all save one, had been taken instead.* He wondered why this had been God's will.

"Now what?" Jan asked. David was the squadron commander.

"Captain Schellinger, please fire one cannon. Just powder, no shot. I am returning to the *Walvis* for the night."

"Yes, sir."

Heyndrick looked at David quizzically.

"I am telling the Indians that I would like to negotiate," David explained.

"Negotiate? With those savages? After they massacred our people?"

"We will hear what they have to say. After that, there will be time enough to take vengeance, if that is called for. Trouble is..." David bit his lip.

"Yes?"

"I knew Gilles Hosset, God rest his soul. I don't like to speak ill of any man, but never was there a man less suited for command. Slow of thought and quick to anger."

✧   ✧   ✧

The next morning, David was awakened early.

"Captain, the lookout saw a column of smoke. From the pine woods outside Zwaanandael."

"I'll be right up."

David checked his pistols and cutlass, and came out onto the main deck. He pulled out a spyglass, a Dutch invention. "I don't see anyone in the open. Still, we accomplish nothing by sitting here. Mr. Vogel, on the double, please!" Vogel had been the interpreter on the *Walvis'* last trip to Zwaanandael.

"First mate, detail seven men to join us in the longboat. All fully armed, muskets and cutlasses, if you please. Heyndrick, kindly bring your shotgun. Come along, Vogel."

Some minutes later, they were past the breakers, in water they could wade in. David had decided not to land until he had seen the reception committee. They waited, sure that they were under observation, but saw nothing but the lapping of the waves on the beach, the wheeling of the birds in the sky, and the caress of the wind on the branches of the woods beyond.

The gulls cried overhead, like lost souls, and still the Dutchmen waited for the Indians to reveal themselves. David pointed out a particularly large bird to his cousin. "Heyndrick, bring that fowl down." Heyndrick, readied his shotgun, and waited for the gull to fly near. He fired, and the hapless bird fell to the beach below. The crewmen cheered, and an answering cry came from some riverside weeds.

The Indians rose, with broken stalks littering their long hair. They waved their arms, and shouted something. The sailors gripped their weapons with white-knuckled hands.

"What are they saying?" David asked Vogel.

Vogel grinned. "They applaud our Heyndrick's prowess as a hunter." At this, the boat party gave its own cheer, and relaxed a bit.

David held up his hand to quiet them. "Tell the Indians to come down to the beach."

Vogel cupped his hands, and shouted this invitation. The Indians conversed among themselves, and then answered. "They say to come ashore."

"Hah! It will be a fine day in Hell before I do that. Tell them the tide is too low now, we will visit them at high tide tomorrow morning."

✧　　✧　　✧

At dawn, David transferred to the *Eikhoorn*, and had it sail close to the fort, into waters a fathom or two deep. He had Vogel urge the Indians to come to him. "Tell them we have a fine present for one who comes to us."

One fidgeted, and then walked slowly toward them, hands open. He stood on the strand for a moment, watching them. Then he swam out, coming alongside. "I am Temakwei—the Beaver. Because I am a good swimmer. What do you have for me?"

The crew threw down a rope to him, and he climbed up. David handed him a blouse and breeches. Temakwei held each up, and compared it to what David and his shipmates were wearing. At last he laughed, and pulled them on.

David held up a bottle. "Perhaps you'd care for some schnapps?"

"So Temakwei, why did your people slay mine?"

"Your *sakima* Hosset put a metal shield on the gate of your village. It was small, but very beautiful. It showed a great golden panther with the sky behind it. It walked on two feet like a man, and carried a white knife in one paw, and seven white arrows in another."

"He means a lion, not a panther. And a sword, not a knife," said Heyndrick. David shushed him.

"One of our chiefs, Taminy, thought that it was a great waste that this pretty thing sit on a gate. So he borrowed it to make a tobacco pipe, so we could smoke it together and honor the peace between our people."

Heyndrick reinterpreted this statement. "Stole it, he means."

David sighed. "The Indians don't have much of a property concept. Stealing isn't a crime, so far as they're concerned. It is a chance to demonstrate that they are cleverer than you. If you don't like it, steal it back."

"Your Hosset said many bad words to us. He told us we had taken a . . . I don't know the words."

"Coat of arms?"

"That sounds right. A 'Koh-Tah-Ahms' of the Dutch people. He told us that this was a terrible insult to your chief of chiefs, and to your Manitou, your great spirit. That the thief must be punished.

"That was when we realized that we had committed a great wrong. Clearly, the 'Koh-Tah-Ahms' was strong medicine. To take it away was to hurt the Dutch people, our friends.

"So, the next day, we brought the head of Taminy to your Hosset."

Heyndrick's eyes widened. He started to speak, but David raised a finger in admonition, and Heyndrick subsided.

"Your chief told us that he didn't mean for us to kill Taminy, only to make him bring back the spirit-shield and apologize. Still, he was pleased that we had punished Taminy, and he sent us home with pleasant words. But the brothers and sons of Taminy were angry that Taminy was dead. And the sister-sons of Taminy were angry, too. They waited and waited, but Hosset did not send them any wampum to atone for the death of Taminy.

"It was an insult not only to Taminy's kin, but to his entire clan."

"And then what?"

Temakwei fidgeted. "They did what they must. They wiped out the dishonor in blood."

David and Heyndrick watched Temakwei jump off the *Eikhoorn*, and swim back to shore. They couldn't see any other Indians, but they knew there had to be some there.

"So much blood spilled, over a stupid piece of tin," David said. "I hesitate to waste more."

Heyndrick protested. "But surely you can't let the Indians think that they can get away with pillaging our colonies."

"That's true. But we could go on playing tit-for-tat indefinitely. Like Italian families with a vendetta. And we aren't going to make a profit that way.

"So we need to be conciliatory, but at the same time, show we are strong. Temakwei is carrying our message to the chiefs. When they come, we will give them a demonstration of the power of our cannon, it will seem pretty strong magic to them, I think. Then we will offer them presents, propose a peace pact, and pass around the pipe."

Heyndrick looked skeptical. "You think that will solve everything?"

"No. We must forgive, but not forget. We must be friendly, but always on guard. They will trade with the strong, but prey upon the weak.

"In which regard, to be blunt, they aren't very different from us."

Grantville, Winter Break, 1632

Maria had actually welcomed the coming of winter. It gave her the chance to catch up on her pleasure reading. In particular, she was finally able to tackle Elva's book on woman artists.

Her friend Prudentia's mother, Artemisia, was in it, of course. And Maria was pleased to see that the book mentioned the work of Clara Peeters, a Flemish still-life specialist, and Judith Leyster, the portraitist and genre painter from Haarlem.

But what truly caught Maria's attention was the description of two other artists. One was Rachel Ruysch of Amsterdam. Her father was Anthony Frederick Ruysch, a professor of anatomy and botany. Much like Maria's father. And apparently, he passed on some of his scientific knowledge to her, because the book said, "Ruysch brought a thorough knowledge of botany and zoology to her work."

Maria also thought much about Maria Sibylla Merian. She had come to art by the more usual path, being the daughter of an engraver and the step-daughter of a flower painter. Merian had published her first book, a collection of flower engravings, when she was only twenty-three—younger than Maria. But Merian's great passion was to understand and depict the life cycles of insects, especially moths and butterflies.

In 1699, Merian actually traveled to fabulous Suriname, in South America, on what the Americans would call a "government grant." The result was her masterpiece, *Metamorphosis Insectorum Surinamensium.*

"Lolly, about the Ring of Fire. I know that it has already changed history. Gustavus Adolphus doesn't die at the battle of Lützen, and all that. What happens to the people who would have been born after the Ring of Fire? Are they still destined to come into the world?"

"It depends on when and where they were born," Lolly replied. "The effect of the Ring of Fire diffuses out from Grantville. We think it would change the weather around the world in a matter of weeks, even though actual news would travel more slowly.

"And it doesn't take much to change who is born. A soldier leaves his mistress a day earlier than in the old time line. A couple fails to meet, and the two marry other people. A person's father or mother dies earlier than in the old time line, because an army takes a different path, or a plague ship comes to a different port."

"The people I am thinking of, one was born in 1664, and the other in 1647."

"Not a chance, then. Even if their parents were alive in 1631, and married to each other, they will have different children."

After Lolly left, Maria thought further about the question she had raised. Neither Rachel Ruysch nor Maria Sibylla Merian would ever brighten the world. Their contributions would be limited to the fragments imported from the old time line.

The more Maria thought about it, the more it seemed that, though born in an earlier age, she was their intellectual heir, and that it was her duty to posterity to make a similar contribution. And, with her father and husband both dead, she had a degree of independence that was unusual for women her age.

Suriname. Also known as Guiana. The Wild Coast of South America, between the Maracaibo and the Amazon. There was a Dutch settlement there, she was sure. Her ex-husband, a merchant, had mentioned it more than once. And Catarina, Adolph's wife, was from a commercial family; she and her kin might know more.

Perhaps it was worth consulting one of the Abrabanels, too. Maria could do more than just draw nature, she could collect it. Was there something in Suriname that the up-timers wanted badly enough that they might pay to send Maria there to look for it? The Abrabanels would know, she was sure. And, as the daughter of a Dutch doctor, she didn't have the usual Christian prejudice against Jews. Well, some, she admitted, but after more than a year in Grantville, she had been forced to rethink a lot of what she had been taught.

And she mustn't forget that the library might have books, or at least encyclopedia entries, that would reveal facts not naturally known to anyone of her time.

What would Adolph say if she announced that she was going to Suriname? Even if she were joining a Dutch household there? Oh, the conniptions he would have.

That was just the icing on the cake, as far as Maria was concerned.

Delaware River, near modern Philadelphia, January 1633

David took command of the shallow-drafted *Eikhoorn*, and left its former skipper, Jan, with the crew of the *Walvis*, to build and run a shore-based whaling operation. He also had the *Walvis* and its boats, should he need to take refuge from the Indians.

David, in the *Eikhoorn*, sailed up the Zuidt River, and, near Jacques Island, the going became rough. The temperature dropped sharply overnight, while they were at anchor, and, the next day, the nineteenth of January, they found the river to have almost entirely crusted over with ice. They had to pick their way, looking for open leads or, if those were absent, areas where the ice was thin enough for them to crash through. The ship shuddered at each attempt, making the crew more than a bit nervous. If the ship foundered, they wouldn't survive long in the icy water.

"A whale (*walvis*) would be more at home here than a squirrel (*eikhoorn*)," David joked. The crew laughed, but their mood soon turned somber again. David tried heading back downriver, but the ice there seemed even thicker.

David pointed out a creek to the helmsman. "Turn in there."

"You think our chances are better in that kill?" Heyndrick asked.

"Yes, the current's stronger, that will tend to keep it from freezing solid. Unless it gets colder." The *Eikhoorn* crept into this uncertain haven.

The Dutchmen needed to conserve food, if possible, so David sent out a hunting party, led by Heyndrick. He was whistling, slightly off-key, when he returned, and all of his followers had something in hand.

David thumped him on the back. "The hunting went well, I see."

"Very well. We bagged several wild turkeys. Look at this one." He held up a carcass. "Must be a good thirty-six pounds.

"And that's not all. There are wild grapevines everywhere, so we did some picking."

"Hopefully we won't be here long enough for the grapes to ferment. But let's call this creek 'Wyngard Kill.'"

The weather worsened, and great chunks of ice came down the creek and battered their hull. David had the crew cut down some trees and construct a raft upstream of the *Eikhoorn*, to serve as a bumper.

On the third of February, the weather relented, and the *Eikhoorn* headed back toward the coast. But the respite was a short one. Ice reappeared, and once again the *Eikhoorn* took refuge in a swift-running kill. This cold spell was worse than the one before, and even the creek froze over.

They were trapped in the ice. But at least there were no signs of Indians nearby, hostile or otherwise.

Not until a week later. Fifty Indians, carrying their canoes, walked across the frozen river.

David turned to Vogel. "Order them to halt."

The Indians looked at the leveled arquebuses and the steel breastplates of the sailors, and stopped, lowering the dugouts onto the ice.

One stepped forward. "We mean you no harm."

"But you are dressed for war," David declared.

"We are Minquas, and yes, we are at war, but with the Armewamens, not you. Six hundred of us have come, and the Armewamens flee in terror. We have burned their homes, and their women are now ours. We hunt the few braves who escaped into the forest."

"There are no Armewamens on this ship, so you have no reason to linger here."

"No reason," the spokesman acknowledged. However, the Minquas did linger, carefully inspecting the *Eikhoorn* and its crew, before they finally trudged on to the far bank.

"Tide's coming in, sir," reported a crewman.

"Good," David said. "Let's get this ship out in the mouth of the kill, where the water is widest. Preferably before nightfall."

David divided the men into two parties, and sent one to each bank, with a heavy rope in hand. There, they started hauling the *Eikhoorn* downriver. They moved it twenty-five painful paces, no farther.

David went out on the ice and studied the lie of the ship. "The creek's too shallow, we must lighten the *Eikhoorn* to make more headway. I need four men to go to the ship and toss out the ballast."

"We can't do that, Captain," said the helmsman. "The *Eikhoorn* is tall-masted, prone to listing."

"That's right, sir," said one of the mates, "we'll capsize before we reach the *Walvis*." There was a general murmur of agreement.

David frowned ferociously. "It's a risk we must take. Did you see those painted savages, the Minquas, eyeing us? They'd love to take our guns, our gold, our food. And do you know what they'll do to us? You'll be lucky if you are just shot with an arrow, or toma-hawked, in battle. If they take you prisoner, they'll torture you for their evening entertainment. You must lighten the ship, and trust to Divine Providence to save you from the river's embrace."

The mate was unimpressed. "If we are going to trust to Divine Providence anyway, why not trust it to save us from the Min-quas, instead?"

"What do you want me to do, David?" whispered Heyndrick. "Start throwing out ballast myself? Shoot the ringleader of this mutiny?"

David ignored him. "The tide's going out, men, even as we argue, and soon the Minquas will be coming in, with blood in their eyes. I have three demijohns of rum in my locker, and I'll share one out tonight if you throw the ballast overboard. But you must act now."

Sullenly, the crew came aboard, and jettisoned the ballast. The ship slowly rose in the water, and lurched downstream. It reentered the main river, but proved difficult to control. A thousand paces below the kill, it was swept toward the bank, and the bowsprit was wedged in between the horns of a double-crested hillock of ice.

At dusk, the Minquas attacked. Several feet of icy water still separated the exposed part of the ice from the actual bank. Hence, they had to first leap across the water, onto the midget iceberg, then clamber onto the bowsprit, which pointed landward.

Two of the Indians made it onto the ice, but were confronted by all eight of the crew, armed and armored. They retreated. Throughout the night, David kept two men on the alert at the bowsprit, and the others slept on deck, in their armor, with their weapons beside them.

At dawn, they were still alive. Standing, half-asleep, David read to them. "Let us, with a gladsome mind, praise the Lord, for He is kind."

The river rose. The ice floated away from shore, carrying the *Eikhoorn* with it. The iceberg ran aground on a sandbar, and the river swirled angrily around them. The ship creaked in response, and David wondered how long it could endure this treatment.

Then the Indians who were their foe unwittingly became their saviors. The lookout spotted two dugout canoes, unmanned, float-ing toward them. At David's order, the crew caught them, and pushed them under the bow. As the waters rose still further, they buoyed up the canoes, and thus the *Eikhoorn*'s bow as well. At last, when David had almost given up hope that this ploy would succeed, the *Eikhoorn* was freed from the ice.

By the fourteenth, the wind shifted to the southwest, and brought in warmer air. The ice softened into slush. At their first opportunity, the crew gathered stones for ballast, to restore the yacht's balance. Soon, they were back in Zuidt River Bay.

By the end of March, it was clear that the whaling had been a failure. Jan's people had harpooned seventeen whales, but had little to show for it. Most had been struck in the tail, whereas a Basque or Cape Verde harpooner would have aimed for (and hit) the fore-part of the back. As a result, only seven carcasses had been brought in, and those were the puniest of the lot.

David sighed. "Thirty-two barrels of train oil. My partners will be furious."

"It's not your fault that they didn't give you experienced harpooners, or proper whaleboats, or strong enough cables or winches to handle the larger whales," said Heyndrick. "Godijn chose the ships and the whaling expert." They were back on the *Walvis*, where Jan couldn't hear them. Still, he kept his voice down.

"Godijn won't remember that when I return," said David gloomily. "I will be thrown to the sharks. The financial kind, that is."

"But that's how it goes." David raised his voice. "Helmsman, set a course for New Amsterdam. Pieter, signal the *Eikhoorn* to follow."

David turned to Heyndrick. "After we reprovision there, we'll head home. And then I am going to find myself a new patroonate, and new partners. Ones with more trust in my judgment."

Grantville, July 1633

The theater at the Higgins Hotel was packed with people. The men wore everything from a twentieth-century jacket, pants and tie, to seventeenth-century breeches, blouse and cloak. The women were even more varied in their appearance; black cocktail dresses for some, bodice and bell skirts for others. And of course there were those who wore some combination of up-time and down-time styles, or who had decided to copy a garment of the eighteenth or nineteenth centuries.

"This is a madhouse," said de Vries. He was seated at a small table near the front of the theater.

Kaspar Heesters, an Amsterdamer who had escorted David to Grantville, shrugged. "There's method in their madness."

Hugh Lowe, standing at the podium, tapped the microphone. The loudspeaker squealed. "Can everyone hear me? Welcome to the Grantville Investment Roundtable.

"I am sure that many of you know me already. I used to be the president of the Grantville Chamber of Commerce, and I am now the chairman of the Roundtable.

"Our first guest is Captain David Pieterszoon de Vries, a patroon of the Dutch West India Company. He has an investment proposal for us. Remember, Captain, we limit the summaries to two minutes. My assistant will bring the portable mike to you."

De Vries took it and stood up. "Thank you, Herr Lowe. My proposal is to establish a colony on the Wild Coast, the area of northern South America between the Orinoco and the Amazon. Your English compatriots call it the Guianas. In your late twentieth century, there were three countries there: Guiana, Suriname, and French Guiana. My colony would be in Suriname. What was once called Dutch Guiana.

"I intend to transfer my patroon privileges in the West India Company from America to Suriname. I would be entitled to a patroonate of, oh, about twelve hundred square miles." There was a gasp from somewhere in the audience.

"This would be, primarily, an agricultural colony. It would grow tobacco and cotton, of a surety. Orlean, too, that's an Indian dye plant. Sugar cane, if we can find a suitable teacher. And I hope that there may be plants not yet known to us which are of value.

"As to other possibilities, once the colony is established, I can take a yacht upriver, to look for the gold which Suriname is reputed to possess." He was referring to the legend of El Dorado, and the Lake of Manoa. "Or I can take my squadron privateering; that can be very lucrative."

David finished off by discussing how much money he was trying to raise, and what it would be spent on. "There is a—" He looked blank for a moment.

"Handout," whispered Kaspar.

"—handout by the door. Thank you for listening to me." He sat down.

"Are there any questions for the captain?" said Hugh.

David Bartley stood up. "Aren't you worried that the Spanish will wipe out your colony?"

David de Vries was surprised that a youngster would ask questions in such a gathering, but answered his question politely. "There are already Dutch, French and English settlements on the Wild Coast, and the Spanish have simply ignored them. Well, most of them."

"And where are you going to get your colonists? I don't think you're going to find many here in Grantville."

"There are many displaced peasants in Germany and Flanders, thanks to the wars. This would be their big chance to own land of their own."

Chad Jenkins, one of the major landowners in Grantville, stood up. "Captain De Vries, you are going to have to find a suitable site for this colony of yours. Do you have experience as an explorer?

"Yes, in the Barents Sea, in my youth, and more recently in the Americas, between the Zuidt and Noord Rivers."

"The South and North." Kaspar Heesters explained. "What uptimers would call the Delaware and Hudson Rivers."

Chad wasn't finished. "And have you been in more tropical climes?"

"I spent several years with Coen in the East Indies, and I also visited several islands of the West Indies on my last voyage."

Claus Junker raised a newspaper. "Joe Buckley says here that you were involved in the Zwaanandael disaster. The attempt to found a colony in Delaware."

David's face reddened. "That was hardly my fault. I had sought the command of the first expedition, but it was denied. Indeed, I had to stay at home, trusting to the leaders picked by my partners. And on the second trip, it was the so-called whaling expert who failed, not me."

Endres Ritter chimed in. "You know all about financial disasters caused by picking the wrong partners, don't you, Claus?" It was a reference to Claus' ill-fated investment in microwave ovens. The two men glared at each other.

Claus returned to his original target. "But even if it weren't your fault, your . . . association with a failed venture has made it difficult for you to raise money for your latest enterprise, hasn't it?"

David folded his arms. "It made it difficult for me to fund it myself. But I do have prospective investors. Jan Bicker of Amsterdam, for one. And two of his friends." There was an answering murmur from the financiers in the room. "Coming here was not a necessity. I was hoping to raise more money, to be able to give the colony a more secure foundation.

"And I hoped that there might be some Germans here who had a yen to own their own farm in the New World."

An up-timer stood up. "And I imagine your colonists are going to steal their new farmland from the natives. And then either force them into labor, or kill them outright."

"That's Andrew Yost," Kaspar whispered to David. "He's manager of the Grantville Freedom Arches, and one of the leaders in the local Committee of Correspondence. I told you about that."

"Herr Yost, if you examine the history of what someone earlier referred to as the 'Zwaanandael disaster,' you will find that despite great provocation—the murder of thirty settlers in America while I was still in the Netherlands—I did not retaliate in kind. I was able to trade for furs, with the Lenape. And I kept all of my crew alive, without having to kill any Indians."

A gentleman with a moustache and a goatee stood up. He was dressed in a staggering variety of colors, leaving David with the impression of a somewhat cadaverous peacock. "Captain, I am Doctor Phillip Theophrastus Gribbleflotz. You mentioned mining for gold. But there is a mineral, prolific in Suriname, which is a necessary precursor to the preparation of the 'Quinta Essentia of the Human Humors.' This mineral is called bauxite. Perhaps—"

"No," Tracy Kubiak moaned. "Not aluminum, again." Bauxite was the principal ore of aluminum, an up-time metal that fascinated the alchemists because of its silvery appearance and extraordinary lightness.

Doctor Phil sighed. "Perhaps we should talk about it privately. I will call upon you."

There were no more questions. Hugh Lowe repositioned the mike. "Okay, our next speaker is going to bring us an update on the concrete project...."

"Captain, I am Johann Georg Hardegg, an attorney from Rudolstadt. My clients were quite interested in your presentation last week. They think there could be some commonality of interest."

"I beg your pardon?" said David. He had learned English in his youth, but he wasn't sure whether that was what Hardegg was speaking.

"He thinks you can work together," Kaspar explained.

"If you will follow me, I will introduce you to the principal members."

They walked down an elegantly decorated corridor of the Higgins Hotel, and Hardegg knocked on the door. David heard a muffled "About time."

There were both up-timers and down-timers in the room. David recognized several of them, and exchanged greetings with Hugh Lowe and Endres Ritter. There was no sign of Claus Junker.

The nobleman at the head of the table said, "My name is Count August von Sommersburg." David bowed.

"Our group has some interest in that part of the world. For example, in Trinidad. It has great deposits of tar."

"The place Sir Walter Raleigh visited when he needed to caulk his ships?"

"Yes, that's right. We can use that tar in road building. Then there is a material called rubber. It's used in the tires of our cars. The rubber comes from—call it the sap—of certain trees."

David raised his hand. "I know nothing about trees."

"That's all right. We have a tree expert who wants to go to Suriname to study and do research. As for your proposed colony, Captain, hopefully it will be able to tap the Surinamese rubber trees. If not, we have some other economically interesting plants which we are hoping can grow there. Coconut palms, coffee, a few others. Of course, you should be looking for native plants of value."

"Tell him about the other rubber trees," urged Joseph Stull. He was informally handling transportation matters for the New United States and was likely to be named secretary of transportation when the NUS got around to creating that cabinet position.

The count nodded. "If we can't get rubber from Suriname, you'll have to go into the Viceroyalty of New Spain." That formally encompassed Mexico, Central America, the Spanish West Indies and the southern United States.

David steepled his fingers. "They don't exactly welcome foreigners."

"The source we're interested in is pretty far from the Spanish towns. Here, let me show you on a map." He rolled one out on the table. He ran his finger along the coast from Honduras to Nicaragua. "We can work this stretch. The 'Miskito Coast.'"

"Hmm," said David. "That's convenient. Here—" he twirled his finger over the Bay of Honduras "—that's prime hunting ground for capturing Spanish galleons."

Hugh Lowe shook his head. "We aren't interested in privateering. We don't see a distinction between it and piracy."

"Oh, no? I think Dutch privateers capture a ship a week in that part of the world. Galleons, caravels and coasters. Ship and cargo worth as much as two hundred thousand guilders."

Someone in the back of the room muttered, "Let's keep our options open, then. It's not like the Spanish are friendly to us."

"You have been in sea battles, Captain?" asked the count.

Kaspar interrupted. "Captain de Vries is famous in that regard. He had some great victories against the Barbary pirates."

"But no Spanish treasure ships came my way, unfortunately," David admitted. "Or I wouldn't be talking to you now."

"So, Captain, I understand that your only reservation to our 'counterproposal' is the choice of a woman, Maria Vorst, as your, uh, 'Chief Science Officer.'"

"That's right, Herr Lowe. I am sure that she knows her plants and all, but I don't believe that she can possibly comprehend the rigors of an expedition.

"It is true that there are Dutch colonists already in Guiana—at Fort Kykoveral on the Essequibo—but I doubt that there are any white women among them. It would be one thing if she were going to stay in the new colony, but she intends to join us in exploring the rainforest.

"Moreover, it is quite possible that we will have to go to the Miskito Coast for this rubber, which will put her in hazard of capture, and worse, by the Spanish. How can I agree to put this delicate flower of Dutch society into such straits?"

"Hmm, well, you did agree that it was only fair to meet her before making any decisions."

"Yes, I so agreed. I am not sure why we had to meet out here."

"I think she wanted to show you something."

They stood on a hill near the southwest rim of the Ring Wall. When Grantville was deposited into seventeenth-century Thuringia, it was in such a way that, in general, the Grantville terrain was lower than the surrounding Thuringian land. Nowhere was the transition more dramatic than here in the southwest, where the Ring separated the power plant from the castle of Schwarzburg.

"Well, I can't complain about the view." Where the Ring Wall was intact, it was perfectly smooth, and shone like a mirror in the morning sunlight. Some of the rock had been destabilized by the change, and had fallen onto the American side. The Schwarza river dropped sharply, perhaps ten or fifteen feet, forming the Schwarza waterfall. It was a triangular curtain of water, higher on river left than river right. It then descended, in a series of smaller drops and rapids, over the bed newly formed by the fallen rock, to the Grantville valley floor. The path was not a straight one. First, it paralleled the Ring Wall, then it curved away. Ultimately, the water entered the Spring Branch, a tributary of Buffalo Creek.

"So, when will I meet this Maria?"

"Here she comes now." Lowe pointed upriver, at a lone figure in a bright red kayak at the top of the falls. As David gaped, the kayaker pencilled over. David ran to a better vantage point, expecting to see an overturned kayak, and perhaps a lifeless body spinning in the foam.

Maria was already past the hydraulic at the foot of the falls, and gave them a quick salute with her paddle as she rested in an eddy. She then paddled on. They watched as she "boof-stroked" over a second, smaller waterfall.

"So, I hope you are up to a bit of a hike, now. We have to go down to the valley floor so you can properly question this, uh, delicate flower of Dutch society."

Maria's Mission

September 1633 to Early 1634

Grantville, September 1633

"You've heard the news, Mevrouw Vorst?" A red-faced David de Vries brandished a folded copy of the *Grantville Times* as if it were a club.

Maria Vorst turned to face him. "Who hasn't, Captain? Is it really as bad as the papers say?"

"Probably worse. Over sixty warships destroyed by French and English treachery." To a Dutch captain, especially one with the fighting reputation of David Pieterszoon de Vries, this was the worst possible news. He had friends aboard that fleet, friends now dead or fled to parts unknown. The Republic had needed him, and he hadn't been there.

Belatedly, he added, "Haarlem has fallen to a *coup de main.* And the Voice of America just announced that the northern provinces are said to be in revolt against the prince of Orange."

"What about Leiden?" That was Maria's home town.

"Not yet under siege, so far as the Americans know, but it's only a matter of time. It's bracketed by Spanish forces at Haarlem to the north and Den Haag to the south."

"My brother . . . and his wife . . ." Maria's voice quavered.

"There was no massacre in Haarlem, or Rotterdam, at least.

And Leiden is hardly likely to offer resistance. So there is no reason for the Spanish army to adopt...stern measures."

"And the prince, he will want to protect the university, surely."

"Probably. Although if your family was prudent, they probably fled to the countryside. They certainly had enough warning."

"I hope for the best." Maria paused. "And your wife?"

"She is in Hoorn. The Spanish will probably check to make sure that no warships are hiding in its harbor. Otherwise, I don't think it will be directly affected by the fighting. The Spanish will land more troops at Egmont, and move them south to complete the investment of Amsterdam. Once the siege line is drawn close to Amsterdam, Hoorn will be militarily irrelevant."

"That sounds promising...as much as anything can be promising in these evil times."

"But, Mevrouw Vorst, you realize that this means that we can't go to Suriname after all."

"Why not?"

"It is my duty to fight the invaders. My ship, the *Walvis*, is in Hamburg, and it is well armed; it was outfitted as a privateer. I can attack the Spanish supply ships; perhaps send small boats into Amsterdam."

"That is courageous of you."

David bowed.

"But Captain, is that really the best you can do against the Spanish?"

David bristled. "Surely you don't expect me to attack the Spanish fleet singlehandedly."

"No, no, that's not what I meant at all. From what I hear, the only thing that can prevent the ultimate fall of Amsterdam is if the city is relieved by the Swedes and their American allies. Is that true?"

"Well." David dropped his eyes, then raised them again. "The city is well stocked against a siege..."

"Captain..."

"The fortifications are in excellent condition...."

"Really, Captain..."

"Well, of course, Amsterdam would fall, eventually. If disease, or a Swedish relief force, or some crisis elsewhere, didn't force the Spanish to pull back. But it could hold out for many months."

"It seems to me that your ships could be put to better purpose than sinking a Spanish supply ship here and there. Bringing tar from Trinidad, and rubber from Suriname or Nicaragua, to keep the American APCs running." The APCs were coal trucks converted into makeshift armored personnel carriers, and they had played a major role in Grantville's past military operations.

David took a deep breath, expelled it slowly. "I suppose there is something in what you say. I see it is not enough for you to be a science officer, you have aspirations to be a general, too."

"War is too important to be left to men," she quipped, smiling. "Logistics is not their forte."

"Okay, I'll think about it."

David's original plan had been to simply transfer his rights as a patroon of the Dutch West India Company from Delaware to Suriname. The Dutch defeat at Dunkirk, and the subsequent fall of most of the Republic, had changed all that.

Raising the Dutch flag over a new colony was now more likely to invite attack by English and French opportunists than to deter it. So after extensive negotiations, a "United Equatorial Company" had been formed, under the laws of the New United States. Those laws were based on the U.S. Constitution, and thus banned slavery. The up-time American backers insisted that the corporate charter also ban slavery, since the political fate of the NUS was somewhat uncertain.

There was the practical problem that the NUS flag might not be recognized. Hence, as a additional diplomatic fig leaf, David obtained the right to have his ships, and the colony, fly the Swedish flag, too. Not that David was getting any troops or money from Gustav Adolf. Still, it would be a warning that Sweden might officially take notice of any harm done the colony, and the better Sweden did in the wars, the more others would fear to give it an excuse to retaliate.

"Thanks, Philip," said Maria, balancing a stack of books. "This will really be helpful."

"You're welcome," he said with a smile. He blinked a few times. "Do you like Westerns? They're showing *High Noon* this Friday."

"That might be nice. I'll have to ask Prudentia what her plans are."

"She can come, sure."

"I'll ask Lolly. She'll appreciate the excuse to get out of the house." Maria was staying with Lolly, the middle school science teacher. Currently pregnant.

"Uh...I was thinking that we could celebrate your completing the sugar report."

"That would be nice. So we should ask Irma and Edna. They told me so much about sweet sorghum and sugar beet. And Rahel should come, too."

Philip blinked again. "I suppose."

"And of course the Bartollis. Lewis and Marina, I mean." She gave him a wink. "Don't forget to invite your sister Laurel. Evan, too, perhaps?"

"Yeah...I'll ask them. Well, uh, see you Friday." He turned toward the door.

"It's a date!" she called out after him.

It's a date, she said, Philip thought. *Yahoo!*

Philip needed something to cheer him up. It had only recently hit him that in just a few months, his gang, the "Happy Hills Six," would be split up; most would be going into the military, and who knows where they would be stationed. Or what would happen to them there.

His mother had been driving him nuts about it, too. It had been bad enough when Laurel went into the army—and jeesh, she was in Telephone and Telegraph, not exactly on the front lines—but Philip was the baby of the family and Momma was always bringing it up.

And then there were Grandpa Randolph's health problems. He was seventy-five years old, but until recently in great condition for his age. Thanks to all that hunting and fishing, Phil figured. But he was bed-ridden now, and Momma fretted over that, too.

Phil wished, really wished, he could just, like, *move out*. If it hadn't been for the Ring of Fire, he could have solved the problem by going to college some place far away. Like Cleveland.

"How's your report coming along, Maria?"

Maria greeted her friend Prudentia with a kiss on each cheek. "Almost done. It would help if the investors didn't keep changing their mind as to what they wanted to know."

Prudentia smiled. "Believe me, painters working on commission have the same problem."

Maria showed Prudentia the report. "As you see, it covers pretty much everything the colony might grow, for itself or for export. Various kinds of rubber trees, sugarcane, cacao, coffee, cotton, dye plants, rice, pineapples, bananas, manioc, oranges, coconuts—you name it."

Prudentia gave it a once-over. "Impressive."

Maria shrugged. "I couldn't have done it without Philip Jenkins' help. He knows so much about trees, and of course he's actually seen, and eaten, pineapples and bananas."

Prudentia gave Maria a knowing look. "I bet he's been helpful."

"What do you mean by that?"

"Don't pretend to be obtuse. You know what I mean. I think he likes you."

"Yes, we're friends."

"That's not what I meant. I think he's courting you."

"That's ridiculous. I am in my mid-twenties, and he is what? Fifteen?"

"Sixteen. And a half."

"That's right. He did say that the first time we met."

"He has probably been saying it to *someone* every day since attaining that lofty age."

"Anyway, he's not the only lad who helped me. There's Lewis Bartolli, the chemistry 'whiz kid,' who did the write-up on aluminum, bauxite and cryolite. And his sister Marina has done a lot of typing for me." She paused. "You know, maybe Phil is interested in Marina, and is using his visits as an excuse to see *her*. She's pretty, in a dark sort of way, and just a little younger than Philip, so she's the right age for him. And she is the daughter of the Bartolli of Bartolli's Surplus and Outdoor Supplies, while Philip is a hunter and fisherman. Since Lewis Bartolli isn't going into the family business, perhaps Philip sees an opportunity there. That would be sensible."

"Yes, that *would* be sensible." Prudentia didn't sound convinced.

"By the way, who's that kid that's been making googly eyes at you at Dinner and a Movie?" asked Maria.

Prudentia blushed. "His name's Jabe, and he's not a kid. And he's not making googly eyes. In fact, he can hardly look at me."

Maria was walking down Buffalo Street, on her way to Hough Park. She stopped suddenly. Wasn't that Rahel's friend Greta in front of her? And the guy she was with was, what's his name,

Karl? He was handsome, but Maria had heard bad things about him. Should she join them? No, that probably wouldn't work. She could follow them, but what could she do if there was trouble? She was no martial arts expert.

Then she saw Philip on a side street. The answer to her prayers. "Philip, come join me." Philip was brawny—he played American high school football—and knew how to fight.

She linked arms with him. "Walk with me," she commanded. "And talk."

"About what?"

"Umm. Coconuts. Pineapples. Tropical stuff."

"Okay." She let him drone on while she kept her eyes on Greta and Karl. At last, Greta and Karl parted—not without some squirming on Greta's part—and Maria breathed a sigh of relief.

"Did you say something?" asked Philip.

"Thank you, this was lovely. Sorry, but I have to run. Bye!"

If it wasn't one thing, it was another. The latest problem was a political one. The Company had been chartered under the laws of the New United States, which, at the time, was a sovereign state. But now the NUS was merely a part of the United States of Europe. So was the charter still valid? And if the NUS prohibited slavery on its soil, but the USE had yet to speak on the issue, was slavery forbidden in the colony?

The lawyers whom David consulted gave him an extremely learned, expensive and authoritative "maybe."

When David arrived in Hamburg, where his ship was docked, he discovered a letter waiting for him. He opened it. It read, simply, "Bring back bauxite." The letter was unsigned.

But he recognized the handwriting. It was that of cousin Jan. Who, last David heard, was in the employ of Louis De Geer. Mr. "I-am-sending-ships-to-the-Davis-Strait-to-hunt-whales-and-maybe-mine-a-little-gold-in-Greenland." Even though he was a metals magnate, with no previous interest in whales. And even though the up-time books said nothing about gold in Greenland.

But they sure said plenty about Greenland being the only source of cryolite. The critical flux for making aluminum from alumina. Which in turn was made from bauxite.

David decided to buy some more shovels and picks. Right away.

North Sea, December 1633

David and his band of sailors and colonists left Hamburg on a blustery, rainy December day. It was an uncomfortable time of year to venture out on the North Sea. But that was an advantage, too; the Spanish war galleons weren't especially seaworthy and tended to spend the winters in port.

David was once again captain of the *Walvis*. As its name implied, it was a whaler, but it was also a licensed privateer. And, just as on his last journey, the *Walvis* was accompanied by the yacht *Eikhoorn*.

The Company had doubled his force by adding the *Koninck David*, a two-hundred-tonner with fourteen guns, and a second yacht, the *Hoop*.

It was the ideal combination of ship types for making the dangerous run south to Africa to pick up the trade winds for the Atlantic crossing. The Barbary corsairs ranged from the English Channel to Cape Verde, always hoping to capture an imprudent European ship. If they did, all aboard, crew and passengers, would be held for ransom, or simply sold as slaves at the marts of Sallee or Algiers.

The yachts could scout ahead, warning the flotilla of danger, and in turn they could shelter under the big guns of the fluyts if they encountered any formidable foe. They would come in handy in the New World, too, being ideal for inshore work.

Some investors in the Company had been more intrigued by David's descriptions of the profits to be made from privateering than by the more prosaic plans to tap rubber and mine bauxite. They had prevailed on their fellows to beef up the crews, so that David would have additional manpower for working the cannon, adjusting sail, and boarding enemy ships (or repelling boarders). That was good.

Unfortunately, David felt a bit betwixt and between. He had more men than was truly economical for the operation of a fluyt, but not so many as would be on a true privateer on a short range hunting mission. And his ships were larger, and therefore less handy, than the piratical ideal.

David was well aware that this uncomfortable compromise was the natural result of decision-making by committee.

"Captain, we have a stowaway."

David looked at his cousin, Heyndrick. "He must be very ingenious to escape detection this long."

"I suspect it was more that he was very generous to a sailor or two. He is a young American, and many of them are rich."

David started swearing. "And no doubt he is on board without parental permission, and his parents will be raising bloody hell with my investors. Bring him to my cabin."

A defiant young American teenager was brought in a moment later.

"What's your name, and age?"

"Phil Jenkins. I'm sixteen. And a half."

"Sixteen, huh?"

"And a half," Phil reminded him.

"That's young for an American to leave home. Do your parents know that you are here?"

"I mailed them a letter. From Hamburg. Anyway, I'm old enough to join the army, so why can't I go overseas?"

"So...you stowed away because you want to see the world? Or perhaps you have seen one of those romantic American movies about pirates, and fancy yourself with a black eye patch and a parrot on your shoulder?"

"I know a lot about trees, and stuff like that. I thought I could help Maria—"

"Maria, huh? Would you be as keen to look at trees in Suriname if Maria weren't on board?" Phil colored. "I knew having Maria on board was going to mean trouble," David muttered. "I don't suppose you have any nautical skills?"

"Well, Grantville was located about two hundred miles from Chesapeake Bay. But I know how to hunt and fish, and I can handle a small boat..." Phil paused. David's stern expression was unchanged. Phil's voice trailed off. "On a river or lake."

David waved toward the porthole window. "Does that look like a lake to you?"

"No, sir."

David studied Philip, and decided that he was not entirely unpromising material for a colonist, or a mariner. Still...

"All right. You're more trouble to me than you're worth. I can't afford to turn around—we waited a long time for a northeast wind—but as soon as we see a friendly ship heading toward

Hamburg or Bremen, you're out of here. If you can't pay for the passage, you'll write me a promissory note, and I'll give you the money."

"But sir—"

"No buts. This is not your American legislature; there is no debate. Cousin, find a place for him to swing a hammock, and keep him out of my hair."

Maria couldn't believe it. Philip had snuck on board to be with her.

It made her feel like, like . . . reaching into his throat and pulling out his intestines. Not that his *intestines* were the root of the problem, anatomically speaking. Teenage boys, *arggh*!

She admitted to herself that it made her feel good that he was so interested in her. After all, she was ten years older than him.

But did he have any idea what sort of position it put her in? The crew and colonists would have had difficulty enough accepting an *up-time* woman in a position of authority. But the up-timers all acted as if they were nobles. Maria was educated, and of good family, but not of the nobility, nor someone whose past achievements would force them to overlook her gender. The captain had only grudgingly accepted her, after witnessing her kayaking stunt . . . not that the demonstration had the slightest bit to do with her competence as a botanist, a healer, an artist, or a geologist!

And now the captain would be wondering if this trip to the New World was just her excuse for eloping with Philip. Why, everyone else on board would be wondering the same thing.

Well, she was going to have to have a little talk with Philip. Once she had calmed down enough not to throw him overboard and make him *swim* back to Hamburg.

But it was nice to know that he thought she was attractive.

Carsten Claus sat on a capstan and watched the sailors going about their work. The other colonists had decided that the water was a bit too rough for their taste, and had retired to the *zwischendeck*. Carsten, however, had once been a sailor himself, and he had quickly recovered both his sea legs and his "sailor's stomach."

His fellow colonists were mostly Dutch and Germans, displaced by the war. Happy people don't pack their belongings and make a long and difficult journey to a wilderness reportedly populated by cannibals and savage beasts. Even if rumor also had it that there is gold to be found somewhere in that wilderness. The practical Dutch and Germans just didn't put much stock in stories of El Dorado. So the colonists were people with problems back home that they needed to escape, or with more than their fair share of wanderlust.

Of course, there was a third possibility. A few could be spies, or agents provocateurs. Carsten was an organizer for the Committees of Correspondence (CoC), the revolutionary organization that, with American encouragement, had spread across much of central Europe.

Andy Yost had briefed Carsten on how important it was to have a colony that could export rubber, bauxite and oil to the New United States. Oops, Carsten meant the United States of Europe. Just before the expedition left, the once-sovereign NUS had become a member state of the USE.

In Carsten's opinion, some of the CoC members greatly exaggerated the ubiquity of Richelieu's spies. In fact, at a CoC meeting, Carsten had once rapped on a closet door, and yelled, "Cardinal, come out right this minute." That had a gotten a laugh, albeit a somewhat nervous one.

Carsten had to admit that it was at least conceivable that the colonists had been infiltrated. So one of Carsten's jobs was to check their bona fides. By now, Carsten was sure that they were all okay. Well, reasonably sure.

He had also made some progress with respect to his long-term business, which was "education." Gently indoctrinating them in democratic principles, and forming a new CoC cell to make sure that the colony didn't venture onto dangerous ground. Like slaveholding.

When their ship entered the dangerous waters between Cape Finisterre and the Cape Verde Islands, he had reminded the colonists that these were the haunts of the Barbary Corsairs.

He acknowledged that they couldn't have a better captain than David de Vries, who was famed for having fought off the Turks when they outnumbered him two-to-one. But he asked them to pray for his fellow sailors who were less fortunate, who had been forced to surrender and whose families could not ransom them from slavery. They did so, and if they added a prayer or two for themselves, he couldn't blame them.

And then, as they prayed, he asked them to pray for the Africans who had been enslaved in the New World by the wicked Spanish and Portuguese.

When one of the colonists was bold enough to retort that the Africans couldn't expect better treatment, being pagans, and probably cannibals at that, Philip had hotly complained that putting chains on the blacks wasn't the best way to teach them about the benefits of Christianity. As an up-timer, Philip's opinions were accorded respect, despite his youth and inexperience.

So Carsten, at least, was glad that Philip had joined their expedition.

The ship was running before the wind, which meant that the captain's cursing was carried down the length of the ship. The crew was practically tiptoeing.

Philip gave Heyndrick an anxious look. "What's got the captain upset? It isn't me, again, I hope."

"No, no, it's not you. The captain got all these newfangled navigation instruments in Grantville. Most of them work fine. The sextant, it beats a cross-staff any day. Maybe ten times as accurate, and you don't go blind trying to sight the sun."

"So what's the problem?"

"The clock. It's supposed to keep Nürnberg time, so we can calculate our longitude. It worked just fine...on land. And it's supposed to work at sea. Uses springs, not a pendulum."

"But..."

"But whoever designed it never tested it at sea. Or at least, not on waters this rough. We know where we are, more or less, from soundings and sightings, and either the clock is wrong, or our computations are. And since the captain's figures and mine agree..."

"How bad an error are you talking about?"

"Well, the old pendulum clocks, if you took them to sea, accumulated ten or fifteen minutes error a day. This one, oh, a minute or two. But an error of one minute clock time still throws off the longitude by"—he frowned for a moment—"seven and a half degrees. A few hundred miles. And after a month at sea, the clock won't even tell you which *ocean* you're in."

"Really. In that case, I have a proposition I want to put before the captain."

"Pardon me if I wait here. I have no desire to join you on the execution block."

"Captain, you don't want me to leave," Philip said.

David turned to face him. "Oh? Why the hell not?"

Philip took a deep breath. "Because of this." He pulled back his sleeve.

David didn't understand, at first. Then he did. Philip was wearing a self-winding wristwatch. A timepiece which worked at sea would let David accurately determine his longitude each day. If the timepiece kept the correct time for a place of known longitude, like Grantville, then it could be compared with the ship's local time, inferred from the position of the sun, to find the ship's longitude.

"How accurate is your watch?"

Philip hesitated. "I'm not sure. I guess it might lose or gain a few minutes a year."

"A year," repeated David dumbly.

"Yep," Phillip affirmed, this time more confidently.

David took a deep breath. "You are offering me your watch in return for the passage, and your maintenance in the colony?"

"Are you kidding? I bet this watch is worth more than your entire ship."

"Not this ship." David said. But he couldn't help thinking, *But it is perhaps worth as much as one of the yachts. And it would be worth a lot more if only I could shoot the sun with equivalent accuracy.*

Philip clarified his position. "What I meant was that I—and my watch—would be at your disposal for the duration of the voyage."

"Aren't you worried that I might just seize it from you? Or perhaps contrive your murder?"

Phil took a step back. "I . . . The things I heard about you . . . I didn't think you'd do something like that. You could have killed the Indians who wiped out the Zwanandael settlement, and you didn't. At least, Joe Buckley said you didn't."

"You might bear in mind that Joe Buckley got the story from me. But you're right, I didn't. And I won't. But I would advise you to be very cautious about whom you show that watch to."

"Philip." She stared at him, eyes half-slitted, fists on hips.

He either didn't recognize the warning signs, or chose to ignore them. "Hi, Maria, I'm—"

"Why are you here?"

"Isn't it obvious? We've been seeing each other a while, and I couldn't stomach your being away for a year, maybe forever."

"Seeing me? You mean courting me? Dating, as you call it?"

"Well, yeah."

"But you never wrote to my brother, and asked his permission to court me. Or even asked Lolly, whose roof I live under."

"Jeesh, guys haven't done that for, I dunno—"

"Centuries? Almost four centuries? As in, the way it was done back in 1633? Oops, it *is* 1633, isn't it?"

"Well, you've lived in Grantville for two years, so it didn't occur to me—"

"Didn't occur to you to say anything to me, either."

"You mean, like saying, 'Will you be my girlfriend?' or 'Would you like to go steady?' That's so old fashioned, you know. Kids my age just hang out, and that's what we were doing."

"Philip. Listen to me. What do you think *my* age is?"

"I don't know. College age? Nineteen? Twenty?"

"I am twenty-six, Philip. I am ten years older than you."

"Not quite. I am sixteen and a—"

"Yes, I know! Sixteen and a half!" Maria took a deep breath, let it out slowly. "I have been married once, and widowed, already. My husband was lost at sea, in Asian waters."

"Sorry, I didn't know. Gee, you look terrific for someone your age."

"Thanks—I think." Maria felt herself losing control of the conversation. "Philip, yes, you came to visit me a lot, but I thought that was because we were friends, not boyfriend and girlfriend. And because you were interested in my work. And maybe because Marina was helping me."

"Marina? She's never said a word to me in school." Philip paused. "Do you have a boyfriend already? I mean, someone other than me."

"No, Philip." He looked relieved.

Maria decided to seize the bull by the horns. "So what did you hope to accomplish by coming on board?"

"I guess...I guess I really wanted to impress you. You know, make a really big romantic gesture." Philip's cheeks were as red as apples.

"Well, you impressed me, but not with your maturity. You didn't try to find out how I felt first, you left your parents worrying—"

"I left them a note."

"Believe me, that just gives them something new to worry about." Maria threw up her hands. "Really, Philip. This is like, like *stalking* me. Go think about it. In private."

Philip was not a happy camper. Everything had gone dreadfully wrong. Maria thought he was a *stalker*, for crying out loud. Philip thought he would *die*.

He lay in his hammock, listening to the creaking of the hull, and tried not to cry. Eventually, he fell asleep.

When he awoke, he resolved that he would ask the captain to flag the next Hamburg-bound ship, after all. He went up to talk to David.

David didn't buy it. "We made an agreement, young man, and you need to stick to it. Unless you are willing to give up your watch."

"Well..."

"I thought not. You have skills that are useful to this expedition, and I expect you to apply them. Whether you love or hate Maria is of absolutely no interest to me. The two of you work it out."

"Heave-to!" The *Walvis* turned into the wind, and stalled. A few minutes later, the other ships followed suit. David sent more lookouts aloft, in case Barbary corsairs came sniffing around, and went to the poop deck.

Philip had no particular duties at this moment, and decided to see if David was in the mood to explain what was going on. He found David peering across an odd-looking compass. It had the usual compass needle and card, but mirrors and slotted vanes were mounted on an outer ring. "What's that?"

"An azimuth compass. One of your up-time ideas, but made in Nürnberg. It's for measuring the compass bearing of an object. A landmark, or, if you fiddle with the mirror, a heavenly body."

David turned the ring, and squinted through an opposing pair of slits. "There's the Pico de Fogo, the 'Fire Peak' of Ilha de Fogo." A plume of steam rose from it. Plainly, it was a volcano. He adjusted the azimuth circle, and took a second reading. "And Pico da Antonia, on Ilha de Santiago." The two islands lay near the southwestern end of the Cape Verdes island chain.

"With cross-bearings, I can find our exact position on both your up-time map—it has a little inset of the Cape Verdes—and on my old chart." David looked up at the sky. "It's getting close to noon, we'll take a sun-sight, and then see how good your timepiece is." David waited until the sun seemed to hang in the sky, and then measured its altitude. Philip called out the time. Grantville Standard Time, that is. GST had been proclaimed by the government after Greg Ferrara had determined Grantville's new longitude.

"Follow me." David walked across the gently tilting deck to his cabin, Philip following in his wake. Philip watched as David laboriously calculated the latitude and longitude.

"Hmm, pretty good. In fact, so good as to earn you an invitation to the captain's table for dinner tomorrow."

By then, Mount Fogo, the highest peak of the Cape Verdes, had disappeared below the horizon, to the north and behind the *Walvis* and its companions. Its volcanic plume was just a smudge, almost lost in the horizon haze. The great mass of Africa lay only four hundred miles to the east; the wide Atlantic separated them from the Americas to the west.

Over the meal, David explained just how Philip's wristwatch was going to help them on the next leg. He unrolled a map. "Most ships, if Caribbean-bound, would have turned west from Fogo, run down the fifteen degree line to Dominica."

Philip nodded politely. He could see the small speck marking the location of Dominica, on the near edge of the West Indies, but he knew nothing about it.

"But that's not the best sailing for us," David explained. "We'd have to fight our way southeast, against the current, to then get to Suriname from there."

"So why not go farther south, and then turn west?"

"Spoken like a true landlubber," David said, smiling to take out the sting. "If we went south to the latitude of your up-time town of Paramaribo, we would hit the doldrums. Do you understand that term?"

"No wind?"

"Often, nary a breath. Duppy Jonah's Flytrap. You can be stuck there for weeks, as your provisions spoil and your men's tempers do the same. The belt of doldrums moves north and south with the sun; that's one of the reasons we set sail in winter."

David paused for a bite. "With your fancy wristwatch to help us find our longitude, we can curve gradually south as we head west, hit South America here." He jabbed his forefinger against the spot marking the up-time town of Cayenne, French Guiana. "We don't have to sail down a latitude line anymore."

"Philip, congratulations. Heyndrick told me that we made a very difficult sailing, thanks to your navigational help."

"Thanks." Philip kept his back to her.

Maria waited. "Is that all you're going to say?"

"Yep."

"When you're tired of being a jerk, come and talk to me." Maria stalked off.

"Wait, Maria," called Philip, but his voice was lost in the wind, and he didn't want to follow her and endure the catcalls from the sailors.

The Wild Coast of South America, February 1634

Their first view of Suriname was discouraging. As they cruised northwest along the Surinamese coast from Cayenne, they saw mile after unbroken mile of mangrove swamp. It didn't look like a place the colonists would want to visit, let alone live.

At last, David led his small flotilla into the mouth of the Suriname River. Here, it was really more than a river, being several miles in breadth. They headed south for what the maps had shown to be the location of the twentieth-century capital of Suriname, Paramaribo, twelve miles upriver. The "Great Encyclopedia" said that it had been settled in the old time line in 1640, and it seemed that the location couldn't be that bad if it had remained in use for over three centuries. And it added that the site was "on a plateau sixteen feet above low water level, well drained, clean, and in general healthy." Even here, the river was a mile wide, and eighteen feet deep.

They solemnly raised the flag, and David christened the town "Gustavus." Gustavus Adolphus was a hero to the Dutch and Germans, and the christening was a cheap price to pay for the Swedish support.

There were signs of a former Indian settlement on the plateau. Whether its abandonment was a heavenly blessing, or a warning, they couldn't say.

In the days following the landing, they explored the country-side. Despite appearances, the marshes were just a narrow strip on the coast. Behind them lay an area of *zwampen en ritsen*: swamps and ridges. They weren't sure just how far that terrain extended, but the up-time encyclopedias had told them that if they went far enough south, they would find savannas and the great rainforests.

They had deliberately arrived at the beginning of what the encyclopedia called the short dry season. That, they knew, would be the best time to clear ground. And, once they found it, to mine bauxite. In March, when the long wet season began, they would plant their crops—tobacco, cotton, and various food crops, by preference.

There had been much debate back in Grantville as to how to solve the perennial labor problem of tropical America without resort to slavery. It had to be solved, because the tropics had products that Grantville desperately wanted, like rubber. Part of the proposed solution was to use up-time medical knowledge so that Europeans wouldn't die off so readily.

The botanical garden at Leiden, which Maria knew so well, was primarily a garden of medicinal plants for the education of the student physicians. So she knew her herbs. In Grantville, she had learned more about disease, and how to avoid it. On the ship, she had insisted that the sailors and colonists eat sauerkraut, to ward off scurvy. On shore, she lectured the settlers on mosquito control. And sanitation. Several of the colonists had gotten some medical training, too, since Maria wasn't planning a permanent stay.

Carsten Claus and Johann Mueller walked along the wooded ridge line, grateful for the shade that the scrub forest provided. Even though they were miles from the sea, there were shells and shell fragments everywhere.

Carsten bent to pick up a particularly interesting one. It was egg-shaped, and mottled red in color, and it shone as though it was made of the finest Chinese porcelain. It was a cowry, a snail shell. Like the cowries of Africa, which Carsten had seen in a nobleman's collection, it had a ribbed slit opening. In Africa, that made it a fertility symbol.

Frau Vorst was right, Carsten thought, this must be an ancient sand dune. Carsten decided to save the shell for her; she loved to collect curiosities. He also decided not to say anything about its symbolic significance.

Johann Mueller, a glassmaker, was more interested in the sand. Every so often he would pick up a handful and bring it so close to his eyes that Carsten wondered whether Johann was nearsighted.

It wasn't common for fledgling colonies to have glassmakers, although Carsten had heard that there was one in Jamestown, Virginia. But it was the second part of the master plan to make a tropical colony viable without resort to slavery.

The up-timers knew they had to find a way to get the local Indians to work, day in, day out, without coercion. And Captain de Vries, who had been to both North America and the Caribbean, told them that there was only so much one could accomplish with the standard trade goods. An Indian might work to acquire one steel knife, but he didn't need a dozen. Strong liquor was a possible lure, but it had its own disadvantages.

Knowing that glass beads were a good article of trade, the Company had decided to coax a glassmaker to join the colony. That way, they could sell or barter a variety of glass articles, not just beads, and not just to the Indians, but also to Europeans in Guiana and the islands.

On the long voyage over, Carsten had delicately drawn out the details of Johann's background. Johann was a Thuringer from Lauscha, a journeyman with many years experience, who had failed to make master. Solely for economic reasons, he assured Carsten. He hadn't botched his masterwork or been caught seducing his mentor's daughter.

Carsten was inclined to believe him. You could only become a master in a guild if you found a town whose guild chapter had a vacancy. Because of the war, the demand for glassware had declined, and masters who were scrounging for work weren't likely to welcome a newcomer.

"In this Suriname," Johann said, "I don't have to marry an ugly old widow just to get her husband's shop. And I don't have to worry about competition."

Just about pirates, Indians, jungle beasts and tropical diseases, thought Carsten, but he kept the thought to himself.

"Oh, look at this," Johann chortled. "This sand, it's almost a pure white. And look at the size of the grains. They are so even, it's beautiful."

Carsten was reminded of the adage, *Beauty is in the eyes of the beholder.* But that, too, he kept to himself.

"Captain, the plan won't work. It's hopeless. You should just take me back to Hamburg." The speaker was Denys Zager, the master sawyer hired by the Company. They knew that Suriname had plenty of wood, so why not sell wood articles to the Indians? Things they couldn't make with their primitive tools. And Zager's planks would also be used for constructing buildings and furniture for the colonists. Zager would cut the wood and the colonist's carpenter would do the fine crafting.

Unfortunately, the person who *hired* Zager, on the Company's behalf, wasn't the one who had to *work* with Zager. That is, poor David. Zager was the sort of person who, if he found a pot of gold at one end of the rainbow, would complain that there wasn't another pot at the other end.

David sighed. "What's the problem?"

"The Company wants me to build a wind-powered sawmill. Like the one Cornelis Corneliszoon had invented in 1593. A wonderful idea."

"And the Grantville-made saw blades are satisfactory, I suppose." They were, of course, better than anything he had seen before, of course, but Zager would never admit it. They had been provided on the theory that it was better to use steel to make saw blades and use them locally to manufacture wood articles, than to make steel trade goods that would have to be produced at home.

"Only... where's the wind? All we get here is a light breeze."

"What about using a water wheel?"

"Well... the most efficient water wheel is an overshot. Water comes down from above, onto buckets. But you need a decent drop, and where's the drop?" Zager waved his arm toward the placidly flowing Suriname River. "Not there, I assure you."

David shrugged. "Come with us upriver, perhaps we can find you a waterfall there. We know from the up-time maps that there are mountains to the south."

"You want me to live alone in the wilderness, tending my mill by this yet-to-be-located watermill of yours? You will keep me supplied with food and lumber, come instantly to my aid if the Indians attack?"

David started to answer, then thought better of it.

Zager looked triumphant. "I thought not."

David rubbed his chin. "You said, the 'most efficient' wheel. So what are the alternatives?"

Zager said nothing.

"Well?"

Zager sighed. "I suppose we could make do with an under-shot wheel. If we must. It just needs flowing water, to strike the floats." He spat. "But this river is rather slow-flowing. We won't get a lot of power out of it."

"Then we will find you a livelier river. Or we will have to bring you oxen, or donkeys. And, until then, if you don't want to hassle with an undershot wheel, you can saw the old-fashioned way, in a pit with a platform over it."

"Hmmph. At least as the senior man, I'd be at the top of the pit, where I can breathe. But all right, we'll try the undershot wheel. Once I figure out where the current is strongest . . . probably by falling in and drowning."

Heinrich Bender, formerly of Heidelberg, was clutching a piece of sketch paper in one hand, and a rock in the other. "Frau Vorst, Frau Vorst, we found it!"

Maria looked up. "Bauxite, you mean?" The sailors and colonists were searching creek beds and other rock exposures in the vicinity of old-time-line Paranam, some miles south of Gustavus, because the up-time encyclopedias had said that bauxite was mined there. Maria had divided them into groups, and given each a "wanted" sketch showing what bauxite looked like. Maria, who was an experienced artist, had made the drawings back in Grantville, basing them on photographs in various up-time field guides owned by the school libraries.

Heinrich nodded.

"Let's see." He handed her the paper and the rock. Maria compared her sketch with the specimen. The sketch was deliberately done in charcoal, to avoid misleading the searchers—bauxite could be white, yellow, red, or brown. This specimen was red.

For bauxite, the telltale sign was its "raisin pie" texture. Okay, the up-timers called it "pisolitic." Yep, the pisolites—little pea-sized concretions—were present in Heinrich's find.

Heinrich was fidgeting with excitement. Maria wasn't surprised;

David had promised a bounty to the first person to find bauxite. "Well, is it bauxite? Is it?"

"Looks promising, bear with me." Maria tried scratching the rock with her fingernail. She brushed away the white powder to make sure that it was the rock, not her fingernail, which had succumbed. Yes, there was the scratch. That meant that on the Mohs' scale of hardness, the rock was less than 2.5. Bauxite had a hardness ranging from 1, like talc, to 3, like calcite. A bit harder than most clays.

What else? Right, specific gravity. She hefted it; it seemed to have about the right density, two or two-and-a-half times that of water. She could measure it when she went back on board the yacht, but clearly it was in the ballpark.

"Good work, Heinrich," Maria said. "Show me where you found it."

"It was over here...no, over there."

Maria saw a second rock, much like the first. She called over some more of the colonists, and set them to work digging test holes near the find, so she would know how deep the formation was. And then she wrote a note to David, and sent Heinrich off with it to claim his reward.

The formation turned out to be enormous in extent; miles wide, and usually just a few feet below the surface. In places, powdered bauxite, or so Maria presumed it to be, actually turned the soil to a dark purple-red, as if someone had soaked it in beet juice.

Out came the shovels, the pickaxes, and the wheelbarrows. For now, all they did was collect the bauxite. If the market for bauxite took off—meaning, someone succeeded in duplicating the Hall-Heroult process of making aluminum—then they would see about converting bauxite to alumina right in Suriname. Four tons of bauxite made two of alumina. That would reduce transportation costs—if the necessary reagents could be produced by the colony.

The Company even hoped that one day it could harvest the power of the cataracts of the Suriname river to produce electricity. If so, then they might actually be able to produce aluminum locally. Two tons of alumina, with great gobs of electricity and a dash of cryolite to reduce the melting point of the alumina, would make one ton of aluminum.

For that matter, she had been told that alumina made a great refractory. So even without cryolite, the bauxite might come in handy.

It would be nice, Maria thought, if she could carry out a proper chemical test, but she didn't happen to have any cobalt nitrate handy. Hah, she might as well wish Gustavus had an atomic absorption spectrophotometer, while she was at it. At least, wonder of wonders, the high school in Grantville actually had one...an unlikely gift from a large construction material manufacturer. So when they got the ore home, the chemists could definitively determine that it contained aluminum.

Of course, David and Maria would feel rather stupid if they carted twenty tons of bog iron home, when they were looking for bauxite.

Finally. Maria could get on with her real work. Documenting and collecting the extraordinary plants of Suriname, for the greater glory of the Leiden Botanical Gardens. Which she thought of as the family firm. Not without reason; her father Aelius had taken it over in 1599, and then her brother Adolph in 1624.

She would start close to town, on the coastal plain, and ultimately head upriver, to explore the rainforest.

For documentation, she had her pencils, chalks and paints, and her leaf press. But live specimens would be better yet. She collected both seeds and seedlings. The seeds were mixed in with charcoal, or sawdust or sand, and placed in bags. Those, in turn, went into what she hoped were insect-proof boxes. Seedlings could go into cases with glass sides and tops, so they could be kept moist and given the benefit of the sun during the long trip home.

Nor would she ignore the fauna. She drew pictures of some, and they had both live and dead specimens to ship to the savants and curiosity collectors back home. Philip had brought her, no doubt as a peace offering, a curious fish he had caught. It had four eyes. Well, not quite. It had two eyes, but each was divided into upper and lower halves. Philip told her that it swam on the surface, with the upper halves above the water.

Maria never tired of painting the wildlife. The birds, in particular, were beautiful. And even many of the insects.

Other insects, she could definitely do without.

David studied the mark in the sand bar. It was, quite clearly, the imprint of a European boot. He tapped the shoulder of one sailor, whispered to him, and sent him to collect the others.

Soon, they were back on the deck of the *Eikhoorn*. David, an explorer at heart, had taken command of the yacht, leaving its usual skipper to supervise the loading of bauxite ore onto the *Walvis*.

"We're not alone."

"Indians?" asked a crewman. He looked around nervously.

"No, Europeans. We don't know their nationality. If we're lucky, they're Dutch." While the colony was under the protection of Sweden and the United States of Europe, it also had a license from the West India Company. Since David was a patroon of the West India Company, it hadn't been difficult to obtain. Especially since Sweden and the USE were the only Dutch allies remaining.

"Listen up. If they're English or French, they won't know about the Battle of Dunkirk. Well, probably not. And while I am palavering with them, I don't want you to give away the information that they have any reason to fear us." David's crew was almost entirely Dutch. "So, no insults, no glares, no nattering among yourselves as to how treacherous the English and French are. Have your weapons ready, but don't point them until I give you leave. Understood?"

He turned to Maria. "So much for the up-time encyclopedias. First settled by the French in 1640, my eye!"

The *Eikhoorn* continued a mile or two upriver, but its crew didn't spot any signs of habitation, European or otherwise. They retraced their route, and this time went up a creek, rowing with muffled oars. It wasn't long before they heard voices. English voices.

David signaled a halt, and called out. "Hello, be you English?" There was an excited clamor, and several roughly dressed Europeans stepped out of the trees. They looked at him goggle-eyed.

"We are. We are Captain Marshall's men. Who are you?"

"I am Captain David de Vries, a patroon of the Dutch West India Company, currently in the service of His Majesty the King of Sweden and the emperor of the United States of Europe." That sounded impressive enough, he hoped.

They murmured among themselves. One ventured, "I am sure Captain Marshall will want to entertain you. To hear news, if nothing else."

"When did you last have news?" David asked.

"A ship comes once each summer to collect our dried tobacco."

"Really? Do you have any left for sale? How much do you sell each year?" Their answer gave David some clue as to how many acres were planted, and thus, of how many settlers were engaged in tobacco cultivation. It was clear that the crew of the yacht was outnumbered. But not the colonists he had left downriver.

"My friends don't speak English," David said. "Excuse me while I explain to them that I am going to pay a call on Captain Marshall." He then added, softly, in rapid Dutch. "Be on guard. Let none of the English on board in my absence. If I don't return by tomorrow morning, make haste to the settlement and warn them. From the extent of the tobacco crop, there must be several dozen English here, at least."

"Why are you visiting them? Wouldn't it be better to just come back in force?" asked Maria.

"It's a calculated risk. I need to see just how many of them there are, how well fed and armed, whether they have a fort, and more. And much more. Are the local Indians friendly or hostile? Are the English of the royalist or parliamentary factions? Are they Church of England, or Puritans, or even Catholics?"

David was gone the rest of the day. A lone Englishman came back to the creek and informed them that David had been invited to dine with Captain Marshall and spend the night.

Maria and the others could only hope that the messenger was telling the truth. Two men remained on watch at all times.

The next morning, while mist still shrouded the creek, David emerged, together with two of the English. They were better dressed than any of the men seen the day before. David said something to them, and they waited at the forest edge as he came up to the yacht. "Captain Marshall and one of his colleagues, a Mr. Francis Scott, will be enjoying our hospitality. Remember what I said about keeping your lips buttoned. I am fairly sure that Scott is being brought because he speaks Dutch—whether he says so or not."

"How many of them are there?"

"Sixty, all men. They have been here since 1630, and they cultivate tobacco. Perhaps half a mile up the creek they have a fort, with a wood palisade. But I need to get back to them, lest they grow suspicious. Fortunately, the custom in the Guianas has been for the few English, Dutch and French in the country to live in harmony, so they aren't expecting trouble."

"Mevrouw Vorst—"

"Please, Captain, by now I think you can call me Maria."

"Maria, ply Marshall and Scott with questions about the Indians, the animals, the plants, the weather, and the like. Philip, you can tell them about the wonders of Grantville. Stay off the topic of politics! All right, I better go fetch them now."

"Ahoy, the *Walvis*! Captain de Vries and party, with two English guests," bellowed the the first mate of the *Eikhoorn*.

The men on the deck of the *Walvis* stopped what they were doing, and stared.

"They don't seem happy to see Englishmen," Captain Marshall commented.

"The Dutch-English relationship has sometimes been a troubled one," David replied. "But you are my guests."

Heyndrick and Philip were both on the deck of the *Walvis*. Heyndrick finished cleaning his fowling piece. Heyndrick looked up, and saw Philip sitting on the railing, a fishing rod in hand. He studied Philip for a moment, and decided he might as well just ask the question he had been thinking about lately. "How are things between you and Maria these days?"

Philip turned. "I dunno. Okay, I guess. I've recovered from my case of hormonal insanity, if that's what you mean."

"Good. If that means what I think it does. So it wouldn't bother you, if . . . if I wanted to be better friends with Maria?"

"I guess not. It's hardly poaching, after the way she told me off. It was nice of you to ask, though."

"Excellent. Come to my cabin, share a glass of brandy with me."

Meanwhile, Marshall and Scott had come down, together with Maria, to David's cabin. "Our colony is a new one, I can offer you better hospitality here," David explained.

At dinner, David came to the point. "I understand your last news of England was from this past summer."

Marshall gave Scott a meaningful look.

"I regret to tell you that King Charles has made alliance with the Catholic powers, with France and Spain."

Scott cursed. "I knew it was a mistake for him to marry that Frenchwoman."

"Worse," David continued, "rather than declare war on the Dutch Republic openly, he and the French betrayed us. The French and

English squadrons that sailed with Von Tromp's Sea Beggars, to meet the Spanish fleet at Dunkirk, pounced on him from behind."

"So England and the Dutch Republic are at war," said Marshall. "Are we prisoners? Hostages?"

"Formally speaking, I am right now in the service of Sweden and the USE," drawled David. "And there has been no attack by England upon either. So while there is no doubt that this alliance is aimed, ultimately, at Sweden, and the USE, I am not *required* to take hostile action against any English ships or settlers I may encounter."

Marshall raised his eyebrows, but said nothing.

"Still, your colony is something of a dagger at the back of mine. As the English fleet was to the Dutch at the Battle of Ostend. And my colonists, many of whom are Dutch, will not be happy to have English neighbors.

"That said, the governor of Virginia, Sir John Harvey, is a friend of mine. He came to my aid in the days when we were both in the East Indies. So, I would do you a good turn, if I could. If you surrender, and give me your parole, I will transport your people to Tobago, or Saint Kitts, or Providence Island, all of which have English colonies, and land you there under flag of truce." David waited for them to respond.

Scott and Marshall exchanged looks; Marshall gave Scott a slight nod. "You certainly have control of the mouth of the Suriname River," said Scott. "I saw that you have emplaced cannon at your town, and of course you have ships of war, too. You can keep reinforcements and supplies from reaching us, and prevent us from selling our tobacco. And you are too strong for us to conquer.

"On the other hand, you wouldn't find it easy to scour us out. Your colony isn't too much larger than ours. We know the terrain better than you do. Your fluyts can't go up our creek, and your yachts don't throw enough weight of metal to successfully assault our fort. We don't need supplies from the outside; we are self-sufficient. The Indians are friendly to us and would come to our aid if you attacked. So it looks like a stalemate to me," Scott concluded.

"Only in the short-term," said David. "Given time, we could bring in troops, land them and march up the creek. And if you huddled in the fort, we could burn your crops. That would be the end of your self-sufficiency. And I wouldn't be too sure of your Indian alliance. The Indians will switch sides if they think you're likely to lose anyway."

Marshall took a sip of wine. "Have you been to Saint Kitts, Captain de Vries?" That was one of the Lesser Antilles, a crescent-shaped chain of the small Caribbean islands, stretching from Puerto Rico to Trinidad.

"Yes, I put in for water there on my last trip."

"Are you familiar with the peculiar relationship there?"

"Indeed." The island was settled by the English in 1623. But a few years later, they had allowed the French, under the command of the ex-privateer captain Pierre d'Esnambuc, to claim the ends of the island, while the English remained in control of the middle. They held the salt pans in the south in common, and they had agreed that they would not fight each other even if England and France were at war.

"Perhaps...perhaps we can do the same? Agree to neutrality between our colonies, regardless of what is happening in Europe?"

"It might not be in my power to conclude an absolute neutrality," David warned. "We didn't know you were here, so we don't have specific instructions from the emperor of the USE."

"But we could at least agree to remain neutral in the absence of a direct order from our sovereign, and, in the event of such an order, give notice of intent to dissolve our pact."

David looked thoughtful. "It wouldn't be easy for you to receive such an order, considering that we control your line of communication."

"No, it wouldn't. So the agreement will be more to your benefit than ours, but at least would save our honor."

"I will think on it. While it is a tempting prospect—trade, and exchange of information, would be mutually beneficial, I think—the feelings of the Dutch of the colony run high. And we won't always have warships in the river; there would be a fear that you would try to take advantage if they were absent."

Maria moved her chair. The screech drew all eyes to her. "But gentlemen, there is another factor to consider. As a Dutch woman, I was of course appalled by the treacherous attack on our fleet. But I understand that the English in turn are still fired by the incident at Amboyna."

"The massacre—" began Scott, but he desisted when Marshall gripped his shoulder.

"Still, in the long-term, they have a common enemy: the Spanish. The French, too. I think that upon more mature reflection, you will realize that your long-term interests lie with us. Us, meaning the USE and its allies."

Marshall steepled his fingers. "How so?"

"I doubt very much that your king cares what happens to you. Because he has already given up North America to the French."

"The French!"

"Yes, by the Treaty of Ostend, which we learned about shortly after the Battle of Dunkirk. Charles discovered that in the Grantville history books, some of the American colonies revolted successfully, and so he was willing to let them be Richelieu's problem."

"You have proof of this?"

"Sorry, no, but you may question the crew or the colonists," David said.

"You can do better than that," Maria interjected. "Didn't you save the newspapers? You said you would save them until the Spanish had been defeated!"

David swore. "You're right, of course." He dug them out and handed them to Marshall and Scott.

When they finished reading, he added, "Charles also found out that, according to those history books, he gets into a fight with Parliament, which ends with his head on the chopping block. So he's brought in mercenaries to control London, and he's been arresting anyone who the up-timers' books identified as a Parliamentarian. Indeed, anyone he thinks likely to have such sympathies."

Marshall winced. "Do you know anything of the Earl of War- wick?" Maria shook her head.

"Warwick, Warwick," mused David. "Oh, Robert Rich. Well, what I know about him is that he is a big investor in New World colonies. Bermuda, and Providence Island, off the coast of Nicara- gua. And, yes, Richneck Plantation, on the James, is his. I spent a few weeks in Virginia in March of '33. Why do you ask?"

"He is our chief benefactor," Marshall admitted. "And a Puri- tan, as are we."

Scott didn't look happy. "He is on the outs with the Court. Opposed the forced loan of 1626. And Laud's repression of the Puritans."

"So what you can expect," said David, "is that either your colony, too, will be turned over to the French, or it will be given as a reward to one of Laud's or Wentworth's cronies."

✧   ✧   ✧

Heinrich coughed. "Begging your pardon, Madam Vorst, but the captain wants to see you."

Maria looked wistfully at the scarlet ibis that stood rock-still in the pond some yards away, watching for an unwary frog. She had just set up her easel, and had been looking forward to painting the beautiful bird. But she doubted it would hang around waiting for her to finish the captain's business, whatever it was. Answering a gardening question for colonists, perhaps. She knew that she wouldn't have had the opportunity to study the natural world of Suriname if it weren't for the colony, but sometimes her role of "science officer" was irksome.

She rose to her feet, and the sudden movement startled the bird, causing it to take flight. "Help me gather up my things, will you?"

The captain didn't beat around the bush. "Scott's staying in Gustavus, as the representative of the Marshall's Creek colonists."

Maria raised an eyebrow. "As a hostage, too, I imagine."

David nodded. "Marshall's going back upriver on the *Eikhoorn*, to explain the situation to them and see if they wanted to throw in with us."

"Really. Then perhaps I should go upriver with him. Their fort is on the fringe of the rainforest. I might be able to find rubber trees with their help. Or at least the help of their Indian allies."

"Are you sure? We don't know how they'll react to the news. The crew of the *Eikhoorn* will be outnumbered."

"Captain Marshall seems a man of honor; I will make sure that I am traveling under his protection. And even the Spaniards, when they attack a foreign colony, will usually spare the women."

"You'll be the only woman there."

"I am sure there were Indian women around, they just stayed out of sight on your last visit. And as I said, I will be with Captain Marshall."

David hesitated.

"It's not just that the USE needs the rubber. If I find them a new product to sell to us, that will help reconcile them to the 'Swedish' presence downriver. Or whatever you want to call it."

"Okay. You've convinced me."

"This is *so* slow," said David.

"Slow but sure," Maria replied.

They were watching latex slowly drip from the gash in the tree, into a waiting cup. With the aid of Maria's sketches, themselves based on illustrations in the Grantville encyclopedias, the Indians had been able to locate several different trees of interest. One, the *Hevea guianensis*, produced true rubber. Another was what the encyclopedias called *Manilkara bidentata*. Its latex hardened to form balata. Balata wasn't elastic, but it was a natural plastic, which could be used for electrical insulation.

"Why don't we just chop the tree down and take all its latex at once?"

"Several reasons," said Maria. "They aren't that common, just a few trees an acre, so we would have to go farther and farther out to find more. If we tap them, each tree will produce rubber for twenty years or more. And finally, it just won't work. The latex is stored in little pockets. It's not like there's a big cavern inside you can chop your way to. If you want a quick return, you need to find a *Castilla elastica*, it has nice long tubes."

"Well, this is too slow for me. It's as exciting as watching paint dry," David declared. "I think it's time for me to head out."

"Back to Gustavus?"

"No, on to Trinidad and Nicaragua. And pick up a Spanish prize or two along the way, if we're lucky."

"If we must," said Maria with a sigh. "But I have such a horrible backlog of plants to study. Lolly told me the rainforest was diverse, and I thought I knew what she meant, but the reality is inconceivable if you don't see it with your own eyes."

"Who said you had to leave?"

"You need me to find the *Castilla* in Nicaragua."

"No, I don't. I have Philip."

Maria opened her mouth, then shut it without saying anything.

"And he has to come with me because he has to go home at the earliest opportunity. Even if he is dreading the parental punishments that await him."

"Philip."

"Yes, Maria?" He eased the rucksack he was carrying down to the ground. "As you can see, I am packed and ready to go back to sea."

"I am sorry it didn't work out. Couldn't work out. You and me, that is."

Philip didn't quite meet her eyes. "I know. I made an idiot out of myself."

"Don't feel bad. You're a teenage male. Teenage males, by definition, are idiots. Whatever century they were born in."

"Thanks. I think."

"Anyway, I have a present for you." She brought forward the object she had been hiding behind her back. It was one of the blank journal books she used for drawing.

"You can use this to keep track of what you see and do. Perhaps it will make you famous. And...and I will enjoy reading it one day."

He took the journal, brushing her fingers as he did so. "Thank you. I mean it. And good luck."

He paused. "Heyndrick seems like an okay guy."

"I think so, too."

David studied his cousin. "You're determined to stay here in Suriname?"

"Yes. I think there is a lot of opportunity here," said Heyndrick, straight-faced.

"You're blushing."

"I am not," said Heyndrick, coloring still more deeply.

"I am naming you as acting governor, but—you intend to escort Maria on her explorations?"

Heyndrick nodded.

"I thought so. We need someone to keep a steady hand here in your absence. I think I will appoint Carsten Claus as your deputy."

"The ex-sailor? Ran away from the farm as a kid, and later thought better of it?"

"That's right. He is CoC. An organizer of some kind. He is chummy with Andy Yost." Andy was the owner of the Grantville Freedom Arches, the first headquarters of the CoC.

"And you let him come on board?"

"There's CoC money invested in this colony. And the up-timers are counting on the CoC to make sure we don't make any, uh, imprudent investments."

"Buying slaves, you mean?"

"That's right. I will leave you one of the yachts. You and Maria can use it for exploring. You'll have to keep the captain, of course,

I don't have good reason to deprive any of them of command. Which one do you want?"

"The *Eikhoorn*."

"I am not surprised." Heyndrick blushed again. The *Eikhoorn* was commanded by Captain Adrienszoon, a man thirty years older than Heyndrick, while the *Hoop* had a young, unmarried skipper.

Heyndrick pulled a map out of its case, and flattened it out. "Are you sure you shouldn't stay until July or August? See the colony through the end of the first wet season?"

"No. If I wait, I will be in the Caribbean in the hurricane season. Not a wise idea."

Heyndrick found Trinidad on the map, grunted, and rolled the map up again. "That's true . . . However . . . David, I have sailed with you for a long time. And there is something I think needs saying, although I doubt you'd like to hear it."

"Out with it, Cuz."

"You want to be a patroon. But we know how often colonies with absentee owners have come to grief. Someone like Jan Bicker can afford a loss, but you can't. You're terrific at managing sailors and settlers and Indians, but you need to manage yourself. After a few months, you go crazy and want to sail off. And next you know it, your colony, your investment, will be gone."

"So what do you suggest?"

"I know you have to, what's the American phrase, 'get the ball rolling' in Trinidad and Nicaragua. And then you want to get the rubber and tar to the Americans as quickly as possible. But after that, please plan on coming back here, and staying as governor. At least for a few years."

"I'll think about it. But it is a waste of my skills as a shiphandler."

"Then perhaps you need to forget about being a patroon, and stick to what you do best."

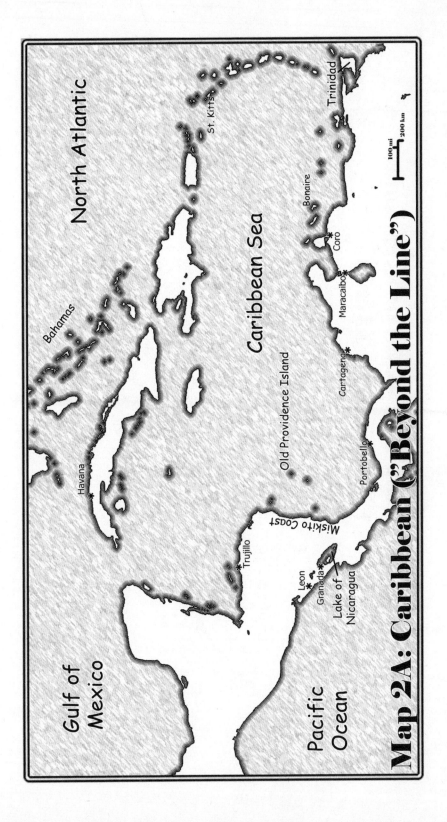

Map 2A: Caribbean ("Beyond the Line")

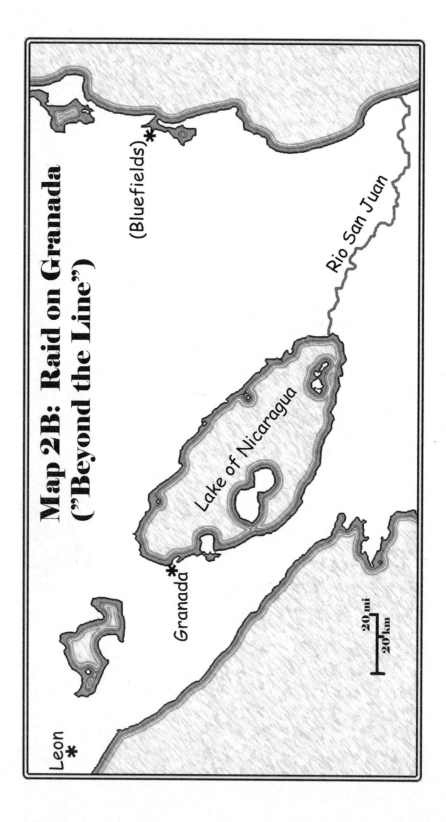

Map 2B: Raid on Granada ("Beyond the Line")

Leon *

Granada *

Lake of Nicaragua

(Bluefields) *

Rio San Juan

20 mi
20 km

Beyond the Line

April 1634 to Late 1634

Trinidad, April 1634

It was a lake, but one unlike any other they had seen. This was the famous Pitch Lake of Trinidad. A hundred acres of tar.

David Pieterszoon de Vries, captain of the fluyt *Walvis*, studied it for a few moments. The lake was nearly circular, perhaps two thousand feet across, nestled in a shallow bowl at the top of a hill. The surface wasn't flat and still, like a mountain lake protected by hills from the wind. Instead, there were broad, dark folds, with clear rainwater lying in the hollows between them. David, in his youth, had worked for a bookseller, to learn English, and the haphazard folding reminded him of marbled paper. Here and there, the folds were festooned with a patch of grass, a few yards in width, with a shrub or small tree rising above it like the mast of a ship.

For Philip Jenkins, born in twentieth-century West Virginia, it awoke other memories. "This is a humongous parking lot."

"Sir Walter was right," said David. "Enough pitch here for all the ships of the world." Sir Walter Raleigh had come here in 1595; his sailors used its tar to protect their ships' hulls from the *teredos*, the wood borers of the tropical waters.

"We have a lot more uses for it than for caulking ships," Philip replied.

"Wait here." Using a boarding pike as a probe, David tested the surface. It seemed firm enough. He took a step forward. The tar sank slightly, but held his weight. He took a second step. No problem.

David turned his head. "Follow me. Test the ground before you trust yourself to it, there may be softer areas at the center of the lake." After a moment's hesitation, the landing party followed him.

Philip was surprised to discover that the tar didn't seem to stick to his shoes or clothing, as he would have expected. Inspected closely, the tar was finely wrinkled, like the skin of an elephant.

David and his landing party walked around a bit, then he called them to a halt. "One spot seems as good as another, so let's start here." The sailors broke up the tar with picks, then drove their shovels into the bitumen, lifting out masses of dark goo. They dumped them into the waiting wheelbarrows. Philip wrinkled his nose; the disturbance of the lake surface had brought forth a sulphurous smell. Nor was the lake quiet; it made burping sounds, now and then.

"The lake is farting," one of the sailors joked.

Philip saw a tree limb sticking out of the tar, and tried pulling it out. It resisted at first, then emerged, a ribbon of black taffy connecting it to the lake, like a baby's umbilical cord. Philip studied it for a moment, then threw down the stick. He walked over to David.

"You know what this place reminds me of?" asked Philip. "The *Welt-Tier.*"

David puzzled over the word for a moment. "German? World-animal?"

"Yes, that's right. It was in a science fiction story by Philip José Farmer. The ground was springy, like this lake. When someone walked across it, it rose up, like a wave, and tried to swallow him. The land was really the skin of the Beast."

The sailors within hearing stirred uneasily. "Philip," commanded David, "you should be shoveling." Philip nodded, and took the shovel that was handed to him.

By the day's end, they had excavated a rectangular pit, some tens of feet long, and several feet deep. David decided against camping on land, it being Spanish territory, and everyone returned to the ship.

When they came back to the lake to continue their labors, they discovered that the pit had partially filled in. Moreover, some of the nearby "islands" of vegetation had moved during the night.

"The lake does act like a living thing," David whispered to Philip, "but an exceedingly sluggish one. Not like your *Welt-Tier.*"

Philip stuck a stick into the tar, and pulled it out slowly. The lake made a smacking sound as it released it. "According to Maria's research notes, tar is usually what's left behind when oil escapes to the surface, and dries out. But for those islands to move, there must be some liquid circulating beneath the surface. Perhaps it's just water, but I think it might well be oil."

"So?"

"We might want to drill for oil nearby. Tar is fine for water-proofing, and roadbuilding, and making organic chemicals, but oil—the liquid form—contains the fuel we need for our APVs. Or for power plants."

David shrugged. "Perhaps some day we may. But I don't see the Spanish letting any foreigners, least of all a pack of Protestants, live here without a fight."

As if David's words were a signal, they heard a whistling sound, and a moment later, an arrow seemed to sprout out of the tar some distance in front of them. The sailors dropped into their trench, which was the only nearby cover.

"Keep your heads low; see if you can spot them." As David spoke, a second arrow plunged into the lake to their left, and was quickly swallowed up. Some seconds later, it was followed by a third arrow, better aimed, which nonetheless fell short of their position.

David mentally retraced their trajectories. He realized that they had most likely come from the vicinity of one of the grassy patches he had noticed earlier. He looked for one, along the estimated path, with bushes or trees for cover. Yes, that one, he was sure of it. It was much too far away for the attacker to have expected to hit anything. They were being warned off, he concluded. Probably, given the rate and direction of fire, by a single Indian. But it was possible that a second Indian was already running for help.

"Joris," he said, "I want only you to fire." Joris nodded; he was the best shot in the party. David pointed out the shooter's putative refuge. "Our target is there, I believe. Give him something to think about.

"The rest of you, let's gather up our tar and head for the ship. Where there's one Indian, there are probably more close by, and they probably have sent a messenger to the garrison at Puerto de los Hispanioles by now."

The men collected their tools and put them in the empty wheelbarrows. They headed slowly back to the ship, with the rear guard, led by Joris, making sure that the Indian, or Indians, didn't get close enough to be a real threat.

"Arwaca Indians," David told Philip. "When I was in the Caribbean last year, I was told that the Trinidados brought them in some years ago. The native Indians had allied themselves with Sir Walter Raleigh, so, after he left..." David drew his finger across his throat. *Snick.*

The *Walvis*, with eighteen guns, was accompanied by another fluyt, the fourteen-gun *Koninck David*, and a yacht, the *Hoop*. They passed through the sometimes treacherous Dragon's Mouth, between Trinidad and the peninsula of Paria, without incident. Another day's sailing brought them amidst the islands the up-time maps called "Los Testigos." Dunes several hundred feet high towered over aquamarine waters, and marine iguanas left footprints and tail tracks as they scurried to and fro.

Some didn't scurry quickly enough.

"Tastes like chicken," David pronounced, and his fellow captains, who had joined him for dinner, agreed.

"Anything to report?" he asked.

"My crew is grumbling," said Jakob Schooneman, the skipper of the *Koninck David*. "It's been more than six months since the Battle of Dunkirk, and we've done nothing to hurt the Spanish. Or to punish the English and French for their treachery."

"It's not as though we haven't been looking for prizes."

"I know, Captain de Vries. But the mood is turning fouler and fouler. We should have sacked Puerto de los Hispanioles, or San José de Oruña, back on Trinidad."

"And where would the profit have been in that? All they have is tobacco, and we had plenty of that from Captain Marshall. So why take the risk?"

Captain Marinus Vijch of the yacht *Hoop*, cleared his throat. "The men weren't that keen on your letting the English stay upriver, either."

"I know. But we're weakened by Dunkirk and we can't afford to fight everyone. The Spanish are the real enemy and we have to focus on them."

"So let's find a Spanish town to raid," said Schooneman.

Vijch nodded. "Portobello," he suggested.

Schooneman protested. "Too tough a nut to crack, for a force our size."

"We could probably find some more Dutch ships by one of the salt flats along the way, recruit them."

"Rely, for an operation like that, on captains and crews you don't know?"

"Perhaps Trujillo," mused David. "We have to go to Nicaragua for rubber, and then from there the currents carry us up the coast anyway."

Schooneman smiled. "The gold and silver of Tegucigalpa is shipped down to Trujillo." He turned his head to look at Marinus. "Might that satisfy you, Captain Vijch?"

David brought up the sextant, bringing the skyline into view on the clear side of the horizon glass. Smoothly, he edged up the index arm until the early morning sun's reflection could be seen on the half-silvered side. He gently rocked the sextant, causing the sun's image to swing to and fro above the horizon. He delicately twisted the fine adjustment until the yellow-white disk, bright even through smoked glass, seemed to just barely graze the edge of the sea. "Mark!"

Philip had been staring at his wristwatch. He announced the time—his watch was set to Grantville Standard Time, which took into account the relocation of the town by the Ring of Fire—to the nearest minute. Comparing the local time to the time at a place of known longitude was critical to the most accurate method of determining a ship's longitude.

"Write it in the logbook. Solar altitude is—" David squinted at the vernier, and read off the altitude. "Record that, too. Take that and the star shot we did half an hour ago, and calculate our position."

Philip stifled a groan. He had made the mistake of admitting that he had taken half a year of trigonometry before embarking on his present escapade. The captain had happily decided that Philip could help with the navigational mathematics. That meant many hours studying *Bowditch*. The Company's *Bowditch* was based on a couple of "attic and basement" editions of Nathaniel Bowditch's famous *American Practical Navigator,* and they included calculation of longitude both with a chronometer and by the method of lunars.

"Boat, ho!" cried the lookout.

David grabbed his spyglass and took a look. Sure enough, a longboat with a makeshift sail bobbed in the waves, several miles ahead of them. Philip eagerly dropped the *Bowditch* and joined.

"That's odd," he muttered.

"What's odd?" asked Philip. Since David's cousin, Heyndrick, had been left behind at the new colony in Suriname, Philip had gradually become David's confidante on the ship. In retrospect, it wasn't surprising; since Philip wasn't a sailor, talking to him didn't create discipline problems. The fact that Philip was one of the mysterious up-timers also gave him a cachet.

"No one would willingly cross the open sea in a longboat. They are used for in-shore work by ship's crews.

"Still...we mustn't get careless. Many a pirate has gotten his first ship by stealing a fishing boat and then coming alongside an imprudent merchant vessel." David gave orders; the crew prepared to repel boarders. The flotilla altered course to bring itself closer to the mysterious small craft.

David hailed them. In English, since it wasn't prudent to do so in Dutch.

They responded in kind. "Help us, please, we're the last of the *White Swan.*" David sent his own longboat over to inspect, and his crew reported back that they did indeed seem to be mariners in distress. Not just English, but Dutch as well. David allowed most of his crew to stand down, and the strangers were taken aboard. If David had a few men still armed and ready, well, that was only prudent in Caribbean waters.

The longboat's crew were brought some food and liquor, and encouraged to tell their tale. Not that they needed much encouragement.

"I am—was, I should say—the carpenter of the White Swan, out of Plymouth. There were two Dutch fluyts with us, all peacefully gathering salt from the pans of Bonaire." That was one of three islands off the coast of Venezuela. "We were sent in the longboat to Goto Meer, a lake in the northern part of the island, to fetch fresh water. We were making our way back when we saw the attack. A squadron of six Spanish warships came through, and immediately attacked the two Hollanders.

"The *White Swan* kept its distance. I suppose the captain, God rest his soul, must have figured the Spanish were just after the Dutch. We should've known better. Once both Dutch ships were safely in Duppy Jonah's Locker, the Spaniards came after the *White Swan*. And sent her down as well."

"So much for peace," said another English sailor.

"'No peace beyond the line,'" David quoted. "And the Spanish think they and the Portuguese own all of the New World."

The carpenter nodded. "We stayed hidden among the mangroves— what else could we do?—until the Spanish moved west, and the sun went down. There was a moon, so we went looking for survivors, and hauled in these Dutchmen, poor wretches. They had found something to cling to, but they were still pretty waterlogged when we took them on." The Dutch survivors were still too weak to make conversation, but they nodded feebly.

"And a good thing for you that you did," David said. "Since I am Dutch, and we are under Swedish colors. Otherwise, we might be less charitable, considering how the English treated the Dutch at the Battle of Dunkirk."

The English wanted to be taken to Saint Kitts, but that was well off David's course, and thus out of the question even if David were sure of a friendly reception. And the American colonies were English no longer. David told his unexpected guests that he could drop them off on Providence Island, off the coast of Nicaragua. There was a Puritan colony there. They would work as crew, in the meantime, of course.

Providence Island was only a few miles north of the route that David had planned originally. However, there was a very good chance that, on that path, they would overtake the punitive Spanish squadron, which was probably en route to Cartagena or Portobello, and more or less hugging the coast. David decided to head deeper into the Caribbean Sea before turning southwest toward Providence. Thanks to the sextant and the wristwatch, he didn't have to limit himself to latitude and coastal sailing. Wind permitting, of course.

Once the Dutchmen recovered enough to speak, they told a grim tale. Not only had the Spanish not made any effort to rescue the sailors thrown into the sea, they had taken potshots at them, for sport. The two Dutchmen had survived by swimming under an upturned chest; it trapped air and hid them from sight.

David knew that if he had reached the area a few days earlier, his three ships, together with the three already there, might well have staved off the Spanish assault. He also knew that it was foolish to blame himself, because there was no way he could have predicted the tragedy.

That didn't stop him from fretting about it, anyway.

The crew likewise became agitated. There was talk of sacking Maracaibo or Coro on the Venezuelan coast, but the more experienced men pointed out the dangers of being trapped against the Spanish coast if the squadron returned.

Philip was uneasy, and it wasn't only because of the Spanish galleons said to be on the prowl. David's temper had changed for the worse. Clearly, his ire had been raised by the report from the survivors of the Bonaire incident.

Not that David was that fond of the Spanish at the best of times. But Philip had always been impressed by David's cool-headedness. Now he was afraid that David might set aside the long-term company goals, in order to take revenge.

His musings were interrupted by Cornelis, the second mate of the *Walvis*. "Captain wants you."

Philip found David on the quarterdeck. "Sir?"

"What do you know about Nicaragua?"

"Just what Maria collected. About the San Juan river being a good place to look for rubber. She gave me a copy of the 1911 encyclopedia article."

"Please leave the copy in my cabin."

Providence Island, off coast of Nicaragua, May 1634

The three peaks of Providence Island slowly rose out of the haze. David's ships picked their way cautiously through the reefs and shoals that surrounded the island, with the shallow draft *Hoop* as their advance guard. The leadsman of the *Walvis* was hoarse by the time they entered the harbor.

The English gave them a guarded welcome. They were Puritans, suspicious of royal intentions, and hostile to the Catholic powers,

Spain in particular. The news of the Battle of Dunkirk, and the Treaty of Ostend, had not been well received. Still, Charles had not yet made any announcement of an intent to hand Providence Island over to the Spanish, and the islanders were determined to keep their heads down and hope the king would recognize the dangers of a Spanish alliance.

That said, they felt no need to engage in outright hostilities with the Dutch, let alone a Dutch-crewed ship flying the Swedish flag. At least until a specific royal command forced them into war.

Several Dutchmen, Abraham and William Blauveldt in particular, had been intimately involved in the founding and maintenance of the colony, and Abraham was on hand to greet David.

David mentioned the roving Spanish squadron to Abraham Blauveldt, and he and David agreed that they should sail out together for mutual protection. "You collect your rubber," said Abraham, "and I will pick up some tortoiseshell from the Miskitos. It sells pretty well."

The coast of Nicaragua was 150 miles west of Providence Island, and the coastal region was dominated by the Miskito Indians. The Blauveldts, and the English of Providence Island, had quickly made friends with them.

"By the way, Abraham, I almost forgot to show you. Look here." David pointed at Bluefields, perhaps eighty miles north of the mouth of the San Juan River. "This town was named after you. Or would have been in our old future, I should say. Really."

Abraham Blauveldt smiled. "That's worth celebrating. Where's the schnapps?"

The English ship's carpenter decided to stay with the *Walvis*. "I'd like to see those rubber trees of yours. And I would even more like to have a chance to pay back the Spanish for what they did to the *White Swan*. You're gunning for the Dagoes, aren't ye?"

"Yes, indeed. And of course, they're gunning for us."

The final addition to their crew was the least likely: a preacher, Samuel Rishworth. He had approached Philip to find out the up-timers' views on the issue of slavery. What he heard pleased him, and he explained why.

Providence Island had started importing slaves the year before. Rishworth's views on the matter had gotten him in trouble with the local authorities. At first, he merely preached against slave-owning. But the company insisted that slavery was lawful for those who were "strangers to Christianity."

Rishworth shrugged. "So God's will was clear to me; I needed to preach the Gospel to the slaves. And tell them that if they became Christian, they could insist on their freedom."

"I bet that went over well."

"I was warned that I was 'indiscreet,' that I should not have made 'any overture touching their liberty' to the slaves, without the permission of their masters."

"Right," said Philip. "So what happened next?"

"Oh, the number of slaves who escaped into the woods increased. Not that I had any idea of how they managed it. No idea at all."

"No idea at all," Philip echoed.

"Of course, getting them off the island is a more difficult matter."

"Can they swim?"

Rio San Juan, and the Miskito Coast, Nicaragua

"Rubber collecting going well, Philip?"

"Well enough." The fugitive slaves from Old Providence Island were willing to work, at least after Rishworth had a word with them, but they were few in number. While the Miskito were willing to cut trees—the fact that it involved using an axe made it a warrior activity—that was only if there wasn't something more interesting to do. If they got bored, they would go hunting or fishing, or just doze off in hammocks, and there was nothing Philip could do about it. And that wasn't the only problem.

"I am worried about the waste," Philip admitted. "Cutting down these *Castilla* trees, I mean. Yes, we get a lot of latex out of them all at once, but if we could just tap them, we could keep coming back each year for more."

"It's not practical, Philip. This is too close to Spanish-controlled territory. All they need to do is put a real fort at the mouth of the Rio San Juan, and give it adequate artillery and troops, and the rubber trees would be as inaccessible to us as if they were on the Moon. And I really can't shed a tear over depriving the Spanish of their *Castilla* trees."

"Well, if they don't build that fort, it means that next time we visit, we're going to have to go deeper into the rainforest to find more trees."

"We'll deal with that if we must."

Philip brooded about the problem. He wasn't worried about the yet-to-be-built fort—he figured that in a few years, the USE would have battleships in the Caribbean, and that would solve *that* problem. But battleships couldn't grow back trees that had already been cut down.

He decided to experiment. He had one of the Miskitos cut V's into the bark, not just near the ground, but all the way up the trunk. The "milk," as the Miskitos dubbed the latex, came running out. A tree with a five-foot diameter might yield twenty gallons of milk. Which was about as much latex as they collected the original way. Whether the tree would in fact survive the heavy cutting, he couldn't be sure. What he was sure was that it wouldn't survive being felled. So this had to be an improvement.

It had the unexpected effect of increasing his labor force. His original guinea pig was one of the topmen from the *Walvis*. Accustomed to climbing a seventy-five-foot mast, he wasn't exactly afraid of heights. The novelty of Philip's experiment attracted observers, both Dutch and Miskito, and Philip overheard what they were saying. And decided to stage a race. The *Walvis* beat the *Koninck David*.

Then the Miskitos wanted in. They had their own climbing tricks. There was a risk of falling, of course. A mature *Castilla* was many feet high. But so far as the Miskito were concerned, the risk was what made the new rubber tapping a *desirable* activity for a warrior.

Rather than draw on the ships' provisions, David preferred to pay the Miskitos to hunt for them. The Indians ranged along the coast, and up the river, bringing back turtle meat, fish, fowl and other dainties. Blauveldt had told David that in their home territory, two Miskitos could feed a hundred Europeans. It wasn't much of an exaggeration.

"One of the hunters is back; seems anxious to speak to you, Captain," Cornelis reported.

"Bring him by. Let's find out what he has to say." David was sitting on the stump of a rubber tree, munching on some fruit.

The report brought him to his feet. "Cornelis, pick the steadiest men. Have them go around, tell the other captains to have their men to quiet down, collect weapons, and assemble by the canoes. There're Spanish upriver."

David pulled a ring off his finger, and handed it to the hunter. "For you, good work!"

He then turned to Philip. "Go with him, get the Miskito chiefs together."

Some minutes later, there was a quick Dutch-Miskito council of war on the bank of the Rio San Juan. The Dutch, with swivel guns brought over from the ships, blocked the path downriver. The Miskitos fanned out in small groups, heading into the rainforest. They would cut off the Spanish escape route.

The ambush was completely successful. It was also completely anticlimactic. The two mestizos the Indians had spotted weren't scouts for a Spanish expedition. They *were* the expedition. In a manner of speaking.

More precisely, they were stragglers from a canoe convoy that had come down the river some months earlier, at the end of the last rainy season. The two had gone hunting one day, gotten lost, and discovered, when they made it back to the river, that they had been left behind. They had built a raft and tried paddling upriver, but decided eventually that it was too difficult and headed back downstream.

The mestizos were from the town of Granada in the interior of Nicaragua. Their convoy's cargo was their region's annual export of cochineal, sugar, indigo, hides and silver; it had been headed for Portobello, three hundred miles to southeast. There, it would have been transferred to the great *flota*, which sailed in January or February to Cartagena, Havana, and finally home.

There was much moaning and wailing among the Dutch when they realized that they had missed an easily captured treasure by just a few months.

The Miskitos were disappointed, too. While the Miskitos did cultivate crops, their general attitude was that it is easier to let someone else do the farming and then rob them. In this regard, they were not very different from their English and Dutch allies.

✧   ✧   ✧

David thought about the treasures of Granada, and its sister city, Leon. He couldn't afford to hang around the mouth of the San Juan until next December or January, waiting for the 1635 convoy. His investors would be unhappy about the delay in the delivery of the oil, rubber and bauxite, and a wait would increase the danger that a roving Spanish squadron would spot his ships.

But...If the convoy left the town half a year ago, that meant that the town's warehouses were half-full again. Right?

Could he ascend the San Juan and assault the two cities? He had started the voyage with perhaps one hundred sixty men. Some of those had been left behind in Suriname, to help the colonists; others had died, through accident or disease. If he were to be away from the ships for a month or more, he would have to leave a strong guard behind, or he could return with much loot, only to find that he had no ships to sail home in. So that meant oh, perhaps, a hundred effectives. That was the bare minimum.

But if Blauveldt joined in...and the Miskitos...he might reasonably lead two hundred men into action. That made the idea...quite practical.

"Captain?" Philip was anxious to report on his successes.

The captain stared into the forest, without a word.

"Captain?"

David grimaced. "I have rethought the situation. We have done enough rubber collecting. It is time to take more direct action against the Spanish."

"The USE military uses rubber—"

"Yes, yes, it will be used by your APCs. But we Dutch need to damage the Spanish more...directly. The Spanish are confident they can do anything they please with our ships and colonies, because they are winning the war in Europe. We need to remind them that the Dutch are not impotent."

"This expedition is funded by USE investors, and flies the USE and Swedish flags."

"And carries Dutch captains and crews. Who want to see the Spanish taken down a peg. Which will make both the Swedes and the Americans happy enough.

"So this is what we will be doing. We will take canoes up the Rio San Juan, to the Lago de Nicaragua. And across it...to Granada and Leon.

"They are towns rich in silver and other treasures. They have never been attacked, and hence are unwalled and poorly garrisoned. I feel confident that they will pay a heavy ransom to be spared the torch."

It was Philip's turn to stare silently at the wilderness.

David put his hand on Philip's shoulder. "You Americans don't seem to have much taste for plunder, I know. When I formed the Company, I was shocked by the up-time lack of enthusiasm for privateering." He stifled a chuckle. "Of course, the down-time investors made up for it.

"So don't worry. I don't need to take you with me. I have to leave a guard for the ships, and I will give you a few additional men to help you continue your rubber harvesting. The ones too old or too sick to be fit for my little excursion to Granada, of course. And you will have some of the Miskitos."

"How long will this take? I am no expert on the Caribbean, but I do know that the hurricanes come in August and September."

"Oh, we'll have you back in the Thuringen Gardens, with your friends buying you drinks, and an admiring young fraulein on your lap, well before then."

It didn't work out that way. Blauveldt urged that if they couldn't wait for the 1635 convoy to come to them, they could at least give the Granadans a few more months to accumulate treasure. Besides, if they waited, he could sail up to Bluefields, and Cabo Gracias a Dios, and recruit more Miskito allies, increasing their chance of success.

The Miskitos told the Dutch that there were several rapids upriver, and that it would be best to make the journey to and from Granada when the rains elevated the water level—July or August.

The captains finally agreed to launch the attack in July—virtually guaranteeing that David would be returning to Europe during the height of hurricane season. Not that David seemed especially worried. "There are only four or five hurricanes a year in the entire Atlantic, according to your up-time books." Since, when they left Gustavus, David had been insistent on the importance of leaving before the hurricanes lay siege to the Caribbean, Philip had to assume that the siren song of Granadan treasure was to blame for David's change of heart. It was ... worrisome.

Nor could Philip conduct rubber-tapping business as usual while David was off freebooting. The nigh-universal Miskito reaction was, "You expect me to fuss around collecting sap from trees when I could be impaling a Spaniard or two on my cane lance? And when your Admiral David says that we can keep the Spanish guns and ammunition we capture? You are a funny boy." It was also quite apparent that Philip would diminish in their esteem if he remained behind.

"Arggh," said Philip to the jungle. "Now all I need are a parrot and an eyepatch." The jungle didn't answer.

July 1634

At last, Blauveldt's ship glided back into the mouth of the San Juan. Some native canoes were carried on its deck, which was crowded with the new Indian recruits. The canoes and longboats were lowered into the water, and they all joined David's group.

The assembled crews and their Indian allies milled about in excited confusion as they waited for David and his fellow captains and chiefs to give the order to begin the ascent. Philip watched as first one, then another alligator, disturbed by the activity, wriggled out of the water and onto a sandbank some yards away. Soon, a score of the big reptiles were sunning themselves. Most of them had their mouths agape.

A sailor from Blauveldt's ship was sure of the reason for this behavior. "They hold their mouths open so as to catch flies," he sagely remarked. "The saliva attracts the insects, and they swallow 'em when enough have landed."

"That makes no sense," said Philip. "Look how big they are! How many flies would an alligator have to catch in a day to keep himself alive?"

"Are you calling me a liar?"

"Certainly not. I'm just pointing out that you are being illogical."

"I think you're calling me a liar." He put his hand on the hilt of his cutlass.

There was a cough behind him. "Is there a problem?" asked Cornelis, his own meaty hand squeezing the man's sword arm into immobility. He was heavily built for a sailor; the sort of fellow who, had he gone to high school up-time, would have acquired the nickname "Tank." He had his share of knife scars and powder burns, too.

Mr. Fly Catcher turned and gave Cornelis a slow once-over. His face took on a more calculating look. The sailors nearest him edged away, ever so slightly, and he shrugged. "Just a friendly conversation."

"That's what I wanted to hear. But we talk when there isn't work to be done. Should I find some work for you to do?"

Fly Catcher shook his head, and, as soon as Cornelis released him, sidled away.

"Thanks," said Philip. "That wasn't looking good."

"Captain told me to look out for you, you being so knowledge-able in some things, but mebbe not in others."

"I was just explaining about alligators."

"Captain also said that if you talked someone into blowing your head off, I was to make sure I retrieved your wristwatch. You want to show me which arm you keep it on, to save me some time?"

While Philip was still worried about whether hurricanes would interfere with their return to Europe, he was happy enough to be ascending the Rio San Juan during the height of the rainy season. The rapids were bad enough even at high water; he didn't like to think about what they would have done to the canoes if the rocks were exposed.

Seeing the rapids reminded him of Maria. "She'll be so freak-ing mad to find out that she missed out on the chance to run some whitewater," he mused. "On the other hand, I am not sure she fancies playing Anne Bonney, so perhaps it's just as well."

The source of the Rio San Juan was the Lago de Nicaragua. Were it not for the maps, they would have thought that they had reached the Pacific Ocean. To their left, they could see nothing but water. Ahead, looking northwest, were several small islands, the Solentinames. Beyond them lay the cone of Ometepec, and farther still, as far as the eye could see, more water. On their right, the lake was hemmed in by a long chain of cloud-capped mountains, but of course you could say the same about the Pacific coast of Peru or Mexico.

The oceanic impression was reinforced when the Dutch-Miskito expedition spotted the telltale dorsal fins of sharks. Bull sharks did enter rivers, but they were now almost a hundred miles from the Atlantic.

The only sign that they were on a lake was that the water was fresh, not salty. No one expressed an interest in swimming.

"About a hundred miles to Granada," David told the other leaders. "I don't know how much lake traffic there is, so we'll hide by day, and paddle by night." They didn't argue. The greatest weapon in warfare was surprise.

"Do your maps show good hiding places along the coast?" asked Blauveldt.

"They're not that detailed. But we have three choices. We can hug the southwest shore. I'm afraid that might be populated, because the land is flat."

"So that's out."

"Or we can go along the northeast coast. There's just a narrow strip of land between it and the mountains."

David swatted, ineffectually, at a mosquito that had dive-bombed him. "But the route I favor is almost directly across the lake."

"Short, but won't we be seen?"

"Besides these specks in front of us"—he pointed at the Solentinames—"there are two big islands along the way. Sneaking along behind the second gets us to perhaps twenty miles from Granada. Then we can edge a bit west, to put a little cape between us and the Granadans, and once we round it we're only five miles out."

"Sounds good to me. We could cut across the cape, if that would keep us out of sight longer."

"We'll have to see. It looked like there might be a mountain spur there. That could turn a short cut into a long cut."

The sun set, and the canoes advanced. They fought to avoid a westward drift; the waves came mainly from the east, no doubt driven by the trade winds. That, too, was a sign they weren't on the Pacific.

It took another week to cross the lake. Several times they encountered fishing boats, but none were allowed to escape and bring warning to unsuspecting Granada. Granada had been founded in 1524, and it had never been attacked by a European force. No mother of Granada warned children that if they didn't go to sleep, the English or Dutch would eat them.

Granada, Nicaragua

David's raiders made the final advance in the darkness and solitude of the wee hours. The city was unwalled, so they marched directly to the great plaza. The few soldiers in the barracks were forcibly awakened, and placed under guard. The powder magazine was emptied. The cannon in the vicinity were appropriated and set up to command the plaza and its approaches.

By the time the civilians knew that there were invaders in their midst, it was already morning. The rays of the rising sun gave the stone outer walls of the Granadan buildings a golden glow. David hoped that this was a portent that they would find gold inside, too.

Several detachments guarded the entrances to the city, to make it more difficult for the inhabitants to escape with their valuables. Others patrolled the main streets and, as the Granadans emerged from their homes, prodded them toward the plaza and into the cathedral. It was soon filled with hundreds of citizens. Some screamed imprecations at their captors, some wept, and others just sat in a state of shock.

The Miskitos had, by this point, taken possession of the weapons in the armory, and were happily firing their weapons at Spaniards so imprudent as to poke their heads out of a door or window, or, if not given the opportunity for such sport, into the air. David's control over them was tenuous, and he thought it best to give them the chance to work off their excitement, as long as they didn't resort to wholesale slaughter.

The Dutch, on the other hand, were more interested in collecting plunder. They did it systematically, starting at the cathedral and the city hall, and then checking out any building that looked well-appointed enough to warrant investigation.

Nor were the Dutch and the Miskitos the only ones taking advantage of the helplessness of the town. The native Indians and black slaves had clearly decided it was payback time. It was futile for a resident to protest that he or she was penniless, or that all his or her valuables had already been taken, for a slave or servant would happily deny the protest, and guide the invaders to the missing items. Perhaps collecting a finder's fee in the process.

✧   ✧   ✧

When the looting was complete, the invaders cheerfully recruited the townspeople to act as beasts of burden, making them tow the municipal cannon to the lake, and dump them in, much to the amusement of their former servants and slaves. The invaders also seized the boats at the waterfront, to prevent pursuit and also to transport more treasure.

Some of the local helpers decided that the invasion offered an excellent opportunity to permanently leave Spanish service. A few decided to see what Miskito or Dutch life had to offer; the rest fled to the hills.

David and the other leaders then had to decide whether to continue on another sixty or so miles, to Leon. Like Granada, Leon had never been attacked, and it lay even closer to the great silver mines of Nicaragua. It was tempting, and, curiously, even the Granadan merchants urged them to do this—apparently there was a serious rivalry between the two cities.

But David knew that some of the Granadans had fled the town. An unwalled place was easier to capture, but harder to then bottle up. David had to assume that word of the sack of Granada would reach Leon ahead of his force, even if they commandeered every nag in Granada. And as a practical matter, they were going to be hard-pressed to get all the Granadan treasure safely across the lake, and over or around the three rapids of the Rio San Juan.

Regretfully, they decided to save Leon for another day.

The Miskitos hadn't gotten much of the treasure but were happy enough with all the ironmongery they had collected. In general, the Miskitos had an extraordinary desire for European goods. David had told Philip that most Indians would work to earn a handful of beads, or a knife, and that accomplished, would disappear into the forest, never to be seen again.

The Miskitos, in contrast, had an insatiable demand for everything European. Weapons, clothes, tools. But the holy of holies, so far as they were concerned, was a firearm. Philip could just imagine them back home in Grantville, discussing the relative merits of a bolt-action Remington Model 700 versus a lever-action Marlin Model 336. For hours.

A few were so fascinated by the really big guns—the cannon—that they joined the crew of the *Walvis*. Considering their skills as small-boat handlers and fishermen, David was happy to have them aboard. He promised that they would have passage when the *Walvis* went back to Suriname, to bring the colonists more European manufactures.

"The Puritans aren't going to be happy, you know," said Blauveldt.

David raised his eyebrows. "Why not? They don't like the Spanish any more than we do."

"While they befriend the Miskitos in almost any way they can, there is one important exception—they never, ever, give them firearms. As a matter of policy."

"Well, then, maybe the Miskitos will decide that we are better friends than the English. Isn't that just too bad?"

Mouth of the Rio San Juan

David was sorry when Blauveldt sailed off, but Rishworth and his charges were delighted. Rishworth had kept them hidden on the *Walvis* when the sailors and Miskitos were assembling for the ascent of the Rio San Juan, fearing that Blauveldt might recognize them as fugitive slaves and insist on returning them to Providence Island. Life had been a bit more relaxed for them while Blauveldt was off on the expedition to Granada, but they had to keep looking over their shoulder, so to speak, so that they wouldn't be surprised by his return. Of course, there were some Miskitos that hadn't gone off a-plundering, and they were recruited to serve as Rishworth's early warning system.

When the Indians came in with the news that the returning warriors and sailors were only a day's journey away, Rishworth hurried his people back onto the *Walvis*.

Once Blauveldt's ship had disappeared over the horizon, the ex-slaves broke into an impromptu dance, much to the bemusement of the *Walvis'* crew. David let it go on for a few minutes, then had a quiet word with Rishworth. Rishworth told them that their choices were to disembark and stay with the Miskitos, or join the crew of the *Walvis*. About half decided on the latter.

Rishworth was pleased. He would have more time to teach them the Gospel.

August 1634,
At Sea

David led his little squadron through the Yucatan channel. The wind freshened, and David ordered the sails reefed. That is, part of the sail gathered up, and tied to the yard by a small cord attached to the sail. Reefing was, for lack of a better term, a "new-old" idea. It was something his great-grandfather had done, but in David's time it was out of favor. Instead, early-seventeenth-century ships normally carried small courses of sail, and added additional pieces if the air was light. The nautically minded up-timers thought it was crazy to fool around with adding these "bonnets" and "drabblers." The more "progressive" down-timers, like David, had switched over to large courses with "reef points." But David predicted that in his own great-grandchild's generation, there would still be old salts who insisted on "bonneting."

As they emerged from the strait, they sighted a ship, hull-down. It disappeared from view without revealing its identity. While it was probably Spanish, given that it was heading west, David saw no reason to risk a fight when his ships were already chock-full of treasure, and the stranger couldn't possibly reach port in time to give a timely alarm. Anyway, David figured it was a straggler from the New Spain flota, bound for Veracruz. If so, it was carrying immigrants and manufactured goods, not treasure.

As they bore eastward into the Straits of Florida, David kept his ships as far from Havana as practicable. The Spanish intermittently posted a *garda costa* there, and he wasn't looking for trouble. He cleared the Straits without sighting anything more ominous than a pod of dolphins, who rode in the *Walvis'* wake for a while.

David was feeling quite pleased with himself.

The three ships threaded their way between Florida and the Bahamas. They had to claw their way northward, close-hauled, fighting against the northeast trades. But at least they had the Gulf Stream to help them along. As they struggled to wring what progress they could against the unfavorable wind, the captains and crews could take comfort in the knowledge that they would eventually escape the zone in which the trade winds, which barred a direct course to Europe, prevailed. Once they reached the forties, they could pick up the westerlies and head for home.

The wind became very light and variable, further reducing their headway. That was common when one passed between the two wind zones, but at this time of year, the area of transition usually lay farther north.

Fortunately, the skies were mostly clear, and the barometer had risen slightly since the last watch. The barometer had once hung on the roof post of a Grantville porch, and David had been very pleased to have it loaned to him.

Soon after they passed the latitude of the northern fringe of the Bahamas, the northeast wind resumed. David didn't like the look of the sea, however. The swells seemed a bit heavier and longer than usual. He took out a one minute sand clock and counted the swells. Four a minute. Eight was norm.

"Go check the barometer again!" David ordered.

"It's level," Philip reported. "But it seems . . . jittery."

The next day, at sunrise, there were white wisps of cirrus clouds, low in the sky. The "mares' tails" seemed to point southeast, and the swells were stronger. The barometer had slowly fallen during the night watches. It usually dipped a bit twice a day, but this seemed to be something more than the usual variation.

"Well, Philip, I am afraid that I think we have a hurricane approaching. The winds are from the north-northeast, and since they spiral counterclockwise about the center, the center should be nine to twelve points off the wind direction. Probably southeast."

"So what do we do? Run to the west?"

"How sure are you of the accuracy of the cross-fix you took earlier today?"

"Pretty sure. Two star fixes and a sun fix, perhaps an hour apart. Why?"

"If I trust the last position fix you took—and I do—we don't have enough sea room between us and the American coast. Only about a hundred miles. Believe me, you don't want to be near a lee shore in a hurricane. So running west, toward land, really doesn't appeal to me."

"Then should we stay put? Throw out an anchor or something?"

"It's not so simple. According to the *Bowditch*, the paths of Atlantic hurricanes are quite idiosyncratic, but they usually move northwest in the Greater Antilles. Sometimes they'll make landfall and disintegrate, but they can also curve north. And they can then recurve and head northeast.

"If I knew that the hurricane was marching northwest, I would head south, and go back the way we came, into the Gulf. And if I thought it was curving north, or recurving northwest, I would head north. Or just heave to."

"What about heading east, or northeast, to get more searoom?"

David shook his head. "That's likely to bring us into what *Bowditch* calls the 'dangerous semicircle,' the area to the right of the hurricane track. Assuming that we're not in it already, of course."

"Why is it dangerous?"

"The wind strength is the sum of the revolving wind, and the forward movement of the storm. And in the forward quadrant, the winds try to push you right into the path of the hurricane."

"Ouch. So there's a 'safe semicircle'?"

"*Bowditch* prefers the term, 'less dangerous semicircle.' Nothing about a hurricane at sea is 'safe.' Anyway, I am going to keep heading north for a little while. Or as close to north as the wind will let us. We're square-rigged, so we can't point close to the wind. No closer than six points of the compass."

Philip scrunched his face momentarily. "Six points from north-northeast, that's northwest. So we're heading toward the coast?"

"Edging toward it," David admitted. "Remember, the coast is curving away from us as we go north.

"We won't outrun the storm, but that course will still buy time for us to figure out which way the hurricane is moving. Right now, we're playing a chess game with the hurricane, but one in which we can't see its moves.

"Anyway, I want get away from the shallow waters between Florida and the Bahamas. Those are more prone to breaking if the wind picks up. And the *Walvis* won't like it much when some breaker drops tons of water on its deck."

David and his mates started giving orders to prepare the ship for the hard blows to come. The crew cleared the scuppers, and checked that the pumps were working. They battened down the hatches, and set up life lines on both sides of the deck.

✧   ✧   ✧

They cautiously continued north, or more precisely northwest by north, making slow progress against the wind. The winds backed to north by east, so they had to angle even more to the west in order to make headway.

Still, the wind change was good news; it meant that they were in the less dangerous semicircle. If they were in the middle of the ocean, their best bet would have been to put the wind broad on their starboard quarter, and edge out. Unfortunately, if they did that here, they would soon be enjoying an unplanned American vacation. So they left the wind farther aft, angling just enough to counter the inward spiral. The *Koninck David* and the *Hoop* did their best to follow the *Walvis'* lead. The chop of the water increased as the new swell fought with the old one.

The sun looked down on them through a white gauze. Despite their plight, Philip couldn't help but admire the halo it had acquired. The ring proper was bright white, with a red fringe on the inside. The sky was darkened for some distance farther inward, and a vaguely defined corona played outside the halo.

Gradually, the sun faded from view. Then a new layer of clouds slid under the old one, darkening the overcast. The sky became a virtually uniform gray. The main topsail split, fabric streaming out like ribbons from a running lass' hair, and the topmen bent in a replacement, and close-reefed it.

It started to rain, tiny droplets that seemed to hang suspended in the air. All at once, there was a downpour, as though someone had suddenly emptied a bucket on Philip's head. It ended within minutes, and the misty not-quite-rain returned. Then came another rain shower.

The wind strengthened. There were many "white horses"— foaming wave crests. The sailors took down the normal sails and raised the storm sails, which were made of a heavier, tougher fabric.

Soon, on the eastern horizon, Philip could see a dark mass of clouds, looking like a sorcerer's fortress, with a parapet of black cotton. If, that is, any fortress had pieces of itself break off and fly away from time to time. That was the "bar," the main cloud mass, where the winds would be strongest.

Not that they were gentle where the *Walvis* and its comrades struggled. The winds were now gale force, and the sea was heavy. The timbers moaned like lost souls. There were flashes of lightning to the east. The only good news was that the barometer was low, but steady. That implied that they were succeeding in keeping their distance from the eye of the hurricane. Philip was sent to join the group who were straining at the whipstaff, keeping the ship on its course.

The stays hummed like a swarm of angry hornets, but they all held.

"Wind's come around to the northwest, Captain," said Cornelis. "Slackened some, too."

David thought this over. Being an old Asia hand had its disadvantages when you were north of the equator; he had to keep reminding himself that almost everything about Indian Ocean typhoons was reversed up here in the northern hemisphere. Northwest, yes, that meant that the storm center was now ahead of them. In effect, the hurricane had swept them up, like an unwilling partner at a dance, and swung them a quarter circle around itself as it continued its journey northward.

"How's the barometer, Philip?"

"Rising, sir." The relief in Philip's voice was evident. And that was fair enough, the pressure change confirmed that they were now in the rear half of the storm.

David sent Cornelis to take a sounding; he didn't want to shoal after surviving this much. And he detailed a half dozen men to act as lookouts, both to watch for danger, and to determine whether the *Koninck David* and the *Hoop* had also weathered the storm.

They soon caught sight of the *Koninck David*, so it, at least, was safe. However, it signaled that some of its precious water casks had been swept off the main deck, and it would need to detour to the American coast to make amends.

There was no sign of the *Hoop*. Whether it had sunk, or merely been driven far away by the tempest, David had no idea.

But there was work to be done. A lot of it. The storm sails, especially the fore staysail, were now somewhat the worse for wear. The fore staysail had so many eyes that Philip likened it to what he called "Swiss cheese." One by one, the crew unbent the storm sails, and set reefed ordinary sails. They found that a stay had stranded, and replaced it, and generally put the ship back into order.

The wind abated further, and they were able to shake out the reefs. But while the ship now looked much as it had before the hurricane, the storm had exacted a toll.

"All hands, bury the dead," David ordered. Here was a sailor who, weakened by some tropical disease, had died of exposure. There was one who had fallen from a spar while trying to put another reef into a sail. A third had been picked up by a rogue wave, and had his skull dashed against a mast. Their bodies were sewn up in their hammocks, and double shotted. The Reverend Rishworth conducted a memorial service. Then, three times, David said the words, "We commit his body to the deep." Three times, a corpse was slid into the waters. There, according to the minister, "to be turned into corruption, looking for the resurrection of the body when the sea shall give up her dead."

After a short but uncomfortable silence, the crew was sent back to work. "Hands to braces," David ordered.

The next day, they found the *Hoop*. It had lost a mast, and was traveling under a jury rig. The flotilla headed for the Georgia coast, to take on fresh water and make those repairs best carried out at anchor. The local Indians didn't attempt to trade, but at least they didn't attack, either.

It was a beautiful day, the hurricane had moved on or fallen apart, the ships had resumed a northward course and were now happily ensconced in the Europe-seeking westerlies, and David was once again at peace with the world.

Philip's navigation had been spot-on, and David invited him to dinner as a reward.

"You know, Philip, it would be bad for discipline for a captain to apologize for an error."

"Yes, sir."

"Like delaying a return trip until the hurricane season was upon him."

"Yes, sir."

"How's the schnapps?"

"Fine, sir."

Late 1634

David and Philip stood in line, waiting for their turn to send radio messages to Grantville. They were at the USE military's radio post in Hamburg. While most of the radio traffic was of an official nature, the post did send private messages on a "time available" basis.

"Philip, I know you expected to go into the army after you finished high school, but I think you'd make a fine navigator, if you'd like the job on a more permanent basis."

"Thank you, Captain. Do you believe in reincarnation?"

"Like the Hindoos? Certainly not, I am a good Christian."

"Well, then it's a moot point. Because when I get back to Grantville, my parents are gonna *kill* me."

Riding the Tiger

Late 1634 to February–March 1635

Marshall's Creek, Suriname River,
Long Dry Season, 1634 (September–November 1634)

Maria Vorst sniffed the wound, and grimaced. "It's infected." Her patient shrugged stoically.

"How did it happen?"

Captain Marshall answered for her charge. "Not sure, but probably just a cut from razorgrass, or a spiny vine."

Maria shook her head. "The men have got to get into the habit of inspecting themselves from head to toe, every day. We're in a rainforest, for heaven's sake; any break in the skin is bad news. If it doesn't get infected, then maybe some fly decides it's a dandy place to lay eggs."

She sighed. "I'll need to clean the wound, and put some antiseptic on it."

"Antiseptic?"

"Yes, from the Latin, 'against rottenness.' You remember my lecture, don't you? The one on the Germ Theory?"

"Indeed," said Captain Marshall. "I had bad dreams several nights in a row. Little armored critters with sharp fangs and claws, hunting us in great packs."

"Back in Grantville, Lolly showed me what they look like under a microscope. Pretty dull actually. Little balls or rods, mostly." Maria, an artist whose family ran the Leiden botanical gardens, had received botanical and medical training in Grantville.

"Well, in my nightmare, they had fangs and claws."

Maria had come upriver on the yacht *Eikhoorn* to visit Captain Marshall and his little tobacco growing colony of English Puritans. And the nearby Indian tribe, who were tapping rubber for Maria's people.

Despite earlier tensions, the colonists at Marshall's Creek had welcomed the latest visit by the crew of the *Eikhoorn*. Especially by Maria. Not just because she was the first white woman most of them had seen since leaving England, but also because of her medical training in Grantville. She had made the rounds, treating the illnesses and injuries of Marshall's people.

"All right, you're going to need to hold still now," she told her patient. She cleaned the wound with a warm decoction of bark. She took out a little rubber pouch—it was easy to come by, now that the Indians near Marshall's Creek were tapping the local rubber trees—and squeezed out an ointment. It was the thickened sap of another tree. Maria had learned about both the bark and the sap from Indians downriver, near the new Swedish colony of Gustavus.

Of course, the Marshall Creek Indians had their own remedies. As the Gustavans' "Science Officer," Maria spent quite a bit of time learning native medicine, everywhere she traveled.

Maria wrapped cotton around the man's leg, to protect the wound while still allowing it to breathe. Even though the local cotton was gray, it still stood out against the black of his skin.

For the first time, she had met Marshall's other people...his African "servants." There weren't many of them, but their existence had been concealed from her and Heyndrick de Liefde on their previous visits. She wasn't surprised. Even if Marshall had not been told, when friendly relations were first established, that slavery was illegal in the Gustavus colony, he might have feared that the interlopers might try to incite the slaves as a cheap means of wiping out their upriver rivals.

Heyndrick, the cousin and agent of the founder of the Gustavus colony, had told Marshall that the Gustavus colony would not, for the moment, insist that Marshall free his slaves, and wouldn't encourage the slaves to flee, but he also warned Marshall that it would not return any fugitive slaves who made it downriver.

But that didn't mean that Maria couldn't attack the institution in subtler ways. "I have tended to this man's physical needs, but what have you done for his spiritual ones? Has he been instructed in the Christian faith?"

Marshall shook his head. "Of course not. He is only an ignorant savage."

"His ignorance can hardly be surprising, if you refuse to instruct him." Maria knew that this was a sensitive point with English slave owners. Since one of the justifications they gave for enslaving the Africans was that they weren't Christian, they feared that if they converted their slaves, they might be forced to free them.

Marshall temporized. "We don't have a minister of our own."

"I understand. I wish I could do something about that. But, I know that as a captain, you have read aloud from a prayer book. Surely your African servants can be allowed to listen and to learn what they can."

"Very well."

"And have you tried to teach any of them to read and write?"

Marshall laughed. "Mevrouw Vorst, few of my Englishmen have their letters."

"That is most unfortunate. In this new world, illuminated by the books of Grantville, being literate is going to be of great importance. Is that not true?"

Marshall nodded slowly.

"Well, I will see what primers we can spare, and all I ask in return is that at least one be dedicated to the edification of the Africans among you."

Based on the reading she had done in Grantville, Maria was fairly confident that there would be trouble over slavery, sooner or later. But for the moment, the colonists in Gustavus had more immediate issues to worry about. Like survival. And she agreed with Heyndrick that it would be better if the confrontation came after Gustavus was bigger and stronger.

The music faltered. The dozen or so Surinamese Indians, resplendent in body paint and not much else, stirred uneasily. Until then, they had been an excellent audience.

"Don't stop!" Maria whispered sharply to her assistant, and made a circular motion with her hands.

The English settler who had been given the honor of turning the crank on her mechanical phonograph nodded sheepishly, and brought the player back up to speed.

The violins, viola and cello played by the musicians of another universe went back to work, and Wolfgang Amadeus Mozart's "Eine Kleine Nachtmusik" once again overrode the clicking and chirping of the insects of the rainforest.

Later that night, Maria tried putting on a Louis Armstrong record. Louis Armstrong had given the world such titles as "Alligator Crawl," "Trees," and "Rain, Rain." Despite this evidence of affinity, the Indians of Marshall's Creek were unimpressed, indeed, a little agitated. It appeared that the rainforest was not yet ready for jazz.

Maria salvaged the situation by hurriedly putting on Mozart's Piano Sonata No. 11 in A, "Rondo Alla Turca." Tempers were appropriately soothed.

Ceremoniously, the chief's wife handed Maria a cup of *piwari*. Maria took a carefully metered sip, and bowed her head in acknowledgment, hoping she had drunk enough to satisfy propriety. Piwari was a brew made with fermented cassava bread. Which wouldn't sound so bad, except the old biddies of the tribe chewed the bread and then spat it into the pot to ferment.

She couldn't help but remember a story Lolly had told her, about a practical joke played on a British diplomat. At some sort of exotic reception, a covered plate was put before him. When he lifted the lid, all that he saw was a spider. He stared at it, as his so-called friends watched him out of the corners of their eyes. A moment later, he grabbed it by the leg, announced, "For the Queen," and dropped it into his mouth.

So it could be worse.

After the meal, presents were exchanged. "And this is for you," Maria said, and handed the chief a strange ornament.

"It is like a piece of the rainbow," marveled the chief.

During her sojourn in Grantville, Maria had listened to CDs on her friend Lolly's player. She had also been introduced to the curious concept of the "coaster," a CD which was no longer functional, and hence suitable for nothing better than protecting the table from water marks. Maria asked if she could have a few of these specimens, and Lolly said, "Sure, why not."

Maria had them cut into quarters, and hole-punched. Maria

gave one only to a chief, or his favored wife. They could be hung from the neck, so all tribesmen and visitors could envy how well, in one light, they acted as mirrors, and in another, they iridesced.

Though tensions had been reduced, there was still a certain amount of casual one-upmanship between the English and the Gustavans, as they both sought to win over the Indians of the Suriname River.

Maria was confident that the Gustavans had won this round. There was no way that Captain Marshall was going to be able to compete with the "rainbow."

Fort Kykoveral (modern Bartica), Essequibo River, Guiana, November 1634

Henrique Pereira da Costa, formerly of the Portuguese-Brazilian frontier town of Belém do Pará, watched as a small caiman emerged from the Essequibo River and rubbed its belly on the riverbank. It didn't have much time left to enjoy the afternoon sun.

"Henrique, would you believe that they only have six books, besides the Bible, in the whole fort?" said his servant Maurício. Maurício had been trained by Henrique's father as a scribe and linguist.

"That many?" Henrique asked rhetorically. "I am surprised." Not that Henrique was much of a reader himself. He was more woodsman than scholar. He looked off to the west, toward the setting sun. Any moment now, he thought to himself.

"Five of them," Maurício continued, "owned by the commander."

The sun at last disappeared below the horizon. The skies darkened rapidly, that was typical of the tropics.

"As for the sixth—"

"Enough, Maurício." Henrique took a deep breath, kneeled, and closed his eyes. "Hear, O Israel: the LORD our God, the LORD is one." Henrique was a *marrano*, a secret Jew, who had, when exposed as a "Judaizer," escaped into the Amazon with his servant and childhood companion, Maurício.

Maurício watched silently as Henrique prayed. Henrique had picked a location some distance from the fort, and out of its direct sight, so as not to give offense to their Calvinist hosts.

At last, Henrique completed the evening *shema*. He rose and looked at Maurício. "There are some serious matters we need to discuss. Like what we do next."

"They don't seem to like us here much, do they?"

"Well, they're Dutch. Mostly Calvinists, too. They hate Catholics and they aren't too keen about Jews, either."

"Or free Africans, of any religion." Maurício patted his pocket. "I keep my letter of manumission with me wherever I go, even in the jungle."

"So, let me review our options." Henrique held up a finger. "First, we can make our home somewhere in the back country."

"Well, Kasiri and Coqui will be happy enough with that idea."

The welcome that Henrique initially received as a great Amazonian explorer had gotten a bit tattered once the Dutch realized he was Jewish. The Dutch were the least prejudiced of all the Christian peoples, but "least" wasn't the same as "not." And anyway, the Dutch didn't know quite what to make of Maurício, let alone their Indian companions.

"But I confess that while I am comfortable in the wilderness, I don't want to cut myself from civilization indefinitely." Henrique held up a second finger. "So the second possibility is that I can return to Europe."

"Right," agreed Maurício, "we need to find you a nice Jewish girl."

Henrique gave him a quelling look. It had no discernible effect on Maurício's smirk.

"We?"

At that, Maurício lost his smile. Henrique, logically, should board the next Dutch ship, and return to Europe. His family had longstanding plans to help them make a quick getaway if they had to, and Amsterdam was the preferred rendezvous point. And it was uncertain that the Dutch in Kykoveral would tolerate the permanent presence of a Portuguese Jew.

But that would mean Maurício would have to decide between crossing the Atlantic with Henrique or remaining on the Wild Coast with Kasiri.

Kasiri frowned. "What's troubling you, Maurício?"

"Nothing."

"Right. My darling Maurício barely speaks. He answers every question with a single word. It's as commonplace as piranhas climbing trees."

Kasiri and Maurício, of course, didn't talk to each other precisely like that. They communicated in a weird mixture of Manau, Portuguese and sign language, with many circumlocutions.

"Henrique doesn't think he can make his home here. He wants to cross the Great Sea to join his family."

Kasiri had never seen the ocean. To her the Great Sea was some sort of extension of the Amazon. And her people, the Manao, traded all along the Rio Negro, down to its confluence with the Amazon. So she just shrugged. A young man of her tribe, like Coqui, might travel hundreds of miles to visit, and perhaps take a bride home from, another tribe.

"And I am his brother and servant. I feel honor-bound to accompany him." Maurício sighed. "Besides, if I don't, then I risk being re-enslaved by the Dutch. They are at war with the Portuguese, so they needn't honor my letter of manumission."

Kasiri smiled. "Fine, I will go with you across the Great Sea." Her frown reappeared. "Unless perhaps you have tired of me?"

"Of course not! It would be wonderful to have you with me. It's just... customs are different in Europe... For one thing, you'll have to wear more clothes."

"Hah! I am already wearing too much. Do I not see how you, and your brother, and these crazy Dutchmen suffer every day? You all need to wear less and bathe more."

"Be that as it may, in Europe, in winter, it is too cold to dress lightly."

"What is cold? And what is winter?"

Maurício abruptly gave Kasiri a hug. "Until a ship comes, we don't have to make a decision. And perhaps we should take a canoe down to the mouth of the Essequibo, so you can see what the ocean looks like, before we decide anything. For now, let's go swimming together."

Clearly satisfied that she had restored Maurício's spirits, Kasiri walked with him to the river. But she didn't know that Maurício was, beneath his surface good humor, still in doubt. Kasiri would suffer in Europe, unless she was willing to wholly adopt the language and manners of a European, like a Amazonian Pocahontas. And even then, as an Indian married to an African, she could expect to suffer all sorts of slights.

Maurício wasn't eager to see white sails billowing over the dark waters of the Essequibo.

Gustavus (Paramaribo), Suriname

Maria returned to Gustavus with rubber, cotton and tobacco from Marshall's Creek, and Heyndrick told the colonists that it was time to do some trading with other Europeans on the Wild Coast. At the town meeting, they announced, "We are taking the *Eikhoorn* to Fort Kykoveral, on the Essequibo." It was the principal Dutch colony in the Guianas, perhaps two hundred forty miles to the west. "We need samples of everyone's products that might find a market there, whether among the traders, the Indians, or visiting ships. And we need your 'wish list' of what to try to get there that we don't have here."

It would, of course, be more than a mere trading voyage. This would be their first chance to explore the coast, and Maria looked forward to seeing and drawing new plants and animals. And perhaps, just perhaps, some of them would be of economic value to the Gustavus colony.

At any rate, it was a chance to escape the ennui of helping to administer the colony. Maria now understood why David de Vries, their nominal leader, spent most of his time at sea.

On the coast of Guiana

They had made camp on a sandy beach, between the Berbice and Demerara rivers. They were now perhaps fifty miles from the mouth of the Essequibo. The next day's sail would be easy, with the trade winds broad on their starboard quarter. As, in fact, they had been every day on their trip westward. Getting back home to Gustavus would be more arduous, of course.

As the tide went out, it became apparent that a little ways down the coast, there was some large object sticking out of the exposed bottom. Maria, Heyndrick and two sailors went out to investigate.

The object was the ravaged remains of the hull of a pinnace, its blackened framing timbers looking like the ribs of a sea monster. It didn't seem particularly likely that any useful artifacts would still be left, but they were now so close that it seemed reasonable to look and see.

"That's odd," said Maria. While Heyndrick and the sailors looked for stray coins, and the like, in the sand, she had been studying the hull.

"What's odd?" asked Heyndrick, who, out of the corner of his eye, had been studying her.

"Look how most of the wood is heavily holed."

"Sure, that's because of the teredo, the ship worm. They're a real plague in these tropical waters."

"Yes, but there is one piece that's barely pitted. You see? I think it's a different type of wood than the rest of the hull."

Heyndrick studied the mystery futtock more closely. He felt and sniffed it, and did the same to the nearby wood. "I think you're right. It couldn't have been part of the original hull, it must have been cut to make a repair."

"Can we take it out, please?" pleaded Maria. "I think it might be greenheart. It's a tree mentioned in the encyclopedias; it's resistant to marine borers. The crew of this hulk must have cut a greenheart tree and used it to make repairs, without realizing their good fortune. Might be a fine export product if we can find a grove to harvest. We can ask the local Indians...once we find them."

Heyndrick scratched his chin. "Even if you're right, the Indians are going to have a hard time figuring out what tree you are looking for, if all they have to go on is a bit of cut wood. They don't cut their trees into lumber, they just hollow them out."

"We can shave off the outer layers of the piece, then they might recognize it as being the same wood as one of their dugouts."

Heyndrick shrugged, and ordered a sailor to cut out the wood of interest. Once he had done so, Maria asked him to chop off a small piece and give it to her. She took it down the beach, to where the waters of the South Atlantic played with the sand, and dropped it in. It sank.

Maria nodded thoughtfully, and turned her head to look at Heyndrick, who was standing a few feet behind her. "It's denser than water. That's true of greenheart, too. One of the reasons it's a strong wood."

"Then you might be right that it's greenheart, Maria, but please don't get your hopes too high. Even a wood that normally floats can sink if it gets waterlogged."

Maria shrugged. "When we find some Indians, we'll get some answers. I hope."

Fort Kykoveral (modern Bartica), Essequibo River, Guiana, Short Wet Season (December 1634–January 1635)

"Well, there it is. A sail," thought Henrique. "Kykoveral" meant, in Dutch, "looks over all," and he had an excellent view of the river from his position on the parapet.

It made him think of the legend of Theseus. Theseus had gone to Crete to slay the Minotaur. He sailed, with the other sacrifices, on a ship with a black sail, but he promised that when he returned victorious, he would hoist a white sail so his father Aegeus would know he had succeeded. Unfortunately, he forgot, and Aegeus threw himself into the sea.

This time, it didn't matter whether the sail Henrique saw was black or white. Either way, it would bring both joy and sorrow.

To Henrique's surprise, the ship, although Dutch-built, wasn't from Europe. Nor was it en route to the Caribbean, or America. Rather, it was from another colony on the Wild Coast, paying its respect to the traders at Kykoveral.

Which meant that perhaps, just perhaps, there was no need for the foursome to separate.

Commander Jan van der Goes of the Zeeland Chamber of the Dutch West India Company cleared his throat. "Mevrouw Maria Vorst, permit me to introduce Henrique Pereira da Costa, formerly of Belém do Pará, the intrepid discoverer of a river route between the Amazon and the Essequibo."

Henrique bowed.

"Senhor da Costa, I introduce to you Mevrouw Maria Vorst. She is the daughter of a physician, and sister of the curator of the Leiden Botanical Gardens. She has received training in natural philosophy at Grantville, the town of the future that you have surely heard of by now. She is attached to the new Swedish colony to our east, Gustavus."

Maria curtseyed.

"And her companion, Captain Heyndrick de Liefde, is of a good merchant family in Hoorn, and has been to the Caribees, Zwaanandael, Virginia and New Netherlands." Zwaanandael was the ill-fated Dutch colony in Delaware. "His cousin, Captain David Pieterszoon de Vries, founded Gustavus, and Captain de Liefde has given us the great pleasure of transporting Mevrouw Vorst to our company."

"Yours must have been quite a dangerous journey, Senhor da Costa," Maria murmured. In the meantime, she was trying to visualize the up-time maps, and guess at its length. Twelve hundred miles? Sixteen hundred?

"Indeed it was, my lady. Giant crocodiles. Poisonous snakes. Deadly rapids. A thousand times, I thought myself at death's door, and took solace in the thought that I would be taken into Heaven. And then I made it here. And now I must wonder whether I died after all, and have come to Heaven, for surely you are an angel."

Heyndrick rolled his eyes.

Maria smiled at Henrique. "Surely it is too warm here to be Heaven."

Heyndrick saw the smile. "I am surprised that you speak so blithely of Heaven, Herr da Costa. The guards told me that you are a Marrano, a secret Jew, wanted by the Inquisition for heresy." Having been baptized, however insincerely, Henrique could not avow Judaism without being considered a heretic.

"I am a heretic only in the eyes of the Catholic Church, not in the eyes of the Lord," Henrique retorted. "And I daresay that the Catholics would consider you, too, to be a heretic, Captain." Heyndrick was indeed Protestant.

Commander van der Goes winced slightly. "Tell me more about your colony, Mevrouw Vorst."

"We have both a sawmill and a glassworks, the first on the Wild Coast, I believe. So we have manufactures that we can sell here and to other colonies. We have shipped home a kind of clay called bauxite. We have planted, as cash crops, cotton, tobacco, and the dye tree orlean. And we are collecting the sap of a strange tree which I doubt you would have heard of, since, until the coming of the up-timers, the only Europeans who knew of it were a few Spanish, and they had no use for it."

"Oh, what tree is that?"

"It is called the rubber tree, the up-timers know much about it. Its sap hardens into a material which is waterproof, and is elastic, an—"

"I know what rubber is!" Henrique interjected. "That is what I was collecting, in Brazil!"

Maria spilled her drink. "In Brazil? How did you learn of it?

Have you shipped any to Europe? Who is buying it? I would have heard if, before I left, someone was selling Brazilian rubber in Grantville. And that's the only market for it."

"Dear lady, I suspect that my family knows about it the same way you do, we have some connection who has studied the books of Grantville. In 1632 I was given a map, and a description of the tree. We started tapping the trees in the summer of 1633, and the first shipment went out thereafter, on one of the sugar ships out of Bahia. When rubber first reached Lisbon, I know not." He was too polite to mention that, beside storms, the likeliest reason for the rubber not reaching Lisbon was interception by privateers. Dutch, French or English.

"And I don't know what my family would have done with the rubber. It might have been some time before they sent samples to business associates outside of Portugal or Spain, and in these troubled times it could have taken many weeks to reach Grantville. It is somewhere near Magdeburg, is that right?"

"Hmm...we left Hamburg in December of 1633. That would explain why we heard nothing about it. Is Belém still shipping rubber to Portugal, you think?"

"It is hard to say. Maurício and I were the only Europeans involved in the tapping operation. We are both here now. The same...incident...that led me to leave Belém, would also have had unpleasant repercussions for my family. I hope they were warned, and fled in time. The Inquisition seizes the properties of heretics. It is possible that they will read the private papers, decide that rubber trees are worth exploiting, and recommend that the Crown send an agent to Belém to take over the business. More likely, they will decide it is too much trouble, or tainted by its association with Grantville, and the Indian *seringueiros* I recruited will just return to hunting and fishing."

"We should ask Henrique and his friends to join us at Gustavus," said Maria.

Heyndrick snorted. "I think that would be a mistake, Maria. Henrique's allegiance is to Portugal, and, so long as Philip rules Portugal, the Portuguese are our enemies."

"But now that they know he is Jewish, he cannot return to Portugal. He must find a new home. He was born and bred in the New World. What would he do in Europe?"

"I still think he would be a bad influence. His whole life has been a lie. We can expect him to have imbibed deceit with his mother's milk."

"Heyndrick...I do believe you're jealous."

Heyndrick took a deep breath. "I have no claim on you... other than one of friendship...and affection." He didn't dare say more, not yet. She was of substantially higher rank than him, although not hopelessly so.

"I have already married once and have been a widow for several years. I have become accustomed to making my own decisions. And the good women of Grantville have taught me that I need be in no rush to remarry.

"Which isn't to say that I don't like you...

"Now then. Back to business. And Henrique, flowery compliments and all, is strictly business. He has run a rubber tapping operation. We could use him to do so for us, up at Marshall's Creek, and at the same time keep a closer eye on Captain Marshall and his men."

Heyndrick nodded slowly. The thought occurred to him that if Henrique were in residence at Marshall's Creek, then Maria wouldn't have to travel there so frequently. And he would be mostly out of Maria's sight and hence out of Maria's mind. Or so Heyndrick hoped.

But suddenly he realized that Maria was still speaking. "And if he was able to cross over a thousand miles of rainforest, he must have impressive survival skills...and no doubt an impressive knowledge of the plants and animals. Some of that knowledge will doubtless be relevant here in the Guianas, too. In fact, I have a question or two to put to him right away."

"Greenheart?"

"Greenheart."

"Senhor Henrique, I am looking for trees with a particular wood, called 'greenheart,' because it is of a dark green color. It grows"—she stopped to consult her notes—"seventy to one hundred thirty feet high, and three feet or more in diameter. It is very strong and heavy, heavier than water. And I think I found some lumber cut from it, in a ship's hull, but of that I am not sure. Here is a sample piece."

Henrique examined Maria's mystery futtock. "It was used in a ship? And it is strong, but too heavy to float? Perhaps it is like the 'stone tree,' itauba, which we have on the Amazon. Coqui had a dugout canoe made from that tree. It is good for running rapids, but if the canoe fills with water, it sinks."

Maurício coughed. "I don't suppose you have any idea what the native word is for this 'greenheart' of yours?"

"Actually, I do. At least if the encyclopedias in Grantville are right. They said that it was called 'bibiru' or 'bebeeru' in one language. And 'sipiri' in another. But I don't know which language."

"Bibiru," Henrique muttered. "Sounds like a word from the language of the Indians who live just north of the Amazon delta. They call themselves Aroo-waks, I think. Are there Aroo-waks, here? 'Bibi' is 'mother,' I think. Or maybe it's just 'woman.' But I don't recognize 'bibiru.' Do you, Maurício?"

Maurício shook his head. "Not 'sipiri,' either. Do the 'encyclopedias' say what the Indians use the tree for?"

Maria wiped sweat from her brow. Guiana was warm even in December. "Not clearly. But the wood is used in the construction of ships and docks, and the bark to make some sort of febrifuge. Probably tastes vile."

"Isn't that something that the physicians insist on?" asked Maurício. "Don't they figure that the worse a medicine tastes, the better it is?"

Henrique laughed. "Presumably on the theory that the patient will get better so he doesn't have to keep drinking the medicine."

Maurício shifted his weight. "Excuse me, Henrique, I have to go," he said. "Kasiri is waiting for me."

Henrique waved him off. "And if the lovely and learned Maria is through questioning me, I have some business with the commander." Maria inclined her head, and he and Maurício both took their leave of her.

"I wonder if Lolly knows any nice Jewish girls I can match him up with?" Maria pondered.

The local tribe was called the Lokono, which of course just meant "the people" or something like that. Henrique, Maurício, Kasiri and Coqui introduced Maria to their Lokono Arawak friends, and helped her with her inquiry. They knew the tree, or at least they knew of some tree they called "bibeera," which sounded close enough. At least, the tree was tall enough, and its wood didn't float. Some young Lokono women led her up the hilly banks of the Essequibo river, and pointed out several "bibeera" trees to her. They had the growing pattern common to many rainforest canopy trees; that is, branching only near the summit. Maria judged these specimens to be a good eighty feet tall.

The Lokono showed her how to remove the cinnamon-brown bark; it had to be beaten before it could be peeled off. The yellowish infusion they made from the bark tasted just as horrible as Maria had expected. It made up for this by smelling nasty, too.

Two of the sailors had come with Maria, and, on her instructions, cut down a few of the trees, trimmed them to logs of manageable size, and skidded them back to the *Eikhoorn*. Back in Gustavus, the carpenter would test them out and, if they were as good as the encyclopedias said, they would send the supply ship on to the Essequibo, with orders to pick up a cargo to take back to Europe for sale. Assuming that Maria and Heyndrick didn't find a greenheart stand closer to their own colony.

Henrique, Maurício and Kasiri decided to go swimming; this stretch of the Essequibo was pleasantly free of piranha, electric eels, and crocodilians. Coqui watched Maria and the Lokono women for a while, then grabbed his bow and headed to the river.

In the meantime, Maria noticed that the larger of the trees were surrounded by nuts the size of apples. She decided that it might be advantageous to collect these, and plant them near Gustavus. If the greenheart trees were useful, it would be better if they didn't have to go each year to Essquibo to harvest them.

As she put the nuts in her basket, the Lokono women started giggling. She tried to figure out why, but her linguistic skills weren't up to the task. One woman did pat her own tummy. Maria took this to mean that the nuts were good to eat, but the Lokono didn't seem interested in sharing Maria's haul.

Maria returned to the fort, basket in hand, and got out her sketchbook. It wasn't until sundown that Henrique and company came back.

"What is it that the Indian women find so funny about me being interested in the nuts of the greenheart?"

"Mevrouw Vorst, it will be an honor and a pleasure for me to find out," said Henrique, bowing. He and Maurício went off in search of their Lokono friends, with Coqui and Kasiri trailing behind.

Curiously, at the dinner table, Henrique wasn't quick to share his findings. Maria managed to contain her impatience until they were all done eating. "Well, Henrique, what did you find out?"

Henrique looked at Maurício. Maurício looked at the ceiling.

Henrique also seemed to have trouble looking straight at Maria. "Mevrouw Vorst. Umm. They use the nuts to, um, keep from having babies."

Coqui wasn't thinking about babies, but he was devoting some thought to the related subject of women.

He had decided to join Henrique, Maurício and Kasiri on their little trip because he wanted to find a mate. And none of the girls of his own village appealed to him particularly.

As they made their way down the Rupununi, they had passed through the lands of the Wapishana and the Macushi. Unfortunately, they had done so at the time that the upper Rupununi was in flood, creating a great lake that bridged it to the rivers of the Amazon. While that made travel relatively easy, it meant that it was hard to fish, and the Indians of the region spent that season mostly in the uplands, where they could hunt land game.

The bottom line was that he hadn't met any eligible females en route. As to the women of the Lokono Arawaks, they fell into three categories. The pretty and available ones, who had struck up relationships with the Dutchmen at the fort. The pretty and unwilling ones, who had prudently moved deeper into the forest, where they could avoid unwanted advances. And the old women who insisted on flirting with him at every opportunity.

Logically, then, he should go deeper into the forest, but he was reluctant to trust his sister Kasiri to the highly dubious wilderness skills of her new boyfriend, Maurício. It was too bad that she hadn't picked Henrique, who was actually competent. For a European.

This Maria said that there were Indian women near her colony. He would have to investigate.

Gustavus (Paramaribo), Short Dry Season (February–March, 1635)

The black schooner rounded the sandy spit that marked the eastern edge of the entrance to the Suriname River. As it continued westward, it came into view of the recently constructed Fort

Lincoln, which lay on the broad vee of land between the mouth of the Comowine River, and the main channel of the Suriname River. Gustavus itself was some distance farther up the Suriname, on the west bank, where the ground was less prone to flooding.

Fort Lincoln, at this point, was more bark than bite. Most of its "cannon" were actually artfully blackened logs. However, there was just enough real ordnance to fool an enemy ship that merely wanted to test the defenses. For all it knew, if the fort didn't fire all its guns, perhaps it was just conserving ammunition.

Captain Dirck Adrienszoon, the original skipper of the *Eikhoorn*, and acting fort commander, lowered his spyglass.

"Slaver," he said.

"How can you tell?" asked Heinrich Bender. He was a member of the colonial militia.

"From the smell. Just wait for the wind to blow this way again. Want a look-see?" Dirck handed the spyglass to Heinrich.

Heinrich adjusted the focus; he was near-sighted. "You think they're here to sell slaves?"

"That's one possibility."

"Hey, that's a Spanish flag they're flying. That means we should shoot at them, doesn't it? Since the Netherlands, the USE and Sweden are all at war with Spain."

"The international law on the subject is a bit complicated. The Spanish supply slaves to all the Caribbean plantations, and so they probably have papers granting them immunity from privateers and warships of any country. At least, those that buy slaves, like the Dutch, the English, and the French. I am not so sure that Sweden would honor the papers, and the USE certainly would not."

On Dirck's command, Fort Lincoln fired a signal shot, warning the visitor to keep its distance, and alerting the settlement upstream that company had come knocking. The schooner prudently anchored several miles away, in two fathoms of water. Soon thereafter, it lowered a longboat.

Dirck walked out to the beach to meet them; he didn't want the Spaniards getting a closer look at his guns.

The longboat crew was led by the first officer of the *Tritón*. Their ship, an eighty-tonner carrying two hundred slaves, had left El Mina several months ago. It had misjudged its position, gotten caught in the doldrums and run out of water. Crew and cargo alike were in desperate straits.

"And so, Senhor, we beg of you that as a good Christian, you tell us where we may find drinkable water, that we may refill our casks and be on our way. We are willing to pay, of course, for the privilege. And naturally, if you wish to buy any of our merchandise, we can give you a special price."

Dirck told him that he would have to get permission from the governor of the colony, at the main settlement, and promised that he would relay the Spanish requests at once, but warned that they must stay where they were until a decision was reached.

Carsten Claus, the acting governor of Gustavus, and a Committee of Correspondence leader, was in favor of attacking the ship and freeing the slaves. Maria, who had recently returned from Kykoveral, agreed, and Heyndrick, though less enthusiastic, admitted that their up-time support would evaporate if they did anything else.

But it wasn't as though Carsten had a company of Marines he could order into battle. What he had instead was the crew of the *Eikhoorn*, some additional recuperating sailors, and the settlers themselves. Some of these had served in village militias, and a smaller number were ex-mercenaries, but it was hardly a professional force. Carsten decided that he would have to persuade the colonists to take action. So he called a meeting of the town council.

"What's the problem?" asked Denys Zager. "Make them pay through the nose for the privilege, and send them on their way. It's all profit and no risk."

"If you are worried about risk, why did you come to the New World?" complained Michael Krueger. "You're Dutch, aren't you? Here you have a heaven-sent opportunity to combine patriotism with profit. Capture the ship, and then sail it to a neutral port— Saint Kitts' perhaps—to ransom off the crew and sell the slaves."

"Do you remember our journey here?" asked Heinrich Bender. "How, as we passed the Canaries, we feared that every ship on the horizon was a Turkish slaver? If it be wrong for them to make you a slave, though you be their enemy, how can it be right for you to take as a slave an African who has done you no harm? Who has not consented to serve you? Can that be Christian?"

"Of course it is Christian," said Krueger. "Did not Abraham own slaves?"

"In the time of the up-timers, all of the great nations made slavery unlawful," Maria added. "Every religion condemned it as sinful. History judged us, and found us wanting. Now, through God's grace, we have the opportunity to choose a more righteous path."

"Have any of you brave souls considered that these slavers are heavily armed, in order to keep the slaves in line, and stand off pirates?"

"I have," said Heinrich. "What of it? Captain Adrienszoon says there probably aren't more than twenty to thirty of them. We outnumber them perhaps ten to one. And we have more and bigger cannon than they do."

"Wearing a militia badge on your hat doesn't make you an experienced fighter," Zager warned. "They may be more trouble than you think."

Krueger was unimpressed. "They have been dying of thirst for days, maybe weeks. I doubt they'll put up much of a fight. And we have our own 'sea beggars,' the crew of the *Eikhoorn*, and the men the other ships left behind. As well as the town militia. The profit from capturing the ship, and the cargo, is worth the risk."

"I agree that we should capture the ship, if we can," said Carsten. "But it is wrong to keep slaves. And anyway, slaves aren't very productive. Give them farmland and tools, and we and they will both profit more in the long run."

"I agree," said Johann Mueller, the glassmaker. He had been doing well enough trading beads with the Indians.

"Give them farmland," said Zager, "and they will steal the tools and disappear into jungle. Probably after cutting our throats." Zager, their sawyer, had a tendency to see the worst in human nature. Probably thanks to the years he had spent, as an apprentice, as the low man on the saw. The one in the saw pit.

Maria held up her hand. "They will see us tie up the slavers and strike off their chains. Surely they will understand, 'the enemy of my enemy is my friend.' Freeing the slaves would double the size of the colony. And we have Maurício to interpret for us, to make sure there are no misunderstandings."

Carsten nodded. "They can be settled on the other side of the river. Less friction that way." And so it was agreed. Although not without some lingering dissent. Mostly with respect to freeing the slaves. The *Tritón* was no mere *jacht* like the *Eikhoorn*; it would come in very handy even if they didn't sell it off.

✧   ✧   ✧

There was still the practical issue of how to assault the ship. The *Eikhoorn* just had six swivel guns. Fort Lincoln and Gustavus both had cannon, brought over when the colony was established, but the *Tritón* was out of their range.

Consequently, the following morning, the Gustavans invited the *Tritón* to go up the Suriname River and dock at Gustavus pier. The pier was brand new, with pilings made of the greenheart brought back by the *Eikhoorn*.

"You can't stay anchored out here, the bottom won't hold the anchor if a storm comes in. As often happens this time of year. Just tie up at our dock."

And once they docked... "Ordinarily we would sell you our water, but it is the dry season now. There is a very reliable spring, upriver. You go up the river until the river turns sharply through twenty-four points of the compass. It then enters a long straightaway, and then veers to port. Just there, you will see a hill in front of you, on the right bank. There is a tree which was split by lightning just below the spring, you can't miss it. If you leave before the tide goes out, you can probably make it back tomorrow." Carsten paused for effect.

"Only, the natives there give us trouble from time to time, so be sure to bring plenty of men, well-armed."

"Can you give us a guide?"

"Certainly, if you can wait until the day after tomorrow. That's when we expect the fellow back."

The first mate of the *Tritón* looked at his captain, and said softly, "I don't know if we can last that long."

Carsten had thought that would be the reaction. And if it hadn't been, Carsten could have stalled a bit more, without fearing that the *Tritón* would try to seize a guide. The *Tritón* was under the guns of Gustavus, after all.

"Go at once," ordered the captain. The first officer of the *Tritón* crammed the longboat full of empty water casks, and sailors armed to the teeth, and headed upriver.

"So, Captain," said Carsten, "perhaps you would care to join me for dinner. I am sure you will be surprised at the hospitality which our rude young colony can afford you."

He was surprised all right. He had just recovered from bowing to Maria when he was quite conclusively coshed from behind. The burly Heinrich Bender, their blacksmith, smiled with satisfaction.

A plank connected the *Tritón* to the dock. It was guarded on the ship's part by two sailors, armed with pistols and cutlasses. And the town in turn guarded itself from an unwanted incursion from the ship by posting watchmen at the shore end of the dock.

The townspeople thoughtfully hung a lantern on the dock, so the *Tritón*'s guards could see what was happening there. If, incidentally, it destroyed their night vision, so they couldn't see anything moving in the water on the far side of the ship, well, so be it.

The town watchmen were far enough from the lantern so they couldn't be seen too clearly by the deck guards. However, they were clearly enjoying their night out under the stars, laughing and drinking.

The *Tritón*'s deck guards could watch this in silence only so long. One looked at the other, received an affirmative nod, and stepped onto the plank. It creaked, and the town watchmen immediately stopped celebrating and looked up. Very slowly, the approaching *Tritón* sailor set his pistol and cutlass down on the dock, and then walked toward them.

"I couldn't help but notice . . . that you seen to be drinking something. Perhaps you have something to spare?"

"I don't know," said the head watchman doubtfully. "Do you have coin?"

"I wish," the slaver responded dolefully. "We don't get paid until we get to Hispaniola."

The head watchman sighed. "Well, in the interest of international amity, we can share."

He handed over a skin. "This is our little local specialty. It's made from a fruit that grows here, ananas. Some people call it pineapple." He declined to mention that the little beverage was then distilled—it was handy having a glassmaker in the colony—to ninety proof.

So far, so good. Carsten had told him, "Don't just go up and offer them a drink, let it be their idea. And feign reluctance."

The mood of the erstwhile ship defenders passed from celebratory to somnolent. The head watchman gestured to the waiting assault team. The two *Tritón* crew members were quickly gagged, bound and dragged off.

From a point out of view of the deck of the *Tritón*, a colonist used a hooded lantern to signal to the *Eikhoorn*, which was waiting quietly downstream. It slowly approached the other side of the *Tritón*, moving on muffled sweeps.

With the *Eikhoorn's* swivel guns commanding the deck of the *Tritón*, there was no reason for further delay. One of Coqui's arrows, six feet long, took down a man who came up on deck as the assault team, lead by Heyndrick, snuck onto the dock. It was the wrong time to use the head.

The assault team came across the plank, and spread out quickly. The most experienced fighters opened the hatches and jumped down. The second mate was surprised in his hammock. The most resistance came from the cook, who was obviously both a light sleeper and a man who liked to keep the tools of his trade close at hand. The cook managed to grab one of his knives and threaten to carve Henrique into little pieces. Henrique maneuvered him so his back was to the entranceway, and another Gustavan put the cook back to sleep.

The rising sun reddened the waters of the Paramaribo.

"The slavers' longboat just came around the bend." said one of the Gustavans, crouching beside the readied cannon. There were perhaps a score on board.

"Good," said the gunner. "The angle is set. When it comes even with that rock—the one whose top looks like a parrot's beak—light the fuse and blow the sucker out of the water."

The longboat crew couldn't possibly have seen the lit fuse. But they may have caught a glimpse of the men hiding by the cannon. For whatever reason, at the last moment, they backed water, and the ball missed them. Just barely; they were still sprayed.

With surprise lost, the Gustavans brought other cannon into action. A second shot was fired, then a third, bracketing the longboat.

The longboat might nonetheless have tried to reach the *Tritón*—figuring, with some justice, that the colonial militia probably weren't skilled artillerists—but at that point the *Eikhoorn*, which had been downstream, swept past the prow of the *Tritón*, her swivel guns all manned. They were formidable antipersonnel weapons.

The longboat swung around, trying to claw its way back upriver, and out of the range, at least, of the fort's cannon. The first officer of the *Tritón* might well have intended to beach the longboat as soon as he was safe from cannonshot, and lead his men inland, to neutralize the *Eikhoorn*'s swivel guns, too.

However, in changing direction, the longboat lost speed, and that made it a better target. A cannonball holed it, and it sank quickly.

The *Tritón*—newly dubbed *Der Vrijdom*—was now anchored in two fathoms of water, off the east bank of the Suriname River. The slaves were brought up from the hold as gently as possible, still shackled.

They stood blinking in the sun, knowing that there were strangers on board, but not knowing the significance. Then the former crew of the *Tritón* were brought before them, in shackles. Even the captain, his mouth gagged because he had demonstrated an amazing gift for continuous invective.

The slaves' eyes widened as they took in this sight.

Then Maurício, the only black among the Gustavans, came aboard. Heyndrick had loaned him a military uniform. Maria had put a harpy eagle feather in Maurício's hat, and hung one of her iridescent CD quarter-slices around his neck. The inner circle—Carsten, Maria, Heyndrick, Dirck and, to Heyndrick's annoyance, Henrique—had decided that Maurício would be their most convincing spokesman, and that he should be "dressed to impress."

Maurício knew several of the African languages. He gave the slaves the same message in each of them. They were about to be set free. Their captors were now captives, but were not to be harmed. The Africans were now among people who wanted to be their friends. Their new friends couldn't take them back across the sea, but could give them a new place to call home, so long as they behaved as good neighbors. They would help each other.

Maurício made a grand gesture. Heinrich Bender produced the key—taken from the second mate—and unlocked the shackles on the nearest slave. The poor fellow virtually collapsed, but Heinrich caught him. Henrique gave him water to drink, and another colonist led him down to a waiting dinghy for transfer to the shore.

Maurício motioned the next African forward.

✧   ✧   ✧

"We are riding the tiger, Maria," said Heyndrick softly. "We don't know if these ex-slaves are warlike or peaceful, thievish or law-abiding. They are in a strange land, and they will have a hard time surviving. They will be tempted to prey upon us. Even if they don't, their gratitude may ebb quickly, and we may find that they refuse to trade with us, and occupy lands which we could put to better use ourselves."

"It is safe to ride a tiger if you have friends to help you dismount," said Maria.

King of the Jungle

February–March 1635 to August 1635

Paramaribo (Gustavus), Suriname,
Short Dry Season (February–March, 1635)

"My children. Help find?" The Dutch words were painfully enunciated, clearly learned by rote.

Maria Vorst put down the chalk with which she had been drawing, and studied the questioner. The tall black man, by his markings, was Coromantee. They were the people living in what the up-timers called Ghana. He was one of the two hundred or so slaves whom the Gustavans had freed from the distressed slave ship *Tritón* when it had come hunting for drinking water.

Perhaps half of the slaves knew some Portuguese, either because their tribes had traded with the Portuguese, or because they learned it after their capture. Only a few knew Dutch, the Dutch presence in Africa being more recent and more limited.

Unfortunately, the Gustavans were mostly Dutch and German, and hardly any of them knew Portuguese. Maria, despite being far better educated than the rest of the colonists, didn't know much herself, although she was trying to fit language lessons into her schedule.

Fortunately, her teacher was nearby. "Maurício, come here please!" Maurício, a freed mulatto, born in Portuguese Brazil, had been trained there as a scribe and interpreter. Because of the large

155

slave population in Brazil, he knew African, as well as European, languages. Once, he and Henrique had lived in Recife, and Maurício had gone time after time to the dock to meet and greet, in his capacity as interpreter, the "wild" slaves, just delivered there to work on the sugar plantations. Most came from Angola, but there were slaves from all over Africa.

Maria remembered that there had been a few children among the slaves they had freed. She explained the situation to Maurício and had him translate. "What are your children's names? How old are they? What do they look like?"

Maurício turned to the Coromantee. They spoke rapidly together, first in Portuguese, and then in the Twi dialect of Akan.

"I am Kojo of the Ashanti. My boy Manu has seen thirteen summers, and his sister Mansa, eleven." Kojo described them.

"Where did you see them last?"

The answer was not what Maria expected.

"In Edina."

"Edina?" interjected her companion, Maurício. "You mean São Jorge da Mina?" The man nodded.

Maurício turned to Maria. "He was separated from his children back in Africa, in the Portuguese fortress you Dutch call Elmina."

"Elmina? My husband, may God rest his soul, spoke of it once, as a place of great trade. Somewhat enviously, I must say."

Maurício nodded. "Enviously? That's for sure. The Dutch tried to take Elmina in 1625." He paused. "Where is this husband of yours, by the way?"

"He was lost at sea," Maria said.

"I'm sorry."

"Thank you. It was years ago. And to be honest, I didn't know him all that well."

"Anyway," Maurício continued, "Elmina was the first Portuguese base in Africa. On what we call the 'Gold Coast.' A century ago, it accounted for a tenth of the entire gold trade. There's still gold mined in that area, but nowadays Elmina is mostly a slave depot. Dozens of slave ships visit every year."

"Does he know which ship they were put on? Not the name, of course, but can he describe it? The number of masts? Or of its gunports? The figurehead?"

"I'll ask." He questioned Kojo further, then shook his head.

"Sorry, Maria. They don't give the captives the run of the fort, you know. The children were taken first. He saw them at one point, in a different pen, so they were there when he arrived, but the guards didn't let him join them and they were sold off before he was. When he was put on the *Tritón*, he hoped that it would take him to the same place."

"So, is it hopeless? What do we tell him, Maurício?"

Maurício suddenly looked much older than usual. "I don't know. It does seem hopeless. If I think of something, I will let you know. In the meantime, all I can do is say that we will pray that they are safe, and that if we learn anything about their whereabouts, we will tell him right away."

"That seems so ... ineffectual."

Maurício shrugged.

"Wait," said Maria. "If he can provide a good enough description, I can draw them. Then you and he can show the drawings around, see if anyone knows more. And at worst, perhaps the drawings will give him some comfort."

Maurício explained what Maria wanted to do. Maria didn't want to waste her precious paper, so she drew on a piece of slate. It was easier to erase that way, too. She decided to try to draw the boy first, guessing that his features would be similar to, but younger than, his father's. She erased a line here and added a curve there until the father seemed satisfied.

Then she pulled out a second slate, duplicated the boy's picture, and then had Maurício find out what needed to be changed for it to represent the girl. That took quite a bit more give and take, but at last it was done.

Then she made a copy to paper of the images of the boy and girl, for Maurício, and gave the slates to the Coromantee. She had plenty of slate from one of her expeditions upriver.

"I hope this helps," said Maria.

The Coromantee reverently set down the slates. He had been pleasantly surprised to discover that one of the whites was a *tindana*, a priestess of the Earth Goddess. Who else would place a magical incantation on a rock?

Now she had blessed him with a talisman by which he could speak to his children. Perhaps even call them back to him.

He had almost lost hope, had contemplated walking into the Great Sea.

He wondered how he could possibly repay her.

"Blue or red?" said Johann Mueller, spreading his hands, each pointing at a different pile of beads.

The young Eboe woman reached slowly toward a blue bead, then jerked her hand back. Two Eboe matrons, baskets on top of their heads, watched the interplay. Johann had no idea what they were saying, but he fancied they were placing bets on which color his customer would settle on.

Business had been good. The Eboe were very fond of beads. Both men and women were accustomed to wearing beaded necklaces. Since they had come to the New World as slaves, they had only whatever they had been wearing when they were sold to European slavers. And once they were freed, they wanted to adorn themselves, to distinguish themselves from their companions.

To buy beads, or anything else, they needed something to trade. And that meant that they needed to fish, hunt, grow crops, mine, or craft artifacts. Either on their own account, or as contract labor. Samuel Johnson's epigram—about liberty being the choice of working or starving—was known only in countries exposed to up-time literature, but the Africans were quick to appreciate the limits of the liberty the Gustavans had conferred upon them.

Of course, thought Johann, they were no worse off than the Gustavans in that regard. It was fortunate that the slave ship still had several months' supply of food. Better yet, they had seeds to plant. Maurício had told Johann that there was an Eboe insult, "I bet you even eat your yam seeds." The colonists had supplied water, and they had made and sold farm implements to the Africans, but they were expecting a return.

"Hello, Johann, how's business?" asked Maurício.

Johann jumped. If Johann were a superstitious man, he might worry that his thoughts had summoned Maurício.

"Fine, fine. Would you ask this young lady whether she has made up her mind?" Maurício did so. She ended up trading for an equal number of both colors.

Maurício walked over to the watching women. He held up the

drawings Maria had made. "Did you see these Coromantee children before you boarded the giant canoe with the white wings?"
That was, more or less, the proper way to describe a European
sailing ship.

They shook their heads.

He heard a cough behind him. He turned, and saw Heinrich
Bender. "Teach me some Portuguese, Maurício. I need to be able
to bargain with the blacks."

"What do you want to know?"

Heinrich smiled. "You can start with 'How much?' and 'Too
much.'"

Maurício laughed. "I should start a school."

"You should, Maurício. You've been teaching Portuguese to
Maria, I know, so why not teach a bunch of people at once?"

"I could, I suppose. Although Maria knows Latin, which makes
it much easier for her than it would be for you German peasants." Maurício smiled to show he was joking.

"I mean it, Maurício. Teach Portuguese to us, and English or
German to Africans. Earn some money."

"Perhaps I will. I can teach the Mandinka trade talk, too. The
problem isn't just us talking to the Africans, it's getting them
talking to each other."

The Eboe stood up, shading his eyes with one hand and hefting
his fishing spear in the other. He kept his balance in the canoe
with the ease of long practice. He had often gone fishing on the
Niger and its tributaries. The dugout canoe, made by one of the
local Surinamese Indians, was made from a strange tree, but he
had learned to handle it quickly enough.

It was a good time to fish; early on a Sunday morning, when
the colonists of Gustavus, across the river, were at prayer, or
enjoying their day of rest.

There. A dark shape in the water. He threw.

Missed. The float bobbed in the water, as if it were laughing
at him. He shrugged philosophically, and pulled on the retrieval
line. He took in a few feet and then it resisted. Clearly, the spear
was caught in something.

Back home, he might have chosen to abandon the spear. Here,
he couldn't afford to do so. The Gustavans had freed the blacks,
but that didn't mean that they felt obliged to give them much

in the way of goods. For anything more than water, and a bit of food, they expected the blacks to work. The hospitality of the Indian tribes also had its limits.

He didn't care about the spear shaft—there was plenty of wood around—but a metal spear point, made by the Gustavan smith... that was another matter.

He tied the near end of the rope about the canoe, as best he could, and then dived into the water.

When he emerged, his teeth were chattering. Not with cold, but with fright. There was a boat, with dead men, resting on the shallow river bottom. And not just any men, but the terrible white men who had taken them across the Great Sea. Had they turned into river demons?

He clambered into the canoe and just lay there, trying to calm down. The pleasant warmth of the sun had a lulling effect. He drew a knife, and was about to cut the rope away and head back to shore, when he had a change of heart.

If the bad men turned into river demons, surely they would have drowned someone weeks ago. And there would have been talk.

So these were just dead men. Dead men still holding their weapons, and with other valuable goods on their persons.

Who needs a spear shaft, if one has a sword? he thought. And with that, he paddled the boat closer to the sunken longboat, and then jumped back into the water.

Some time later, he beached the canoe, and gazed with satisfaction at the pile of goods heaped beside him. A half dozen cutlasses, a gold bracelet, and other odds and ends. He was rich now, by the standards of the ex-slaves. Rich beyond his wildest dreams.

With this, he would be an *ozo*, a big man. A giver of great gifts. And when he ran out, he could slip back here, and collect more goods. He would have a round stool, with three legs, and a stool carrier. He would have the town smith make him an iron staff, with bells attached. He would wear a red hat.

As he mused over these attractive possibilities, he was grabbed from behind. He tried to reach for one of the weapons so close to his feet, but the attackers pulled him back, away from the canoe, and tapped the side of his head with a war club.

When he came to, he was hanging, head down. One of his fellow ex-slaves, from an unfamiliar tribe, was studying him.

Three others, who seemed from their markings to be of the same tribe, lounged nearby.

"Ah," the warrior said to his fellows, "our fish is squirming. Should we toss him back into the water, or throw him into the pot?" His filed teeth suggested that this was not a metaphor.

The Eboe had no idea what they were saying, but was pretty sure it didn't bode well for him. He began pleading for his life, first in his native tongue, then in Mandinka trade talk.

The warrior held up one of the weapons. "Where did you get these?"

"Spare me, and I will show where to find more."

Near modern Paranam, Suriname

Heinrich Bender held up the chunk of rock. "This is what we are looking for." Kojo had asked Maurício whether the Gustavans had any mines, and one thing had led to another.

Kojo, and the two Coromantee he had brought with him, studied the specimen. Kojo took it in his hand, then returned it with a moue of distaste.

"Worthless clay. We gold miners, not dirt farmers."

"This is bauxite," said Henrich. "Very useful. The Americans can make it into a metal which looks like silver but is as almost as light as wood. They call it 'aluminum.'"

"You smelt it?" The Coromantees had been smithing for centuries.

"Not exactly. Uh—Maria, could you explain?"

Maria had researched the possible products of Suriname before the expedition was launched. She knew more about aluminum than anyone else west of the Line of Tordesillas.

"We wash the bauxite with hot lye to make alumina, and then we run electricity through a mixture of alumina and cryolite to melt it down and transform it."

"What is cryolite?"

"It is a stone that it is found in Greenland—that is a land far to the north, where it is so cold that the water is hard like rock."

The Coromantees digested this information. *Magic stone*, they thought.

"And electricity?"

"That is like lightning."

Any doubts which Kojo's fellow Coromantees had, as to whether Maria was as powerful a priestess as Kojo had told them, were now dispelled.

"Anyway," said Heinrich, "don't worry too much about the color—it can be white, yellow, red or brown. It is soft, so soft I can scratch like this, see?" He scratched with his fingernail. "But the real proof is that it has this funny 'raisin pie' texture." He pointed at one of the little pea-sized concretions.

"And where do we find it?"

"It is usually easiest to dig it up from the sides of stream banks."

Kojo flashed his teeth. "Fine. Now let's talk price."

The Gustavans didn't care for digging in the constant heat and humidity; it was worse than farming. So they were happy to give the Coromantee the opportunity to mine the bauxite.

Of course, that meant that the Coromantee had to be allowed to shift their village to the west side of the river, the Gustavus side, since that's where the known deposits were. The colonists debated this a bit, but Carsten Claus, the acting governor of the colony, pointed out that the deposits were still more than a day's march south of Gustavus, and so the Gustavans didn't have to worry about casual thievery on the part of their new neighbors.

What really clinched the deal was when Heyndrick de Liefde, who was the cousin of the colony's founder, David de Vries, suggested that the Coromantee would act as a buffer if the English colony farther south, at Marshall's Creek, got restive. There were many Dutch among the colonists, and given the treacherous attack by the English on the Dutch fleet at the Battle of Ostend, they weren't happy about the proximity of the English, who had come before them to Suriname.

Borguri, who had been the highest ranking of all the Imbangala on board the *Tritón*, had declared himself their chief when they were freed by the Gustavans. He fought two duels to secure his position, but in view of their small number, had declined to kill either challenger. To make sure that they didn't consider this a sign of weakness, he beat them to within an inch of their lives. They now obeyed him with seemingly doglike devotion.

It was a pity, he thought, that the guns recovered from the longboat were unusable. But he kept them. If his warriors carried them openly, their opponents would think that they worked, and would respond accordingly. They might flee, instead of charging, perhaps. And, if they weren't fooled, well, the guns were reasonably good war clubs.

The freed slaves had divided into groups along tribal lines, and spread out in the area east of the Suriname River. The Imbangala had raided the weakest of the nearby groups, for provisions and tools that might be used as weapons, but since the Africans started with little in the way of possessions, they weren't very productive targets. Not yet, at least.

For the moment, while the Imbangala regained their strength, they concentrated on stealing, not killing. The only exception was if they encountered any of the Ndongo, who they had fought back in what an up-timer would call Angola. 'Ngola was the title of the Ndongo king, Nzinga. Who actually was a queen.

The white traders who circulated among the African settlements were more tempting prey. But Borguri wasn't ready to attack the whites yet. Not even those traders, let alone the white colony west of the river. The whites were too well armed, he didn't want to draw their attention yet. His warriors could steal from the whites, if they could avoid being spotted, but no more. If spotted, they must just flee. No killing. Yet.

The Indians, now . . . At first, the Imbangala had avoided confrontations with them. After all, this was their land. Who knew what spirit protections they had? And of course they had missile weapons, which the Imbangala had to make for themselves. But the Imbangala's contempt for the Indians grew. They were clearly primitives, like the upriver Africans the Imbangala once captured for sale to the Portuguese.

The Imbangala chief studied the Indian villages nearest to the Imbangala camp. When did they hunt, what weapons did they carry, did they make war on other villages, did they set sentries when they held festivals. After some time, he picked the Imbangala's first native target.

The Indians had been drinking *piwari* all day and night. They were ripe for the plucking. There was just one more matter to attend to.

Borguri looked at the Eboe fisherman. His head had been shaved, and ashes from the Imbangala hearth fire sprinkled over it, to erase his old identity, to remove him from the protection of his ancestral spirits. Assuming that they cared what happened to him across the Great Sea. In the ordinary course of things, in a few weeks he would go through a binding ritual which would make him property of Imbangala's lineage, and drive thoughts of escape from his mind.

But no war party could set forth without at least one human sacrifice, to please the gods and feed the warriors.

Maurício spoke to the sentry. "I need to talk to him." The guard shrugged. "Watch your step."

Maurício took a deep breath and entered the hut. The change in illumination, from the high tropical sun to the indoor gloom, was stunning. It was several minutes before he could see much beyond the tip of his nose, and he said nothing until his eyes adjusted. At last he could make out the dark figure sleeping, or pretending to sleep, at the far end of the hut, his arms and legs both shackled, and the leg shackles in turn fastened to a chain which circled the great tree trunk that rose from the ground, piercing the roof of the hut.

"I have a few questions for you."

"Do you now? Come a little closer, so I can hear you better." The erstwhile slaver captain rattled his chain. "It's not as though I can come closer to you."

"I'll just speak louder, thanks," said Maurício. The first day after his capture, the captain had half-strangled the man who brought him food. The captain was then punished, by being given nothing to eat for several days, and was fed only after he apologized properly. Maurício was not especially reassured by this expression of contrition.

The captain laughed and laughed, then stopped abruptly. "Well, well, I am a busy man, as you can see. So be quick about it."

"It's a small matter. One of the Coromantee said that his two children were kidnapped and taken to Elmina for sale. He pursued the kidnappers and was captured in turn."

The captain snickered.

"He spotted the children in a pen, but that was all."

"How old were they?"

"The boy twelve, the girl eleven."

"Ah, a good age. They can be trained as domestic servants, or be taught a trade and hired out. Of course, they are long-term investments."

Maurício suppressed the urge to strangle the captain. "So, do you know what happened to them?"

"I can make an educated guess. But what's in it for me?"

Maurício hesitated. He had already read the ship's log, and quizzed all of the other survivors of the slaver's crew. The captain, damn his soul, was Maurício's last hope.

"I suppose I could do something about your rations, if I thought your answer was sufficiently helpful."

"My rations, eh? Well, that's not good enough. I want my freedom."

Maurício turned and started to walk out.

"Wait, young fellow." Maurício stopped.

"They can put a ball on this chain and let me walk about a bit, outside. Where would I run to, after all? If the Africans didn't get me, the Indians would."

"I promise that if you give me the information I need, I will speak to the governor, and request this boon."

"Not on *my* behalf. As a favor to you. To redeem *your* word."

"Yes, as a favor to me! Now talk, damn you!"

The attack took the Indians by surprise. The men were too drunk to put up a fight at all. The women weren't in much better state.

The men of warrior age were slain and eaten, to the horror of their kin. Not that cannibalism was unknown in South America, but of course the Africans had different rituals and so far as the Indians were concerned, what the Imbangala were doing was completely wrong!

The younger boys were gathered together. They would be taught, brutally, that they were now Imbangala. The young women would become wives of the senior Imbangala warriors, and the older men and women would be put to work, as slaves, in the fields. If the old men thought that farming was beneath their dignity they would be beaten until they rethought the matter.

A week or so after the assault, one of the young women managed to escape. Tetube hid in an old hunter's shelter that her brother had once pointed out, until the Imbangala tired of searching for her. Then she slipped downriver.

Long Rainy Season (April to August, 1635)

Carsten raised his hands. "All right, I can't hear anyone if you all talk at once."

"We've had goods stolen, time and again," one colonist, who frequently made trading forays across the river, complained.

"Anyone killed?"

"Not yet," the trader admitted.

"That's not all," said a second colonist. "The Africans are already killing each other."

"Are you surprised?" asked Henrique, Maurício's white half-brother. "It's not as though they were all that friendly back in Africa, you know. That's how at least half of them ended up as slaves in the first place. They fight these little wars, and the prisoners get sold."

"So the villages are armed camps, now," added the trader. "It makes it tough to do business. The Africans are thinking more about fighting than about farming, I assure you. They have less to trade and sooner or later some nervous sentry is going to shoot an arrow or throw a spear into one of us."

"We just find out who started it, and teach them a lesson," said Heyndrick. "That's what cousin David did with the Indians in America."

"You mean kill them?" asked Michael Krueger. "I have a better idea. If a tribe can't keep its people from stealing or killing, then I think it should be considered lawful to re-enslave them all."

"Ah, lawful war," said Maurício. "The Portuguese did that in Brazil, with the Indians. Funny thing was, there always seemed to be a lawful reason to enslave any tribe which was too weak to resist."

Henrique held up his hand. "There's worse news."

Carsten gave Henrique his full attention. He knew that Henrique was a woodsman, and he and Maurício's Manao Indian brother-in-law, Coqui, moved freely among the Indians in the affected region. "What?"

"We've had reports that some of the Africans have real weapons. Steel swords. Guns even. Some Indian villages have been attacked."

"Where could they get them from?" Carsten wondered, aloud.

"The Spanish. Or the Portuguese," Denys Zager suggested. He scowled at Henrique and Maurício.

Henrique scowled right back. "We are wanted men in Brazil.

And Maria and Heyndrick transported us here, from hundreds of miles away. They can vouch for the fact that we brought only our personal weapons with us."

Zager folded his arms across his beer barrel chest. "You say you're refugees, but how do we know? Perhaps your Indian friends are helping you smuggle weapons here from your friends in Brazil."

"Enough," said Carsten firmly. "The accusation is ridiculous. Please don't distract us from the real problem."

"Perhaps," Maria offered tentatively, "we should help the good Africans, the ones who are just trying to defend themselves, deal with the troublemakers themselves."

"You mean, give arms to the 'good' Africans? That's crazy."

Carsten clapped his hands. "We will try to figure out which Africans are the source of the problem, and deal with them. With or without African allies, as seems best at the time.

"For the moment, the Africans who wish to trade will have to come to us, not us to them. We'll set up a trading post just outside Fort Lincoln. We'll strengthen the inland defenses there, too. And I think we better institute river patrols. Hopefully, the blacks'll all calm down after a while."

Borguri held out his favorite whetstone, and one of his new Arawak wives dutifully poured water over it, letting the liquid cascade down into a waiting basin. A tied-up African watched in fear, not knowing what would happen next.

He pointed to the basin. "Drink," he ordered. The cowering captive complied.

Borguri then hit him over the head with the stone. "My sword serves me, my stone serves my sword, my water washes my stone, you have drunk my water. Your ancestors have forgotten you; mine watch your every move, your every thought. You are mine."

He gave the slave a playful cuff, and ordered, "Back to work."

The slave should be thankful. Now that he was officially part of Borguri's lineage—albeit at the lowest level—he was unlikely to be picked as a pre-battle sacrifice.

Borguri frowned. The process of assimilation just wasn't fast enough. Borguri needed a cadre of true Imbangala to serve as role-models for the coerced recruits, and to discipline those who didn't comply with the rules. There were only so many new recruits he could absorb within a period of a few months.

But if he took too long to build up his strength, the Ndongo would make or buy themselves decent weapons, and counterattack.

So Borguri had made a decision. Just as the Imbangala of old had allied themselves to the Portuguese, Borguri would ally his tribe to one of the Carib Indian tribes. One which, he had learned, was not happy about the white presence in their vicinity. Borguri felt confident that they would be delighted by the prospect of revenge and plunder that Borguri would hold out to them.

Of course, once the whites were driven out, the Caribs would no doubt turn upon the Imbangala.

Except that the Imbangala would turn on them first.

Maurício walked up beside Maria, coughed. "About that Coromantee man."

Maria looked up. "Yes? You thought of something?"

"I questioned the crew. Even the captain. They didn't remember the children, of course. What're two slaves among hundreds? But they did know which ship left Elmina before they did. And where it was headed."

"Well?"

"The *Fenix*. Bound for Havana."

"Well, that's something. I imagine there would be records of who was sold out of which ship, to which plantation. And there can't have been that many children. But he certainly can't go there and ask, can he?"

"He would need to learn Spanish, of course. And if he didn't want to be a slave within seconds after stepping onto the dock, he would need a letter of manumission. Preferably, from a Spanish source."

"Henrique could write the letter, couldn't he? Portugal being under the Spanish crown, they would honor a Portuguese document. And I wouldn't think a minor port official in Havana is going to have been informed that Henrique is a heretic."

"Probably not. But then there's the other problem. The financial one. He would have to buy his children. And he doesn't have any money."

"Well, it's going to take him months, if not years, to learn Spanish, and more important, how he must act if he wants to be successful. The important thing is that we can give him a reason to hope."

A moment later she added, "A reason to live."

✧   ✧   ✧

Carsten Claus looked out across the expanse of the Suriname. The river was perhaps half a mile across here. The vegetation on the far bank was dense; there could be an army of Africans hiding there, for all he knew. He wished he knew how the troublemakers were arming themselves. He suspected that the Portuguese in Belém do Pará, or the Spanish in Santiago de León de Caracas, were involved, to harass the USE. But would they arm slaves who had been taken off a Portuguese-crewed, Spanish-licensed ship? Could any of the colonists have been so short-sighted as to sell arms to the ex-slaves without permission?

To reassure the colonists, he had put the *Eikhoorn* on river patrol duty, and banned the Africans from fishing within a mile of the colony. He was waiting for the *Eikhoorn* to return from upriver; he had some questions for its skipper. But what he wanted most of all was for David de Vries to show up with a ship of force, and more colonists, so that they clearly outpowered and outnumbered the Africans. David should have been here a month ago.

At least, if their African informants were correct, he could now put a name to the problem: Imbangala. Maurício, sitting beside Carsten, had just explained to him that since 1615, the Portuguese of Luanda had used the Imbangala as mercenaries in their wars with Ndongo. Ndongo warriors, if captured in battle, were exported to the New World to work on plantations and in the mines. But the Imbangala? Since they were allies of the Portuguese in Luanda, Maurício hadn't expected to find them sold into slavery. Perhaps these had disobeyed orders? Or had the Portuguese beaten the Ndongo into submission, and decided the Imbangala had outlived their usefulness?

Carsten expressed the hope that the Gustavans' African friends were, indeed, friends. Maurício nodded, but offered no reassurances on that score. They sat in silence for a few minutes, then both realized simultaneously that they were no longer alone, and turned their heads.

"Forgive the interruption," said Maria.

Carsten forced a smile. "How can a visit from you be considered an interruption?"

"You perhaps know that Maurício and I have been researching the whereabouts of the children of one of the Coromantees? We think it very likely that they were shipped to Havana. I wondered—could the Anti-Slavery Society send someone there, to find and redeem them? I am sure it would be very good publicity, to reunite the children with their father."

Carsten swatted a mosquito. "The Society has discussed the possibility of redemption."

"And?"

"Decided against it. First, because our financial resources are limited. Second, because we fear that any concerted policy of that kind would just encourage the slavers to fetch more slaves so they could sell them to us for a quick profit. We would be, what's that American term, a 'revolving door.' Once naval resources can be spared to stop the slave trade at its source, and we have better funding, we may reconsider redemption."

"So what would you recommend?"

"Well—" Carsten was distracted by the appearance of the *Eikhoorn*, just coming around the upriver bend. It reminded him of the exciting day that they had seized the *Tritón*, and sunk its longboat, not many yards from where the *Eikhoorn* was plowing back downriver.

The longboat. He started cursing.

"Carsten, what's wrong?" asked Maria.

"We know from the reports that the Africans who have been causing trouble have weapons. I just figured out where they got them from." He pointed upriver.

"I don't understand... oh... the longboat? But wouldn't the weapons all be rusted?"

"By now they would be. But if they were found early enough, not irretrievably. The rust could have been scraped off."

"But how would they have known where to look? You don't suppose a colonist told them?"

"Perhaps. It might not have been evil in intent. A colonist might have bragged about the battle. Anyway, I will have the damn boat brought up. We'll take a count of how many bodies, guns and swords are still there, and that will let us make a good guess as to what was taken."

Carsten stood up. "The crew of the *Eikhoorn* is going to have to wait a little longer for their supper, I'm afraid. As for your problem, I think you are going to have to find a way for your Coromantee protégé to find the money himself. If he does, then the Society could perhaps find a trustworthy agent to send. A priest, perhaps."

✧   ✧   ✧

The three Ndongo warriors, Mukala, Aka, and Miguel, studied the bodies of their fallen comrades. Both bore diagonal gashes on their foreheads, but their death wounds were elsewhere.

"Imbangala," Mukala said. The Imbangala were in the habit of distinctively marking their kills so that each warrior could claim the bodies of the enemies he had slain, have them carried back to the camp by his slaves, and then eat them with the proper formalities so that their ghosts couldn't haunt the slayer.

Miguel pointed to the death wound. "That wasn't made by a spear."

"No," Mukala agreed. "It's a slash, not a thrust."

"And look how clean the edges are," said Aka. "That wasn't made with sharpened wood, or flint. It was a cut from a steel blade."

"This is very bad news," said Miguel. "The whites are arming the Imbangala with cutlasses. That is the only possible explanation."

"We should have wiped out the filthy Kasanje Imbangala right after we landed," said Mukala. "We had the advantage of numbers then." Many Ndongo, warriors and farmers alike, had been captured and shipped to the New World, to work Portuguese sugar plantations and Spanish silver mines. There were relatively few Imbangala on the slave ship because most were Portuguese allies. But Kasanje, who led one of the Imbangala bands, had set up an independent state in 1620, and so his people were fair game.

"That is easy to say now," reproved Aka. "But we were so thirsty we could barely move our limbs when we were freed." The slave ship had gone first to Angola, and tried its luck, even though it didn't have a proper license and therefore had to collect slaves on the sly. It ventured farther north, among the Coromantee, Eboe and Mandinka, only because it hadn't been able to fill its hold. So the Angolans had endured the privations of middle passage longer than any of their brothers in suffering.

Mukala made a gesture of propitiation to the gods. "Powers forbid we suffer so again!"

Miguel added thoughtfully, "If we had attacked the Imbangala immediately, the whites might have feared that we would attack them next, and turned their swivel guns on us."

"Do you think the Imbangala have guns, too?" asked Mukala. "If so, we are in big trouble."

"Don't know, but we better tell the elders what we found." Aka pointed at the bodies. "In the meantime let's rig a sled for these bodies. I'll not leave them for the Imbangala. And be quick about it; we don't know when they'll be back."

A few days later, the Ndongo moved their encampment some miles farther east, away from the Gustavans and, they hoped, the Imbangala.

The Gustavans' spirits were lifted by the somewhat belated arrival of the four-hundred-ton, eighteen-gun *Walvis*, their lifeline to the USE. It was commanded by Captain David Pieterszoon de Vries, president of the USE-chartered United Equatorial Company—their employer. It was accompanied by a *jacht*, the six-gun *Siraen*.

He brought news that was both welcome and unsettling. Welcome, in that peace had finally come to the Low Countries. Unsettling, in that there was now a Catholic king in the Netherlands, Don Fernando. The colonists, many of whom came from the Nether-lands, were mostly Protestants, and therefore not inclined to trust the ex-cardinal infante's promise of religious tolerance—even if Fredrik Hendrik was now a "trusted advisor."

On a personal level, Maria was overjoyed when David brought word that her brother Adolph and his wife Catarina had survived the Spanish invasion. Her cup of happiness overflowed when David gave her a letter from Adolph.

This reaction was somewhat tempered once she had read the letter. Adolph was a professor of medicine, and the curator of the Leiden Botanical Gardens.

He complained about the damage the Spanish troops had done to the garden. He complained that the students weren't paying attention in class. And he complained that the administration had unfairly reprimanded him for not showing more activity.

It was, he pointed out, all Maria's fault. He would have sent his *Catalogus plantarum* to Elzevier for publication two years ago if Maria hadn't sent him all those new plants from Grantville, thus throwing him off schedule. And then made matters worse by sending him exotic specimens from Suriname.

To add insult to injury, since she was gallivanting around the New World, without the slightest regard for her reputation (and for the damage she was doing, by association, to his dignity as a professor), that meant she wasn't back home drawing the plant illustrations for him.

At the end of this litany, he closed by hoping she was well.

Maria crumpled up the letter and tossed it into the Suriname River. "If it isn't one thing, it's a brother," she announced.

David digested the news without any more change of expression than an up-timer might have seen on the faces carved upon Mount Rushmore. But he knew that the Imbangala couldn't be allowed to get away with killing colonists, even ones who foolishly ventured into their territory.

"All right, this is what we'll do. First, we need to fortify the town and Fort Lincoln. Fortunately, I brought cement, and instructions on how to use it to make concrete. Concrete is stronger than wood, and doesn't need to be carved like stone. Besides cement, we need sand, gravel and water, but I believe this country has those materials in abundance.

"I also have the materials for a proper gatehouse, that is, I brought a portcullis and the like. And I have cannon in ballast. They are *pedreros* that were being sold off and replaced by newer designs, but they should be fine for fighting these Imbangala.

"We will need the Africans or the Indians, or both, for fighting in the forests. While the colonists are seeing to the defenses, we will send out emissaries. Heyndrick and Maria, you'll take the *Eikhoorn* upriver to talk to the Coromantee. And see if Captain Marshall, or his Indians, are willing to offer any assistance.

"Henrique and Maurício, you'll go to the Mandinka and the Eboes."

"The Ndongo are much more numerous, and they are already at war with the Imbangala," interjected Maurício. "Wouldn't I be more use talking to them?"

"Perhaps, but we know that they are also more hostile to Europeans, thanks to what the Portuguese have been doing in Luanda the last hundred years. I can speak Portuguese—I was Jan Pieterszoon Coen's right-hand man in Asia. But I can tell them honestly that I am Dutch, and the Portuguese are my enemies. Present company excepted, of course.

"Also, we hear that they've moved pretty far to the east. We'll need a big ship like the *Walvis* to force its way back to windward, find them, and move them some place more useful. And I'd be needed to skipper the *Walvis* in any event.

"Coqui will come with me, to talk to the local Indians. And also—what's her name?"

"Tetube?"

"Right. The lass who witnessed Imbangala atrocities first hand. Anyway, we'll organize a Grand Alliance, and put down the Imbangala for good."

"He's coming, he's coming!" the Mandinka children shrieked, running up the path to their village.

"Who's coming, children?" said the adult on guard duty.

"'He Who Talks'!"

The Mandinka had quickly realized that Maurício was one of the select few who had more than the usual mortal allotment of *nyamo*, the secret energy that allowed one to practice sorcery. It was held by great hunters, skilled blacksmiths, *gree gree* men, and of course the *nyancho*, the hereditary warrior aristocracy from whom they drew their rulers.

Had not Maurício presided over the ceremony in which their shackles were removed? No doubt his *nyamo* had subdued the cruel whites who had crewed the slave ship, forcing them to yield up the key and accept the loss of their property.

When they learned that Maurício spoke the languages of all the Europeans, and seemingly all the Africans, that was further proof of his power. The Mandinka did argue as to whether this was a natural, spontaneous manifestation of his *nyamo*, or whether he actually cast a spell when he wanted to learn a new language. But either way, he was a man to be respected, even feared.

Henrique, watching the fuss made over Maurício, was privately amused. He knew of the epithet, "He Who Talks," which had been given to Maurício, and had told Maria that once the Africans knew Maurício better, they would no doubt change it to "He Who Talks Too Much."

But for the moment, it worked to the Gustavans' advantage. Henrique and Maurício were ceremoniously ushered into the hut of Faye, the leader of the Mandinka.

"So," concluded Heyndrick, "the people who freed you now call upon you to fight with them against the Imbangala threat."

The reaction of the Coromantee miners wasn't quite what he had hoped for.

"What's in it for us?" asked Antoa.

"That's right," said Owusu. "We're here on the west side of the river, and the Imbangala are on the east. Let the Imbangala and the Ndongo kill each other."

Heyndrick tugged nervously at his earlobe. "Maurício tells me that the Imbangala have crossed rivers before."

Antoa shrugged. "They're afraid of your ships with the cannon, so they aren't going to cross."

"Perhaps not this month, or next, but they will cross once they have enough numbers. If only to get at our goods," Heyndrick warned.

"The good whites are helping me find my children," interjected Kojo. Heyndrick gave him a quick smile of thanks.

"Fine, when they bring the children to you, we can talk again," said Antoa.

Maria whispered to Heyndrick.

"Let us talk more after dinner," Heyndrick declared.

"That didn't go quite as well as I had hoped," Heyndrick muttered. "What makes you think that they will be more receptive after dinner?"

"Actually, it's tomorrow morning that they will be more receptive," said Maria. "So don't press too hard after dinner."

"I would think that tonight, when they're drunk, they'll feel more martial than tomorrow morning, when they're all nursing hangovers."

"Trust me, I know the Coromantees. And now you must excuse me." Maria rose.

"Where are you going?"

"I must be polite and help the Coromantee womenfolk prepare dinner."

Heyndrick followed Maria's advice. The next morning, Owusu and Antoa were the first to lay their spears at Heyndrick's feet.

Heyndrick was dumbfounded. *What had happened?*

Maria gave him a nudge. "Uh, thank you," said Heyndrick. "Take up your weapons, warriors." He raised his pistol. "Victory!"

They brandished their spears. "Victory!"

"What just happened there?" asked Heyndrick, as the *Eikhoorn* made its way upstream toward the Marshall's Creek settlement.

"I had a word with the womenfolk, as I told you. And they made it clear to our valiant warriors that if they didn't go off to war, the ladies would make them *wish* they were *already dead.*"

The crew of the *Walvis'* pinnace pulled at the oars. They picked their way through the mangroves, and stared into the verdant growth of the Suriname coast. Now and then the leaves were disturbed as a bird landed or took flight, but they saw no sign of the presence of man.

David de Vries, sitting beside the helmsman, wondered just how, exactly, he was going to find the Ndongo, let alone bring them into the alliance.

Coqui stood at the prow, and occasionally gestured to turn one way or another. David hoped that he, or the local Indian woman, Tetube, who sat behind him, had some idea of where to look.

Eventually, they beached the boat, and left a couple of guards behind. The rest followed Coqui and Tetube, who led them to a trail. Tetube, it seemed, knew of a friendly Indian village in the area.

Friendly to her tribe, at least.

But there wasn't cause to worry. The Indians were indeed friendly. And while they had no contact with the Ndongo, they knew another tribe, which traded with them. David distributed a few presents, and acquired a new guide, who went back to the pinnace with them and directed them to the mouth of a nearby creek. Not far up it, they encountered a Ndongo fisherman.

When he spotted them, he immediately sat down and reached for a paddle. Clearly, his trust in the good intentions of a party of white men, even here in Suriname rather than in Africa, was minimal. However, after a moment he obviously decided that there was no way he could outpaddle the crew of the pinnace, even for the moments needed to reach the bank and disappear into the forest. He set down the paddle and slumped, head bowed.

David identified himself as the "Father" of the Gustavans. The fisherman recognized the name of the colony and this seemed to soften his attitude toward them. At least fractionally. David rummaged in a chest and produced a metal fishhook, which he presented to their new acquaintance. That finally loosened the fisherman's tongue.

He told David that if he brought the visitors to the village unannounced, his people would assume he was acting under duress. He asked David to let him bring word of David's arrival to the villagers, and assured him that he would receive a proper welcome if he did this.

After a moment, David agreed. Although not without some anxiety as to what, precisely, was the Ndongo concept of a "proper welcome" for white men.

The fisherman headed upriver, and, once he was out of sight, David had Coqui and the other Indians in the party climb trees on either side of the creek, to warn David if the approaching party appeared to be hostile.

Perhaps an hour later, several dugout canoes came down the river. The first canoe had just a few men in it, unarmed. Behind them, but obviously holding back, were two more canoes, both carrying bowmen and spearmen. Clearly, the Ndongo were ready to either parley or fight, as the situation dictated.

David, an experienced explorer, managed to persuade the Ndongo of his good intentions, and the Ndongo invited the Gustavan party to follow them back to their settlement.

The Ndongo, of course, didn't need to be convinced to fight the Imbangala. Their concerns were over how did the Imbangala get European arms and was David willing to supply their equivalent to the Ndongo.

David explained Carsten's theory as to the Imbangala windfall, and assured the Ndongo that the Gustavans would give them weapons, provided they came back with him to his ship.

"No, not your ship," they cried. "You might be trying to put us back in shackles."

David told them that they didn't have to come on board, they would be given the arms on the beach. But the arms could only be handed over where the crew of his ship could see the interchange and see that the Ndongo weren't up to any tricks.

The Ndongo saw the sense of this and agreed.

They came to the beach and admired their new cutlasses. "Guns?" one of them asked hopefully.

"Some other time, perhaps," said David.

Beginning of Long Dry Season (September to November, 1635)

With the Gustavans' support, the friendly African and Indian tribes built up their defenses, and set up patrols, curtailing the expansion of the Imbangala. But it was all a big distraction from more productive activities, and it wasn't long before the allies were debating how to bring the Imbangala to a decisive battle. Especially now that the rains had stopped, and it was easier and safer for the Europeans to enter the forest.

David summoned a grand council of the score or so of tribal leaders, African and Indian, large tribes and small ones.

"Can your scouts locate the Imbangala encampment?" David asked the Ndongo leader, Lucala.

"Perhaps. But destroying the camp does not defeat the Imbangala. They are not a settled people, they are a mercenary troop. We would, at best, deprive them of their slaves and their women, and perhaps the children they are training for war."

Faye, leader of the Mandinka, stood up. "A thousand pardons for the interruption. But rather than search the jungle for these pestilent Imbangala, why not bait them into a trap?"

"What kind of bait? And what kind of trap?"

Borguri trembled with rage. "Who has seen this, besides you?" he asked the warrior.

"Just a slave, oh great and wise leader."

"Kill him."

Borguri tore down the sign, and mutilated it with his sword. He then got out his tinder and flint, made a fire, and burnt it. Finally, he collected the ashes and tossed them into the nearby stream.

The next day, a second sign was found. Like the first, it featured a caricature of Borguri, wearing woman's clothes, and surrounded by various Ndongo symbols of ridicule. Maria was good at drawing things other than plants and animals. And her Ndongo informants had thought instructing her to be great fun.

A necessary skill for drawing wild animals, especially those of the rainforest, was the ability to draw from memory, from a fleeting glance. Maria had remembered Borguri from the deck of the slave ship—despite the ravages of thirst and imprisonment, he was formidable, and received deference from the other Imbangala—and, when the Ndongo described Borguri to her, she realized who they were referring to, and could draw him. Especially with the Ndongo by her side as she drew, quick to point out errors to her.

This sign was seen by a large party of warriors and slaves. Borguri had it chopped to pieces, and burnt, and then he peed on it. He then ordered an immediate raid on the nearest African village, and the sacrifice of six slaves to achieve success.

They arrived at the village only to find that it had been deserted, with all the inhabitants and their moveable possessions gone, and the crops destroyed. They did leave behind a lot of signs, however.

Borguri had to kill one of his warriors that night, who, in his cups, made derogatory remarks about Borguri's leadership. It was clear that Borguri had to take quick action, but it wasn't so clear what his target should be. The source of the signs was clearly Gustavus, but Borguri knew that a direct attack on Gustavus, or on Fort Lincoln, would be suicidal.

The answer came a few days later, from one of his spies. This fellow prudently remained in his dugout canoe as he conveyed his news. A dozen or so miles east of Fort Lincoln, in the strip of land between the Great Sea and the Commewijne River, a fetish hut had been built, at a site which the European leaders and the African sorcerers deemed propitious for that purpose. Inside the hut, there was a wood statue of Borguri, surrounded by curse objects and more of the insulting signs. In exactly a week's time, there would be a ceremony at which the statue would be burnt, in a ritual that would assure the ignominious defeat of Borguri and the Imbangala.

Borguri asked him more questions, assuring himself that the fetish hut was out of cannon range of Fort Lincoln. Then he gave his orders.

Wait. Was that a smirk he saw on the face of his spy? He grabbed a spear and threw it.

The insufficiently prudent agent toppled into the water.

The Imbangala and their Indian allies crossed the Commewijne River in a swarm of dugout canoes. Borguri left behind the children trainees, with a few wounded regulars to supervise them, as a rear guard.

Borguri led the rest of his war party in the direction of the reported fetish hut. His Caribs scouted ahead and to the flanks, watching for an ambush. They found no one.

At last, the war party entered the clearing that held the fetish hut. They milled about it, singing war songs and building up their courage. At last, one of the Imbangala strode into the hut, and triumphantly grabbed the infamous statue.

His triumph didn't last long. With the statue dislodged, a spring-loaded pan rose. Inside the pedestal, a concealed trigger mechanism, protected from the tropical damp by rubber and tar, struck a spark, igniting priming powder inside. This lit a safety fuse, which in turn set off the barrels of gunpowder arrayed beneath the floor of the hut. The wood planks fractured, and the shards hurtled upward.

The bold Imbangala, still peering curiously at the statue in his hand, was impaled. So, too, were several of his companions. Others simply fell into the pit.

Borguri wasn't one of the victims of the trap. He immediately ordered the Imbangala back to the boats (and didn't trouble himself as to whether his Indian allies were doing the same). They got there, only to discover that their escape had been cut off.

The fluyt *Walvis*, the captured caravel *Vreedom* and the *jacht Eikhoorn* had taken advantage of the the great depth of the river Commewijne, even well upriver, and were already patrolling it, and firing their cannon and swivel guns at any likely targets.

Borguri briefly considered attacking the ships. It was true that his warriors only had to cross some five hundred feet of water, from the north bank of the Commewijne to the sides of the ships, to attack them, but the high tumblehome hulls of the *Walvis* and *Vreedom* would be difficult to assault from the low-slung canoes. The *Eikhoorn* was a more manageable target, but it, like the larger ships, had boarding nets out. For that matter, their decks were packed with Coromantee, Eboe, Mandinka and Arawak warriors, and there were musketeers in the rigging.

Where are the Ndongo? he wondered.

He got his answer. The Atlantic Ocean, the Suriname River, and the Commewijne River formed a horizontally stretched C, facing east. The Ndongo had been hidden, screened by friendly Indians, far enough to the east to escape detection by the Imbangala's scouts. Once the Imbangala attacked the fetish hut, they surged westward, driving the Imbangala against the reinforced defenses of Fort Lincoln at the confluence of the Suriname and the Commewijne.

Borguri was one of the last to fall. He had his back to a great tree trunk, and several Ndongo approached him. Borguri dared them to pick a champion to fight him, one on one. The Ndongo backed off slightly, and heatedly argued whether this challenge should be accepted and, if so, which had them had precedence.

At last Faye arrived, a Dutch cutlass in hand. "What is the problem here?" They explained.

"Young idiots," he muttered. The Ndongo stiffened.

"Bowmen!" Faye's people raised their bows.

At that, Borguri charged. To no avail. The Ndongo danced back, taunting him and pricking him with their spears, and first one arrow and then another plunged into his body.

Borguri sank to the ground. Faye moved forward, and swung his cutlass. Borguri sank to his knees. "This is real life, not a song," he admonished the spearmen. "Defeat your enemy at the least cost to yourself." Faye made a final sweep, beheading Borguri.

Akan village, Paranam

"Kojo, months ago, we spoke of what must be done to recover your children."

"I remember, Maria. At home, I had gold. I was an *obirempon*, a holder of an elephant's tail." It was the Akan way of saying that he was a gold-mining tycoon. "Here, I am but a leaf in the forest. How will I ever be able to buy back my children?"

"There is a way of getting gold from streams, rather than by digging holes in the ground. My friend from America, Lolly, calls it 'panning.' You take a shallow dish—"

"You need not explain this 'panning,' Maria. All the women and children of the Ashanti know how to gather the flecks of gold which the River God has scattered amidst the gravel."

"And do you know how to do this?"

"Of course. I was a child once. And I watched my wife teach our children, and saw my Mansa find her first nugget."

"Well, I wish I could just give you the gold you need, but I can't. But I have consulted our oracles"—that was how the Africans interpreted her references to encyclopedia articles—"and learned that there is river gold in this land." She started drawing in the sand. "This is our river, the Suriname." She added two more sinuous curves. "And the Saramacca to our west, and the Marowijne to the east.

"Upriver, the Marowijne forks like so." She drew in the Tapanahoni and the Lawa, and then added an "X" between the locations of the up-time towns of Grand Santi and Cottica. She twirled her finger around it. "Here, somewhere, there is gold."

Maria then swept her hand over the upper Suriname and Saramacca. "Here, too, but I can't be more specific."

"How do I get to these places? How long is the journey? How friendly are the Indians?"

"You will need to go by canoe. Tetube said that she can guide you. And Coqui said he will go, too, he is bored." Maria suspected that Coqui's offer had less to do with boredom than with the chance to get to know Tetube better.

"We Akan usually don't mine gold alone. It's most often a family enterprise. I will see if any of my people want to come along."

Maria grimaced. "I must ask you not to. I want this kept a secret. I don't want all the Gustavans running off to look for gold when they should be farming to keep themselves fed."

Fort Lincoln, Suriname

"Getting the colonists to follow orders without griping was hard enough. But if every plan you make has to be presented to every kinglet in this Little Africa you have created, in some kind of grand palaver, you will go insane before the rains return," said David.

"What do you suggest I do?" asked Carsten.

"Get the chiefs together and tell them that you want them to meet and pick a paramount chief. Someone to represent them on all save the most important matters."

"Right, I'll do that."

The chiefs had been huddled in the great ceremonial hut for twelve hours straight. Carsten had told them a few hours earlier that none of them would be leaving it until they picked the chief of chiefs.

Now and then, Maurício was called in to clarify some point or other that they were arguing about. No one wanted an error in translation to get a blood feud started. Finally, after a long waiting period, he decided to snatch some sleep while he could.

Perhaps an hour later, the curtain that had been hung over the hut opening to keep mosquitoes out was pushed back once again, and Faye stuck his head out. "Maurício, please," he said.

Carsten sighed. "Maurício!" he called.

"He's asleep," said Henrique.

"Well, wake him up. We want them to finish one of these days." Still rubbing his eyes, Maurício arrived, and entered the hut.

He emerged a few minutes later, looking wide awake, even a little wild-eyed.

"Well? Have they picked a paramount chief, yet?"

"Yes," said Maurício. "For the love of God...Me."

Maria gave a whoop. "All Hail Maurício, King of the Jungle!"

Tears of the Sun, Milk of the Moon

Winter 1635 to Early 1637

*Surinamese Short Wet Season (December 1635–January 1636),
On the banks of the Coppename, Western Suriname*

Maria Vorst, artist, botanist, and author, mulled over the tribulations of life in the Suriname rainforests. Frequent downpours. Oppressive heat when it wasn't raining. Hungry crocodilians looking for a human-sized snack. Venomous snakes that didn't take kindly to passers-by. Hordes of biting, stinging and otherwise annoying insects. Tropical diseases that could kill you or make you wish you were dead.

She loved it anyway.

But all good things must come to an end.

Maria peered into the bush. "Just a little farther, Henrique, and we'll be through."

The down-time Europeans thought the jungle was impenetrable, hundreds upon hundreds of miles of dense vegetation. In fact, Maria suspected that all too many up-timers thought the same, their knowledge of the jungle being based primarily on vague recollections of Tarzan movies.

As she had explained to the readers of her popular travelogue, *Into the Rainforest with Musket and Paintbrush*, "the rainforest floor is dark, shaded by the rainforest canopy. Since it's dark,

185

there's not a lot of vegetation." To Maria with her artist's eye, the true jungle was like a cathedral, with an emerald roof, and great open chapels for the worship of nature.

The "jungle" only looked like an up-time Hollywood movie jungle if you were on the river, where there was plenty of sunlight to make plants happy. But if you wiggled or cut your way through the "jungle wall" bordering the river, you entered the true jungle, the Green Cathedral.

Henrique da Costa raised his machete and took another swing.

Henrique and Maria first met in Fort Kykoveral, back in 1634. Henrique was a Marrano, a Jew who had practiced his religion in secret in Catholic Brazil, and Maria was a steadfast Protestant, of the Arminian persuasion. In a world divided by religion, it didn't bode well for romance. An early flirtation had fizzled out.

Still, they were close friends, with a love of the outdoors, and so they talked as they settled into their respective hammocks that night. Henrique, who had lived in the Amazon for many years, had taught her the trick of rocking oneself to sleep. You fastened a rope to the side of the hammock, and led it off at right angles. Wrap it halfway around a convenient tree trunk and lead the free end back. Give it a couple of pulls, and the hammock would rock back-and-forth for many minutes.

But Maria wasn't ready for sleep just yet. "Henrique, I received a very interesting proposal from the Danes. The Danish East India Company wants to set up rubber plantations in Asia. Preferably near their trading post at Tranquebar, in southeastern India, but if need be, elsewhere. We know that rubber can be grown in plantations in Malabar, Ceylon, Burma, Siam, Cochinchina, Malaya, Sumatra, Java and Borneo—it's in the up-time books."

"So they want us to teach them how to tap the milk of the rubber tree, huh?"

"They don't just want tapping lessons, they want rubber tree seeds."

"Why should we help them kill off our rubber industry? Isn't that what the British did to Brazil in the old time line?"

"They have pointed out to David's shareholders that it is only possible to harvest wild rubber in South America, because the South American Leaf Blight spreads too easily when the trees are

close together." An up-time book on South America had mentioned the failure of the Ford rubber plantation at "Fordlandia"
and a modern edition of *Encyclopedia Britannica* had made more
general reference to the blight. "Gustavus will get shares in the
rubber plantations as compensation. And in addition, the Danes
will bring us seeds and cuttings for other tropical plants: cacao,
sugarcane, and perhaps even coffee. So we'll have plantations of
our own."

"Ah. Something for everyone."

"But the rubber tree seeds they want aren't those of the local
species, *Hevea guianensis*. They want *Hevea brasiliensis*."

Henrique stopped rocking. "So that's why you're talking to me."

"That's right. You ran the rubber tapping operation in the
Tapajós before the Portuguese discovered you were Jewish. So
you know exactly where to look for good producers."

"And I also know the 'back door' into the Amazon." Henrique
and his servant Maurício, with the help of the Manao Indians
Coqui and Kasiri, had discovered a connection, the sometime-
lake Rupununi, between the Amazon and Essequibo river basins.

"We can retrace your escape route."

Henrique pondered this for a while. "I don't know whether to
hope for a final encounter with Bento Maciel Parente, or not."
Henrique had sought to protect "his" Indians from Parente, and
it was Parente who had been Henrique's most dogged pursuer
during his flight.

"He's not worth your taking unnecessary risks, Henrique."

Henrique grunted. Maria couldn't tell whether it was a grunt
of agreement.

"Wait," said Henrique. "Rubber tree seeds have to be planted
within a few days or they just die. At least, the ones here do.
And it will take months to pack them out of the Amazon by
my 'back door.' And a couple more months, at least, to get them
back to Europe."

"A few days, if they aren't protected from dessication or fungal
attack. But the encyclopedia says to pack them in dry soil or
charcoal, and I have done experiments with our native Guianan
seeds that suggest that with the right packing material and containers, we can keep them viable for a month or two. Maybe
longer with a fungicide."

"But surely we can't get them back to Europe that soon."

"The Danes have promised me a very fast ship, although I am not permitted to reveal details, and I think that I might even be able to plant the seeds in soil while still on board, as long as I do it once I am sure we are outside of the range of the leaf blight. Then I can keep the seedlings alive in Wardean boxes."

"Well, I'm glad for you, Maria. I know you have wanted to see the Amazon, and it's nice that you will be able to do so at someone else's expense."

Maria sat up in her hammock. "Henrique, look at me. After we go to the Amazon, I am returning to Europe. The king of Denmark has decided that he should have a botanical garden and he wants me to be the curator. He is going to build me a greenhouse, since the winters are so cold in Copenhagen, and I will be able to go on expedition to Asia. To Asia, Henrique!"

"I see."

"Don't look glum. You could come with me. I would welcome a partner of your experience."

"I don't know, Maria. In the Amazon, I am an expert. But in Asia, I would be a, a . . . what is that American term?"

"Greenhorn?"

"That's the one."

"I think you underestimate how quickly you would adjust. I know that I have read up-time books about naturalists who traveled all over the world. Gerald Durrell, for one."

"I'll think about it."

African Market Village, Near Paramaribo

Carsten Claus ducked his head as he entered the audience room of the "Jungle King" and then stood for a moment in appreciation of its rude grandeur.

The jungle king was seated on an ornately carved stool, and an attendant was briskly waving a large palm branch. The great monarch wore a loincloth, a cavalier's hat with a rakishly positioned harpy eagle tail feather, and a necklace whose pièce de resistance was a pierced fragment of an old CD.

"Well, Maurício, you've certainly come up in the world."

Maurício made a deprecating gesture. *"Tempore felici, multi numerantur amici. Cum fortuna perit, nullus amicus erit."* It was a reminder that despite his present appearance, he was one of the better educated men in the colony.

"So how's the king-ing business going for you?"

"Well enough. With great regret I had to dismiss the proposal that as chief-of-chiefs I should take a wife from each of the African tribes making up our little confederation."

"You didn't fancy yourself the Sultan of Suriname, complete with seraglio?"

"It sounded good in theory. And among Kasiri's people, the chiefs are polygamists, so she didn't reject the proposal out of hand." Kasiri was an Indian from Manao in the Amazon. "But there weren't a lot of women among the slaves we freed; perhaps one in three. And most of the ones who were of marriageable age got hooked up pretty quickly after the landing. So I'd have to either to take another man's wife away, which is asking for trouble, or pick from the few unattached women of each tribe. Who of course are the ones who didn't get picked already, if you get my drift."

"Well, I have a little project to take your mind off political marriages, or the lack thereof. I got an interesting letter from the Danish East India Company—"

"The East Indies are half a world away from here."

Carsten shrugged. "There's no Danish *West* India Company to tell them to bugger off. It has come to their attention that plants grow rather vigorously here. Perhaps you can interest some of your tribesmen in going into the vegetable oil business? Palms, perhaps?"

"For cooking?"

"I think the Danes are more interested in biofuel." His eyes strayed to the bowl of fruit on the table beside Maurício.

"Help yourself," said Maurício. "As you said, plants grow rather vigorously here, so there're plenty more where that came from."

Carsten reached for a passion fruit, and took a quick bite. "What a luscious juice it has." He spat out a seed. "The fuel's to support a pet project of Maria's, that they've been corresponding with her about."

"Well, if it's for Maria, and it's paying work, by all means."

Surinamese Short Dry Season (February to March) 1636, Gustavus (Paramaribo)

Lorenz Baum, the colony's master carpenter, rolled up the plans. "And what did you say this structure was for?"

"A watchtower," Carsten Claus, acting governor of the colony of Gustavus, said.

"Well, you certainly want a watchtower that isn't going to fall down anytime soon. It is quite..." The carpenter hunted for the word he wanted. "Substantial."

"It's forty-plus feet tall; I don't want it blown down."

"It will have tripod supports fixed in concrete. It would take a hurricane to blow it down. And Maria said that according to those up-time encyclopedias, hurricanes never hit this coast."

"Well, if you really want to know..." Carsten lowered his voice, and the carpenter involuntarily leaned closer. "It's Maria's idea. Make it fancy enough, and we can put it about to the Indians and the Africans that it's a magic thing, that it will do all sorts of bad things to anyone who attacks the town, and even worse things to anyone who tries to burn it or knock it down. And that way, if we have a falling out, they will think twice before attacking."

"Oh. That makes a strange kind of sense. Well, I best be getting back to the shop and make sure that apprentice of mine is working and not trying to spot the Indian girls skinny-dipping."

Fort Lincoln, Near the Mouth of the Suriname River, Suriname

It was nearly sunset when the strange canoe slipped up the Suriname river. The sentinel in the watchtower at Fort Lincoln blew on a conch shell, summoning his sergeant.

"Well, I hope this was worth interrupting my dinner," that worthy grumbled.

"It's a canoe," the sentry said, handing over the scope. "It has a sail, but it doesn't look like a Carib sail. Don't they use a square sail, with a mast up front?"

The sergeant squinted. "That's a spritsail; European influence, for sure. I see two...no, three people.... You don't suppose there's a Spanish army hiding in that palm-thatched hut at the stern?"

The sentry started to apologize for disturbing the sergeant.

"No, no, you did the right thing. By the markings on that sail...I think our intrepid explorers have returned. Coqui, Tetube and Kojo, that is."

"Where from?"

"Maria told me that she had sent them to explore the Marowijne." That was the river that, in the world the Americans came from, had marked the border between Dutch and French Guiana. "She said that Tetube had kinfolk among the tribes there."

"Wonder if they found anything interesting?"

The sergeant raised his eyebrows. "Like El Dorado?"

The sentry grinned sheepishly. "There's always hope..."

"Perhaps. Given the course they're on, I don't think they plan on stopping here, so I guess we aren't going to find out anything tonight."

Gustavus Colony, Paramaribo, Suriname

Coqui, Tetube and Kojo arrived at the Paramaribo dock, tired but pleased with themselves, some minutes later. They asked the dock guard whether their friends were in town. He told them that Maria Vorst and Henrique da Costa were out exploring the Coppename River in western Suriname, and intended to visit the Dutch at Fort Kykoveral, farther west. Maurício, Henrique's former servant and the present "chief-of-chiefs" of the rescued Africans, was visiting with the Eboe, whose village was on the Commewijne some miles to the east. And his wife Kasiri, Coqui's sister, was with him.

Kojo was disappointed at the news, but he invited Coqui and Tetube to come back with him to the Ashanti village, farther upriver. The village was a circle of huts. The smell coming from the cooking pots in the center started Coqui's stomach rumbling, much to Tetube's amusement.

The travelers might have preferred to sleep, but there was food, drink and dancing. And more drink. Soon, Coqui and Tetube fell asleep.

"More *piwari* for the rest of us," Kojo commented.

Antoa, the leader of the local Ashanti, grinned. "Well, how was the trip?"

"I told you—"

"Yes, yes, I know about the color of the Marowijne, and the strange birds, and the Indians you met. But you know what I am really asking about. And you owe me a debt, you know. From before we were taken by the Bad People." By which he meant slavers.

"Tell no one else," said Kojo. "At least not until Maria gives permission."

"She is a powerful seeress, I will do nothing to offend her."

Kojo sat in front of Antoa, his body hiding his actions from the rest of the villagers. He pulled out a pouch, and carefully shook out the contents. Several nuggets of gold came to rest on his outstretched palm; the largest was the size of his thumbnail. "See? I found enough of these to pay for the release of my children from the Spanish. More than enough, actually."

Antoa licked his lips. The Ashanti were gold miners and warriors, not farmers. "And was there more?"

"I am sure there's more. Much more. I could smell it."

Antoa was thinking, once again, about Kojo's gold. Antoa had promised not to tell anyone else about it. No, he remembered, he had promised to do nothing to offend Maria, the seeress. Well, then what was wrong with telling the other Ashanti, and looking for gold themselves? If she were a seeress, then she would know that they were going to do that, wouldn't she? And she couldn't take offense at something that was fated to happen.

With this exercise in sophistry completed, at least to his own satisfaction, he went off in search of his hunting partner, Owisu.

Beginning of Long Rainy Season (April to July) of Suriname, 1636, Near modern Paranam, Suriname

Heinrich Bender set down his shovel with a grunt of relief, and turned to his fellow bauxite miner, Erasmus Stein. "It's getting late. Where are the Ashanti?"

Erasmus shrugged. "Perhaps it's some religious thing."

"Wouldn't they have told us in advance?"

Erasmus swung his pick, not bothering to answer.

Perhaps an hour later, Kojo arrived.

Heinrich waved. "Where are your buddies, Kojo? We could use some help!"

"I am sorry, my friend," said Kojo. "They are gone."

"Gone, why?"

"When a drum has a drumhead, one does not beat the wooden sides," he said mysteriously.

Heinrich took a moment to think this through. "They found a better occupation than mining?"

"Better than bauxite mining," Kojo admitted.

"Better than—they found gold? Where? When?"

"They didn't find it, I did. Where Maria told me to look."

Erasmus raised his head so abruptly that Heinrich thought it was a wonder it didn't fly off.

Kojo ignored him. "She is going to be very angry with me when she finds out I told them. But they are my kinfolk, I had no choice. And I had to tell you why they are gone, lest you think that something bad happened."

"So why are you here, and not looking for more? Or spending what you've got?"

"I must wait for Henrique. He is to take me to Havana, so I can find and buy back my children."

"So, uh...just what was it that Maria told you?"

Kojo hesitated.

Heinrich put his arm around Kojo. "When Maria said not to tell anyone, I am sure she meant strangers. You have known me since you came to this place. And I helped free you. It was I who unlocked your shackles on the slave ship."

Those were the magic words; they unbound Kojo's lips.

"She said...she said that it was near the dream-place Cottica, on the Marowijne. And she was right."

"Dream-place, are you—oh." Heinrich suddenly realized it was the best the Ashanti could do with the difficult concept of a town that would have come into existence in the up-timers' old timeline, but didn't exist now, and probably would never exist. The town was undoubtedly on the maps that were displayed in what passed in Gustavus for a city hall.

"Can you...can you show us what you found? And tell us where to find more?"

On the Marowijne, between modern Suriname and French Guiana

As the Ashanti ascended the Marowijne, they encountered several Indians, presumably Arawaks of some kind. The Indians were naturally alarmed to see such a large party, and black men were totally outside their experience. However, the Ashanti were able to trade for fresh food by dumb barter.

Perhaps ninety miles from where they had entered the Marowijne, the train of Ashanti canoes neared a place where two smaller streams came together to form the Marowijne they had been ascending. The right one was the Tapanahony, and the left, the Lawa.

Recalling Kojo's instructions, Antoa gestured with his paddle toward the left branch. "That one."

Just then, a pink-bellied river dolphin leaped into the air, crossing their path, and landing with a great splash.

All the canoes came to an abrupt halt so that the Ashanti could decide whether this was a good omen or a bad one. While dolphins could be seen off the Gold Coast, the Ashanti country began a good fifty miles inland, and their band knew no old tales about them.

After some minutes of fruitless discussion, they decided to make an offering to Tano, the God of Rivers, and keep going.

Soon thereafter, a small Ashanti hunting party came across a lone Indian. He proved brave enough, or foolhardy enough, to come close enough to talk. The Ashanti knew something of the language of the Arawak Indians who lived near the Suriname and Commewijne rivers, and that was good enough. The Indian confirmed that one could find what he called "tears of the Sun" in the creeks that fed into the Lawa, especially after a hard rain, and he agreed to guide them in return for a glass bauble that Antoa offered him.

The Indian also told them that the river dolphins were shapeshifters, who delighted in seducing humans of the opposite sex. Worse, if the object of their attention was married, they could imitate the appearance of the spouse. Leading, he told the Ashanti, to conversations along the lines of, "Again? Didn't you get enough this afternoon? What do you mean this afternoon, I was out fishing all day!"

The Ashanti agreed that for the next few nights, until they were well away from the river junction, no one, man or woman, should be left alone.

Gustavus

Heinrich Bender heaved another bag of provisions into the canoe. Last one, he thought with relief. Now where's Erasmus? The sun's only a couple of handwidths above the horizon.

But the person who next greeted him was someone other than Erasmus. Someone quite unwelcome, in fact.

"Where's the party?" asked the dock guard, Nikolaus.

Heinrich made a vague wave in the general direction of Fort Lincoln. "Just a private party in New Carthage." That was the local name for the Africans' market town, at the confluence of the Suriname and Commewijne rivers, and it was of course Maurício's fault. At least he had failed to convince the colonists to call it *Carthago Nova*.

Erasmus ran up. "I bought us another shovel, and—" Erasmus suddenly noticed Nikolaus.

"Going to do the shovel dance at the party, huh, Erasmus?" said Nikolaus.

"None of your goddamn business, Nikolaus!"

"Oh really, Erasmus. You've been here less than a year, didn't even fight the Imbangala, and you think you can tell me what questions I can ask. Well, I'm the Dock Guard"—his voice capitalized the words—"and I think you're behaving suspiciously. I can ask all the questions I please."

"Take it easy, Nikolaus," said Heinrich. "I came here on the first ship, so I have seniority over you."

"So you do, but I need to know that you aren't off to bury a body somewhere. In fact—"

He blew a whistle. "I have called for reinforcements."

Two more guards arrived, seeming pleased by the break in routine.

"Okay, let's see what's in the canoe," Nikolaus ordered. Heinrich and Erasmus slowly laid the contents out.

"Two pans? You can't share a pan?"

"It's, it's a hygiene thing," Heinrich explained. Nikolaus' sniff suggested that he was unimpressed by this explanation.

The solar disk was touching the ocean by the time they were told, "You're free to go."

Heinrich and Erasmus tossed their goods into the canoe, without worrying about being neat about it, and pushed off.

"I told you sneaking away was a dumb idea," Heinrich whispered to Erasmus.

Nikolaus had been on duty the day that Kojo, Coqui and Tetube had returned, too. As he tried to fall asleep that night, he wondered again why Coqui and Tetube would have brought an African miner from the Gold Coast with them.

The next day, Nikolaus went looking for Kojo. And told him that the regulations of the colony required that all gold discoveries, including their amount and location, be reported to a duly appointed officer of the law, such as—he preened slightly—himself.

Kojo sighed, and made the report. "I expected this," he admitted.

"Oh?"

"Under Ashanti law, all gold mining must be reported to the king. How much must I pay the governor?"

"Uh... I'm not sure," Nikolaus back-pedaled. "What's the royal cut back home?"

"One-third."

"That sounds reasonable, but I will have to ask the governor. Be patient, and I'll let you know."

"Take your time," urged Kojo. "There's no rush."

"This paddling is more work than mining was," Erasmus complained. "I wish we could use a sail." The wind was then blowing from the east, and would have made eastward progress impossible even with a sail far more sophisticated than that of their canoe.

Heinrich snorted. "So do I, Erasmus, so do I. But be thankful that we are paddling against the puny current of the Cottica, not the great ocean current off the coast of Suriname." The Cottica was a tributary of the Commewijne. In one of the monthly lectures that she gave for the entertainment and edification of the colonists, Maria had mentioned that according to up-time encyclopedias, in the flood season, you could cross over from the Cottica to a tributary of the Marowijne, and follow that down to the latter. Which was a good thing, because the entrance of the Marowijne was pretty dangerous. Not just because of the Caribs, but also because of rocks and odd currents.

Some days later, Heinrich and Erasmus were in the swamp, really a seasonally drowned forest, which bridged the two river systems.

Heinrich and Erasmus felt pretty much drowned themselves, having just gone through a downpour that felt like sitting under a waterfall. But the sun had come out, and they were drying out gradually, with a renewed appreciation of why the natives didn't bother much with clothing.

Now, birds were chirping... and Erasmus was cursing. "I always thought Hell was all fiery and red, but now I know it's watery and green." He had just pulled on his oar and struck some obstruction, a submerged log or tree root, and the impact had jarred him badly.

"It grows on you," said Heinrich, giving Erasmus only a fraction of his attention. He was trying to read the primitive compass he had brought along. "And don't jostle me, damn it; if I drop this compass in the muck, we'll never find our way out." He waited for the needle to steady.

"Okay, we're still bearing east..." Heinrich picked up his own paddle. Soon it was his turn to complain. The waters were even shallower now, and it seemed as though they were hitting an underwater obstruction every few strokes.

Some monkeys howled overhead.

"Shut up!" Erasmus yelled at them. In response, they bombarded him with clots of shit. Erasmus grabbed his musket and tried to sight on them, but it was hopeless. They were well hidden in the green canopy above the colonists.

"I wish I could climb after the little buggers and throttle them. In fact, I wish we could just swing through the trees like them and not have to paddle at all..."

"Not have to paddle..." Heinrich repeated. "Put down your paddle, Erasmus, and try this." He reached up and pulled on a stout liana hanging in front of him, pulling the boat forward. After a moment, Erasmus imitated him. There was no lack of vines to choose from. It was slow, but it was easier on the anatomy.

Ashanti Village

"Hey, Kojo, we'd like a word with you." The three colonists formed a triangle around him.

"What do you want?" His eyes measured the gap between them, and the distance to where he had set down his machete.

"We'd like to see this gold you found."

He shook his head vigorously. "Didn't find gold."

In the privacy of his thoughts, he groaned. Heinrich and Erasmus must have gossiped about it! After they promised to keep it secret, too!

"Don't worry, we're not going to take it from you.... But we want to see it."

Kojo had an unpleasant vision of what they might do if he continued to stonewall. "I gave it to the governor. For safekeeping." That was true.

"Shit!" said the shortest of the three. "He's probably got it in the Company treasury-house."

"Doesn't matter," said the tallest. "Now we're sure that the story's true; there's gold to be found. So where'd you find it, Kojo?"

Kojo didn't answer quickly enough, and "Shortie" punched him in the stomach. Kojo whooshed.

"He can't talk if he can't breathe," admonished "The Tall One."

The third man spoke up. "Listen, Kojo, we colonists freed you and your kinfolk from those slavers. You find gold, you have to tell us where you found it."

Kojo started to explain.

"Fuck, this is too complicated," said Shortie. "Why don't we just take him with us? He can guide us every step of the way."

The Tall One shrugged. "Sounds good to me, if you're willing to guard him. Gag and hogtie him for tonight. Tomorrow we'll hide him under a tarp, and paddle down to the Marowijne."

Soon Kojo was tied to a tree, with only his thoughts to keep him company. *The spirits have punished me for disobeying Maria. I shouldn't have told Antoa. I shouldn't have spoken to Heinrich. I shouldn't have believed that guard who said that the law required that I report any gold finds.*

Tetube pointed at the canoe tied up a mile downriver of the Ashanti village. "Why would the Ashanti leave a canoe there? There are better places right by the village." Tetube and Coqui had decided to visit Kojo.

"I don't know," whispered Coqui. "Perhaps someone wanted to surprise them." He stopped paddling and grabbed his bow. He let the current carry them back downstream until the mystery canoe was out of sight around a bend. Then he put the bow down again, and brought their own canoe to the water's edge.

"Stay in the canoe, keep a paddle in hand. I will check out what's going on." He grabbed his bow and machete.

Coqui crawled through the brush. In due course, he came close enough to hear Kojo struggling with his bonds. He motioned for Kojo to stay still, and cut him free. Kojo then whispered to him what had happened.

"You're sure they left the paddles in the canoe?"

Kojo nodded.

"Then our best bet is to make our escape in their canoe. On my signal..."

Coqui studied his surroundings with his eyes, ears, even his nose. Then he made a sharp arm gesture, and he and Kojo ran, half-crouched, for the canoe. Coqui cleaved the tie line with his machete, and Kojo jumped in and grabbed a paddle. As Coqui pushed the little craft into the water, they could hear the colonists rouse themselves. "Huh, did you make a noise? Wasn't me! So what was that snap I heard? You stupid shithead, you just stepped on me! Hey, where's the prisoner! Shit, they're stealing our canoe!"

Coqui pulled himself into the canoe as the first kidnapper stumbled down to the bank and fired in the wrong direction.

Once he was sure he was out of range, Coqui yelled, "have a nice walk back home!"

After they were safely away, and had beached and hidden the canoes, they talked about what to do next. Kojo told them that these weren't the first colonists to harass him, only the nastiest. And predicted that it was only a matter of time before like-minded whites went after his fellow explorers Coqui and Tetube, even though they weren't gold miners like Kojo.

They decided to leave the Suriname River—there were too many potentially gold-hungry Gustavans traveling on it—and enter the swamp-and-ridge country to the east. There were African and Indian camps there, and they could take refuge with them. They would have a message taken to Maurício, Coqui's brother-in-law, at New Carthage, and he would let them know when Maria and Henrique returned. Maria and Henrique would protect them. At least, if Maria forgave Kojo for breaching her trust.

Gustavus

The acting governor, Carsten Claus, looked up from his paper-work. "Heyndrick. How may I help you?"

"Carsten, something very odd is going on. First the Ashanti stopped mining, and then the whites."

"What are they doing instead?"

"Doing? I have no idea. They have disappeared into the forest."

"Without explanation?"

"None that any of their friends are willing to share with me, at least. I am afraid that as the boss' cousin, I'm not likely to get a straight answer."

Carsten stood up, and started pacing. "Shit, I don't need this now, I have to go upriver to check on the English at Marshall's Creek. Dirck'll be in charge in my absence, so tell him what you've told me...."

He stopped in mid-stride, and laughed. "I hate it when I do that." He sat back down, and leaned back. "I suppose it's not the end of the world. They'll tire eventually of whatever it is that has caught their fancy, and we can go a few months without bauxite mining. It's just being stockpiled until Essen Chemical gets the kinks out of their aluminum refining process."

With this rather tepid assurance, Heyndrick left.

Not for the first time, Carsten Claus wished that the official governor, Heyndrick's cousin David Pieterszoon de Vries, had as much enthusiasm for governing as he did for exploring, trading, and starting colonies. He had not skippered the last supply ship to service Gustavus, and the captain of that ship had not been willing to venture a guess as to when David might deign to reappear.

The next day, Carsten took the *Siren* upriver, leaving the colony in the hands of Captain Dirck Adrienszoon, the commander of Fort Lincoln. On the journey south, he thought about Heyndrick's warning. Adrienszoon was competent, if a bit on the unimaginative side. But Carsten didn't think it likely that anything would happen that Dirck couldn't handle. It wasn't as though the Gustavus Colony was producing anything that the Spanish or French would deem so valuable as to justify the expense of a major invasion force.

✧　　✧　　✧

Elias, the carpenter's apprentice, was thinking, for once, of gold, not skinny-dipping Indian girls. Rumors were circulating, whispered by one lad to another—always under an injunction of secrecy—that Kojo had found a gold nugget. As big as an up-timer's baseball. Unfortunately, the rumors disagreed as to where this golden baseball had pitched itself into his lap. Some said the gold was farther up the Suriname, others remembered Kojo's little expedition and favored the Marowijne. And still others agreed that Kojo had found gold on that trip, but urged that he only pretended to go to the Marowijne, and in fact had sailed westward, to the Saramacca.

They couldn't ask Kojo, because he had apparently gone into hiding. Or perhaps returned to his El Dorado for more gold.

On a tributary of the Lawa River, in Eastern Guiana

Afia ever so carefully transferred the remaining river sand, and a bit of water, to her smallest *calabash*. This one she had dyed black, to make specks of gold easier to spot.

Ama, Antoa's wife, came up beside her. "*Mena wo akye.*" Good morning.

Afia bowed her head respectfully. "*Yaa Ena.*" Thank you, Respected Elder Woman.

She swirled the water around a bit, rinsing the sand.

"Ah." In her hair she had several feathers from various Suriname birds. They weren't there purely as ornamentation. The tips had been cut off and the hollows inside plugged with wild cotton. She pulled out one of these quills and unplugged it. Then, with wood tweezers, she carefully teased out the shiny grain of gold she had just spotted, and stored it inside the quill.

"Keep up the good work," said Ama. She then showed the other Ashanti a sample of the sand that Afia had been panning.

"What's this? What's this?" asked Antoa. "Yes, it is gold." He raised his voice, "Afia has found a fine nugget. Let us dam this creek, so we can dig into the mother-of-gold." He meant the richest layer of gravel.

Ama put her lips beside Afia's ear and whispered. "The hen knows when it's daybreak, but allows the rooster to make the announcement."

✧   ✧   ✧

Elias finished writing his note, and left it where the master would find it. Hopefully not right away, however.

He swung the sack containing the last of his gear over his shoulder, and slowly opened the door a crack. He stuck his head out and looked both ways to make sure the coast was clear.

Then . . . he gurgled as the door was closed and held, trapping his head.

"Where do you think you're going, young Elias?" And then his master's hand closed on the nape of his shirt, and pulled him inexorably back into the room.

Elias sat on the floor in the corner of the room, eyes downcast, as Master Carpenter Lorenz Baum examined the contents of the sack. "It appears you are ready to embark on some great adventure. Care to tell me about it?"

The silence grew.

"If there's anything a carpenter can find quickly enough, if needed, it's a nice, long, hefty stick. . . ."

"Note." Elias muttered.

"Note what?"

"I put a note in your Bible. Thought you wouldn't find it until Sunday."

"You're in no position to be critical, Elias. Let me see . . . uh-huh . . . uh-huh . . . Very generous of you, offering to pay me double the usual apprenticeship release fee once you returned victoriously from the gold fields of the Marowijne." He crumpled the note, and tossed it into Elias' lap.

"Tell me, Elias, did you listen to Maria's lecture on gold mining?"

A vigorous nod.

"I suppose I am not surprised; I remember it was well attended. It was doubtless more romantic sounding than the ones on rubber or bauxite. I can assure you that I paid close attention to what she said. I bet you've forgotten that she said that even in a gold rush, most miners made less money than they would have digging ditches."

"But if you struck it rich—"

"Well, Elias, I'd bet my last thaler that it's easier to get rich selling equipment to the gold miners, than trying to find it yourself.

"So this is what I propose. You tell me who is planning to go treasure hunting, and help me make and sell them wooden pans and rockers and whatnot. And once one of the colonists—not an Ashanti—finds gold, I will release you from your contract, if that's still what you want.

"But for now, put this stuff back where it belongs, get some sleep... and don't forget that we old master craftsmen are very light sleepers..."

Sometime later, the *Patientia*, a small Dutch fluyt, made its way up the Suriname River. The captain's intent had been to make his New World landfall in the Windward Islands of the Caribbean. However, a hurricane had forced him to divert southward, out of harm's way. He then decided to make just a short stop at Gustavus, for drinking water and fresh fruit.

But Lorenz and Elias had set up a stall in the market square, where they were selling dugout canoes, mining equipment, instructions, and maps.

Within twenty-four hours, the entire crew of the *Patientia* had bought prospecting gear, deserted, and crossed the Suriname like a swarm of locusts looking for crops to devour.

A day later, the first and second mates decided that the crew would not be reappearing any time soon, and joined the gold rush.

The *Patientia*'s captain held out until the end of the week.

African Market Village

Maria Vorst spoke. "I understand you're running a witness protection program, Maurício."

"Maria, you're back!" They embraced. "What in the name of all the saints is a 'witness protection program'?" Maurício inquired.

"Something I heard about when I was living in Grantville. I understand that since a certain gold rush started, you've had the three principals in hiding."

"I do."

"I'd like to speak to them."

"I wish we had never found the gold, Maria," said Coqui. "It drives your people crazy." Kojo vigorously agreed.

"Sorry about that." Maria noticed that Tetube was standing protectively close to Coqui. "I see you have a girlfriend."

Coqui grinned and put an arm around Tetube. "I have a wife, once it's safe for me to leave Maurício's village and bring her home for a proper ceremony."

"I am glad you mentioned that," said Maria. "Henrique and I would like to help you do just that. Take you by ship to Fort Kyk-Over-Al, and then you can paddle back from there. You remember the way?"

Coqui nodded curtly, and Maria blushed. She realized that it was the equivalent of asking a burgher from Amsterdam if he remembered how to get to church. Or to the neighborhood tavern.

"Excellent. I think you told me that the trees with the sticky milk, the ones that we saw near Marshall's Creek, also grow near your own village."

"Cousin trees. Not quite the same. But they have the sticky milk inside."

"I understand. We would like you and your people to collect the seeds for us, and cover them with banana leaves, or something similar." The banana had been brought to Brazil from West Africa in the sixteenth century. "And keep them dry, very dry, but without putting them in fire.

"We will come get them, and give you and your people something nice in exchange. What do you think they might like?"

Coqui considered this. "Steel knives and axes. Iron fishhooks. Glass beads."

"What about me?" asked Kojo. "Should I go with you, or stay here?"

"Stay here. Captain de Vries will return, soon enough, and I have letters for him about your situation. You have your gold, so you can buy back your children. But we need to find a trustworthy Spanish agent to handle the matter, and that's best done in Europe. You'll go to Hamburg with him."

"I am sorry I told the others, Maria," said Kojo sorrowfully. "I was afraid you would punish me."

"Some secrets are too big to be kept."

Near the River Lawa, Eastern Guiana

The Ashanti continued to work the creeks along the Lawa. They had decided that they would wait at least for the middle of the wet season before heading back to their village on the banks of the Suriname.

In Ghana, their homeland, it was customary for whole households, even whole villages, to relocate to the goldfields when the rains began. They would loosen the deposits in the streams, making them easier to work, whether by panning or the usually more productive shallow pit mining. But later in the rainy season, the pits would be flooded and unworkable, and at that point they would take advantage of the higher water level to paddle back the way that had come.

Some of the Ashanti thought that there was no point in heading back, that they should found a new village here on the Lawa, or at least somewhere nearby. But the chief decided that they couldn't do this without at least giving some kind of notice to Gustavus. After all, they had agreed to help the colonists mine bauxite.

"Dammabo" Creek

They heard it over the rustlings of the leaves and the gurglings of the water: "*Kro kro kro kro ko kyini kyini kyini kro kyini ka ka ka kyini kyini kyini kyini ka.*" The Ashanti froze for an instant, then the men set down their tools and reached for their weapons, as the women took cover in the vegetation lining the Dammabo. What they had heard was the call of the *kokokyinaka*, the "blue plantain-eater," the "clockbird" that greeted the morning, the "drummer's child." It was a bird of their forest homeland, and in the two years they had lived in Suriname, they had never seen one.

To hear it now, late in the day and far from Ghana, could mean only one thing: the lookout they had posted where the creek waters mingled with those of the Lawa had spotted hostile, or potentially hostile, intruders.

Most of the Ashanti men crouched behind the boles of the great trees, with muskets or bows readied. Owisu and another man crawled through the jungle wall and headed down toward the Marowijne, seeking more information.

Exchanging bird calls, they caught up with their sentry, who explained why he had raised the alarm. "Two men we know, Heinrich and Erasmus, were panning where the Abonsuo meets the Lawa." An *abonsuo* was what they called a *calabash* when it was used for gold panning; the Abonsuo was the creek immediately downstream of the Dammabo. "I saw them when I did my walk-around. I came back here.

"At mid-day, I heard arguing from the direction of the Abon-suo. I went back there and saw that there were three new white men there. All of the whites had hands near their weapons, and their faces were snarly. They complained that Heinrich and Erasmus had had plenty of time to pan the Abonsuo and it was time they gave someone else a chance. They said that they should 'help' Heinrich and Erasmus, and split what was found. Heinrich and Erasmus kept telling them to go away. Finally, they did. I followed them, and heard them talking to each other. They plan to wait until it is dark and then kill Heinrich and Erasmus, and take their gold dust and their panning place."

The two Ashanti reinforcements exchanged looks, then Awisu ordered. "Tell Antoa. We will watch now." The sentry picked his way back up the creek.

Some minutes later, the sentry returned with Antoa and many of the Ashanti warriors.

"These are very bad men," said Antoa. "They will try to kill Heinrich and Erasmus, who are our friends. I think we should kill them instead. But let us talk to Heinrich and Erasmus first, so they can tell the other whites that we are not starting a war with them."

Near Fort Lincoln, Mouth of Suriname River

David de Vries hadn't a care in the world. He was at sea, with a clear sky, the trades blowing firmly on his starboard quarter, and a flying fish had just jumped on deck in front of him.

By day's end he should arrive at Gustavus, the colony he had founded, and he expected to be fawned over. He was the governor and founder, after all.

The lookout called down from the masthead. "Captain, you better take a look at Fort Lincoln. It just don't look right."

David sighed. So much for a life without care. He raised his spyglass. The fort seemed deserted. What did it mean? Had the Spanish, or the Caribs, attacked and killed everyone? Had there been an outbreak of plague?

Not an attack. The fort looked too, too neat. And even if plague killed everyone in the fort, it wouldn't wipe out the entire colony, and the fort would be reoccupied. Well, unless it were, what did Maria call it? Septicemic or pneumonic plague.

Wait. There was someone at the fort. And that person was hopping about, therefore not sick, and yet had not raised the yellow quarantine flag to warn off visitors.

David ordered his dinghy lowered, and made his way down the rope ladder.

"Thank God you're here, David," said Captain Dirck Adrienszoon.

"So what happened?"

"I think we should talk in private," Dirck replied, minutely jerking his head in the general direction of David's coxswain.

David ordered the coxswain to go up to the fort's watchtower, and stay there until David called for him or he saw something that ought be reported.

In Dirck's office, David got the bad news.

"We've had an attack of the fever, David."

"Malaria? Yellowjack?"

"No, *gold* fever. One of the Ashanti, Kojo, went exploring with Coqui and Tetube, up the Marowijne, and apparently they came back with some nuggets. Then the rest of the Ashanti decided to try their luck, followed by many of the whites. There's no bauxite being mined, and no one wants to play soldier any more. We still have most of our craftsmen, and farmers at least. Not because they aren't gold-hungry, but because they're not willing to abandon the comforts of home on the say-so of an African or Indian. And the women have stayed here, too. But once a white man comes back with gold, this place'll be a ghost town, I'm sure."

"But how the hell did they find out about the gold?"

Dirck shrugged. "I don't know.... Hey, wait a minute. You said, 'find out,' not 'find.' Did you know it was there?"

David nodded. "It was in the American encyclopedias. But I was under orders to get food, rubber and bauxite production ramped up before letting the colonists get involved in anything as chancy as gold panning."

"Well, the cat's out of the bag now, that is for sure, David. In fact, it may be more of a tiger than a cat. There's a deserted fluyt in port right now. Sooner or later, its crew will return to Europe, and start spending their gold. That will attract attention."

"You're right about that. We need to get a fort built at the mouth of the Marowijne, *tout de suite*. So no other power claims the gold fields."

"Good thinking, but there's one catch. Who's going to labor at building a fort, when there's gold to be had?"

David pondered this for a time. "Someone whose labor earns them gold," he answered. "Because the fort gives them the privilege of charging a toll to fortune hunters. And selling them supplies... at wilderness prices.

"In the meantime, while hardly any ships come by here, other than our own, we best stop doing an imitation of a sitting duck. I'll lend you some men who are too sick for traveling, let alone gold hunting, to wear uniforms and swagger around your parapets. You might put some of our female colonists in uniform, too."

"Women soldiers?" Dirck's tone made it clear that he was horrified to the very depths of his by-the-book soul.

"Think of them as Amazons. Anyway, they probably won't need to fire a shot, just look properly martial at a distance."

Next, David had his own crew to worry about.

"All hands on deck!" bawled the high boatswain. The watch below roused itself, and blearily made their way up the hatches. Their expressions were puzzled; there was no storm, and no foes, to be seen. But Captain de Vries was dressed in his best uniform, and standing on the poop deck with his hands clasped behind him. Clearly the captain wanted to address them about something important.

David cleared his throat. "Lads, we've got a fine opportunity for fame and fortune before us, but only if we use our heads. There's gold to be found up a nearby river but it will take time and effort, and the gold won't do us much good if we don't have a ship to return to. That gold'll spend much better in Europe than in this blasted jungle.

"There are plenty of fools who have left their ships to rot while they chased gold, but we won't be among them. The problem, of course, is that no one wants to be left behind while others make their fortune. And the solution to that problem is that we will sign a compact that it's share-and-share alike, whether you're panning for gold or manning the cannon to make sure the damned Spanish don't come along to rob us of what we've earned.

"So what say you? Shall we have a compact?"

The roar left no doubt of the answer.

While at New Carthage negotiating with Maurício, David learned of Kojo's predicament. David persuaded Maurício to set up a meeting, and then sweet-talked Kojo into coming aboard the *Walvis* as a guide. He had three cogent arguments. First, as "patron" of Gustavus, he had more authority over the colonists than anyone else, and hence could protect Kojo from the greedier Europeans. Second, by coming along, Kojo would be more quickly reunited with his fellow Ashanti. Third, that on the way to the goldfields, Kojo could learn how to use the fancy gold mining equipment that David had bought from Master Baum, and then be the "expert" for the benefit of his fellow tribesmen.

It was David's intention to resell much of that gold mining equipment at a stiff markup to the colonists already upriver, and have Kojo provide, what did his up-timer friends call it? A "celebrity endorsement."

Jan Smoot cleared his throat. "It has pleased the eternal and immutable Wisdom of Almighty God to call Dirck van Rijn to His bosom. He has passed from this sinful world to the blessed joy of God's Eternal Kingdom, where the great street of the Eternal City is of pure gold. Revelation 22:21."

Like Master Baum, Jan had decided that it was more profitable to sell goods to the miners than to pick up a pan or shovel himself. Unlike Master Baum, he had decided that the road to riches was to bring his goods to the goldfields, where competition was scarcest.

Near the old-time-line town of Grand Santi, Jan had found an island where, thanks to the poorness of the soil, there were few great trees, just ground cover and some small shrubs. There, he had built a small building to serve as both dwelling and shop. He had an Indian to serve as a go-between with the nearby tribes, and two Ndongo boatmen to ferry supplies up the Marowijne.

Jan looked around at the assembled miners, mostly colonists. "Anyone have anything they want to say about Dirck?" He paused. "Anything nice, I mean."

"He was a hard worker," said Pieter, Dirk's former partner. They had split up in a dispute as to whether the stretch they were working was producing enough; Pieter had stayed and Dirk had moved on. Unfortunately, Dirck had picked a new location that had been recently worked by a pair of crewmen from the *Patientia*. When they returned, he insisted that they had abandoned the location, and they thought otherwise. The words became heated, he made a move they thought threatening, and one of them clubbed him in the noggin with a reversed pistol. He picked himself up, and walked off, seemingly wounded only in his pride. A few hours later, he lost consciousness.

The sailors had found Dirck when they were on their way to Jan's shop to resupply, and brought him to Jan for treatment. Unfortunately, while Jan had learned some first aid from Maria, he couldn't do much more than keep Dirck comfortable. Dirck died the day after his arrival.

This might have started a feud between the colonists and the crew of the *Patientia*. Fortunately, the sailors had tried to help Dirk once they realized he was seriously injured, and Pieter admitted that Dirk had a temper and might well have acted imprudently. Still, Jan was troubled by the larger implications of the incident.

By now, there were perhaps a hundred Europeans on the Marowijne and its tributaries, looking for gold. More arrived, usually in twos or threes, every week.

Some of the newcomers respected the knowledge of the first arrivals, and worked for them for a few weeks, in a rough and ready apprenticeship, before finding their own panning spots. Others, like the three the Ashanti had disposed of, tried to intimidate their predecessors into giving up part, or all, of their territory. Even those that didn't intend to take what wasn't theirs could get into honest disputes, fueled by fatigue, frustration, and fermented Indian drinks.

Jan raised his voice. "Folks, it's obvious that we need some rules, or miners'll spend more time arguing and fighting than they do mining. And some are going to end up dying, like Dirk. So think about what would be fair, and let's talk about it on the next full moon."

The *Walvis* anchored about fifty miles up the Marowijne, just below the whitewater that David christened Maria Falls. It wasn't, strictly speaking, a waterfall, but rather a series of rapids by which the river dropped about fifteen feet over half a mile. Still, there was no way that the *Walvis*, or any other blue water vessel, was getting past it.

David was more than a little concerned about the risk that a European warship would come upriver and attempt a hostile takeover. But he had to worry about the local Indians, too. Hence, the *Walvis* was anchored with springs on her cable, so that by heaving one spring and paying out the other, she could be turned readily to fire her broadside at an opponent downstream or on either bank.

To protect the *Walvis*—and to make sure that any would-be gold seekers from other colonies paid for the privilege of going farther upriver—David left a guard force on board. He sent an advance party upriver, to the head of the rapids, and they established a camp there. The crew spent several days ferrying supplies and portaging canoes up to this camp. Finally, they were ready to follow Kojo and David to the supposed El Dorado of the Lawa.

Kojo suddenly stood up in the canoe. "Heinrich!" he called out. He had seen Heinrich as the German's canoe came around the bend a few hundred yards upstream.

Heinrich waved back. Soon, he brought his canoe alongside Kojo's, and grasped Kojo's arm, hand to elbow. "Good to see you!"

"Well, did you find gold?" asked David.

"We found what we were looking for," Heinrich admitted. "Enough to make the trip worthwhile, I'd say. And I think a fair number of the creeks off the Lawa have gold. You just have to know where to look, and how to pan, and be willing to work hard and long. You glean a speck here, a speck there. It's not like capturing a treasure galleon."

Some of David's men bristled. They perhaps had a different view of what it took to capture such a ship.

"We brought tools to make it easier," said David. "What they call—" he gave Elias a quick glance.

Elias recognized his cue. "A rocker. Like the ones the Forty-Niners used. Perfect for use by a pair of miners."

"That's good news," said Heinrich. "Although I am done for this season. But Captain, there's been trouble here. Three men tried to take our creek and our gold dust, and it might have turned out badly if the Ashanti hadn't shown up and stopped them."

"The Ashanti?" asked Kojo. In his excitement, he nearly fell out of the canoe. "Where, where did you see them?"

"I will tell you in a moment. But that's not all, we've had a killing."

"A killing?"

"Of one of the colonists, by a couple of crewmen off a visiting Dutch ship."

Seeing David's scowl, Heinrich hastily added, "it was something of an accident. Still, there's going to be more trouble if we don't have some kind of mining law here. Remember Jan Smoot? He came up with a proposal. It might have been accepted if it had been made up front, before anyone started panning. But now folks can see immediately how the law will affect them, and if they don't like it, they don't want to give their consent. So they make a counterproposal, and of course that displeases other miners. Instead of fighting over the claims, now we're wrangling over the rules for making the claims."

"I'm going to be honest with you all," said David. "Those of you who are from Gustavus, you were brought to the New World by my ships, under contract. Those of you are from the *Patientia*, you are now in the USE Territory of the Wild Coast, of which I am the appointed governor, and your mining rights are what I say they are."

The captain of the *Patientia* glowered at him. "This is the first I've heard of a 'USE Territory of the Wild Coast.' It's not marked on my charts, I saw no USE flag or other marker anywhere along this river. The land was unclaimed."

David shook his head. "Permit me to remind you, Captain, that the gold was discovered by an expedition from Gustavus, composed of the Ashanti Kojo, and the Indians Coqui and Tetube. They were sent by Maria Vorst, who is the 'Science Officer' of our colony, and they thus constituted an official USE expedition." *Whether they knew it or not*, mused David.

"They claimed the Marowijne River, and all its tributaries, for the USE, by right of discovery.

"The Ashanti are allies of Gustavus, and residents of the Territory, by treaty, and were brought here by Kojo to pan for gold. Thus, through them, the USE claims these lands by right of occupation. And indeed they, or some of them, are settling here permanently." *Have to remember to tell them that*, David told himself.

"And lastly, Captain, I have a warship here. So the Marowijne is ours, by right of conquest."

David laughed abruptly. "Even if it weren't, you abandoned the *Patientia* in Gustavus. It has been lawfully seized for failure to pay dockage. So unless you think you can *swim* back to Europe with your gold dust, you had best recognize my authority and comply with our mining laws."

That silenced the man. Or perhaps it was the dark looks that he was receiving from David's well-armed crew and the Gustavans.

"Anyone else wish to question my authority?" David paused. "I thought not.

"There is going to be a mining law. If the colonists, sailors and Ashanti can agree on its terms, well, that'll be fine, as long as the government get the fees it sets for recording a claim. If not, then I'll decide. I want each group to pick a representative today. And the representatives have three days to reach agreement.

"Dismissed."

The treasure seekers' representatives eventually agreed that every miner would have to put up some kind of monument, several feet tall, that gave his name and the date of the claim, and place boundary markers to show where the claim began and ended. And that the claim would have to be worked for at least one month each year, or it would be lost. Jan agreed to keep record of all the claims, in return for a recordation fee. And he would collect the government tax that David had insisted on, too.

The biggest issue was how large a claim could be awarded to a single miner. Initially, the thought was that the claim should be as wide as the creek itself, and one hundred fathoms long. An up-timer would assume a fathom was exactly six feet, but in seventeenth-century Europe it was the distance between the finger-tips of a sailor's outstretched arms and was five or five-and-a-half feet. A wag suggested that since they were so far from the sea, it would be more appropriate to measure the "run" in "smoots." Jan obligingly lay down on the ground and those miners who had rope knotted them at intervals of a "smoot."

David approved the mining law, with only a few changes. One of them was that the miners could pool their claims. While all the claims would still need to be worked, they could be recorded at one time, for a discounted fee, as jointly owned. This obviously was to the advantage of David's sailors.

That settled, David had quizzed the Ashanti as to where and how to pan for gold. His men were raring to go.

"Big Chief David, we are so sorry for you," said Antoa.

"Why? Is all the gold gone already?"

"No, no. When we came here, it was the beginning of the Time of Daily Rains. When it rains, the Crabs of the River God scurry about, and bring the gold out of the River God's palace and leave it where the river shallows or turns.

"But now, the waters are so high, that it is difficult to reach the sands where the gold is. This is the time to paddle home."

"Perhaps we can divert some of the water..." David suggested, somewhat doubtfully. "We have the apprentice carpenter from the colony, as well as the ship's carpenter."

"I cannot say if that will work," Antoa told him. "It is not our way."

David's cousin Heyndrick spoke up. "So you don't mine gold in the dry season at all?"

"Oh, I didn't say that. Between harvest time and planting time, we dig shafts in the hills. But we don't yet know where to dig in this land."

"Until then, look for falling water when the water is low," Kojo said suddenly. Questioned further, Kojo and Antoa explained that when a gold-bearing river reached a waterfall, the gold was deposited at its base, underwater, but the base might be more or less exposed at the height of the dry season. It wasn't likely to be as productive as the lode gold mined by shafts, but it was better than nothing.

"I think I can depend on my fellow colonists to honor the agreement with the Ashanti." said Heinrich. "The most experienced miners among us are those, like me, who worked alongside the Ashanti at the bauxite pits, and we became friends. Most of us, at any rate. But what about the sailors from the *Patientia*? Or your sailors? Or the treasure-seekers who'll come from Europe, next year or the year after? Who's going to keep the law after you sail off?"

"I've thought about that," said David. He raised his voice. "By the powers vested in me as governor of the USE Territory of the Wild Coast, I hereby appoint you president of the Marowijne Mining District, including the bed and banks of the Marowijne River, and of all waters tributary thereon.

"There. You'll keep them honest."

"But I have no experience—"

"You're one of the original colonists. You're a miner. You're a friend of the Ashanti. You can make it work. We're going to build a fort right above Maria Falls, and I will leave my cousin Heyndrick there as militia commander of a mixed militia, composed of white colonists and Ashanti. I persuaded the Ashanti to settle here, so they don't have to travel as much to reach the gold field each year. We'll find other people to dig for bauxite back in Paranam."

Low Water Time, Central Amazon (August–September 1636)

Coqui smacked his lips. "Any moment now."

He and Tetube stood on a beach, their back to one of the creeks feeding into the Rio Negro, holding spears and improvised nets. Moonlight glinted off the sand and water.

"Here they come!"

The young river turtles, hatching in synchrony, made a mad dash for the water. Birds dive-bombed them, and caimans, dolphins and fish waited for them to take the plunge.

Coqui and Tetube became separated as they chased first one, then another hatchling.

Suddenly, Tetube found herself face to face with a jaguar. It snarled. She back-pedaled, and found her feet squishing into wet sand.

Agony! Her right leg cramped and collapsed under her.

She looked about fearfully for the jaguar but it was already trotting off with a turtle in its mouth.

"Coqui! Help!" she screamed.

He came running, and lifted her up. Once they were on higher ground, he inspected her foot.

The moonlight was bright enough to reveal the characteristic wound left by an angry stingray. Coqui winced in sympathy. Many fishermen bore stingray scars, on foot, ankle or calf.

The sting was serrated as well as venomous, and the pain was intense.

He hugged her. "I am here. It will be all right."

In the morning, when there was light enough to gather the right plants, he made a poultice for her.

Even so, it was two weeks before the pain went away.

Lawa River region, Inland Eastern Guiana, September 1636

David had noted, with some curiosity, that the rains came and left at different times here, on the upper Maroni, than they had back in Gustavus. By the time the dry season began on the Lawa, in September, the colonists, and the crew of *Patientia*, had left the gold fields. David wondered whether they would make it back safely. And whether the *Patientia* would cause any problems for the Gustavans. Its cannon had been confiscated before David left Gustavus, but the crew could still be dangerous. David had to hope that Dirck and Carsten had taken the necessary precautions— they could call on Maurício for assistance—and of course as the colonists returned home the colony's defenses would be stiffened. In any event, it was out of his hands.

David's larger worry was the temper of his men. Initially, they had sought gold in high spirits, constructing wooden dams and chutes to control the high waters. However, the rainy season of the Guianas was at quite a different scale than anything the Forty-Niners of the American history books had to put up with. The waterworks had to be given up as a lost cause. Perhaps some other year, with better tools and more men, and begun sooner, it would work.

Then his men had dug shallow pits in the riverbanks and higher lands, wherever some peculiarity of vegetation or earth color led them to fancy that gold might be present.

No luck.

His third mate caught two men plotting to sneak back to the new Ashanti village, near Maria Falls, and force one of the Ashanti to divulge the secrets of gold mining that they had obviously held back from the whites. Those men were summarily executed.

David wished, fervently, that they would find a waterfall, as Kojo had suggested. But there were no waterfalls marked on David's map of French Guiana—the American atlases hadn't shown much interest in that region—and the highlands, where one might reasonably expect to find a waterfall, were well to the south.

"Captain, come quick!" One of David's sailors was shouting.

David wasn't the only man to rush over, but he was the first to speak the word that was in everyone's thoughts.

"Gold?"

"Yes, sir. Look." The sailor held out a small nugget. He pointed at the base of a boulder, in the middle of the stream they had been following. "That's where I found it."

David realized that the stream had changed grade here, from steep to shallow, depositing gravels and even a few small boulders. "Spread out, men! Along the rock line!"

It proved to be a very respectable pay streak.

Buoyed by this find, David and his crew continued to explore southward for the rest of the dry season, then returned to the established gold field.

Surinamese Short Wet Season (December 1636–January 1637), Gustavus

A distant boom drew the attention of everyone in the Gustavus town square. A sentry called out, "Signal cannon from Fort Lincoln."

The townspeople who were members of the militia dashed into their homes to grab their weapons, just in case hostile warships had been sighted.

"I see smoke on the horizon," said Johann Mueller. "Is the forest on fire?"

"Is the fire on this side of the river?" asked another.

"I can't tell," said Johann. "You know how the river twists and turns."

They heard a chugging sound, one totally outside their experience, and then a great whistle. His Danish Majesty's Armed Steamship *Valdemar* came into view.

"So that's the little secret you've been hiding," declared Henrique. "A steamship. I should have guessed; you did tell me that Henry Wickham got rubber tree seeds from Brazil to London that way."

Maria smiled sweetly.

"How long will it take to steam back to Europe?"

"About a month, according to the letter that told me to expect it."

"Amazing. A sailing ship captain would count himself lucky to make the passage in two months. That will certainly improve your chances of making it there with viable seeds.

"But how are you planning to get up and down the Amazon without the Portuguese stopping you? You must enter by the Canal do Norte or the Canal do Sul. On the northern approach, you pass Fort Cumau." This was the modern town of Macapa. "We took it from the English, and left it in ruins, but when I fled Belém, there was talk of rebuilding it.

"If you come from the south, then on the south bank of the main channel you will find the fort of Gurupa. The channel there is narrow enough so that you are within cannon range.

And they'll hear your engines from far off. The garrison is fifty Portuguese and perhaps twice that number of Indians.

"The *Valdemar* has sails as well as a steam engine, so I suppose that if the winds are favorable it can sail up quietly. But there are many Indians living by the banks, and boating in the water. The *Valdemar* cannot escape detection, especially since you must enter in daylight in order to see where you are going. Perhaps it will have the advantage of surprise when it arrives, and can pass the forts before the cannon are loaded, but when it returns downstream, the Portuguese will be ready for it."

"Not to worry," said Maria.

"It doesn't look like one of the ironclads that the last supply ship told us about. But it has some American superweapon on it, yes?"

"In a manner of speaking."

"You're just going to be infuriatingly reticent, aren't you?"

"Yep."

The varnished cotton skin quivered like a living thing. Hydrogen bubbled out of the generator, traveled through a hose into a scrubber, and then by a second hose into the envelope of the slowly inflating airship.

Henrique snorted. "So that's your superweapon."

Maria nodded. "Notice the hoses? Made with *our* rubber."

"What are the Manao Indians going to do when this damned thing flies overhead? Run away in terror, I would think."

"I told Coqui that I would come to him in the belly of a giant bird. He will tell them that the bird is friendly."

"When did you—I suppose you told him when we were in Fort Kyk-Over-Al, and I was off buying supplies."

"That's right."

"Why didn't you tell me?"

"And ruin the surprise? It's just too bad I couldn't arrange things so that the first you saw of the airship was it in the air, and me waving from it."

Henrique watched the airship envelope as it slowly inflated. The nose cap had been hoisted up and attached to Carsten's alleged watchtower, now revealed to in fact be a short mooring mast. The hind part of the airship was covered with a large net, weighted around the edge, so it wouldn't rise up too high and place unnecessary strain on the mooring connection. "So how much longer will the fill-up take?"

"Captain Neilsen said, 'About four hundred hours.'"

Henrique's face creased as he did a rapid mental calculation. "Sixteen days?"

"Something like that."

Henrique picked up his walking stick. "Tell me when it's over."

Maria pointed. "There! His Danish Majesty's Airship *Sandterne*." It was an apt name for an exploratory vehicle, as the gull-billed tern wintered in the Caribbean, northern South America, Africa, southern Asia and even New Zealand. The tethered airship, attached to the mooring mast, faced into the steady northeast trades.

"The gondola looks about the size of a Grantville school bus," Maria commented. "Not much privacy, but fortunately the flight time to Manaus is only about thirty-five hours."

Henrique executed an exaggerated formal bow. "We will all gallantly look the other way when you use the head, milady."

"Talking about ladies, you know, most of the female colonists here at Gustavus are already married. And none of them are Jewish."

"Ahem." Henrique wasn't sure he liked where this was going.

"Has it occurred to you that the pickings might be better in Amsterdam? Or Grantville? Or Prague? Or even," she added slyly, "Copenhagen."

"Ahem."

"You're just going to be infuriatingly reticent about your plans, aren't you?"

"Yep."

With the envelope inflated, and the air in the ballonets adjusted to level it off, it was time to attach the gondola. This had been disassembled for shipping, and had been reassembled in the meantime.

"Fuck! We need it about a foot to my left," yelled Lars. He and his ground crew had come over on the *Valdemar*. "Lift on my command. Three...two...one...LIFT!" The gondola lurched into place, and the ground crew climbed up and attached it to the suspension cables that secured it to the envelope of the airship.

Nearby, in a makeshift roofed shed, the engineer was testing the engines that had been brought over on the *Valdemar*.

✧   ✧   ✧

There was a knock on the door, which Henrique answered.

"Maurício!" The two half-brothers embraced.

"Follow me," commanded Henrique. Maria and I were just going over the route. Looking for landmarks that should be visible from the air.

Maurício peered over Henrique's shoulder. "Do you have time to talk, Maria?"

Maria looked at him. "I'll make the time, Maurício. What's up?"

Maurício shuddered. "Another Americanism... Language as we know it is doomed...."

Maria sighed. "Get to the point, Maurício."

"That's King Maurício, chief of chiefs, don't forget. And now that I am involved in politics, I have discovered the cardinal rule of being a successful politician."

"Finding someone else to blame if something goes wrong?" asked Henrique.

"That's rule number two. Rule number one is, there's no such thing as bad publicity."

Maurício pointed toward the mooring mast. "And what I think would really enhance my status is to ride that airship of yours."

Henrique snorted. "'He Who Flies' makes a better epithet than 'He Who Talks,' you think?"

Maria fingered her chin. "I'd have to ask the captain, but I suppose that he might let you do a quick tethered ascent, if it can be managed without wasting any gas."

"Tethered ascent? I had in mind that Kasiri and I could join you for your little flight. We do a little air show over my villages, to remind them of how awesome I am, and then we fly to Manao so she can visit her family."

"I am surprised that someone who deplores Americanisms would seek to bring the political junket to the New World."

"Seriously—"

"Seriously, it's not going to happen, Maurício. Let me explain the facts. It takes a thousand cubic feet of ninety percent pure hydrogen to provide about sixty-four pounds of lift. Our total lift is less than three hundred times that. That lift, at a minimum, has to support the envelope, the ballonets inside, the gondola, the fins and rudder, the engines, the fuel, and the crew. What's left—less than half of the gross lift—is what carries the passengers and cargo into the air. Henrique and I have to go; we know how to tap rubber, we know if a rubber tree is healthy or sickly. We can tell whether a seed is from a rubber tree or not. The airship doesn't have room for tourists. Not even a royal one."

Lawa River, Beginning of Wet Season

At last, the crew of the *Walvis* decided that it was time to return to their ship, head back to Europe and transform their Lawa River gold into the good things in life. They would have to stop at Gustavus first, to resupply, however.

They rowed back to Maria Falls, the current helping them along, and boarded the *Walvis*.

David inspected the ship and somewhat grudgingly pronounced himself satisfied with how it had been cared for in his absence.

"Up Anchor!" David ordered.

Surinamese Short Dry Season (February to April 1637)

The gas envelope was an elongated teardrop, with a side panel bearing the Danish coat of arms: three lions passant in pale Azure, crowned and armed. The gondola slung beneath it was painted red and yellow, the colors of the House of Oldenburg that ruled Denmark.

And a spy basket hung below the gondola. In it, from a height of a hundred feet, King Maurício waved to his people.

The idea for the spy basket had come from a 1930 Howard Hughes film, *Hell's Angels*. A German zeppelin is shown flying over London, and it lowered an observer in a little streamlined observation car. This wasn't a wild fancy on Hughes' part, there were German spy baskets that could be lowered as much as several thousand feet below the zeppelin, on steel wire paid out with a winch. The support wire doubled as a telegraph line. The *Sandterne*'s spy basket was a more primitive affair.

Maurício heard a horn from above, and waved acknowledgment. It was time to descend. The "spy basket" he stood in was slowly winched down, and when the bottom swung a couple of feet above the ground, the ground crew grabbed and steadied it so Maurício could clamber out.

Once he was free, they signaled the airship, and the basket was raised back into the bowels of the *Sandterne*. The name painted on the *Sandterne*'s drop basket was, rather irreverently, *The Yo-Yo*.

As his wife, Kasiri, hugged him, Maurício told Carsten, "Now all of my people will tremble when they see me. King Maurício dared climb into the Heavens!"

"More daring than you realized, my dear King Maurício."

"What do you mean?"

"Lars just told me that the *Sandterne* has not previously used the spy basket to carry a person. You are a true pioneer!"

It was fortunate that Kasiri had her arm around Maurício, as it wouldn't have looked very kingly if he had fainted.

En route to the Central Amazon by Airship

"I can barely hear the engines, Captain."

"I am not surprised, Mevrouw Vorst. We are just letting them idle, the northeast trade winds are carrying us in the direction we wish to go."

"Then why run the engines at all? Doesn't that use up fuel?"

"Oh, yes, but if there's a sudden wind change, or other hazard, we don't want to cold start the engines. If you want to ride out at a moment's notice, it's best that the horse already be saddled and bridled, yes?"

The airship was progressing southwest, at a height of about six hundred feet. They had already passed over the Coppename and skirted the northern tail of the Bakhuys Mountains. They passed south of Blanche Marie Falls, on the Nickerie, and then directly over Tiger Falls, on the Courantyne. This gave them a precise navigational fix, because its latitude and longitude were known from an up-time atlas. At their present height, they could easily see Frederik Willem IV Falls, perhaps thirty miles upriver.

"Right rudder!"

The rudderman pressed the right rudder pedal, beginning the turn to the right. Since the airship lacked wings, it didn't roll into a turn.

"Engines one-half forward," Captain Neilsen spoke into the speaking tube.

"One-half forward," the engineer, in the engine compartment acknowledged.

The captain kept his eye on the compass. "Neutralize rudder." The ship's angular momentum kept it turning, but ever more slowly.

"Heading two seventy," the captain said with satisfaction. The course change avoided the Kanuku mountains, farther south. While the *Sandterne* could easily climb high enough to cross them, Henrique and his party had come from the Rupununi, to the west.

They ran west along the fourth parallel north for six hours, then turned south. In still air, their cruising speed was twenty miles per hour, but they would have a bit of a westward boost from the diminished trade winds. It wasn't too long before they spotted a key landmark, the Rio Branco.

They followed this guide to the mighty Rio Negro, the largest blackwater river in the world. Continuing downstream, they came at last to the confluence of the Rio Negro with the Solimoes, forming the Amazon. Here, on the north bank, in another universe, the 1669 Fort of São José da Barra do Rio Negro had become the nucleus about which the nineteenth-century town of Manaus had aggregated. And that town was the home of the rubber barons, who built an Opera House to prove that they were equals of the plutocrats of America and Europe.

Now, in the year 1637, there was no fort, and no European town, but there was a village, a small settlement of the Manao Indians. "Manaus" was their word for the confluence; it meant, "mother of the gods."

Above Manau, Central Amazon

The *Sandterne* lurched upward, caught by an updraft, and the elevatorman adjusted the elevator to compensate. He checked the variometer, a barometer modified to measure the rate of change of altitude. "Holding steady again, Captain."

Captain Neilsen eyed the rainforest below. "Looks good."

Maria spoke. "Can you bring us down any farther?"

"Not a chance," said Captain Neilsen. "I have to keep at least thirty feet above the treetops. There's no telling when a downdraft might send us down."

"But if that happened, couldn't you adjust the elevator wheel, or drop some more ballast?"

"Sure. But there are limits to how much, how fast."

Maria studied the ground. "But Henrique and I need to get down there, and pick the rubber trees whose seeds we want to harvest. And of course we'd like to get back up again, too, it's a long walk back to Gustavus. And the canopy is a good hundred feet high. I am not going to manage a hundred-thirty-foot descent, even in that 'spy basket.'"

"Then we will need to find a clearing," said Captain Neilsen. "That would be best in any event, since I wouldn't want the wire to snag on these giant trees."

"Does the river count as a clearing?" Henrique asked abruptly.

"This gondola is waterproof, so we can 'land' on water. And you could then lower a canoe. But we have only practiced landing on a lake, I am not comfortable about landing on a river, except for an emergency."

Nature might or might not abhor a vacuum, but Nature *qua* rainforest most definitely abhorred open spaces. A tree struck by lightning might fall over and, connected by lianas to neighboring trees, cause a chain reaction that cleared a considerable area, but the sudden exposure to sunlight would cause seedlings and saplings to burst into frenetic activity, and soon the clearing would be erased by a green explosion. They found a clearing, close to the Rio Negro, a major tributary of the Amazon, but it was at least a day's hike away from Manaus.

It would have to do.

Maria gazed out over the coffee-colored waters of the Rio Negro. She knew, from her studies in Grantville, that the color was the result of tannins leached out of decaying vegetation.

"Henrique, I think I have spoken of movie night at the Higgins Hotel in Grantville."

"Moving pictures, yes. What about them?"

"This place reminds me of a movie called *Creature from the Black Lagoon*. The creature was a Gill-man—"

"Excuse me?"

"A Gill-man. Half-man, half-fish. My friend Lolly said that it was based on a merman legend from the Amazon, so naturally I thought of it here."

Henrique pondered this for a moment, then gestured with his gun. "If it comes here, I'll shoot it."

The next day, as they approached the outskirts of the Indian village of Manaus, Coqui and several of his fellow Manao Indians jumped in front of them.

Henrique lowered the rifle he had just pointed at Coqui. "You idiot, I could have killed you."

Coqui was still grinning. "We saw the great bird, and I see it laid two little eggs."

Coqui held out a reed basket. "Here are many seeds, all from a tree that gave much tree-milk when I cut it the way you taught me."

"'Milk of the Moon,'" she dubbed it.

"Milk of the Moon," Coqui repeated. "But the Man in the Moon is male, a warrior. How can the moon give milk?"

"How does the moon enter into it?" asked Henrique. "I know that the moon makes the tide, and that affects fish, but I don't remember seeing any change in the flow of latex according to the lunar phase."

"There isn't," said Maria, "I just like the alliteration. It works in Dutch as well as English. 'Melk' and 'Maan,' you know."

Henrique pondered this. "It even works in Portuguese," he said in a surprised tone. "'Leite' and 'Lua.'"

"Besides," added Maria, "the Indians up north call gold the 'Tears of the Sun,' and the encyclopedias say that latex was once called, 'white gold,' and the moon is 'white'...I just like the imagery."

"Well, you're an artist...I'm not surprised...."

Coqui rapped the trunk to get their attention. "There is evil news from downriver. Where the Cuyari meets the Mother of Rivers, there are many bad white men." The Cuyari was the Indian name for what the Portuguese, and the up-time atlas, called the Madeira. "The whites make war on the Tupinamba.

"And the Tupinamba told us that before this happened, the white men had returned to the Tapajós." That was where, a few years ago, Henrique had taught the Tapajós Indians how to tap rubber.

"Describe these white men, if you can. Especially what your scouts said about their leader," said Henrique grimly.

✧   ✧   ✧

The next day, gifts for the Manao Indians were lowered in the spy basket, and Henrique and Maria rode it back up to report to Captain Neilsen.

"My best guess," said Henrique, "is that they are led by Bento Maciel Parente the Younger, who is a scoundrel of the first order, but also a good woodsman. And very well connected, his father having been the captain-major of Grand Pará. I presume that he was sent out to restart the rubber tapping in Tapajós."

"But how did he know how to do it?"

Heinrique shrugged. "Perhaps he was sent encyclopedia descriptions. Perhaps he tortured the Tapajós until they showed him the technique. I know the rubber trees there are rich in latex, so we should collect their seeds. We just need to use this airship to destroy Bento and his men."

"Impossible," said Captain Neilsen. "First, this is not some kind of aerial dreadnought. We have no bombs, no cannon, no rockets, no volley guns, just a few small arms. Second, my orders are to facilitate your mission, but only to the extent commensurate with the safety of this extremely expensive airship."

"It seems very strange to me that so expensive an airship would sail without any armament," said Henrique.

"My dear sir, you have walked the entire deck of this gondola. Have you seen, heard, or even smelled the slightest hint of a substantial weapon of any kind? We don't need armament because when we are six hundred feet in the air, no enemy can touch us. At least, none that I know of."

Henrique looked down at his feet for a moment, then glared at Captain Neilsen. "I accept your word. But we could still sail to the Tapajós, trade weapons for seeds with the natives there. Bento Maciel Parente can shake his fist at us as we pass overhead, but it's almost four hundred miles to old time line Santarem, at the mouth of the Tapajós, and we can fly that distance faster than he can paddle it, even with the Amazon current helping him."

Captain Neilsen scratched his chin. "But why go to the trouble? Aren't the right kind of rubber trees available here?"

"Yes, but all we know is their yield of the moment, since we arrived," said Henrique. "And we are at the end of the tapping season, so the figures are unpredictable. On the Tapajós, I know how each tree performed, day in and day out, for a whole season. We can go straight to the best producers and collect their seeds."

"You are certainly correct that we can outrun a bunch of canoes," Captain Neilsen admitted. "But it will take time to make contact with the Tapajós Indians, especially since the appearance of this airship would probably scare them out of their shoes, if they wore them! Moreover, the trees you're most interested in may have already dropped their seeds, or not be ready to oblige you for another week or two. That's time enough for the Portuguese to paddle down to us. And isn't it likely, if the Portuguese have resumed your old tapping operation, that they left soldiers there to keep the Indians working?"

Henrique sighed heavily. "Very likely."

"Then it seems to me that the value of a trip to the Tapajós is outweighed by the danger to the ship. Not to mention the risk that if Parente arrived while you were on the ground, I might have to abandon you!"

"Of course I could not let Maria take the risk. But I could go down alone."

"I will need your help getting plantations started," said Maria. "Please, Henrique, don't consider this further. At least, wait until we see how much seed we can collect here before doing anything rash."

Bang!

Henrique and Maria exchanged looks, and moved cautiously uphill toward the sound. This wasn't foolhardiness; their ears, tuned by experience to the sounds of the rainforest, recognized that what they heard was not a gunshot, it was the noise made when seeds burst from a ripened rubber tree seed pod.

The tree's genetic blueprint called for the seeds to be flung as much as a hundred feet away from their parent, carried off by the rising waters, and at last to germinate miles, perhaps many miles, away.

But the sound had been heard by other creatures, and they had their own genetic blueprints, which told them to consider the "bang" to be a dinner bell. Some of the seeds fell into the water, where they were eagerly snapped up by the *tambaqui* and other fish. The *tambaqui* mostly fed on falling fruit, but its favorite meal was the rubber tree seed. Indeed, the Indians could trick it to the surface by imitating seeds falling into the water, and then harpoon it.

Others seeds came to rest on land, and insects and rodents hurried to the feast. As did Maria. She walked, then ran, basket in hand, toward the base of the tree, where there were many seeds. There, an agouti was already greedily stuffing seeds down its gullet, as fast as it could. Maria's seeds, damn it!

"Wait!" ordered Henrique, grasping Maria's shoulder.

An instant later, the predator that Henrique had spotted, a *jararaca do norte*, struck. The agouti shuddered in the six-foot-long pit viper's fangs. It didn't suffer long; the snake, what an up-time biologist would call *Bothrops atrox*, a kind of fer-de-lance, could deliver a large dose of a quite potent venom. Enough to kill an agouti quickly... or an overeager Dutch naturalist more slowly.

"I didn't see it...." Maria murmured.

"Neither did the agouti."

"Remember, I agreed only to a flyover, as far as the Madeira," said Captain Neilsen. "This mission is just so we can warn our Manao friends of what they are up against, we are not here to make war on the Portuguese or try to sneak over to Tapajós. You have a ton of seeds on board. That's plenty."

"Understood," said Henrique.

"That's him," said Henrique grimly, spyglass in hand. "In the rear of the first canoe. Bento Maciel Parente, the scum of the earth.

"Captain, did you really mean it when you said that this airship was unarmed, or were you holding out on me?"

"Sorry, we just have a bay for lowering the spy basket. I suppose it could be used to drop bombs, if we had them. The designers may even have had that possibility in mind. But it's a moot point, since there are no bombs aboard."

"Maria, you're the science whiz, can you improvise something?"

"The target's a little canoe, traveling in a mighty river. At our present altitude, the chance of setting it afire with a fused fuel flask is remote, I think, even if we managed to hit it in the first place."

"But you can take us lower?"

The captain shook his head. "I am not going to bring our gas envelope within Portuguese musket range. We're a much bigger target than they are, and if we're holed, hydrogen can leak out and air can leak in."

"But a bullet, fired upward, can hardly have much force," Henrique pleaded. "And surely the hole made by a bullet is very small compared to this giant gas bag. How much leakage could there be?"

"If we lose just one-sixth of our hydrogen, and it's replaced with air, the hydrogen-air mixture in the gas bag will become flammable. If lightning strikes—" The captain shuddered.

"Dammit," said Henrique. "Is there nothing that can be done?"

"You could—never mind," said Maria.

"What were you going to say?" Henrique demanded.

"You got that fancy rifle as a present from Captain de Vries. You could go down in the spy basket and shoot from there—while our envelope stayed safely out of harm's way. But I think it's too risky."

"I'll do it."

"But the basket might be swinging like crazy. The airship would have to keep up with the speed of the canoes—which is the rowing speed on top of the current. It's not like hovering in one spot and lowering Maurício."

Captain Neilsen had listened to the interchange with unconcealed interest. "We can use our speed to get downstream of the canoes, then hover. You can shoot them as they come toward you. It will be an interesting experiment. I can imagine circumstances in which knowing that we can use a rifleman to clear enemies from a proposed landing site might come in handy."

Maria looked anxiously at the winch. They had paid out several times as much steel wire as they had for Maurício's test run. Would the wire hold, or would Henrique drop into the turbulent waters below?

Captain Neilsen has done well by me, thought Henrique. There had been a bit of oscillation, but the captain had managed to damp it down somewhat. It helped that there wasn't much wind, here in the doldrums, and over land to boot. The basket still swung, a bit, but Henrique remembered a bit of reminiscence from Captain de Vries. *We fire cannon at the peak of the upswing, when the ship seems to stand still, for an instant.*

Henrique squeezed the trigger.

The *bandeirante* standing next to Parente slumped. "What the hell," the leader said, scanning the trees on the nearest bank for signs of an enemy. He hadn't thought to look up, and even if he had, the spy basket at least was lost in the glare of the sun.

Henrique fired again.

Bento clutched his breast. Slowly, like a giant tree blown over by a gust of wind, he toppled into the depths of the Amazon River.

"Good-bye, Bento," said Henrique. "And good riddance."

Below, one of Bento's men, eyes shaded, was pointing upward at the airship.

A telegraph wire connected Henrique with the airship, and he clicked out a quick signal. As the spy basket lurched upward, and Parente's men fired wildly into the air, Henrique remembered one of Maria's odd American phrases. "Beam me up, Scotty," he murmured.

Gustavus (Paramaribo)

Captain David de Vries stared up into the sky in amazement. A small airship floated there, like a cloud. The airship delivered by steamship to Maria Vorst, for an aerial raid on the botanical treasures of the Amazon.

Carsten Claus beamed at him. "Quite a sight, isn't it?"

"Carsten, I am tired, fucking tired, of being a governor. You're the one interested in politics. On behalf of the Company, I appoint you as my successor."

Carsten nodded sympathetically. "I always knew you were more interested in adventure than colonial management. Going to go privateering in the Spanish Main?"

"No need. We did well in the gold field. It's time to head back to Amsterdam. But after that, I am going to learn to sail one of those things." He pointed upward. "I want to be an *airship* captain."

The *Sandterne* faced into the wind, and slowed down its propellers just enough to hover, the gondola a few feet off the ground. Lars and his ground crew grabbed hold of the mooring ropes attached to the *Sandterne*'s nose cap.

The airship fought to remain airborne, like some wild animal resisting capture. For a moment, the ground crew found themselves with their feet dangling in the air. Fortunately, there was still mooring rope on the ground, and colonists, watching the landing, ran over and grabbed hold. The ground crew regained their footing and with the colonists' help eased the *Sandterne* into its mooring position, nose almost nuzzling the metal ring of the airship's mooring mast. Then a couple of crewmen raced up the stairs of the tower and fastened the bowlines to the mooring ring.

Maria had intended to watch the entire deflation of the *Sandterne*, but left after a few minutes. She couldn't help thinking of the *Sandterne* as a living thing, a "she," not an "it."

It was like watching a beloved mount be put down.

Henrique had refused to talk about her proposal that he join her in Copenhagen, and later in Asia. She wasn't sure why he hadn't jumped on the idea. After all, if he secretly wanted her, despite their difference in religion, he should want to come along, as otherwise they might never see each other again. And if the religious difference was insurmountable, then he should come along at least as far as Copenhagen, and then travel to one of the Jewish enclaves of Europe.

Was he afraid of joining society—real society, not the crude community life he had experienced in Belém and then Gustavus? Well, then he could go with her to Asia, soon enough.

Or was it that he couldn't bear to be parted from Maurício? Maria had thought that with Maurício's new role, that he needed Henrique to step away and let him become the man he could be, not just Henrique's shadow. But perhaps Henrique didn't see it that way. And perhaps Maurício wasn't ready to let go, either.

"Thank you for the letter of introduction, Captain Neilsen."

"My pleasure, Captain de Vries. The airship service would profit from having a skipper of your maritime experience. But please remember that there will be much to relearn. You will need to first serve as a crewman on an airship, under another captain."

"I understand. Flying is not sailing. But the freedom... To travel as easily over the land as over the sea."

They exchanged knowing looks. "It's too bad they won't let you sail this airship across the Atlantic," de Vries added.

Captain Neilsen shrugged. "The *Royal Anne* could do it, I think. It made it to Tranquebar, with a refueling stop in Venice. I was a crewman on that flight. Perhaps you will fly to Asia, or back to the New World, one day."

"I hope so, Captain." He touched his hat in salute, and Neilsen returned the honor.

Maria stood on the dock as the *Valdemar* made its final preparations for departure. Many colonists had come to personally thank her for her services. But where was Henrique?

"Do you need any help, Maria?" It was Kojo. The Ashanti was traveling with her to Copenhagen. There, she would make arrangements with friends in Amsterdam for him to go to Havana, in the guise of a free servant of a Spanish gentleman. The gentleman in question was a trusted colleague of Captain de Vries, and he would carry a letter of credit with which he could buy Kojo's children... assuming they could find them. She had been taught Kojo Spanish... enough to get by, at least.

"No, I am fine." She motioned him closer. "Don't forget what I told you," she whispered. "Don't show your gold to anyone on board, or even speak about it."

"I will remember." She watched him board the *Valdemar*.

Hearing a commotion behind her, she turned. Ah, there Henrique was, with Maurício and Kasiri. The lesser African chiefs followed, at a respectful distance.

Maria sighed. She could only offer Henrique a professional partnership, not a marriage; she couldn't compete with his relationship with his half-brother. But at least he was here in time to say farewell.

"Here you are at last, Henrique. I was afraid you weren't coming."

"It would be very difficult for me to get to Copenhagen, if I didn't come. I am not that good a swimmer, you know."

"You're coming!"

"Someone has to keep you out of trouble. You'll go to Asia, see a butterfly perched on top of a tiger's tail, and next thing you know, you'll be holding that tail..."

"It will be a splendid adventure."

Henrique turned to his half-brother. "Goodbye, Maurício." He offered his hand.

Maurício took it. "I am glad to know that you'll keep Maria out of trouble. But who, exactly, will keep you out of trouble?"

"Come, Maurício," said Henrique, "is that the best you can do? There must be a Latin maxim that is apropos to this occasion."

"*Ubi bene, ibi patria,*" Maurício declared. *Where you feel good, there is your home.*

The Rising Sun

Where the Cuckoo Flies

February 1633 to January 1634

*Where the cuckoo flies
till it is lost to sight—out there
a lone island lies.*
—Matsuo Basho (1688)[1]

Nagasaki, Island of Kyushu, Japan, Kan'ei 10, first month, sixth day (February 14, 1633)

Four down, one to go. Yamaguchi Takuma felt sweat beading on his brow, but he didn't dare wipe it off.

The *hissha*, the ward scribe, called out the next name: "Hiraku." Hiraku was Takuma's son, the youngest member of the household and therefore the last to be summoned. He had only recently turned seven, the age at which a Japanese child was considered a member of the community. Until that age, "children belong to the gods."

Mizuki, Takuma's wife, took Hiraku by the hand and led him in front of the *otona*, the ward headman, and his assistants. When she started to leave, he clutched her uncertainly. She gently took

---

1   Translation by Harold G. Henderson, *An Introduction to Haiku: An Anthology of Poems and Poets from Basho to Shiki*, 38 (Doubleday & Co., Inc., 1958)

his hands in hers and whispered to him, "Remember what you must do." Then she let go of his hands and backed away.

Hiraku stared down at the carved stone blocks which the *monban*, the bearers of the images, had placed on the floor. One showed the crucified Christ, the other, a praying Mary.

He started to cry.

The *otona* frowned. One of the assistants whispered to him. Takuma bit his lip, wondering whether saying something would make matters worse.

Mizuki made a deep bow to the council. "He is only a small boy, seeing the images of the 'Evil Sect' frightens him. Allow me to assist him." The *otona* nodded.

She took Hiraku by the hand, and led him so that he walked over the Christian images, thus desecrating them, just as his mother, father, and grandfather had done already.

"There, it is done!" she cried.

The *otona* clapped his hands, and beckoned to Yamaguchi. The scribe pointed to a blank spot on the register, and Yamaguchi applied his name seal to it. The *otona* coughed, and all the members of the household bowed. Then the *otona* rose, somewhat creakily, to his feet. "This *efumi* is concluded. You have reaffirmed your status as good Buddhists, and good Japanese. I congratulate you. Remember to report any suspicious activity to one of my assistants."

He turned to his *nichi gyoshi*, the ward messenger, who was seated near the door. "Go at once to the house of Matsumoto the matmaker. Tell him that we just finished with Yamaguchi-san, and we are on our way to Tanaki-san. Tell Matsumoto-san that we expect to visit him at the hour of the monkey. Then meet us at Tanaki's house."

The *nichi gyoshi* bowed, and departed on his errand. The *monban* packed up the *fumie*, the Christian images, in their cases, and began the procession to Tanaki's. They in turn were followed by the scribe, the assistant headmen, and lastly, the *otona*.

After they were out of earshot, Takuma whispered to his wife. "Tomorrow is the last day of the efumi. The following night, we'll perform the rite of atonement."

Edo Castle, the residence of the Shogun, in Edo (Old Tokyo),
capital of Japan,
Kan'ei 10, fifth month (August 1633)

Pieter van Santen, the chief Dutch factor in the Land of the Rising Sun, shook out the exotic garment. "And this, Great Lord,
is what the up-timers call a 'rain poncho.' They wear it to keep
dry when it rains."

Tokagawa Iemitsu, the *Taikun*, the shogun, the ruler of Japan,
looked at it doubtfully. "What is this material it is made of?"

"I am told that they call it 'plastic.' It is manufactured, not
natural. Is it not marvelous? It folds up into a small package,
even though it covers the wearer as well as a *haori*." That was
the three-quarter length kimono-shaped coat of the samurai. "It
has the transparency of glass, but it is flexible like cloth. And it
is far more waterproof than any cloth."

"Hmm. Put it on."

Van Santen complied. Iemitsu made a twirling motion with his
hand, and, after a moment's hesitation, van Santen pirouetted, slowly.

Iemitsu snapped his fingers, and a servant appeared. Iemitsu
whispered to him, and he returned a moment later, carrying a pail.
He stood behind the Dutchman, who was unaware of the servant's
exact position, since protocol required that (unless commanded to
do otherwise) the visitor remain facing the shogun at all times.

Iemitsu made a second gesture.

Splash! The servant had upended the bucket over the Dutchman. Iemitsu laughed with great vigor. A beat later, the rest of
the court joined in.

Iemitsu held up his hand, and the laughter stopped, in mid-
titter. "Let's see how well this 'rain poncho' worked."

The servant carefully lifted it off van Santen, then felt the material. He reported his findings to the chief of the attendants, who
in turn confided them to a junior councillor. Finally, the senior
councillor, on duty, Sakai Tadakatsu, made his report to the shogun.

"Dry."

Van Santen bowed.

"What else do you have for me?"

"A barometer, it is a up-timer device for predicting the weather.
A kind of artistic marvel; I believe it is called an 'Etch-a-Sketch.'

A globe, showing the entire world as it existed, or I should say would have existed, in the time of the up-timers. And one of their firearms, Great Lord. On the instructions of your guards, it was locked in this chest." He pointed to one held by a servant.

"You may open the chest, but do not touch the firearm without my permission."

Van Santen unlocked the chest, and held it so the shogun could see its contents.

"Come closer." Van Santen, head bowed, shuffled forward until he was close enough for the shogun to reach in.

The shogun held up a strange-looking firearm. "What is it?"

"In Grantville they call it a twelve-gauge pump-action shotgun. There are four hundred rounds in the small container which accompanies it. It is most often used for shooting birds, but it can be used in combat. Of course, it is not loaded."

The shogun mimed shooting at a moving aerial target. Then he lowered the barrel.

"Who used it in combat? Samurai? Ashigaru?" Ashigaru were foot soldiers, usually commoners.

"Horse warriors, Great Lord. In the American *Sengoku*."

Iemitsu, nodded, satisfied. Horse warriors, by definition, had to be samurai. The Sengoku was the most recent period of civil war in Japan, brought to a close in 1600 by the victory of Iemitsu's grandfather Ieyasu in the Battle of Sekigahara.

Iemitsu examined the buckshot in the chest.

"May I humbly beg that the *Taikun* not test *this* present on my person?" said the envoy.

"No problem," said Iemitsu. "We can always find a criminal. Or a peasant," he added thoughtfully. "In the meantime, it can go into my firearms collection.

"Do you have any other presents for me? I am feeling a bit tired." That was understood by all to mean that Iemitsu was bored and wanted to go hunting or hawking.

"Just some books. These are volumes of what the Americans call the *World Book Encyclopedia*. This one includes articles on Japan and Korea. Written in the Americans' day, which, as we have told you, is four centuries in the future. And knowing of your interest in happenings in the Middle Kingdom, I also brought the volume with the essay on China. This third volume has an article on Asia, which covers the Kingdom of the Mughals, and the Kingdom of Ayutthaya, and many other places of interest. And the fourth one speaks about the rise of the Buddha. And I also have pages copied from other encyclopedias. And atlases."

"I am sure it is all very interesting. Give it to Tadakatsu-san." He clapped his hands, and everyone quickly prostrated themselves. A moment later, he was gone.

Tadakatsu directed van Santen to a small chamber near the audience hall. There, van Santen handed the four volumes to the chief councillor, who looked through them quickly.

Tadakatsu paged through the first volume, without saying a word, or even changing his expression.

This made van Santen uneasy. He pointed to the "J-K" volume. "The *World Book Encyclopedia* has a very interesting map of Japan. One which shows where gold, silver, copper and iron occur. Perhaps some of the localities are not yet known to you? There is also a map copied from the *Hammond Citation World Atlas*. And then I have a list for you of Japanese towns which, according to the *Columbia Encyclopedia*, are mining centers."

He lowered his voice. "The Americans have only two originals of what they call the Great Encyclopedia. They don't permit them to leave Grantville, but we have compiled the information which they provide on Japan. I have the compilation in manuscript form. It is in English, but I can translate it for you. It was sufficiently... sensitive... that I thought it best not to have it translated into Japanese, or even into Dutch."

"What sort of information?"

"Information regarding certain, um, difficulties, which lie in the path of the shogunate. Difficulties that might be avoided if the shogunate knew about them in advance.

"And proof of both the perfidy of the Portuguese, and the loyalty and friendship of the Dutch."

Kan'ei 10, ninth month (October 1633),
Shikoku, Japan

"So, now that there is no competitor to hear your great secret, please explain to my unworthy and lowly self: why are we slogging up a mountain instead of drinking sake at an inn, and flirting with the serving girls?" said Nakamura Takara.

His companion, Sumitomo Tomomochi, kept walking. "A friend of a friend... (breath)... of my esteemed father... (breath)... has a new diviner..." Abruptly, he decided that it was no use trying to talk and walk at the same time. Stopping, he explained. "This diviner says that there is a lode of copper somewhere around here."

"Which father would that be?" This question was not as peculiar as it sounded. Tomomochi was the natural son of Soga Riemon, a coppersmith in Kyoto. Riemon had married the daughter of Sumitomo Masotomo, a former priest, who ran a bookshop-cum-pharmacy in the same city. To strengthen the alliance between the two families, Masotomo had adopted Tomomochi. Since Tomomochi and Takara were of samurai descent, they had true surnames.

"Riemon. Can we continue, please? I would like to get back down by nightfall."

His hiking companion didn't move. "And what do you mean, a 'friend of a friend'?"

"You want us to be here all day? My father was called to the office of the Kyoto deputy." That was the Tokugawa official who made sure that the emperor stayed out of politics. "To meet with a visiting superintendent of finance, out of Edo." That made a bit more sense, since Soga Riemon had invented *nanban-buki*, the method of extracting silver and gold from blister copper. "And he had gotten his marching orders from some shogunate bigshot."

"Really, who?"

"He was very careful not to say. Anyway, my father said, 'So sorry, I am too old for climbing. Please speak to my son in Osaka after he gets back from Shikoku.' And the superintendent said, 'Funny you should mention Shikoku. The diviner I spoke of says that there is copper south of Niikama.'"

"Whoever that shogunate bigshot was, it's a pity that he didn't make the diviner slog along with us."

"Save your breath for the climb, please." Tomomochi resumed his struggle up the mountain trail.

"Oh, all right. Even if we don't find copper, perhaps I'll find some dragon bone." Takara was, like his father, a physician. His father was one of Masotomo's regular customers, and Takara had set up his own practice in Osaka. Naturally, he had been instructed to look up Tomomochi. That was how business was done in Japan.

Takara and Tomomochi had traveled to the island of Shikoku for the *Shikoku Hachiju-hakkasho*, a pilgrimage to eighty-eight temples on that island. At Mount Koya, they had put on the traditional garb: the white *hakui* coat, the purple *wagesa* scarf, and the conical *sugegasa* straw hat. And then each took a firm grip on his *kongotsue*, his walking stick, and headed for the first temple, Ryozenji.

When they planned the trip, they had expected to be able to complete the circuit in two months. However, when they reached Matsuyama, the halfway mark, there had been a sealed message waiting for Tomomochi. One whose contents he had refused to reveal to Takara, until now. At Niihama, they had deserted the pilgrimage route and headed deep into the mountains, guided by a local "mountain master." Much to Takara's amazement.

They were now on the south side of the Dozan ridge. The "mountain master" ahead of them halted abruptly. Then he resumed his progress, this time scuttling slowly forward in a peculiar half-crouch.

"What is it?" said Tomomochi.

"I saw... promising colors. In the small stones. Which may have fallen from someplace higher."

"I wish they could have fallen from someplace lower," said Takara.

They continued journeying. Tomomochi stopped from time to time to rub his hands. Even though it was summer, they were high in the mountains, above the timber line.

Then they stopped in amazement. Before them lay a massive buttress of stone, and in it, plain to see, was a vein of copper ore. The mountain-master prostrated himself before it, as if it were some *kami* of the mountain. Takara whooped. "You've hit the bullseye, my friend!"

"I will call this place *Kanki*," replied Tomomochi. It meant "cheers of joy."

"So, at least some of what is in the up-timers' encyclopedias is true," Tadakatsu told the shogun. "And since we do not allow the Dutch or Portuguese barbarians to roam freely, and we have not given them maps, their detailed descriptions of the geography of Japan must come from the future."

"Could they not merely have very good diviners?"

"If they have diviners good enough to find copper mines in Nippon, while standing somewhere in Europe, then that is almost as remarkable."

"The copper will certainly come in handy. What about the gold and silver? And the iron?"

"We have found the iron, too. Near Kamaishi. As to the rest—" Tadakatsu shrugged. "It is disappointing that we haven't found them yet, but the maps and descriptions are of a very general nature. We must search a dozen *ri* in every direction from each town mentioned." A *ri* was about two and a half miles. "And over mountainous terrain, to boot.

"But in view of our successes with copper and iron, I have ordered that additional surveying parties be sent out to look for the rest of the deposits."

Beppu, on the Island of Kyushu, Japan

The Christian prisoners stood on the brink of Hell. There were five of them, all peasants, stripped naked, their bodies still bearing the red stripes of the lash.

But even though the sun had set, they weren't shivering. To the west rose the great caldera of Mount Aso. Far beneath their feet, according to the Shinto priests they disdained, the *yama no kami*, the mountain spirits, tended gardens of fire in deep grottos. Like seeds blowing in the wind above, seeds of fire escaped from these grottos and heated the nearby lakes to fever pitch.

The *kirishitan* were held on the rocks above one such cauldron: *Chino-ike Jigoku*, the Hell of Boiling Blood. Steam rose from its rust-colored surface, first in wisps and then in great billows, and the air smelled of rotten eggs. The Hot Springs of Beppu were considered one of the *Sandaionsen*, the "Three Great Hot Springs" of Japan, but the *kirishitan* didn't seem to be admiring the view.

Hasegawa Sadamitsu studied his prisoners, his expression suggesting that he had just bitten into an unripe persimmon. His superior had been broadly hinting that he wanted Sadamitsu to try throwing Christians into a snake pit, as the inquisitor in Arima was wont to do. Sadamitsu was much opposed to the idea. First, he would have to either buy or catch the snakes. Then they would have to be transported to the place of trial, and thrown in the pit. When the Christians' ordeal had ended, either in death or recantation (or both), someone would have to recover the serpents and bring them back home. And then they would have to be cared for until the next batch of Christians was arrested. If he lost some of the snakes, there would be paperwork to fill out. And if the snake bit one of his men, who then died of the venom... more paperwork. Sadamitsu quietly cursed all hotshots who made unnecessary work for their colleagues.

Sadamitsu debated whether he should prod the Christians off the cliff one at a time. That would give the others time to reconsider their position. The shogunate wanted recanters, not martyrs.

On the other hand, it was getting late, and he really, really wanted a cup of sake.

He caught the eye of his second-in-command, and made a broad sweeping motion.

Edo (Tokyo), Japan

"You are sure of your translation?" demanded Sakai Tadakatsu.

"Most sure, my father taught me well." The speaker was Magome Anjin... known to a few as Joseph Adams. His father was William Adams, the English pilot who became a *hatamoto*, an upper-level retainer, to Ieyasu, Iemitsu's grandfather. Ieyasu valued William's advice on dealings with foreigners. After Iemitsu's recent edict restricting foreign trade, Joseph had thought it prudent to use his mother's family name, Magome, rather than the English Adams. And the Japanese given name that Ieyasu had conferred on his father. Anjin, "pilot." Joseph, too, was *hatamoto*, but he didn't have any real influence with Iemitsu.

"I will have to think about how to present this to the shogun, and the Council. In the meantime, speak of it to no one without my permission."

"Of course not. My heritage puts me at risk, if the information creates more ill will against the *gaijin*."

Tadakatsu knew that the Dutch had their own goals; he hadn't wanted to rely on a Dutch translation of the up-time texts. Hence, he had located and enlisted Anjin.

Thanks to Anjin, Tadakatsu now knew several explosive secrets. First, that in 1637, secret Christians had revolted in the Shimabara peninsula. Disgruntled ronin had joined them, and it had taken an army of two hundred thousand to crush the rebels. Perhaps thirty thousand rebels had lost their lives, either in the fighting or in the mass beheadings that followed.

Secondly, the shogunate had reacted by kicking out the Portuguese traders, and limiting the Dutch to the tiny islet of Deshima, in Nagasaki harbor, save for an annual journey to the shogun's court in Edo.

And thirdly, that while the policy of seclusion—*sakoku*—had bought Japan over two centuries of peace, during that time, the Western powers had grown knowledgeable and mighty, and had finally humiliated the Tokugawa by forcing open the Japanese ports. Leading, in turn, to the overthrow of the shogunate by "outside lords" allied with the once-powerless emperor.

Tadakatsu believed that Iemitsu had no deep-seated hatred of Christianity per se. The Tokugawa concern was that the Spanish and Portuguese had a reputation of using missionaries as a fifth column, subverting the people and the lords and preparing the way for invasion. When the Tokugawa were still at war, the trade contact with the West was useful, as a source of weaponry. Once they had pacified the country, they concluded that Western guns and cannon were more likely to strengthen the outside lords, who had only grudgingly accepted Tokugawa rule, and stopped the trade in weapons. The Western traders remained convenient for conveying silks from China to Japan, but there was little else that the Tokugawa had still wanted from them.

But that was beginning to change. Iemitsu was not the only one who was fascinated with the up-time artifacts. There was also the newest senior councillor, Abe Tadaaki. Tadakatsu was confident that Tadaaki would, if properly approached, support the new policy Tadakatsu was thinking of proposing. And that he would be willing to dare the displeasure of the shogun by voicing his position before Iemitsu himself announced a policy change. It was Tadaaki, after all, who had refused to throw a fencing match to the shogun, back in 1630.

Still, once Iemitsu heard of the Shimabara Rebellion, he might lose his new-found enthusiasm. But should he? Tadakatsu feared that, with the dissemination of up-time knowledge, there would be Spanish or Portuguese steam warships off the Japanese coast in a decade, rather than two centuries. In which case seclusion wasn't the solution. But free intercourse with the West might be equally dangerous. Tadakatsu wasn't sure what he should recommend to the shogun.

He decided to go to the Senso-ji temple and pray to the Bodhisattva Kannon for guidance. And then perhaps call on Abe Tadaaki.

"Great Lord," said Tadakatsu. "I have been thinking."

"About the game?" asked Iemitsu. They were playing Go.

"About the parable concerning the sound the hare heard."

Iemitsu placed a stone, threatening one of Tadakatsu's formations. "What parable is that?"

"In one of his incarnations, the Bodhisattva was a lion of the forest. A hare lived in that forest. He was something of a philosopher, as hares go, and was thinking about how the Earth might come to an end. At that very moment, a ripe fruit fell nearby, but out of sight, and it made a loud sound. 'The Earth is crumbling!' the hare cried, and he started to run, without even a glance back in the direction of the sound that had startled him. Another hare saw him running and asked, 'What's the matter?' The philosopher-hare answered, 'There's no time to ask or answer questions; run for your life!' And the second hare ran."

Tadakatsu took a sip of sake. "Other animals saw their flight, and started running too, without questioning whether they fled a forest fire, a stream of lava, or a tsunami. Soon, all the animals of the forest were fleeing, save for the Lion Bodhisattva. He forced one after another to stop and explain why he ran, and each referred him to another animal for the answer. At last he was directed to the hares, and the first hare told him what he had heard. The great-souled Lion told the other animals to wait, while he and the hare investigated further. With the Bodhisattva by his side, the hare found the courage to return, and there the Wise One found the ripe fruit, and the untroubled ground, and realized what had happened."

Tadakatsu counterattacked in another part of the board. "And thus it was that the animals of the forest learned that they must not listen to rumors, they must learn the truth before they act."

November 1633

The senior members of the *Roju*, the Council of Elders, were assembled in the *yobeya*, the "business office" of the shogunate. It was in the central citadel of Edo Castle, near the shogun's daytime apartment. The councilmen in attendance were Inaba Masakatsu, Naito Tadashige, Morikawa Shigetoshi, Aoyama Ukinari, Matsudaira Nobutsuna, Abe Tadaaki, and Sakai Tadakatsu.

A page entered, and announced the impending arrival of the shogun. The *Roju* made the appropriate obeisance and Iemitsu entered.

Iemitsu cleared his throat. "You are of course aware that an extraordinary event has been reported to have occurred in the land of the Southern Barbarians. A so-called 'Ring of Fire' transported a town from four hundred years in the future into our time. And from the place the Barbarians call 'America' to their Europe.

"The Dutch and Portuguese agree that this Ring of Fire is real, and they also agree that such a prodigy could only be the result of divine action. Such agreement on the part of barbarians so hostile to each other is of course a miracle in itself.

"While they did not dare to say so to us, I am sure that they credit it to their Christ. We of course know that it must be the result of the action of the buddhas, or the kami, or perhaps both acting in concert.

"It is of course essential that we fully understand the significance of this event in the context of *Ryobu Shinto*." The term referred to the amalgamation of the Shinto and Buddhist religions, peculiar to Japan.

"We believe that this requires firsthand observation. But even if there was a barbarian whom we trusted, they are all ignorant of the true nature of the universe, and could not be expected to make intelligent observations. Hence, we have decided that a proper religious delegation must be sent to this, this Grantville.

"So, I have decided to license a Dutch ship to sail under the Red Seal, and bear my embassy to Amsterdam, and, ultimately, to Grantville." He paused, then added nonchalantly. "While the delegation is in Grantville they can of course also consider whether the up-timers have any suitable gifts for us. Like the 'rain poncho.' Or the 'barometer.'" "Gifts" was a euphemism for trade goods, it being uncouth for any of the *bakufu*, let alone the shogun, to show open interest in any mercantile dealings. The *bakufu* were the ruling class, that is, the shogun's close relations, high shogunate officials, and the daimyo and their most powerful retainers.

Osaka, Japan

"So, is it ready yet?" asked Takara.

"Not yet," Tomomochi replied. They stood outside a sword-smith's shop. There, they could hear the impacts of the hammers as the swordsmiths pursued their sacred art. In his mind's eye, Tomomochi could picture them. They wore robes, like those of Shinto priests, and their work area was marked off by a rope from which paper streamers hung, like the enclosure of a Shinto shrine.

A messenger had come from the capital a few weeks ago, informing Tomomochi that in view of his discovery of the great new copper mine, he had been awarded the right to wear the *daisho*, the "long and short." A commoner usually could only carry the short blade, the *wakizashi*, and then only when authorized to do so by a travel permit. Only samurai, and a few privileged non-samurai, had the right to carry the longsword, the katana.

"Have you decided on the *tsuba* design?" The *tsuba* was the sword guard, and would be made by another craftsman.

"An 'igeta,' of course." The igeta was the frame placed around a country well. A stylized igeta, four crossed lines in a diamond pattern, appeared on the shop-sign of Riemon Soga's smithy in Kyoto, and also, of course, on that of Tomomochi's satellite establishment in Osaka. Both of their stores were named *Izumi-ya*, that is, "spring-shop."

Tomomochi's thoughts went to the other news brought by the messenger. News of risk and opportunity. He had been invited to join a mission halfway around the world, to study the arts of Grantville. Not one Japanese in ten thousand even knew the name, so closely had the shogunate guarded the information about it. But he had been told that the general location of the copper mine he had found had been divulged in a book from Grantville, a book supposedly written hundreds of years in the future. And that the shogunate had resolved to find out if Grantville really came from the future, the spiritual significance of its appearance, and finally, whether they had any useful arts which the Japanese should acquire. As it had acquired gunsmithing from the Portuguese almost a century ago. The messenger hinted that the up-time craftsmen exceeded the Portuguese as much as the Japanese did the primitive Ainu to the north.

It was the opportunity of a lifetime. But who would care for his father if he fell ill? Who would run his shop while he was away? What if the ship was sunk by a typhoon? Or, returning, he found that politics had shifted again, and that they were barred from reentering Japan?

He had not, of course, been formally offered the position. He would have to make a decision soon, and send word of what it was. If, and only if, he said he intended to accept, would he receive the offer. No Japanese official would make such an offer without knowing in advance that it would be accepted. Embarrassment must be avoided.

December 1633,
Edo (Tokyo), Japan

The guardsman approached. "There is no one else in the garden, my lord."

"No one?"

"No one, anymore, I mean. We chased out a pair of lovers."

"Very good. Post a guard at the entrance of the garden. Allow no one to enter, save for the one who presents the token I told you about."

"Yes, sir."

The lord, wearing a large hat that shadowed his face, looked up at the moon. "It is a pity that it lacks a handle. On an evening this sultry, I would like a silver fan with which to cool myself." It was an allusion to one of Yamazaki Sokan's verses, written a century earlier.

His cloaked companion smiled. "We *are* in a garden. You could break off a stick of bamboo, and use that."

They stood in silence for a few moments.

"The *kirishitan* are a great threat to Japan, and to the *Bakufu*."

"I heartily agree with Your Excellency."

"Suppose that the *kirishitan* have devised a devilish scheme."

"What sort of scheme?"

"To set up gunpowder mines all over Edo. Then, on a windy night, light the fuses, and burn down the city. The shogun would die, as would all of his councillors, and those of the daimyo that were in attendance upon him. The emperor, in Kyoto, would be taken captive, and he would become a Portuguese puppet."

"How horrible! You have found evidence of such a plan?"

"Alas, no. Hence, for the good of the realm, we must...create... such evidence. Before the dreadful event can in fact occur. Give the shogun reason to rethink his policy once again. Think of it as a *kabuki* play, in which the characters suddenly step off the stage and walk among the audience."

His manner became abrupt. "It should be simple enough for you to obtain the gunpowder. Inside the barrels, place Christian symbols. Then all that is needed is an anonymous tip to the police, before the explosion can be triggered, and soon thereafter...the vicious *kirishitan* conspiracy is unveiled." He smiled thinly. "And of course, I will be promoted for unveiling it. Perhaps even to the *Roju*."

His spymaster raised an eyebrow. "Planting the gunpowder will not be too difficult. However, the problem is that the conspiracy will be faceless. The Great Lord will want *kirishitan* to confess to the crime and be punished appropriately." In Japan, where most buildings were of wood construction, the penalty for arson was to be burnt alive.

"Every few months, we find a few more cowering *kirishitan*. If we ask them...vigorously...enough, they will admit that they were involved. Problem solved."

"Indeed. But wait. I have spies among the *kirishitan*. They wait for the opportunity to catch a big prize, a Spanish or Portuguese padre. But suppose I have one of them try to recruit a few fools to become part of the 'conspiracy'?"

"Ah, I see. They will be sent somewhere to await the explosion...with the explanation that once it occurs, they are to seize what is left of the castle...the police will arrest them, and they will think they were part of a *real* conspiracy."

"My Lord is most perceptive."

"But what if no one volunteers?"

"They will still remember the visit of the recruiter. And they can confess *that* to the inquisitor."

"Excellent. Now let's discuss where and when."

Kodama Katsuo would live to see another sunrise. Katsuo wished he could one day tell his grandchildren that his survival had been the result of his wisdom, or his keen senses, or his swordmanship. In truth, it was because he didn't snore.

Lying under a bush, so that the light of the full moon would not disturb his beauty rest, he had heard the entire plot. He had remained as still as possible, his breath slow and shallow and above all, silent.

He had heard the lord and his spymaster leave. He hadn't seen their faces, but he didn't have to. He had seen the *mon*, the family crest, on the sleeves and back of the guards' *haori*. And the voice was one he recognized from the time that he had been samurai, not ronin. It was that of Inoue Masashige. As one of the sixteen *metsuke*, the "inspectors" of the Tokugawa intelligence service, he had decided that Katsuo's former master was untrustworthy, and persuaded the shogun to cut his estate in half. Which in turn had meant that he could no longer afford to keep Katsuo in his service.

Since the Tokugawa had taken power in 1600, they had confiscated property from many a lord, in the process demoting many samurai to ronin. There were now perhaps four hundred thousand ronin in Japan, and, with Japan at peace, they had few opportunities for respectable employment.

Katsuo wrinkled his nose. Masashige had been rewarded for his diligence with promotion to the lower junior rank of the court nobility; he now styled himself *Chikugo no kami*. And earlier this year he had been promoted to *ometsuke*, chief inspector, with a fief having an income of four thousand *koku*. A *koku* was the rice needed to feed a man for a year.

The ronin wondered why Masashige was so virulent in his hatred of the Catholics. Did he really consider them a threat to the *bakufu*? Did he see persecution of the Christians as a stepping stone to power? Could he be a relapsed convert, contemptuous of his former teachers?

The safest thing for Katsuo to do was to forget what he had

heard. It wasn't as though he cared a hoot what happened to the *kirishitan*.

But the opportunity to deal a blow to Masashige was tempting, and who knows? Katsuo might be rewarded, perhaps even become a direct retainer of the shogun.

Katsuo couldn't exactly walk up to the shogun and say, "one of your junior ministers is plotting to trick you into thinking that there is about to be a Christian uprising. And putting the whole city at risk of fire in the process." Even if he could get into earshot, and the shogun believed him, the shogun would thank Katsuo and then have him beheaded for his impertinence.

Nor was Katsuo on an intimate basis with any of the Council of Elders.

Logically, Katsuo should go to the Edo magistrate. There were two, the "North" and "South," and they alternated months of duty. The magistrate on duty met with the councillors every morning.

But perhaps he was too high a personage to receive a visit from a humble ronin. Under the magistrate, there were the *yoriki*, also samurai. With a suitable gift, a *yoriki* would certainly introduce Katsuo to the Edo magistrate.

Unfortunately, Katsuo didn't have any money.

Well, it was easy enough to find a *doshin*. They were the officers who actually patrolled the streets of Edo, and each carried a *jitte* as his badge of office.

But time was short, given what he knew of the plotter's plans. By the time he worked his way up from a *doshin* to a *roju*, it would be too late for the information to do any good. Worse, the authorities might decide that *he* was part of the plot.

Wait. This was still the term that the magistrate of the north was on duty, the magistrate of the south didn't take over until next week. That meant that the magistrate of the south should be reachable at his home. And he knew a merchant who was likely to know where that was.

Katsuo waited outside the magistrate's home for the right opportunity. At last, he saw a maid walk out, bamboo basket in hand. He sweet-talked her into letting him into the anteroom. He explained to a higher servant that he had urgent, confidential information for the magistrate. Something about his voice and gestures must have been convincing, because he was told that the magistrate would see him as soon as possible, and he should just wait.

At the Hour of the Dog, he was ushered into the private office of the south magistrate. The official listened closely to Katsuo's story.

"Inoue Masashige? You are sure it was him?"

"I would stake my life upon it."

The magistrate stood up. "You have done the government a great service, Katsuo-san. I must ask you to remain here while I make the necessary arrangements. I assure you, you will get your just desserts."

"Thank you, Your Excellency."

The magistrate left, sliding the door behind him. Some time passed, with Katsuo lost in a reverie about the possible rewards. Suddenly, a nasty thought struck him. The south magistrate would be the magistrate on duty at the planned time of the mock attack. The police would make their reports to him. Might he actually be involved in the plot?

Katsuo ever so slowly slid the door open a crack. He could see the higher servant was outside, holding a cudgel. *Fuck*, he thought. *But let's see if we can profit from the experience.*

He carried out a lightning search of the judge's papers, looking for anything that could possibly relate to the plot. One of the papers was a map, with locations in Edo marked that Katsuo figured were the planned sites for the explosives. The map wasn't labeled "plot to overthrow the shogun," of course, but it would still lend support to Katsuo's tale. And it wasn't signed, but Japanese calligraphy was distinctive, and he thought, thinking back to that terrible order his daimyo had received, that it might be the work of Inoue Masashige himself.

That done, he drew his katana with one hand and . . . cut his way out through another wall of the office. It was convenient that Japanese used so much paper in building construction.

The problem now, of course, was that the magistrate knew his name. He could be described to others, like hordes of *doshin*. Katsuo didn't fancy matching his katana against a *doshin's jitte*, if he could avoid it. The original *jitte*, the "weapon of ten hands," was a polearm with tines for trapping an opponent's sword. The Edo police carried a shorter one, with a single hook near the base.

But it was still effective enough, as many a disorderly samurai stumbling around the pleasure district could attest to.

Katsuo needed a place to hide.

Shimabara Peninsula, Island of Kyushu, Japan, Kirishitan Feast Day

So far as the police in Nagasaki knew, the Yamaguchis were in the country, visiting relatives in Shimabara. And that was true, so far as it went.

What the police didn't know was that the relatives were secret Christians. Like the Yamaguchis. Each had a statue in a household shrine. To Buddhists, the statue seemed to be *Koyasu Kannon*, protector of women and children. To the *kirishitan*, she was the Virgin Mary.

There was no church, of course; they met in the home of one of the villagers. This feast day, one of the few that brought the entire community into one place, commemorated the birth of Christ. All evening, prayers were said to encourage Santa Maria Sama, and to aid the birth. At midnight, prayers of thanskgiving were recited. And of course, special foods were served.

Takuma wasn't in a good mood. There was a visitor, someone who claimed to be a "Brother," even though he looked Japanese. He admitted he was native born, but said that he had been made a brother by Diego de San Francisco Pardo, the Franciscan superior. Brothers were almost as hard to find at their ceremonies as padres, given the prices on their heads, so he was receiving much attention.

So why was Takuma displeased? There was something unsavory about this "Brother." Takuma was a merchant, and this brother reminded him of one who had tried to cheat him by mixing shoddy goods in with a shipment.

The brother talked mysteriously about a great new Christian quest, and tried to persuade the younger men to meet him up the hill the next morning to discuss it. That afternoon, after he left, Takuma made an effort to un-persuade them. He hoped he was successful.

At least Hiraku was too young to get involved in any such nonsense.

Edo, Japan

Her name was Hanako. She was a *bikuni*, that is, a member of the order of wandering nuns, and owed a loose allegiance to the nunnery at Kamakura, perhaps ten *ri* south of Edo. Katsuo had met her a few months ago, on the road from Yokohama to Edo. He was then working as a *yojimbo*, a bodyguard, for a merchant.

Like almost all of the *bikuni*, she was pretty, despite having to shave her head to comply with the rules of her order. When Katsuo met her, she was wearing a black silk cap, and gloves without fingers, and carrying a shepherd's crook. Her modus operandi was that if she saw a prosperous traveler, she would approach him, singing some rural ditty and with her kimono artfully arranged to show part of her bosom. The better endowed of the *bikuni* had found that this tended to encourage charitable giving.

What she had seen in Katsuo, he had no idea. Certainly, not even the slightest hint of wealth. But she had sung to him, and he had responded in kind, and one thing had led to another.

"You want to get a message to the Edo magistrate." Hanako sounded doubtful.

"That's right. The magistrate of the north, to be precise. Well, really to one of the councillors. Preferably Sakai Tadakatsu himself."

"That's easy."

"What do you mean that's easy? If I went up to the castle door, do you know how many hands I would have to grease to get up that high?"

"No, and I don't care. I have a cousin who works in the Yoshiwara." That was the pleasure district of Edo. Some of the *bikuni* were the daughters and wives of mountain-priests, but others, like Hanako, were ex-courtesans who had bought the privilege of entering the religious order.

"She'll know who Sakai Tadakatsu's favorite bed partner is, and get the message through to him plenty quick. You like?"

"Yes, I like, but I can't afford a Yoshiwara girl. Even on a strictly intangible basis."

"So you'll have to convince her that conveying your message will gain her a reward."

"I think I can do that."

"Great. Let's see how persuasive your tongue is." She snickered.

Early January, 1634

Inoue Masashige, once an honored and feared *omotsuke*, an up-and-comer in the Tokugawa bureaucracy, sighed. Hands which had once been stained with ink were now grimy with the dark soil of Hachijo Island. Fingers once callused only by the rigors of sword practice now were blistered from the unaccustomed demands of the shovel.

He looked down at the pillar hole he had dug. Tomorrow, with the help of the local farmers, he would set the pillars in place and place a thatched roof above. Eventually, he would have a hut to call his own.

At least he would not have to farm the land himself. He had just persuaded the peasants that they should feed him in return for lessons in reading, writing and abacus-arithmetic. He might even aspire to be the village's official scribe. Hah! His *yashiki-gami*, the guardian spirit of the Inoue, must have been drunk on sake when Katsuo slept in that confounded grove!

His erstwhile ally, the Edo magistrate of the south, had been executed. *Good riddance*, thought Masahige. Were it not for his incompetence, the plan would have succeeded. Masashige might at this moment be sitting in Edo Castle, in the chamber of the junior councillors, an honored protégé of the shogun.

But the magistrate, instead of simply slaying that busybody ronin, Katsuo, on the spot, had left a fool of a servant to guard him, armed only with a cudgel. Moron. Imbecile. Idiot.

When that sanctimonious prig of a senior counselor, Sakai Tadakatsu, revealed the anti-*kirishitan* plot to the shogun, Masashige had prepared to commit *seppuku*. Indeed, he wondered now whether that was what he should have done in the first place, rather than concoct the "gunpowder plot." That is, carry out *seppuku-kanshi*, the ritual suicide to reproof one's lord.

But Masashige's friends had insisted that he go quietly into exile. His life had been spared at the urging of Iemitsu's only friend (and former lover), the junior councillor Hotta Masamori. Masamori was one of the leaders of the anti-Christian, pro-seclusion faction within the *bakufu*, "Do not waste our efforts on your behalf. The Christians will make a mistake, and the shogun will remember that you tried to warn him of their threat. He will forgive you; you will return to Edo in triumph," Masomori told him.

And Masashige vowed that if he ever got off the island, he would make sure that Katsuo regretted his meddling with affairs of state.

The privileged Tadakatsu sat with the shogun in the Great Interior, the inner section of the Edo Castle. Through the walls, he could hear the clacks as the shogun's ladies practiced with the *yaginata*, the halberd.

Tadakatsu's star was in the ascendant. He had enriched the shogun by identifying new mines, and making sure they came under Tokugawa control. He had learned of various beneficial political practices which, in the old time line, would soon have been adopted by the shogunate, and was able to gain credit for recommending them at this earlier date. And finally this ronin, the Katsuo, had alerted him to Inoue Masashige's plot, allowing Tadakatsu to discredit the reactionaries at court. Now, he thought, it was time to tell the shogun of the kernel of truth unwittingly concealed in that plot, and recommend a new course of action.

"What would you say, Great Lord, of a farmer who ate all his saved seed?"

"I would say that he is very foolish, he fills a stomach for a short time, but he dooms himself to starvation in the long term."

"Ah, and in that lies the genius of Japan, which distinguishes it from the Southern Barbarians. Thirteen hundred years have elapsed since the time of the Emperor Jimmu. How old is the oldest of the barbarian nations? A few centuries at most.

"Their rulers think only of what will profit them over the next month, or year, or perhaps a decade."

Iemitsu interrupted. "Whereas we also concern ourselves with the tale of centuries."

Tadakatsu inclined his head. "Such is the genius of the Japanese... and the Tokugawa. Now reading these up-time texts, I have found that there was a policy established which served our nation well for many years, but which in the end was our downfall. By this Ring of Fire, the kami and the boddhisatva have given us the opportunity to perceive this pitfall and to moderate that policy for both short and long-term good."

"What is that policy?"

"The policy of *sadoku*, in a more stringent form than it exists now. We thought that the greatest threat to the stability of Tokugawa rule was the threat from within, from the missionaries and their converts. And indeed, in the old time line there was an incident, four years from now, which fueled our fears." The Shimabara rebellion started in December 1637, the end of Kan'ei 15. "But instead it is the threat from without which we must meet, and because of the changes in the world, mere exclusion of western ideas is insufficient. Permit me to explain further."

Iemitsu heard him out. Finally, he said, "So what do you propose?"

"Of course, Great Lord, you can put all the *kirishitan*, whether in Shimabara or elsewhere, to death. And I agree that so long as the Southern Barbarians use missionaries to conquer from within, we must keep them out of our homeland and forcibly repress Christianity."

"I hear a 'but.'"

"But I think we can defend the homeland better by exiling the *kirishitan*, rather than killing them. Exile them far away, to a place where, in the defense of their new homes, they would be an obstacle to the expansion of the Southern Barbarians, rather than a threat to Nippon."

Iemitsu thought about this. Exile was a classic Japanese punishment. Depending on the severity of the offense, and the offender's connections, a criminal might be forbidden to enter Edo, banned from coming within twenty-five *ri* of Edo, or exiled to some remote and uncomfortable island. Iemitsu's grandfather Ieyasu had sent Ukita Hideie, the daimyo of Mimasaka, and one of the Five Elders of the defeated Toyotomi faction, into perpetual exile on Hachijo, an island guarded by the dangerous currents of the Kuro Shio, the Black Tide. He would have been beheaded if he had not been the husband of a Maeda and the friend of Lord Shimazu.

"Are you sure that the *bakufu* won't see such a pronouncement as a sign of weakness?"

"Not if properly presented, as a veiled attack on the Spanish domains. We will of course either occupy Hara castle with a strong force, from a domain known for anti-Christian sentiments, or pull it down altogether." Hara was the castle where the Christian rebels, in the Shimabara rebellion, had made their last stand. "We can concentrate the *kirishitan*, or most of them at least, on an island, where we can keep them isolated until we are ready to transport them. And we should remove Matsukura from office, since it was his stupidity that triggered the rebellion."

Iemitsu closed his eyes for a moment. "I will appoint Abe Tadaaki—don't look surprised, I know that you and he are thick as thieves, lately!—to supervise the operation. With the understanding that it is a temporary appointment, that I want him back in Edo as soon as it is completed.

"Once the *kirishitan* are gone, we can open the Shimabara pensinsula to peasants from the more crowded of the other domains. And we can leave the daimyo guessing as to who will get rulership over it. They'll be intriguing against each other, instead of against me."

Tadakatsu smiled slightly. It was becoming *Iemitsu's* idea, which was a good thing indeed.

But Iemitsu's next remark made it clear that he wasn't completely convinced. "Still... the Spanish, they keep sneaking in missionaries. Even if we completely replace the population of Shimabara, the problem will be back in another generation or two."

Tadakatsu clapped his hands together. "Let us again use one problem to solve another. The ronin are restive, that is why some were recruited into the rebellion. So give the ronin something to do that will bring them back into service, and will also solve the missionary problem."

"Ah. Manila."

"Toyotomi Hideyoshi asserted sovereignty over the Philippines almost four cycles ago. And four years ago, you... um... 'encouraged' Matsukura Shigemasa's plan to attack Manila." Shigemasa was Katsuie's father, and a warrior who had distinguished himself at the battle of Sekigahara and the siege of Osaka Castle. "Without actually promising to give him the one-hundred-thousand *koku* fief he wanted."

"Ah, poor Shigemasa. He died that very year."

"Not before obtaining Dutch support. Maps. Espionage reports on the Spanish garrison. Offers of cannon, troopships, and warships. I daresay the Dutch would still be... cooperative."

"I must think about it. Is it better to move against Manila before we deal with the *kirishitan* here, or only after they are in exile? Do we trust the Dutch, or wait until we can build a fighting fleet of our own?" He didn't wait for an answer. "How many *kirishitan* do you think there are?"

"Two to four tens of thousands, according to the up-timers' encyclopedias."

Iemitsu frowned. "That many? We don't have many ocean-going ships. Do we have enough?"

"The Dutch and the Chinese have more. But even if we hired their vessels, we will have to transport the *kirishitan* in shifts, since otherwise there will be too many of them for the new land to support. A few thousand each year, over a twelve-year cycle."

"Too long."

Tadakatsu bowed. "I will speak to the shipbuilders."

"Ask the Dutch for help if you must," said Iemitsu.

"Let me show you where we might send the *kirishitan*, on the up-time globe the Dutch gave you." Tadakatsu turned the sphere, and jabbed down his finger. "Here is Nippon." He moved it lightly over the surface of the globe, following the ocean currents marked upon it. "And here, I propose, is New Nippon, the place of exile."

The shogun gave the globe a spin, and laughed. "So be it...Tairo."

Tadakatsu bowed deeply. There had not been a *tairo*, a "great elder," since the time of Hideyoshi. He was now the chief of the senior ministers of the State.

Negi-Cho district, Edo

Hanako studied her lover. "Wake up, Katsuo."

No response.

"Katsuo, we'll be late."

Grunt.

Hanako reached for a pitcher of water near their bedding, and poured a thin stream onto Katsuo's upturned face.

He rose with an oath, and reached for his sword...which Hanako had prudently first positioned out of his reach.

"Hanako, are you trying to drown me?"

"I am glad to see you're awake now."

"What time is it, anyway?"

"The sixth time." That was what an up-timer would call six a.m. "Can't you tell by the light? Didn't you hear the shopkeepers sliding open their doors?"

"The sixth...I didn't sleep at all last night. Let me go back to sleep." He reached for the quilt, and pulled it over his head.

She pulled it back down. "You're taking me to the theater, to celebrate. Remember?"

He reached for her. "I have a better idea..."

"Oh, no you don't," she said, taking evasive action. "It isn't every day I get the chance to see Nakumura Kanzaburo perform."

Grudgingly, he got dressed. Done, he grabbed a fold of his *kataginu* jacket, twisting his neck to get a better view of the insignia recently sewn on. "Wish we had a mirror."

"What did you expect? It's just a restaurant that earns some extra coin by letting people sleep here that want to get to the theater when it opens."

The insignia was the triple hollyhock, the *mon* of the Tokugawa clan. Katsuo was now a *gokenin*, a direct retainer of the shogun, with a stipend of one hundred *koku*.

Hanako wouldn't dream of saying so, but she was happy that he hadn't been made a *hatamoto*. He might then think himself above consorting with a *bikuni*. "Hurry, Katsuo. Nakamura could come on stage any moment now."

Kyushu, Japan

Hasegawa Sadamitsu pointed with distaste at the base of the stake. "Too much tinder," he rebuked. "The *irmao* will burn too quickly. Since his crimes are greater, he should suffer longer." The Franciscan brother tied to that stake waited impassively as the actual executioners, of the abhorred *eta* class, made the necessary adjustment. The missionaries who had come openly to Japan had been kicked out in 1614. Perhaps thirty had gone underground, but most of those had been captured, and had either recanted their faith or gone to their martyrdom. This brother was one of the handful who sneaked into Japan each year on Portuguese or Chinese ships.

Sadamitsu also waited, but more impatiently. It didn't appear that he would have any last-minute apostates in the present lot of condemned *kirishitan*, and that meant that Sadamitsu wouldn't receive the bonus for causing a Christian, especially a priest, to renounce his faith. It was enough to unsettle his stomach.

Gradually, Sadamitsu became aware of a commotion, coming closer and becoming louder. Nonetheless, he raised his hand, ready to command the executioners to light the piles.

"Halt!"

Sadamitsu turned angrily, but quickly swallowed his words.

A special messenger from the shogun, as the man's uniform and banner proclaimed him to be, was not to be trifled with.

"Edict from the shogun."

"Thank you, make yourself comfortable, I will read it as soon as I have this execution under way."

"You must read it aloud to the prisoners before proceeding."

"Very well. But it's a waste of time giving them another chance to repent, if that's what it's about." Sadamitsu cleared his throat, and began reading aloud.

"*This edict is to be read aloud and posted in every place where it is customary to announce an edict.*

"*1. The padres of the Christians have disturbed the tranquility of the realm by advocating the destruction of the shrines of the kami and the temples of the buddhas. Such cannot be permitted.*"

That was in Hideyoshi's edict in the fifteenth year of Tensho, Sadamitsu recalled. 1587 in the Christian reckoning. Why was the shogunate wasting his time with this?

"*2. They also spread a pernicious doctrine to confuse the right ones, with the secret intent of changing the government of the country and giving ownership of the country to a European king.*"

Well, that hadn't been in an edict, but the apostate's oath required that he admit that the purpose of the padres' teachings was to justify and facilitate taking the lands of others.

"*3. However, we know from the example of the Dutch that it is possible to be Christian without acting outrageously.*"

Sadamitsu didn't like where this was going.

"*4. Hence, the Japanese-born followers of the padres will be allowed to worship according to their conscience, and Japanese-born padres and brothers will be permitted to teach the Christian faith, but only in duly constituted Christian settlements in New Nippon, a land across the sea.*"

Exile! What was the shogun thinking? It was true that exile, whether from Edo, or one's home province, or to some desolate island, was a time-honored punishment in Japan, but if the *kirishitan* were sent into exile, wouldn't they just sneak back?

And where was this New Nippon? North of Korea, perhaps? Across the Sea of Okhotsk? Well, at least they would freeze their butts off.

The prisoners were praising their Lord, now. How irritating.

"Keep reading," said the messenger. Was he smirking? It wasn't as though *his* job was at risk!

"*5. In order to be permitted to go to New Nippon, they must take oath, on pain of eternal punishment by the Father, Son and Holy Ghost, as well as by Saint Mary and all Angels and Saints, as follows:*

"*a) they will not return to the homeland without permission of the shogun, or assist any Southern Barbarian in going to the homeland without permission of the shogun.*

"*b) they will defend New Nippon against the Christian powers, obey the daimyos duly appointed by the shogun to govern them, and support their daimyos as is customary, save as they may be excused during the first years of settlement.*

"*c) they will not oppress the worshipers of the buddhas and kamis, or the followers of Confucius, in that land, or prevent any Christian from renouncing that faith and returning to any of the traditional religions of Nippon.*

"*d) they will repay the cost of their transportation to New Nippon as soon as is reasonable.*

"*e) they will provide the inquisitors with any information they have as to the whereabouts of Christians still in hiding.*"

Sadamitsu turned to the messenger. "How are we going to enforce this oath?"

He shrugged. "They will be shipped in batches. Those still in Japan will be punished if the first to be sent are disobedient. And they will need supplies shipped to them if they are to survive, let alone prosper. Gunpowder, if nothing else."

"Still—"

"Please, finish reading the edict."

Sadamitsu took a deep breath. "*6. Those who timely accept exile, and cooperate with the authorities, will be permitted to take all of their possessions to New Nippon. Those who do not, will forfeit, depending on the circumstances, some or all of their possessions before being sent into exile, and will be required to work as servants, for an appropriate period of years, for those who behaved properly.*"

Oh, I like that, Sadamitsu thought. Create a schism in the Christian community between those who surrendered quickly and those who tried to stay in hiding, with the ones we prefer on top.

"7. Any informer revealing the whereabouts of followers of padres that have not timely surrendered themselves must be rewarded accordingly. If anyone reveals the whereabouts of a high ranking padre, he must be given one hundred pieces of silver. For those of lower ranks, depending on the deed, the reward must be set accordingly."

Sadamitsu thought about this for a moment. Perhaps he would go into the padre-hunting business, now that he couldn't execute them.

"8. Any apprehended padres who are Southern Barbarians shall stand surety with their lives for the good behavior of the followers permitted to go to New Nippon. If all goes well, then in twelve years they will be permitted to pay for their transport to a Southern Barbarian land. Any who afterward return will be executed in the most painful way imaginable."

Good, good. Sadamitsu prided himself on his imagination.

"9. Any Japanese-born followers of the padres who fail to take the oath, or to apostasize, within three years of this edict, are to be executed.

"10. Books teaching the Christian faith may be taken or sent to New Nippon, but only if they are in the Japanese language, are offered for inspection by the inquisitors, and are found to not contain teachings contrary to the required oath."

The edict closed with the formulaic, "You are hereby required to act in accordance with the provisions set above. It is so ordered."

Sadamitsu looked at the Christian captives. "So, do you wish to take the oath?" They nodded their heads.

"Don't be hasty," he admonished. "New Nippon is probably thousands of ri away, too cold in the winter and too hot in the summer, filled with savage monsters eager to dine on kirishitan flesh."

They assured him that they would prefer to take their chances with the monsters.

Nagasaki, Japan

"Can it really be true?" Mizuki asked her husband. "That if we go on these ships, that we will be taken to a land where we will be free to worship the Christ?"

"That's what the proclamation said," Takuma admitted. "But it might be a trick, to get us to reveal ourselves. Then they kill us. Or perhaps they will let us board the ships, but then, once we are out of sight of land, throw us overboard."

"How long do you think we will live if we stay here? There are spies everywhere," said Mizuki. "And what of our son? You know how precocious he is. He has learned his catechisms so well. But that makes it all the harder for him to carry about the pretense that he is Buddhist. What will happen at next year's efumi? Will he refuse to desecrate the images?"

"Oto-sama, what do you think?" Takuma was addressing his father, who had retired as head of the household a decade earlier, but of course was still consulted on all major decisions.

"If you don't throw the dice you'll never land sixes."

"So, soon we will leave for New Nippon," said Mizuki.

"Indeed," said Takuma as he packed his wares. "More precisely, we will be helping to *create* New Nippon. Right now, it's just a wild land, according to the Red-Hair merchants I have done business with. The Red-Hairs call it—" he struggled visibly to recall the strange Dutch word—"America."

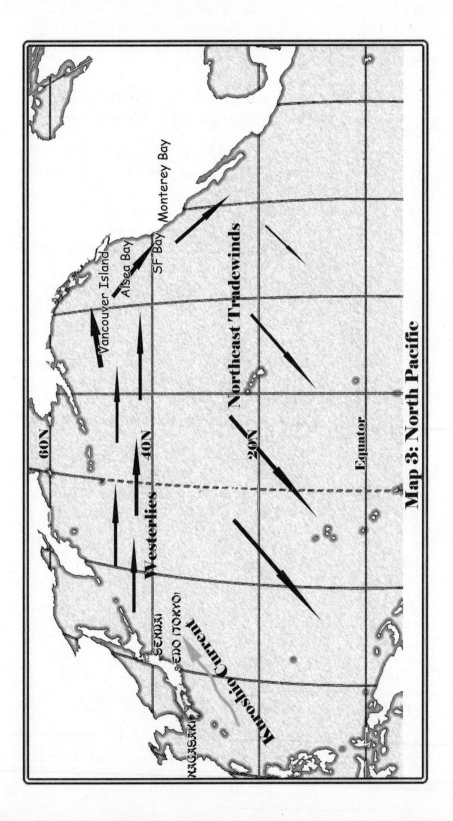

Map 3: North Pacific

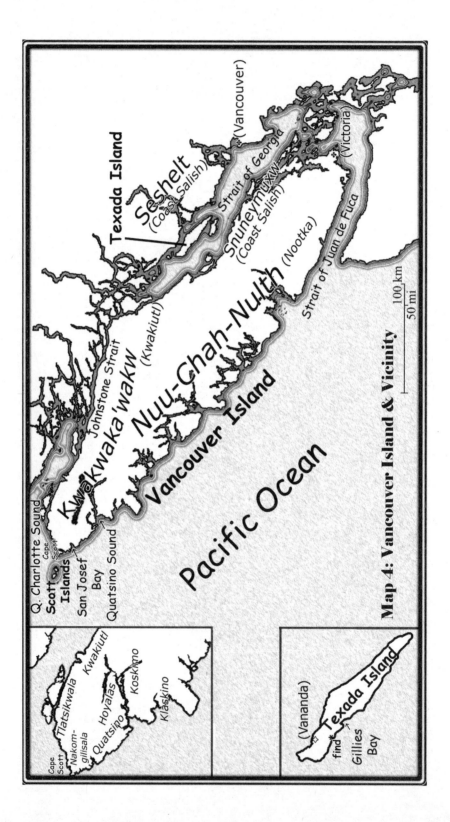

Map 4: Vancouver Island & Vicinity

Pacific Ocean

Vancouver Island

Nuu-Chah-Nulth

Kwakwaka'wakw (Kwakiutl)

Texada Island

Seshelt (Coast Salish)

Snuneymuxw (Coast Salish)

(Vancouver)

(Victoria)

Strait of Georgia

Strait of Juan de Fuca

(Nootka)

Johnstone Strait

Q. Charlotte Sound

Scott Islands

Cape Scott

San Josef Bay

Quatsino Sound

100 km
50 mi

Cape Scott

Tlatsikwala

Nakom-gilisala

Kwakiutl

Quatsino

Hoyalas

Koskimo

Klaskino

(Vananda)

Texada Island

find

Gillies Bay

Fallen Leaves

February 1634 to August 1634

If a west wind blows,
They pile up in the east—
The Fallen Leaves.
—Taniguchi Buson (1715–83)[2]

February 1634,
Osaka Castle

"Isn't it marvelous? I have the old plotter just where I want him." With a sudden movement, Tokugawa Iemitsu, shogun of Japan, snapped his fan closed and then open again, as if driving off flies.

His tairo and chief councillor, Sakai Tadakatsu, smiled thinly. "Forgive me, Great Lord, but Nippon is not merely the Land of a Thousand Kami, it is the Land of a Thousand Old Plotters." The shogun snorted in agreement, and Tadakatsu continued, "Which particular old plotter do you have in mind?"

"Date Masamune."

"Ah."

---

2   Translation by Harold G. Henderson, *An Introduction to Haiku* (Doubleday & Co., Inc., 1958)

Iemitsu paused for a moment, admiring the play of light on the Tokugawa mon, three encircled hollyhock leaves, set out in gold leaf on one side of the fan. "He perplexes me. In the barbarian year 1614, he dared to send an embassy to the king of Spain, without my father's permission. The act was proof that his ambition to be shogun was not dead. But in 1632, when my father was near death, and publicly voiced his fear that I was too young to prevent the return of civil war, Masamune declared before the assembled daimyo that he would defend my right to rule."

"Perhaps his ambitions mellowed with age."

"Perhaps. But who knows what long-banked fires have awakened, thanks to the tidings of Grantville? I have no doubt of his sagacity, but I would prefer it to be exercised across the Great Ocean. Hence, I put him in a position where he couldn't reasonably refuse the appointment."

"You think of this as if you are playing a game of Go with him, and have found a *kikashi*." That was a forcing move. "But perhaps you are really playing *kemari*." That was the courtiers' kickball, a cooperative game, played in Japan for a millennium. The players had to keep the ball in the air, each giving it a few kicks before passing it to the next one.

Iemitsu gave his back a quick scratch with the folded fan. "How so?"

"You need someone who can keep the *kirishitan* under a firm hand, yet is respected by them. And Date Masamune...he is an old warrior in a land at peace. Perhaps his dream is to die on horseback in the middle of a battle. In New Nippon, fighting the Indians or the Spanish, perhaps he will do so. So this appointment may be to the benefit of both of you."

Spring 1634,
Kirishitan Internment Camp,
Hashima Island, outside Nagasaki, Japan

Doctor Zhang knelt in front of young Hiraku, the Yamaguchis' only child. Hiraku was already kneeling. He was also trembling.

His mother, Mizuki, kissed his head. His father, Takuma, frowned, but didn't rebuke Mizuki for coddling Hiraku.

Zhang very carefully took a vial out of a pouch wrapped against his skin, and set it on the floor. Then he reached into his bag and pulled out a two-foot-long silver tube, slightly curved at one end. He ground the curved end of this inside the vial, and held the straight end by his mouth.

"Tilt your head back, boy," said Zhang. "More, more, look at the ceiling. That's good. Hold it right there."

He carefully inserted the curved end of the tube into Hiraku's right nostril. "This won't hurt a bit." Zhang blew the dried pox material into the boy's nose.

"There, like sneezing in reverse, eh?" he said to Hiraku.

Zhang turned to face the parents, and they bowed to him. "Remember, he may only be visited by those who have already had the 'heaven flowers.'" That was the Chinese euphemism for smallpox. "In six or seven days he will have a fever, and you may treat him with the herbs I gave you. The eruption will occur a few days later. Scabs should form after two weeks. I will return then, so I can collect the material. The scabs should fall off after another week or so, and he can then live a normal life."

"We have prayed that it will be so."

Zhang sniffed. "To your Christian God?" They nodded.

"And to Mary, the Mother of God," Mizuki added.

"Well, I hope that's sufficient. I still think you should have let me conduct the normal ritual." That involved praying to the Goddess of Smallpox, who in turn was an incarnation of the Goddess of Mercy.

Zhang was a Chinese practitioner, from a medical family, who had come to Japan a few months earlier. A chance encounter with a *bakufu* official had led to him being questioned about his methods of preventing smallpox. Zhang claimed that dried and aged scabs, mixed with appropriate medicinal herbs, and warmed in his armpit pouch for a month, were efficacious.

He assured the official that if, on a lucky day according to the calendar, the preparation was blown into the nostril of a child (right for a boy, left for a girl), it provided immunity against the dread disease. Asked about survival rates, he asserted not even one in a hundred failed to recover from the treatment.

The *bakufu* official was impressed, and suggested to his superiors that perhaps condemned criminals might be allowed to volunteer, their lives spared if they survived the immunization. The suggestion made its way up the chain of command, and one of the junior councillors of the shogun had the bright idea, why not test Zhang's methods out on the *kirishitan* instead? If they were successful, they could be adopted more generally. If they caused smallpox, well, then there were a few less Christians to worry about.

The first uses of Zhang's *han miao fa* were limited by the supplies that Zhang had brought with him, but of course each patient became the source of fresh material.

Hiraku was one of Zhang's first *kirishitan* patients; his parents had lost their first two children to smallpox. Their prayers were answered; Hiraku survived the immunization.

After several hundred were treated successfully, the *bakufu* invited Zhang to Edo, to treat selected members of the shogun's household.

Date Masamune's agents had quietly monitored Zhang's experiment. After Zhang left, Masamune's own physicians continued the immunizations, among the Christians as well as the people of Rikuzen, as they had been instructed by Zhang.

Some Christians objected to Zhang's rituals, others permitted it, figuring that as long as it was Zhang praying, not them, they were committing no sin. And of course, in the shogun's household, only the Buddhist ritual was practiced.

This came to Masamune's attention, and he questioned his doctors as to whether it made a difference who was prayed to. "It didn't appear to," he was informed.

His reaction was just one word. "Interesting."

May 1634,
Sendai Castle (Date Clan Family Home)

Captain Abel Janszoon Tasman of the Dutch East India Company earnestly hoped that this would not be a long meeting. He had not been in Japan long enough to feel at all comfortable squatting for hours. He tried as best he could to copy how the Japanese captain sitting beside him had locked his heels under his buttocks, but feared that his imitation was poor.

A flunky announced the coming of the great lord, bellowing "All kow-tow for Date Masamune-sama, Echizen no Kami,

Mutsu no Kami, Daimyo of Rikuzen, Taishu of New Nippon."
Taishu meant "grand governor," and was, according to Tasman's
colleagues, the local equivalent of a Viceroy.

Of course, the title by which Date Masamune was best known
was *dokuganryu*—"one-eyed dragon." This was a reference to the
loss of his right eye. According to Tasman's sources, Masamune
had gone blind in that eye as a result of childhood smallpox. It
was a common enough consequence of the disease. What wasn't
so common was Masamune's reaction; Tasman had been told
that Masamune had plucked it out so that an enemy couldn't
take advantage of it in battle.

And he was in battle frequently enough. The shadow of his
famous helmet, bearing a crescent moon, had fallen on scores of
battlefields. And he was a successful general, serving first Hideyoshi in Korea, and then Ieyasu when he unified Japan.

Perhaps too successful. He was one of the most powerful
daimyo in Japan, and the Tokugawa had suspected that he had
ambitions to become something more than a mere daimyo...a
shogun. They were particularly irritated when he sent his own
embassy to the pope in faraway Rome. Still, they had grudgingly
found him to be indispensable.

Tasman's superiors were certain that Shogun Iemitsu had been
ecstatically happy when he realized that he could give Masamune
a position of immense prestige...thousands of miles away.

Masamune addressed the Dutch captain in slow but under-
standable Portuguese. "Please explain."

"Explain what, milord?"

"The proposed sailing route. Look!" Masamune pointed to the
globe that his aide had reverently placed in front of him. It was
a duplicate, as near as skilled Japanese craftsmen could make
it, of the "Replogle" globe presented to the shogun the previous
summer.

"This is the world according to the wizards of Grantville that
your people spoke of. Now look." He held a string taut across
the surface from Sendai, the capital of his *han*, to Monterey,
California, then released it. "This is the shortest path, neh?"

Tasman nodded. "That's true, milord. But it's not a route we
can easily sail."

"No? But the globe shows that the currents are favorable. See—
Masamune's finger traced out a chain of dashed blue arrows on

the globe—this is marked, 'Kuroshio Current.' 'Kuroshio' is Japanese, meaning 'Black Stream.' Our sailors know it well, it is very fast and very dark. The short route should also be a fast route."

"May I touch it, please?"

Masamune swept his hand in a graceful arc from Tasman to the globe.

"There are two problems, milord. Here is the North Pole, at ninety degrees north latitude, and this is the equator, at zero degrees. These smaller circles are the lines of latitude. Sendai is at about thirty-eight, and the up-timers' Monterey a little farther south. Now, may I have that string, please?" Masamune silently handed it over.

Tasman laid it down between Sendai and Monterey. "See how close it comes at the middle of the journey to the fifty-degree line? It will be very cold there."

"Even in summer?"

"Even then. There are likely to be more storms, that far north. And there could be icebergs." When Masamune failed to react, Tasman quickly explained, "great masses of ice, some larger than ships, that float in the water. Most of the ice is below the water, and can't be seen. They are very dangerous to shipping."

The Japanese captain interjected, "Excuse me, Great Lord, but I have heard of such floating ice. Each year, some wash up on the beaches of Hokkaido." These icebergs in fact came from glaciers calving into the Sea of Okhotsk. The North Pacific was virtually free of icebergs, as those of the Arctic ran aground in the Aleutians, but none of the participants in the meeting knew this.

"And the second problem?"

"Staying on course. We steer by the compass. If we run down a latitude eastward, we just make our way east as best as the winds allow, and we can tell from the height of the sun at noon whether we are too far north or south.

"But if we take this path—and indeed your lordship is most astute to recognize that this is the shortest path—then we start on a northeast heading, and mid-cruise we are heading east, and near Monterey we must bear southeast.

"Alas, since we cannot tell our longitude—" the Dutchman moved his hand back and forth between Japan and North America—"that is, our easting or westing, we would not know when to change the course."

Masamune stated at Tasman. "Why can't you tell your longitude?"

"We could if we had a clock that could keep time even at sea. Then we could set the clock to Sendai time before departing." Tasman turned the globe slowly. "This is how the Earth turns. As it turns, the sun seems to climb in the sky, then sinks. When the sun has reached its highest point in the sky, we call that noon. Noon will come earlier in San Francisco than in Sendai. En route, at noon, we would look at the clock to see what the time in Sendai was, that is, how much before noon. And from that we would know the distance in longitude."

"And you cannot build such a clock?"

"We can't. Our clocks use a pendulum to keep time, and the rocking of the boat plays havoc with it." Tasman shrugged his shoulders. "Perhaps the up-timers can do better."

Masamune stared at the globe. "They must have, in order to draw these longitude lines, neh? Well, if you can't build such clocks yet, we can't either." The Europeans had brought clocks to Japan.

Tasman didn't belabor the point, but the clocks made for use in Japan wouldn't be useful for voyagers even if the waters of the Pacific were as quiet as those in a bathtub. The Japanese didn't have a standard hour, but rather divided the day and night each into six equal parts, whether the days were summer long or winter short. The customized clocks presented by the Europeans to the shogun and several of the more important daimyos had complicated mechanisms to adjust for the seasonal variation at Edo or Nagasaki in the length of the day.

"So, milord, our route is a bit of a compromise. We head northeast, passing abreast of your northern island—"

"Ezochi," Masamune interjected.

Tasman inclined his head slightly. "Thank you, Your Grace. The American globe calls it Hokkaido. And then when we are at latitude forty-five degrees, by the sun, even with this island—" he pointed at Iturup, in the Kurile Islands, with his rather grimy fingernail—"we turn east. When we sight the coast of America, we turn south, and this 'California Current' will speed us down to the latitude of Monterey."

Masamune turned to the Japanese captain on his left, and they spoke hurriedly and softly in Japanese. "Captain, please repeat what you just told me."

"Tasman-sama," said the Japanese captain, "why do we need to worry about where the sun journeys? We can follow this chain of islands to this peninsula, then cross to this second island chain, and run along this second peninsula, and finally sail down the coast." The path he outlined was from the Kurile Islands, to Kamchatka, the Aleutian Islands, the Alaska Peninsula, and then along Alaska, British Columbia, and the Pacific Northwest. "According to the distance scale, I think we would always be in sight of land."

"In sight of land, yes, if there were no fog. Are fogs not common in your northern waters?" The Japanese captain nodded.

"Then you don't want to be close to land, I assure you. The island-hopping route, also, takes you even farther north than the shortest path route, to sixty degrees north. And part of the way, you'll be fighting the Alaska current."

Masamune spread his hands. "Perhaps it would be prudent to defer the island-hopping and shortest path routes to another time, after we have more experience in the waters in question. For now, Captain Tasman is our *sensei*."

Tasman bowed in polite acknowledgment. "If I may be permitted a question of my own, Great Lord, why Monterey? It is an open roadstead, and the largest harbor in the world is to the north. San Francisco Bay."

"And perhaps you are also interested in the gold fields of the Sacramento and San Joaquin River valleys that lie beyond that bay, neh?"

Tasman smiled. "Exploration is an expensive pastime. And so is transporting thousands of people across the world's greatest ocean."

Masamune cocked his head. "Consider this, Captain. Which power is the greatest threat to the California endeavor?"

"Spain, of course, they are already in what the Americans called Mexico."

"Indeed. And there are two reasons that the Spanish might send a force to California in the near future. The first is that they learn about our activities from their spies in Asia. That won't be easy. The Spanish have been banned from Japan since 1624. We seized the Black Ships of the Portuguese at Nagasaki a few months ago, and so they have heard nothing since then. The *kirishitan* only know that they are going to America, not where. If the Spanish learn of our interest in California, it will be because some Dutchman tells them."

Tasman stiffened. "My lord, we have fought the Spanish for our independence since 1568. While I do not doubt that the Spanish

have spies in our ranks—as of course we do in theirs—only a few
of us, the participating ship captains, and senior officials in the
Dutch East India Company, are aware of your great adventure.
And we have kept secrets before."

"See that you do so here. The other reason for the Spanish to go
to California is that they, too, are tantalized by the stories of the
California Gold Rush. They could sail north, never suspecting our
intentions, and enter the Bay. If they find us there, what would do?"

"They would blockade the Golden Gate, or fortify it, and then
hunt down your settlements," Tasman admitted.

"Exactly. And that would cut our supply line, and doom us, if
we were indeed inside San Francisco Bay." He paused.

"If we were settled, instead, at Monterey, what is the chance
that they would discover us while en route to the Golden Gate?"

"Small." Tasman ran his finger lightly over the globe. "The
California Current comes down the coast, as is marked here,
and Sir Francis Drake said that the prevailing winds are from
the northwest. The Spanish surely know that, too. Knowing the
latitude of the Golden Gate—as they would from the up-timers'
maps—the Spanish, coming from Mexico, would swing well out
to sea to avoid the California Current, make their easting above
the Golden Gate, and reach it from the north.

"But there is always the possibility that some Manila galleon
would put into Monterey Bay for shelter and fresh water. Vizcaino
explored it in 1602, and he suggested that the Spanish settle there."

"A suggestion they ignored for 167 years, yes? And don't forget,
we have taken Manila. There isn't going to be another galleon
coming from Manila to Acapulco."

"And indeed we Dutch hope to catch the Acapulco galleon
that even now is en route to Manila."

"Well, you have my blessing." Masamune raised his hand in
the *karana mudra*, the gesture of removing obstacles. Tasman
didn't dare tell him that in the Netherlands, raising the little
and index fingers, and folding down the middle fingers, had a
quite different significance.

Tasman rose and backed out, happy to stretch his legs.

It was a pity he hadn't had the opportunity to study Masamune's globe more carefully. If he had, he might have wondered
about the etymology of the little island off the southeast tip of
Australia...the island called Tasmania.

Nortbeastern Pacific Ocean

The sea has many dangers, but the *Ieyasu Maru* had not fallen to any of them. It was acting on secret orders; that after they had been at sea for at least two months, and by dead reckoning had traveled at least one thousand *ri*, they were to work their way north, as the winds permitted, to fifty degrees North—the latitude of Vancouver Island.

The *Ieyasu Maru* was crewed entirely by Japanese. Its captain was Yamada Haruno, a veteran of the shogun's "Red Seal" trading ships, and the first mate was "Tenjiku" ("India") Tokubei. Tokubei had gone to sea when he was fifteen, and had traveled twice to India, with the Dutch trader Jan Joosten van Lodensteijn. He had a gift for languages, and for adapting to alien cultures.

Jan Joosten himself had taught Tokubei how to use the *hoekboog*, the double triangle. This was a bit like the Davis quadrant of the English, except the sliding vanes traveled along the sides of triangles, rather than the arcs of circles.

Tokubei had been judging the movement of the sun, as the measurement was supposed to be taken when the sun reached the highest point in its trajectory across the sky—local noon. He had adjusted the two sliders to what he guessed, based on yesterday's measurement and dead reckoning, the latitude would be. That way he would only need to "fine tune" the sliders, speeding up the process. Which was a good thing, since holding the hoekboog in position could be a bit tiring.

He stood with his back to the sun, adjusted the sight hole slider and the shadow-casting slider until he could see both the horizon and the shadow. This was best done at the end of a roll, when the ship's motion was least. Then he read off the altitude from the scales.

"I get fifty, on the nose," he announced.

The captain had been making his own reading. "I'm a bit higher, call it fifty and a quarter."

"What should we put in the log?"

"Fifty makes more sense, given our progress. Call it fifty." He raised his voice. "Helmsman, take us due east by the compass."

"Due east, sir," the helmsman acknowledged.

Under ideal conditions, Tokubei could determine latitude to within a quarter-degree or so. But that assumed a calm sea, and a clear sky at noon. "Noon," of course, was simply when the sun was highest in the sky, and was a matter of guesswork. If the ship were heaving about, or the sun was shrouded, the navigational measurement became even more of an exercise in what an up-timer would call "guesstimating."

If the sun could not be seen at all, you had to find the Pole Star at night. Since it didn't cast a shadow, you had to use the old forestaff, instead, to make the measurement. Its accuracy deteriorated at high latitudes, because the scale gradations had to be placed closer together.

And if it were overcast both day and night, well, you were in trouble.

The "First Fleet"—the flotilla of Japanese, Chinese, Dutch and captured Spanish and Portuguese ships that was conveying the *kirishitan*, Date Masamune and some of his retainers, and a small number of hired specialists—had set sail at last. Because of the restrictions on overseas travel of the last few years, the Japanese had only a limited number of ocean-worthy ships. They had built more since Iemitsu's decision to transport the Christians, and more still had been brought up recently from the Philippines. From captured Manila, long a thorn in the shogun's back.

The *kirishitan* didn't have the opportunity to wave goodbye to their homeland. By orders of the *bakufu*, the national authorities, they were to be confined and chained belowdecks until Nippon had vanished below the horizon.

Once that milestone had been passed, they were allowed topside. However, precautions were still taken. These were most extreme on the Dutch and Chinese-operated ships; a wood barrier, with loopholes for guns, had been erected amidships, and the *kirishitan* were required to remain forward of this obstacle. If they pressed against it, they would be met by musket and even cannon fire, several pivot guns having been repositioned for this purpose. If weather conditions required that the sailors come forward, the Christians would be forced back down, no matter how long they had patiently waited for exercise.

On the Japanese ships, the *kirishitan* were allowed more freedom. However, all navigational maps and equipment were kept under lock and key, in a fortified cabin, and they and the navigator himself were guarded at all times by samurai.

It was just as well, for the navigators' peace of mind, that they did not know that the samurai guards were under orders to kill them if the *kirishitan* seemed likely to take over the ship. Or, for that matter, that the Dutch and Japanese warships of the First Fleet, which had plenty of soldiers on board, had orders to recapture or sink any rebel-controlled ship.

June 1634,
Pacific Ocean

Yamaguchi Takuma bowed politely. "Please, most learned brother of the faith, would you please recite to us from the Catechism?" The other Christians on deck murmured in agreement.

Imamura Yajiro wrested his gaze away from the waves. "Surely there is one on board who is more learned in Christian doctrine than I."

"There is not," Takuma assured him. "Indeed, we are astonished by your bravery, that you surrendered yourself to the inquisitors so soon after the edict. None of the padres or *irmaos*, and you may be our only *dojiko*." That was a lay catechist, one who had taken vows, but was not ordained. "The rest hide, and wait for word from those here, on this 'First Fleet,' that the government's promises can be trusted."

"I assured myself that it was God's will that this Edict come, and took it as a Sign."

"So will you read to us?"

"I suppose. Please, give me time to collect my thoughts."

Yajiro pondered the irony of life. He had been, for some years, an *onmitsu*—a Tokugawa spy and agent provocateur, moving among the *kirishitan* as if he were indeed one of them. He was, in fact, a faithful Buddhist.

After the Edict of Exile, his superior had summoned him to a secret meeting. There, he was asked to remain among the *kirishitan* even as they went into exile, and to send reports from time to time on whether they, or the grand governor of New Nippon, posed any threat to the homeland.

His family—his true family—would receive many honors and rewards in recognition of his sacrifice.

So here he was. And he was now not merely a spy, but an

up-and-coming religious leader of the New Nippon *kirishitan*. How droll.

He addressed his new congregation. "Since we are creating a new community, I will speak of the Creation."

He paused and scanned his audience. When he was sure he had their undivided attention, he spoke.

"In the beginning Deusu was worshiped as Lord of Heaven and Earth, and Parent of humankind and all creation. Deusu has two hundred ranks and forty-two forms." The ranking of deities, and their having a proliferation of forms, was a Buddhist concept. This was one of many respects in which the *kirishitan* understanding of scripture had diverged from Catholic orthodoxy.

"Deusu worked for six days. He divided the light that was originally one, and made the Sun Heaven, and twelve other heavens. He also created the sun, the moon, and the stars, and tens of thousands of angels. The chief of these was Jusuheru, and he had one hundred ranks and thirty-two forms. Deusu also made this world, and put his own flesh and bones into all its elements: earth and water, fire and wind, salt and oil.

"On the seventh day, he blew breath into Adan, the first of men, to whom he gave thirty-three forms." Thus, the seventh day was not a day of rest. "Deusu also made a woman and called her Ewa." And so, Eve wasn't made from Adam's rib. "He married them and gave them the realm called Koroteru, which had a value of one hundred thousand *koku*. There they bore a son and daughter, Chikoro and Tanho, and went every day to Paradise, the adjacent *han*, to worship Deusu..."

He continued his sermon, speaking of the temptation of Ewa by Jusuheru, the eating of the Apple, and the loss of Paradise.

"My friends, we seek now an Earthly Paradise..." Moses and the Promised Land might have been an apter parallel, but most of the *kirishitan* had never heard of Moses; he wasn't in the catechism.

The *Date Ni-Maru*, the flagship of the First Fleet, plowed through the waters of the North Pacific. There had been no sign of land for many days, but occasionally they were saluted by passing dolphins or seabirds.

Date Chiyo-hime turned to her maid, Mika. "I think I have made my peace with the sea-god." By which she meant, she wasn't seasick any longer. "Some exercise is in order."

They returned to their cabin, and Mika helped Chiyo take off her kimono and put on her *keiko-gi, obi* and *hakama*—jacket, belt and divided skirt. The front of the black *hakama* had the traditional five pleats, representing the virtues of loyalty, justice, compassion, honor and respect.

They came back on deck, chatting merrily about Teitoku's poetry. Chiyo had brought along the anthology, *Enokoshu*, he had written the previous year, and she and Mika had resolved to attempt to write a verse each day. The maid carried a cloth-wrapped bundle, and she laid it down with a sigh of relief.

Chiyo bent down and pulled away the cloth, revealing a *naginata*—a polearm. This was a practice weapon, of solid oak. The real weapon, still in her cabin, had a seven-foot shaft and a two-foot blade, fitted with a wood scabbard, the *saya*. The *naginata* blade was made the same way as the samurai longsword, the katana... and it was just as wickedly sharp. The butt of her *naginata* had a spiked *ishizuki*, so it was sheathed in leather.

The *naginata* was the only weapon that was traditionally taught to samurai women, and its length allowed them to compensate for the greater reach of a man. If she married, it would be hung over, or beside, the door to her bedchamber, as her final defense.

Actually, not quite her only weapon, or her final defense. She also had a *kaiken*, a dagger. It could be used for close-quarter fighting... or to take her own life. Just as a samurai man was taught how to perform *seppuku*, a painful disembowelment, so he could demonstrate his fortitude, a samurai woman had to know the art of *jigai*, a quick cut to the jugular that would preserve her beauty and dignity.

Chiyo pulled off the leather sheath and handed it to the maid. She handed a chalk to the maid. "Mark off my practice space," she commanded. While Mika bent down and carefully drew a large circle, Chiyo did some stretches.

When the maid was done, she stepped out of the chalked circle. Chiyo raised her voice. "Let none enter the circle without warning, on pain of death." Even the practice weapon could kill.

The second stage of her warm-up were the *happo buri*, the "eight-direction swings" with the *naginata*. After a few minutes of this, she began her *kata*, the standard attacks and parries. Several of her father's retainers stopped what they were doing to watch her. The crew did, too, but more surreptitiously, lest they be beaten or whipped by the officers.

The only Japanese Christians allowed on this vessel, it being a warship, was a small number of single women. They were watching, too.

Her brother Munesane stopped by. He was Data Masamune's sixth son; she, his third-eldest daughter; her mother was one of his concubines.

"Need a sparring partner, Sister?"

"That would be most appreciated."

Munesane told his aide Rusu Nobuyasu to bring up a *bokken*, a wood practice sword having the same size and shape as the samurai longsword, the katana. There was a long list of *kata* for the duel between katana and *naginashi*.

Chiyo repeated the same series of practice forms, this time with Munesane executing the standard countermoves. They had learned from the same sensei, so they knew the same *uchi-kata* and *uke-kata*, offensive and defensive forms.

When they had completed the usual series, Munesane grinned at her and said, "care for some free sparring?" He preened a little bit for the benefit of the watching female *kirishitan*.

"Mika, fetch my practice armor." Mika brought back Chiyo's head, chest, waist, glove and shin protectors, which Chiyo donned.

"Where's your armor?" she asked her brother.

"Don't need it."

"Don't be an idiot." He grudgingly sent his aide to get his own set, and put it on.

"Shall we make a small wager on this *shiai*?" asked Chiyo.

"What did you have in mind?"

"If I win, you teach me archery."

"Archery? How many women archers do you know?"

"None, personally. But what of Tomoe Gozen, or Hangaku Gozen?"

"They lived centuries ago."

"Well, the whole point of women learning the *naginata* is to fight men at a distance. So wouldn't bow and arrow let us kill enemies even farther away? One mistake with the *naginata*, and they could close with us. We have to drop the *naginata*, and rely on the *kaiken*. Which is a close-quarters weapon. It makes no sense."

"Sensei would say, 'So don't make a mistake.' But all right. If Father doesn't forbid it. Remember, all I can teach you on shipboard is the hold and the draw. There isn't room for an archery range, even on this monster of a ship.

"And, let me see, what should your part of the wager be? I know—you must personally embroider a kimono for me. With a design of my choosing." He knew that Chiyo *hated* embroidering anything. "Still want that wager, Chyio-chan?"

"Yes!"

They both bowed, and then began circling each other. Occasionally, one or the other would attack, but these were mere testing moves, without full commitment, and each was sidestepped or parried. Gradually, the attacks increased in frequency and intensity. Victory would go to whoever had come closest to mastering the principles of Budo: distance, awareness, balance and focus.

"I am going to become a Christian," she commented.

He parried her attack anyway, and gave her a quick grin. "I always thought you were a Christian sympathizer."

They exchanged a few more blows.

"Will they still baptize me if I'm pregnant?"

He jerked involuntarily.

"Hiai!" She struck him in the shin, and he tottered. Her next blow took him down.

She looked down at him. "So when's my first archery lesson?"

He looked back up at her. "You aren't really pregnant, are you? Because if you are—"

"I didn't say I was. I simply asked a question. And you made a completely unwarranted assumption. I would be offended, but of course you have already prostrated yourself before me, and so I must accept your apology."

Near Vancouver Island

The sky had been overcast for a week. Worse, *Ieyasu Maru* now had to inch its way through a fog bank, its leadsman calling out the depths every few minutes. Fortunately, they were clearly still in deep water, but Haruno had no desire to be wrecked in the middle of nowhere. Or anywhere else, for that matter.

Suddenly, the ship emerged into full sunlight, its crew blinking their eyes in reaction. As they continued heading east, by the compass, they became aware of changes in their environment. The water had changed color, becoming greener. And they were seeing birds they had never seen before.

Haruno and Tokubei conferred. Could they be nearing the North American coast at long last? Haruno announced a prize for whoever spotted land first.

Before long, land was indeed sighted. At least, there was a long smudge, which the lookout insisted must be the mainland, ahead of them in the east. But more importantly, there appeared to be an island perhaps ten miles away, off the starboard bow.

The wind remained steady, coming from west-northwest. As they continued on their course, the island rose above the horizon. The scenery ahead, however, didn't change noticeably; if there was land in that direction, it was still very far away.

At noon, both Haruno and Tokubei shot the sun. It appeared that they were farther north than they had intended to be, perhaps fifty-one degrees north. If so, then instead of striking the middle of Vancouver Island, they were north of it, in Queen Charlotte Sound. And that suggested that the island they had spotted was one of a small chain of islands, northwest of and leading toward Vancouver Island, that had gone unnamed on their map of British Columbia.

They decided to make for the island, and then use the chain as a guideline. Their map had only shown two islands, but in fact there were five. As they passed to the south of the last little island, they could clearly see Vancouver Island, stretching south-east as far as they could see. Their map referred to the near tip as Cape Scott; they could see that this was one end of a short north-south ridge. This ridge was connected to the rest of Vancouver Island by a rather low-lying isthmus.

Their first destination was Quatsino Sound. The Japanese, when they seized the Portuguese "Japan Fleet" in Nagasaki Harbor, had found a Portuguese copy of the up-time *Hammond Citation World Atlas*. If the captured copy was correct, there was an iron deposit somewhere on the south shore of the inlet.

The *kirishitan* on board the *Ieyasu Maru* came from many places in Japan, but they had one thing in common: prospecting or mining experience. The *Ieyasu Maru* even had on board a mining engineer, Iwakashu. And iron was an ore that was in short supply in Nippon.

But they were not fated to reach the Quatsino Sound that day.

"Captain, a wreck!" yelled a crewman. "And it looks like a junk!" He was pointed to the isthmus; the wreck was lying amid sand dunes. The mast was missing, but the ship had a distinctive hull shape that was decidedly non-European.

There was a mass movement to the starboard rail. No one could see any people, Japanese or native, besides the wreckage or nearby.

Of course, if there were Japanese survivors, they might have reason to be wary. From a distance, the *Ieyasu Maru* looked like a Dutch ship. That was no accident; it was nearly a copy of the 120 ton *Good Fortune* that William Adams had built for then-Shogun Ieyasu in 1610. The *Good Fortune*, in turn, was a slightly scaled-down version of *Der Liefde*, the ship in which Adams had come to Japan. The *Good Fortune* itself no longer existed; it had been loaned to the shipwrecked ex-governor of the Philippines, Rodrigo de Vivero y Velasco, to return him to New Spain, and the viceroy of New Spain had ordered its destruction. Probably muttering something to the effect that the Japanese ought to stay on their own side of the Pacific.

The only concession the builders of the *Ieyasu Maru* had made to Japanese maritime traditions was that the hull, like that of a junk, was divided into many watertight compartments. This was less convenient for stowing bulky cargo, but handy for surviving a holing. Not that this sturdy construction had saved the unfortunate junk that lay before them.

The *Ieyasu Maru* eased its way closer to the isthmus, and then lowered a launch. Tokubei was ready to get in, when Hosoya Yoritaki stopped him. Yoritaki was commander of the samurai "marines" that the *Ieyasu Maru* was blessed, or cursed, with. "You may go along, but first my men check to make sure it's safe."

Tokubei nodded and Yoritaki gestured for three of his samurai to enter. All were armed with handguns. One, after noting the openness of the land, took a *naginata* along, too. All had swords, too, but that was a given. You might as well note that they were wearing clothing, too. Once the samurai were settled, Tokubei leaped in, and the launch made its way toward the wreckage.

The samurai disembarked first. Oyamada Isamu, shouldering the *naginata*, took up a sentry position, facing inland, while the other two circled the wreckage. Satisfied that it was free of threat, they climbed to the top of Cape Scott. They looked around, and then one came back downhill.

"No one in the immediate area, but there are native villages to the east and south. Haru will fire if he sees a threat."

"Thank you, Masaru-san," said Tokubei. "Please join Isamu-san on guard."

Tokubei and his coxswain Kinzo made their way around to where the deck had been. Most of the decking was gone, so they had a clear view into the interior of the ship.

Tokubei made a few interesting observations. First, there were no skeletons. That told him that there must have been survivors, and that either at sea or after landing, they had disposed of the bodies of any less fortunate crewmen.

Second, there was nothing of value left on board. Either it had all been consumed during the voyage, or, more likely, the survivors had taken everything. That implied that they had been in reasonable health.

Third, the wreck was Japanese, beyond question. Every surviving aspect of its construction was typical of a large cargo ship of traditional Japanese design.

Finally, there was no seaweed on the underwater part of the hull. Clearly, it had been out of the water long enough for the seaweed to die and rot away. That suggested that the wreck had been here for a long time, and thus could not be one of the ships of the First Fleet. And that was a relief.

Tokubei and Kinzo collected a few small items, to show to Captain Haruno, and strode back to the launch. They waved Isamu down, and then Masaru and Haru cautiously retreated to the launch. A couple of crewmen pushed the boat back into the surf and then jumped in. Once he was on the deck of the *Ieyasu Maru*, Tokubei made his report.

"These sailors were clearly Nihonjin," Tokubei told Haruno, "we must find them if we can."

"Man the guns," Captain Haruno ordered. "Archers and arquebus-men, to the rails. Prepare to repel boarders." Even the miners grabbed spears. "But not one shot unless and until I give the command, or I'll feed you to the sharks!"

Haruno was worried about those the native villages. According to the Dutch—who in turn drew on unnamed up-time sources—the Indians of the Pacific Northwest built seagoing canoes that could hold more than sixty people, took slaves, and, some of them—the Tlingit farther north, at least—had wooden armor. All of which suggested that the crewmen of the *Ieyasu Maru* weren't going to be greeted by lithe Indian maidens gaily tossing chrysanthemum petals.

Because of the importance of the *Ieyasu Maru*'s mission, there were more than a dozen samurai on board. Until a few months ago, they had been ronin, masterless warriors, but they were accepted into the service of Date Masumune, grand governor of New Nippon. All were unmarried men who had chafed at the peacetime restrictions, and were happy to be offered the opportunity to fight, even in a faraway land.

They were less happy to be under Haruno and Tokubei's command, but they would follow Date Masamune's orders to obey them. At least, Tokubei hoped so.

"So, which of the villages do we check out first?" asked Haruno.

"The one on the west coast," Tokubei answered. "If it's the right one, then it won't take us out of the way."

Before long, a lookout shouted, "Houses. I see houses."

Tokubei had a Dutch telescope, one of the few in Japan, and he was studying the beach in front of the village. "Lot of commotion down there...

"Looks like someone is coming out of the biggest house, wearing some kind of fancy costume. He's dancing now. At least I hope he's dancing and not having a fit of some kind.

"Okay, he's gone down to one of the canoes. Kwannon have mercy upon us, it's big. Lots of paddlers getting in behind Dancing Man. Okay, they're rowing out to us."

"Weapons?" asked Yoritaki.

"None that I can see. Of course, they could club us with those paddles."

Yoritaki snorted. Kinzo had a pivot gun trained on the canoe. He could sink it with a single shot, if need be. And if the paddlers tried to board, they would wish they hadn't. Of course, no one knew what weapons the rest of the villagers might have.

The canoe pulled up alongside the *Ieyasu Maru*, and the Dancing Man danced once again. There was a platform, apparently for this purpose, on the front of the canoe.

"Tokubei, you may invite him on board, if you think it

advisable." said Haruno. It was part of the delicate dance of command aboard the *Ieyasu Maru*; Haruno was responsible for the ship, but Tokubei was in charge of all negotiations with natives, and Yoritaka would take charge if there were any hand-to-hand combat, on deck or on land.

Tokubei checked his short sword, the *wakizashi*, to make sure that it was in place, and would neither get in his way while walking nor be too difficult to draw if he needed it. In Japan, he was considered a commoner, and as such would only be allowed to carry a sword when traveling, and then only after obtaining a license from the authorities. But Date Masamune had told him that once Japan had disappeared below the horizon, the Sword Edict of Hideyoshi did not apply.

Which meant that once again, at least in New Nippon, commoners could be part-time warriors, and samurai could be part-time farmers.

Not that Tokubei was all that confident about his ability to use the sword. He was more apt to rely on the brace of handguns he was carrying. He would, if possible, leave swordsmanship to the samurai on board.

Of course, having samurai along was something of a mixed blessing. He had great faith in their fighting ability. What he wasn't sure about was whether they would follow the orders of a commoner as to whether or not to fight... despite Date Masamune's instructions that Tokubei, given his breadth of exposures to foreign cultures, would be in charge of negotiations.

"Let down a rope ladder, but be prepared to haul it up again quickly if I say so." The rope ladder went down, and Tokubei pointed to the Dancing Man and then held up a single finger.

The canoe edged closer to the ship, and Dancing Man grabbed hold of the ladder. He pulled himself agilely onto the first rung, and quickly ascended.

Tokubei addressed him in Japanese, Chinese, Dutch, Portuguese and several other Asian languages. The Indian responded with an equal lack of intelligibility.

Tokubei noticed that a seagull had landed on deck. "Someone, give me an arquebus." A sailor handed him one. Tokubei loaded the gun, smiled at the Indian, and fired at the bird. *Crack!* It fell over, dead. The Indian froze, obviously terrified. Tokubei carefully set down the gun behind him, and reached into a pouch. He pulled out a necklace of glass beads, put it on for a moment, then took it off and set it down on the deck. Then Tokubei backed away, and motioned toward the beads.

Ever so slowly, the Indian walked forward, then stooped to pick up the beads, all the while watching Tokubei. Then he backed up himself, until he felt the rail behind him, and stopped. He looked over the trinket, smiled, and put the necklace around his own neck. Then he took off his cloak and tossed it in Tokubei's direction.

Tokubei put it on. As he did so, Yoritaki swore.

Tokubei looked at him. "What's wrong?"

"Look what the chief's wearing." Tokubei realized, all at once, what Yoritaka was reacting to. The Indian's ornaments included what appeared to be pierced copper discs, strung on a string of some kind. And there was something oddly familiar about them...

"Yoritaka, be ready to grab him on my say-so, or if he tries to leave."

Tokubei pulled out a copper coin from his own pouch, and held it out for the chief. The chief came closer, and Tokubei handed it to him. As he did so, Tokubei got a better look at the chief's discs. They were one-*mon* coins; Tokubei could see the *kanji*. They had holes so they could be strung together.

"Now," he said quietly, so as not to warn the chief. Yoritaka acted immediately, putting the chief into an immobilizing hold. Another samurai drew his katana, and held it speculatively, in front of the chief's throat. The chief glanced down, at the sword's glistening edge, and then back at Tokubei.

Tokubei grabbed the coin necklace and gave it a shake. He pointed at the village, and made a beckoning gesture. He pantomimed climbing a rope ladder. Then he folded his arms across his chest, and waited.

The chief tried to say something, realized it was futile, then simply bowed his head and waited.

"Well?" asked Yoritaki.

Tokubei took a deep breadth. "We'll have to give him a chance to tell his men to free our people."

Yoritaki snorted. "Hopefully he'll say that, and not, 'Kill the intruders! Turn the waters red with their blood!'"

"Escort him to the side, but don't give him a chance to escape.

Try not to be obvious about him being held hostage, it could complicate matters in the long-term."

"Miracles are my specialty," Yoritaki replied. He called for assistance, and the samurai bound the chief's hands, behind his back, and trussed his feet as well. For good measure, they tied a long line between the feet and the mast, as a leash. Yoritaki and one of the sailors then inched the hobbled Indian forward, as a samurai with the drawn sword came behind, the point nuzzling the chief's back.

The chief spoke, and Tokubei didn't need to wait long to have a response. One of the rowers near the rear of the canoe rose, and worked his way forward. The other rowers didn't make this easy for him; clearly, they suspected that the chief was acting under duress.

He reached the rope ladder, and called out, "*domo arigato gozaimasu*." Japanese for, "I am really, really grateful." He reached the deck, and prostrated himself before a bemused Tokubei.

"Rise," Tokubei commanded. "What's your name, and how many other Nihonjin are in this village?"

"I am Heishiro, and there are five more of us. My two sons, and three sailors."

"You speak the native language?"

"*Kwak'wala*. Yes, of course; I've been here almost ten years. And it wasn't as though the Kwakwaka'wakw were going to learn the language of a slave."

"How did they treat you?"

Heishiro shrugged. "They rarely beat their slaves. But they don't feed us well, we can't earn our freedom by working, and we live in the most exposed parts of the village, where raiders would come first."

"Tell the chief that he is our hostage, but we will free him after he has released to us, unharmed, the other five Nihonjin." Heishiro translated this. The chief scowled.

"Your cargo? Was it valuable?"

"Not especially."

"Say that we appreciate them taking care of you and in return they may keep the cargo that they already have."

"What about us? Shouldn't it go back to us?"

"You can stay here, and make your own bargain, if you wish. No? Then repeat my words. And tell him they are to be brought over in a single small canoe, without any armed men. And his other canoes had best stay out of the water."

The chief's scowl relaxed fractionally. He shouted orders down to his men, and the ceremonial canoe returned to the village. Perhaps an hour later, the Japanese paddled out in a small canoe, with just two of the Kwakwaka'wakw accompanying them.

The Japanese drifters came aboard, one by one, and the chief's bonds were struck off. The chief rubbed his arms and legs, to work the circulation back into them, and in the meantime Tokubei dropped some presents in front of him.

"Tell him these are for him." said Tokubei. And then he dropped the shot seagull carcass beside them. "And tell him that this bird is a reminder that we are beloved of the sky god, who gives us thunder to wield against our enemies."

Heishiro spoke again to the chief, then addressed Tokubei. "I told him that you were the People of Tseiqami, the Thunderbird. Its wings cause thunder, and the flash of its eyes are the lightning. I said that you build ships—'floating houses'—with its help; there are legends in which it carries big cedars for heroes who are building a house."

The chief descended the rope ladder and got into the canoe. It headed backed to the village, his men paddling furiously.

"He looked impressed," said Tokubei. "Keep it up, and you'll be getting some presents yourself."

Heishiro bowed slightly. "I hope it helps, but—" He stared down at his feet.

"But what?"

"To the Kwakwaka'wakw nobility, 'face' is very important. By taking him hostage, you offered him an unforgiveable insult."

Tokubei's skin reddened slightly. "What about the insult he offered me by enslaving my countrymen?"

"He will see only the injury to himself. He will work himself up into a rage, then come after you."

"Hmm... Did you hear that, Captain?"

"I did indeed," said Haruno, who was standing nearby. "Do the Kwakwaka'wakw know where Nippon is?"

"Far away, in the direction of the setting sun, I told them long ago."

"Then let's pretend to be heading straight back home," Haruno decided. He gave orders to bring the ship about. The *Ieyasu Maru* couldn't sail close enough to the wind to head directly west, but it could manage a southwest course. It headed out to sea, its prow knifing through the swells, and then, as soon as the land was out of sight, it cut southeastward.

"Wish this wind were stronger," said Tokubei.

"Better than no wind at all," said Haruno. "Wouldn't want those big war canoes to be able to catch up with us. Especially at night."

But daylight offered its own problems. If the Kwakwaka'wakw canoes followed they would be able to see the tall masts of the *Ieyasu Maru*, from perhaps six miles off—farther, at any rate, than the *Ieyasu Maru*'s lookouts could see them. And in summer, sunset would come late in these northern parts.

About seven miles out, Haruno ordered a sharp turn to port, bringing them to an east-southeast heading. The lookouts thought that there might be a bay in that direction. Haruno also had the upper sails furled; the ship would catch less wind, but since they were heading almost directly to leeward their speed wouldn't be reduced, and with the upper masts naked, they would be quite a bit harder to see. Fortuitously, the sky was overcast, so they wouldn't be strongly silhouetted.

After sailing another five or six miles, the *Ieyasu Maru* slipped into San Josef Bay. It was now hidden from pursuit by a headland—provided, of course, that the canoes had not been able to spot it after the course change. If they did, then the hills that were now shielding it would also break up the wind, making it more difficult for the *Ieyasu Maru* to sail away again.

The first thing the chief had done upon reaching the beach was to ask a nearby commoner for a weapon. With it, he immediately killed the two slave paddlers who had taken him back from the *Ieyasu Maru*, and thus had seen his embarrassment close-up.

He told the now trembling commoner who had loaned him the weapon to keep an eye on the *Ieyasu Maru*, then stormed into his house, and remained there for a time. When he emerged, he was wearing war paint.

It took time, of course, for him to assemble and harangue his tribesmen, and then for them to prepare for war. By that point, the *Ieyasu Maru* had been several hours gone. However, the watcher was able to tell the war party what course it had taken.

Speaking eagerly of the glory and booty they would soon enjoy, the warriors pushed the war canoes into the water, hopped in, and started rowing. They were the Nakomgilisala of the Kwakwaka'wakw, who raided as far south as California.

How much farther away could this island of Nippon be?

Coal torches burned as the sentries on the *Ieyasu Maru* kept watch for a night attack.

Heishiro had been brought to the captain's cabin.

"So, please tell me your story," said Haruno. "I don't want to get it secondhand from Tokubei." He gave Tokubei an apologetic smile, so he wouldn't be offended.

"My name is Heishiro. Our ship was *Yahiko Maru*, a *sengoku-bune*." That meant a ship that could carry a thousand *koku* of rice, about 150 tons in European measurement. "I had on board my wife and two children, and a dozen sailors.

"We began at Osaka with a cargo of rice, and, as we went along the coast, we sold off rice and took on other cargos. Fortunately, we still had a lot of rice, seaweed, and other food when the storm came upon us, off Cape Shiono."

"When was that?"

"In the month of falling frost, the first year of Kan'ei." November 1624, by Western reckoning.

"When we saw the storm clouds, we tried to make for shore, but we couldn't find an anchorage, or even a safe place to beach the ship. The winds rose, and the waves tossed us about, and it became too dangerous to remain near the coast. So we returned to the open sea, and reduced sail, but even there the storm was too much for us. A great wave overtook us, and we grabbed hold of whatever we could, lest we be washed overboard. We heard a terrible snapping sound, and, when we could see again, our *hanaita* was gone." The *hanaita* was the rudder, a giant nine feet by twelve on a *sengoku-bune*.

"The wind came across our beam and pushed against our sail, heeling us over, more and more, until we were sure that we were about to capsize. Then it lessened for a moment, and we all gave thanks to the buddhas and kamis.

"But we gave thanks too soon. Another squall line advanced toward us, like charging cavalry. The winds howled louder as it approached, and we knew what we had to do. In a frenzy, we cut down the mast.

"After that, we were at the mercy of Susanoo, the Bringer of

Storms. When the sky cleared, we were far out at sea. Where, we did not know. We prayed to the buddhas for deliverance. We bailed out the hold and rationed out the food."

"But what about drinking water? Surely you didn't have enough water for so long a voyage."

"At first I just rationed our water. But after it was clear that we would be drifting a long time, I realized that I had to somehow take the salt out of seawater. I poured it into a big cooking pot, brought it to a boil, and put a wooden rice tub on top of the pot."

"On top? What good would that do?"

"So sorry, I am poor at explaining this. I made a hole in the bottom of the rice tub and ran a pipe through it. The steam from the pot went up the pipe and turned back to water inside the tub."

Tokubei thought about this.

"You made a *ranbiki*! A still!"

"If you say so."

"In the Ryukyus, they use a still to make a strong drink, what the Southern Barbarians call brandy." The Ryukyu islands, south of Nippon, were under the secret control of the Shimazu clan of Satsuma. Secret, so that the Chinese would continue to come there to trade.

"I have never been to the Ryukyus."

"Well, it was clever of you to think of such a thing. How much drinking water could you make?"

"Perhaps twelve quarts a day."

Haruno took over the questioning. "I'll have to remember that trick. How long were you adrift?"

"Fourteen moons."

"And you were carried into that bay, where the wreck is now?"

"Yes. Only half of my sailors were still alive. Barely. The Kwakwaka'wakw took us in, and fed us, but they made us their slaves. Three of my sailors were sold to other Indian tribes, up or down the coast. One to the Haida of the north, a second to the Nuu-chah-nulth of the south, the third, I know not.

"My boys are sixteen and twenty-five now. My wife returned to the Wheel a few years ago.

"The 'Kwakwaka'wakw' are a nation?"

"No, it just means, 'those who speak *Kwak'wala*.' The local natives are the Nakomgilisa. And there are several other Kwakwaka'wakw groups."

"All the cargo is gone. Why didn't the Kwakwaka'wakw take the ship timbers?"

"They were going to, but when the salvage party walked on the beach, a great wave came up and knocked them over. They decided that it was a sign that Kumugwe, their sea god, wanted it left alone."

Tokubei raised his hand. "I will need to give your bay a name, for my report to my superiors. May I name it after you?"

"That would be far too great an honor. And it would slight my fellow castaways. Call it, Hyoryumin Bay." In Japanese, *hyoryu* was the action of drifting after a shipwreck, and the unfortunate mariners were *hyoryumin*.

Heishiro took a puff on the pipe he had been offered. "So, what brings Nihonjin, even samurai, in a Southern Barbarian ship to the Land Across the Sea?" He handed the pipe to Tokubei.

Tokubei took a pull and then answered, "We have reason to believe that there are valuable ores on this island."

"What sort of ores?"

"Iron. Copper. Gold."

"The Indians have no iron tools or weapons, and I have no idea what iron ore looks like. I have seen copper ornaments here. Besides the coppers they took from us, that is. I don't know whether the copper is mined on this island, or elsewhere. But it's a big, big island. As for gold, well, the Nakomgilisala are not the richest of the Kwakwaka'wakw. So it could be here without my knowing anything about it."

The *Ieyasu Maru* continued down the west coast to Quatsino Sound, and met the local Indians. These were of different Kwakwaka'wakw groups, the Quatsino and Klaskino, but the dialect of Kwakwala they spoke was similar enough to that of the Nakomgilisala so that Heishiro and his comrades were able to make themselves understood.

These Indians were friendly, and anxious to trade. Well, to be honest, the Nakomgilisala had greeted the *Ieyasu Maru*; it was unfortunate that Haruno and Yokubei couldn't let the enslavement of Nihonjin go unpunished. The Japanese, too, had honor to preserve.

Among the Quatsino and the Klaskino, Tokubei bought supplies,

local products that he thought might find a market in Japan...
and Indian slaves. The last purchase he made with reluctance,
since the Japanese frowned on the practice of slavery by the
Portuguese, Dutch and similar barbarians, but it was a regret-
table necessity. They needed translators who could speak both
Kwakwala and the languages of the Indians to the south. Once
the *Ieyasu Maru* was under way, he could promote them from
slave to retainer.

Unfortunately, the Quatsino and Klaskino claimed to know
nothing of any iron, copper or gold deposits in the area. If they
existed, Tokubei was told, they were deep in Hoyalas territory,
and the Hoyalas were presently at war with the Klaskino. It would
not be prudent to proceed further.

Assuming the Indians were telling the truth, of course.

July 1634,
Pacific Ocean

Jacob de Veer, first mate of the Dutch ship *Blauwe Draeck,* had
his ear to the wall that separated the *kirishitan* quarters from the
rest of the ship's hold. One of the sailors from the watch below
had anxiously summoned him, reporting a "commotion" forward.

De Veer had first rushed to the similar barrier that lay above
deck, to make sure that the *kirishitan* were not already seeking
to take over the ship. The deck lay deserted in the moonlight,
seemingly belying his concerns. Nonetheless, he had doubled the
wall guards.

Then he had gone back down to the hold, hoping that his ears
could find a clue that his eyes could not. It was clear from the
outset that the *kirishitan* weren't attempting to break through the
lower wall; what the sailor had heard was the sound of many
voices, not that of axes or other tools.

De Veer had been to Hirado often enough to learn a smattering
of Japanese. He could only make out a few words, but those were
enough to cause him to flinch: "dead... dead or dying..." And
once he thought he heard a woman say, "... the poor little ones..."

The sailor was close beside him, so close that de Veer could
feel the heat of his breath. "What are they saying, sir? Should
the captain be called?"

De Veer carefully composed his expression. Blandly, he assured the sailor, "nothing for you to worry about. Go back to your duties."

Once the sailor was out of sight, de Veer made his way to the captain's cabin by a different route. As he walked, his mind was in turmoil. Had some dread disease taken hold among the *kirishitan*? If so, it had acted suddenly; they had seemed healthy on his last watch.

Would it just as suddenly inflict itself upon the Dutch?

De Veer couldn't help but wish that he could somehow cut loose the forward third of the ship, and leave the Japanese to their fate.

After a walk that seemed to take hours, but surely was just a few minutes, he knocked on the captain's door. Rap. Rap.

He heard the muffled voice of the captain. "Whoever's bothering me better have a damn good reason, or I'll give him cause to regret it."

"De Veer, sir. And it's important."

"Enter, damn your eyes."

De Veer made his report as matter-of-factly as he could.

"I wonder if it's the smallpox," said Captain Campen. "It's always hardest on the young. And I heard that some Chinese doctor blew old pox dust into our colonists' noses, so they would get a weak form of the disease. Maybe it didn't work as it was supposed to."

"I've had the pox, sir." De Veer's pockmarked face confirmed the truth of this declaration. "So has the ship's surgeon. We can go forward and check out the situation."

"Not tonight, you won't. You'll need to wait until daylight, so we can see that it's safe for you to do so. Perhaps they have the flux, or the ague, or something else that you *could* succumb to. Perhaps they're just faking illness. Get some sleep now. At daybreak, you can go forward, call for just one of the Japanese to come above to speak."

De Veer went below and crawled into his hammock. The hammock swung back and forth, and the sea seemed to murmur with each upswing: "Dead...Dying...Dead...Dying..."

The next day, de Veer summoned the surgeon and the two of them were assisted over the barrier. Both were weaponless; a pistol or cutlass would hardly allow them to escape a hundred

Japanese, and there was no sense in delivering weapons into the hands of potential mutineers.

De Veer went to the forward hatch, knocked, and shouted in Portuguese, "Send up one man to speak with us. One only, or we'll shoot!" He and the surgeon then backed away a bit, to give the wall guards a clear line of fire.

One of the *kirishitan* emerged. "What is the problem? Why can't we all come on deck for our morning exercise?"

"You're not all sick?" said de Veer. "With the pox, perhaps?" He said this quietly; he didn't want the wall guards to hear him. "I have brought our physician." That was something of an exaggeration, since the ship's surgeon was hardly that.

"Sick? No more and no worse than you'd expect, in a group this large, cooped up in a ship for so long. And no cases of pox, thank Deusu. Why would you think otherwise?" He made a Shinto gesture of aversion against evil, without any apparent awareness of his theological faux pas.

De Veer explained what he had heard. The Japanese man looked puzzled for a moment. And then he started to laugh.

"Well?" asked Captain Campen.

"He said that they didn't need a physician," said de Veer, his tone one of profound disgust. "But that if would be a kindness to summon one of the Great Lord's master gardeners."

"What?"

De Veer explained that according to his informant, the "poor little ones" that were "dead" or "dying" were silkworms. The word for silkworm—*kaiko*—also meant child raising. The women of many Japanese villages cultivated silkworms as a sideline, and indeed spoke to them as if they were little children.

The villagers on board the *Blauwe Draeck* had brought silkworm eggs, and freshly collected mulberry leaves. After five weeks or so, the silkworms had spun their cocoons. The best of these were reserved for breeding, and the others were thrown into hot water to kill the insect, and then spun into thread.

The problem had come with the eggs of the second generation. They hatched, but the remaining mulberry leaves were now old, and the tiny jaws of the new larvae weren't equal to the task of chewing them. So most had died.

The captain, all a smile, asked de Veer if he thought that the

Japanese would be comforted if the captain conducted a memorial service for the departed. De Veer rolled his eyes. "May I return to my duties, sir?"

The captain waved him off, and de Veer fled, the captain's laughter ringing in his ears, already red and burning hot with embarrassment.

Coast of Vancouver Island

The *Ieyasu Maru*'s next destination was Nootka Sound. While the atlas said nothing about any mineral deposits there, the copied atlas showed it to be home to an up-time town with a most intriguing name: Gold River.

By rounding Vancouver Island on the ocean side, the Japanese had avoided the narrow channels and tide rips of the Inside Passage, but guaranteed themselves ample exposure to the caprices of Susanoo. The wind, normally blowing from the northwest, backed around the compass until it was from the southeast, and increased to gale force, blocking the *Ieyasu Maru*'s sojourn down the coast.

It was only through skilled seamanship that the *Ieyasu Maru* avoided becoming the second Japanese shipwreck on Vancouver Island. By the time the storm abated, and the wind returned to the northwest, the *Ieyasu Maru* was well south of Nootka Sound. Indeed, they were at about the latitude of the Straits of Juan de Fuca, which separated Vancouver Island from the up-time state of Washington.

Captain Haruno summoned Tokubei. "I think we have to give up on Gold River for this year."

Tokubei winced. "Our patrons will be disappointed."

"You saw how it was on our approach to Vancouver Island. We had winds from the northwest, day after day, for at least a hundred *ri*. So we'd have to sail way offshore, then work our way north and east, as the winds permitted. It could take weeks. Is it really worth it? Our rescued countrymen say that the weather will take a turn for worse once summer's over. So going to Gold River might mean losing our chance at Texada."

"Well..." Tokubei shifted his weight as the ship reacted to a larger wave than usual. "Texada is important. Both the atlas and the encyclopedia say it has iron. And we have nothing definitive indicating that there is actually gold at Gold River."

"Might be a poetic fancy, neh? So named because of the silt in the river gives it a yellow color. Like the Hwang Ho, the Yellow River, in China."

"Yes. Or when the first European explorer saw it, it was gleaming in the sunlight."

"All right, then. We'll set course for Texada."

August 1634,
On the Date Maru

"Munesane."

The young samurai bowed. "Father."

Date Masamune gestured for him to take a cup of tea from a nearby tray. "Your tutors have been pleased with your progress. However, it is time to step up your education with regard to matters of statecraft, as it is surely only a few years before you must succeed me as the Lord of New Nippon."

"May the buddhas and kamis grant you a long life!"

"They already have done so. I am sixty-nine years old, nearing autumn's close. Back home, as my sixth son, you would not have had much chance of being given the opportunity to rule a *han*. Here, you do.... The question is whether you can hold it.

The old warlord inhaled the steam coming from his own cup, then took a sip. "Ah, we must enjoy this while our supply lasts. I wonder if tea can be grown in New Nippon? Well, back to my line of inquiry—what threats must you overcome?"

Munesane thought about this. "Most immediately, the *kirishitan*. They might seek to overthrow the Date family and choose a Christian ruler. The king of Spain, even."

"And how do we prevent this?"

"We have brought many of our retainers. They are trained for war, and the *kirishitan* are not. All the Christian samurai renounced Christianity, or went into exile, to Macao or Manila, many years ago. Our retainers have nothing to fear from a mob of farmers, fishermen, and craftsmen, let alone merchants."

"Hmmph... Well, leave that be for now. Who else threatens us?"

"The Indians, and the Spanish."

"Don't assume the Dutch will always be our friends. They may like what they see in New Nippon, and try to seize it for themselves."

"Thank you for pointing out my oversight, Father."

His father took another sip. "Indeed, this warms my old bones. So, how do we defend against those threats?"

"Well, as I said already, we have your retainers."

The elder Date frowned. "The encyclopedia says that there are three hundred thousand Indians in California. They aren't, of course, all in Monterey, but still we must prepare for the possibility that the settlers from the First Fleet will be heavily outnumbered. And our retainers, even more so. And one day we may face—will face—the forces in New Spain." Mexico.

His son worried his lip with his teeth before replying. "I supposed that means that we will have to teach the settlers how to defend themselves. Use the samurai as a mobile reserve."

"Exactly. Which means—coming back to the point I raised earlier—that the *kirishitan* will then no longer be unschooled in the arts of war."

"So what do we do, Father?"

"It is not so much what we do, as what *you* do. You must become a Christian, yourself."

"A Christian? Well, I suppose I can. Does that mean that all our retainers must also become Christians?"

"No, leave it to their conscience. And *I* will not convert. If I did, they would, too, and if we were all Christian, that would make it more difficult to recruit non-Christian Japanese to come to New Nippon. And I have hopes to attract more ronin here, at the very least.

"You may, of course, be approached by certain of the *kirishitan* . . . who will suggest that it is your duty as a Christian to overthrow your father—"

"I will slay them on the spot!"

"You will listen, feign ambition tempered by fear and conscience, determine the names of their fellow conspirators . . . and *then* you may execute them all."

"Thank you for this very good advice, Father."

"You're welcome. But you have yet to name the greatest threat of all."

"Forgive my slowness. The Portuguese?"

"No, no, no." The old lord lowered his voice. "The shogun himself. We have to walk a fine line. If we produce too little, then he may decide to cut off our supplies. What would we do without gunpowder and metal? According to the encyclopedia, these 'American Indians,' like the Ainu north of Nippon, only have stone weapons. Even if they ally with us, they will not be of much use against the Spanish."

"And if we produce too much of value, he may regret his bargain with you, and seek to replace us with his own clansmen."

"Exactly."

On the Ieyasu Maru

Texada Island was in the Straits of Georgia. These separated the eastern coast of the southern half of Vancouver Island from the mainland of British Columbia. If the atlas copy could be trusted, then the iron was near the middle of Texada. Haruno and Tokubei had hoped that with the help of local Indians, they would be able to find it.

When they arrived at Gillies Bay, midway along the west coast of Texada, they spotted a trio of Indians. They appeared to be watching a killer whale pod. There were at least a dozen killer whales zipping about, and one was a baby. Tokubei's interpreter identified the Indians as belonging to what an up-time anthropologist would call the Coast Salish, a rather loosely defined group of Indians speaking related lanaguages. She explained that the Coast Salish believed that a dead chief, or an ordinary tribesman that died by drowning, could be reborn as a killer whale. Perhaps, she suggested, there had recently been such a death, and the Indians were trying to determine if the baby had any markings that were reminiscent of the deceased tribesman.

Despite Tokubei's technological advantage—the telescope—the waiting Coast Salish became aware of the Ieyasu Maru almost as soon as Tokubei spotted them. Or so Tokubei interpreted the gestures they made in his direction. They nonetheless held their ground; clearly, they thought that monitoring the behavior of the orcas was worth the risk posed by the "flying canoe."

Tokubei had the launch lowered, and he, the interpreter, a miner, two samurai, and several sailors got on board and rowed obliquely toward shore, being careful to keep their distance both from the pod and the Indians. Tokubei's interpreter called out a greeting.

Like all of the slaves Tokubei had purchased from the Kwakwaka'wakw, the interpreter was a "she." Generally speaking, when the Kwakwaka'wakw attacked an enemy village, they killed the mature males and carried off the prime females. The Japanese drifters were actually lucky to have been spared. Their good fortune was perhaps attributable to them being recognizably not of any known enemy tribe, so there were no grudges to work off. It also helped that it was more prestigious to own a slave who was plainly "exotic."

Tokubei had held a big ceremony to free the slave interpreters and "adopt" them into his "tribe." He said that he expected them to respect his authority and that of Haruno, and to translate and in general help out the crew.

The crew seemed very eager to help them learn Japanese.

This particular translator was of the Snuneymuxw, who lived near modern Nanaimo on Vancouver Island. Her name was "Yells-at-Bears," and she proved to be equally effective at yelling at other Indians.

The Coast Salish made a peace sign, which Tokubei and his people mimicked. The two parties slowly sauntered toward each other, pausing now and then to scan their surroundings, until at last they were at a comfortable speaking distance.

The trio were of a different Coast Salish group, the Seshelt, and they were of the Kalpilin band, whose main village was near modern Pender Harbor. If the translations Tokubei was getting were accurate, the Seshelt, or at least the Kalpilin, did not live on Texada, but they hunted and fished there, mostly on the southern third of the island. This group had ventured farther north because they were keeping watch on that group of orca, for pretty much the reasons that Yells-at-Bears had suggested.

Yells-at-Bears was visibly pleased to meet these Coast Salish men from the other side of the Straits of Georgia—indeed, for a moment Tokubei was afraid she would abandon him—but they didn't recognize the iron ore specimens they were shown. Did that mean that there was no iron ore on the island? Just that the local material didn't look quite like these specimens, and therefore they thought they were something different? Or could there be some reason, religious perhaps, not to admit recognition? Tokubei had no idea.

Tokubei gave them some trifling gifts anyway, since he wanted to make a good impression, and signaled to the captain that they could continue on.

They couldn't measure latitude with an accuracy of better than about seventeen miles, and Texada Island was about thirty miles long. But the Indians confirmed that the Japanese were on the west coast of a big island, and from its size and general location, they knew that it must be Texada. So far, it had been heavily wooded, with a steep coast.

They had gone three or four miles beyond Gillies Bay, which appeared to be a passable anchorage, when first one of the miners, and then several others, started shouting. Tokubei spoke to them, and soon thereafter, he was running for the captain.

The miners had seen a large red stain on a hillside. Tokubei and Haruno discussed the significance of this find with Iwakashu. The ship was already sailing close-hauled, so all that was needed to heave-to was brace just the squares on the main mast over to the opposite tack. The maneuver left the hull perpendicular to the wind, drifting slowly to leeward.

A boat was lowered, and Tokubei, three samurai, Iwakashu, one of the rescued drifters, and Yells-at-Bears rowed to shore. As the samurai watched for any threat, Iwakashu scrambled up to the outcrop. He took some samples, and gingerly made his way downslope.

Iwakashu, "singer-to-rocks," was a mining engineer and prospector, and had once been a protégé of Okubo Iwami no Kami Nagayasu. Iwakashu had traveled all over Japan; mining engineers were permitted to cross all road barriers, provided they could pass an examination confirming their knowledge of ores. Iwakashu had even traveled to Hokkaido to look for gold dust in the rivers, but he had been stopped by orders of Lord Matsumae, who jealously guarded access to the land of the Ainu.

Nagayasu, a *kirishitan* actor who had overheard the shogun Tokugawa Ieyasu complain that he needed more gold, had told Ieyasu that he knew how the mines could be operated more efficiently and new mines discovered. He brought in Portuguese and Chinese experts, and succeeded in boosting gold production at

Izu. Ieyasu was impressed, and gave him more authority. When Okubo died in 1613, he was the commissioner of mines, and the collector of taxes, in Sado and Omi.

Unfortunately, Okubo had promised his concubines a large inheritance upon his death, and his heir refused to pay. The concubines appealed, and Ieyasu ordered an audit. This revealed that Okubo had committed embezzlement on a massive scale. Moreover, the auditors discovered letters that showed that Okubo was engaged in a criminal conspiracy to overthrow Ieyasu with the aid of Christian soldiers. The letters implicated Date Masamune's son-in-law, Matsudaira Tadateru, in the conspiracy. The daughter of Lord Matsudaira's chief retainer was in fact married to one of Okubo's sons, and Lord Matsudaira was suspected of Christian sympathies, so this seemed quite plausible to the shogun.

Ieyasu didn't move at the time against Lord Matsudaira, a close relative, let alone the powerful Date Masamune. However, Okubo's seven sons were executed and his fief confiscated, and Lord Matsudaira himself was placed under close surveillance.

Iwakashu had thought it wise to travel abroad for reasons of health, and Date Masamune had arranged for him to travel, under an assumed name, first to the Ryukyu Islands, and then to China. There he had studied Chinese mining technology, and had returned to Japan only after hearing of the death of Hidetada, Ieyasu's son, in 1632.

So Iwakashu owed Date Masamune a great debt of gratitude.

A debt that the lord of Sendai called in when he was named grand governor of New Nippon.

And so it was that Iwakashu had found himself crossing the Pacific to distant Texada Island.

Even before Iwakashu actually clambered back onto the deck of the *Ieyasu Maru*, Tokubei knew from Iwakashu's body language that his report would be favorable. But it would say nothing about copper or gold from Vancouver Island. What they had found was an uncommon mineral in Japan. An iron ore. He proved it when he returned to the ship, and held the ore close to the ship's compass.

As the *Ieyasu Maru* sailed back to the Gillies Bay anchorage to spend the night, Tokubei thought about the implications of Iwakashu's discovery, especially in the light of what Yells-at-Bears had told him. Texada was a perfect mining site. While the Indians visited it, there were no villages there. None that the Japanese had seen yet, at any rate. The island, at least in the northern part, was low in profile, so climbing would be minimal. Snow-capped Vancouver Island blocked the ocean winds from the west and southwest, and other islands defended Texada from the north-west wind. There were several good anchorages. The Seshelt had confirmed that it rarely snowed on Texada, and the fishing was decent. And, best of all, some of the ore was just lying loose for the taking. By the time Tokubei had finished these ruminations, it was dark.

Tokubei found the captain at the stern, eyeing the moon.

"The moon is carrying an umbrella," said Captain Haruno. He meant that it had a halo, which usually presaged rain. "I'd like to get a move on tomorrow morning, if we've accomplished our mission here."

"Well, we've found iron ore, and we can report that to the grand governor when we rendezvous with him at Monterey Bay," said Tokubei, "but... wouldn't it be wonderful if we could start a mining colony here and now?"

Captain Haruno frowned. "We were manned with exploration rather than colonization in mind. Iron ore is all well and good, but where are the farmers to feed the miners?"

Tokubei sighed. "But if we must wait until the Second Fleet comes to take the next step, it will be a long time before Texada is producing iron ore, neh?"

"I don't know see how we have a choice, Tokubei-san."

"Suppose we do this. We leave an exploration party, so that by the time the Second Fleet arrives they will be experts on this island, and its neighbors. The woman Yells-at-Bears speaks Kwak-wala and Seshelt, as well as her own language. We leave one of Heishiro's sailors with her, to translate between Kwakwala and Japanese. Plus a few miners and a couple of samurai. Isamu and Masaru, perhaps. Give them a longboat, fishing and mining gear, and trade goods. They can survey Texada in detail; look for more outcrops of ore, and find out where the land can be cultivated, where the fishing and hunting are good, and so forth."

"And that way, when the Second Fleet ship comes, its colonists won't have to start from scratch," mused Haruno.

"Exactly."

"The participation of Yells-at-Bears and at least one of the castaways is critical. Find out if they are agreeable. And then ask Heishiro, Yoritaki and Iwakashu what they think of the idea."

Yells-at-Bears was more than agreeable. She had been resigned to the prospect of sailing away from her homeland, with the Japanese who had bought and freed her, but this was much better. She suggested that the Japanese could spend the winter with her own people. Or perhaps with her sister's people; she had married a Seshelt.

Isamu was standing next to Yoritaki when Tokubei put the question to the samurai commander, and as soon as Yoritaki gave his assent, Isamu volunteered to lead the little Texada samurai contingent. This might have been out of eagerness to impress Yoritaki, but Tokubei suspected it had something to do with Yells-at-Bears' involvement. They had been surreptitiously eyeing each other for several days now.

Heishiro's crewmen were less enthusiastic—they wanted to be repatriated to Japan as quickly as possible—but Tokubei told them bluntly that they should expect to be in California for at least a year, until they had taught Kwak'wala, and any other native language they knew, to selected colonists. After they absorbed this bit of bad news, he assured them that they would undoubtedly be rewarded for each language they passed on. He then spoke to each of them privately, and eventually found the right lure to keep one of them on Texada.

Tokubei lowered the telescope. They had left Gillies Bay, and Isamu's party, behind them. The latter had drawn up and secured their boat, and found a path up from the beach. They had quickly passed out of sight, and Tokubei hoped that they would be all right. His report would direct the future colonists to Gillies Bay; it would be easy to find, as at the northern point, there was an unusual white patch, two spots like a pair of plum blossoms. There was nothing like it anywhere else along the western coast of Texada.

"Tokubei-san." Yoshitaki had come up behind him.

The mariner started. He hadn't seen or heard the big samurai's approach.

"It's a great thing you've begun here," said Yoshitaki. "The grand governor will certainly reward you." He paused. "If it were up to me, I'd say you should start thinking about what might be a nice surname for your house." A surname ... the sign of samurai status.

Late August 1634,
Oregon Coast

"Where have you been?" demanded Standing-on-Robe, of the Alsea Indians. "You should have been home before the sun stopped climbing the sky!"

His son, Little Otter, was not especially abashed. "I was by the beach, gathering clams, as you told me to, when I saw a white cloud on the horizon."

"A white cloud? How amazing!" said his older brother.

"Stay out of this," said Standing-on-Robe.

"The white cloud was moving straight toward me, not with the other clouds. Then it split into many clouds. The clouds came closer together, and I saw that they were hovering over a forest of pine trees, that in turn were planted on the backs of great whales.

"So I ran and hid in the forest. I waited there a few hours, and then circled back here."

Little Otter was, perhaps, fortunate that his people didn't believe in corporal punishment of children for lying. Even though he wasn't.

The First Fleet had made landfall in Alsea Bay, on the coast of Oregon. Armed parties landed first, to set up a defensive perimeter, and then the passengers were given the chance to come ashore, stand, however unsteadily, on dry land, and to collect fresh water and food.

The Alsea Indians noted the great numbers of the intruders, and decided it was prudent to move upriver. Naturally, they left a few scouts to keep an eye on the Japanese.

One of these was Standing-on-Robe. Little Otter was given strict instructions to stay with his mother. Naturally, he slipped out after the scouts as soon as he saw the opportunity. As he made his way downriver, he saw something truly, truly shocking.

When Standing-on-Robe returned, he found Little Otter telling his friends just how ghastly the visitors were.

"Most of them look like men, but they are ruled by some kind of giant beetle. The beetles had eight legs—"

"Beetles have six legs," said his older brother. "That's it."

"Well, these had eight legs, like a spider, but were armored like a beetle. Anyway, they moved on just four of the legs, but they could run faster than any man. And they had a long sting in front."

"Oh, you're just making this up."

"Am not."

"You couldn't have seen it, you were confined to camp."

"I sneaked out."

"Wait until I tell Father."

Standing-on-Robe sent him to bed without supper. But the punishment was for sneaking out, not lying. By then, Standing-on-Robe, too, had seen what a samurai on horseback, carrying a lance, looked like.

Yamaguchi Takuma placed a white cloth on Munesane's forehead, and put salt, an ancient symbol of wisdom, in his mouth. Then Yamaguchi picked up the pitcher and began to pour.

Water dripped down Munesane's eyebrows as Yamaguchi baptized him with the waters of North America. Every *kirishitan* had to know how to administer baptism, but Yamaguchi was a *mizukata*, the elected baptizer of his group of hidden Christians. The honor of baptizing Munesane had first been offered to Imamura Yajiro, but he had declined and suggested Yamaguchi do it instead.

As Yamaguchi poured, he chanted, "I baptize you 'David,' in the name of the Father, the Son, and the Holy Ghost. Amen."

Yajiro had witnessed many baptisms before, but this one was different. This one, Yajiro knew, could not fail to have an impact on history. Date Munesane—'David Date,' Yajiro corrected himself—was the heir apparent to the province of New Nippon. When, as they no doubt would eventually, the Spanish discovered the Japanese settlement in Monterey, they would discover that it was a Christian kingdom. This wouldn't stop them from attacking it, but it would give them pause. And the delay would allow the Japanese to entrench themselves.

It was because of the political significance of the baptism that he had refused to administer the sacrament. What would happen if his secret—that he was a *bakufu* spy—was revealed? He couldn't risk undermining the religious foundation of David Date's legitimacy as a Christian ruler.

Yajiro's thoughts turned to the conflict between Christianity and Buddhism. Not for the first time, he wondered why Christians were so, so exclusivist, in their teachings. Buddhism, like Christianity, was a foreign religion, and yet it had made its peace with the Shinto priests. The Shinto kami, it judged, were manifestations of the buddhas.

The use of water for ritual purification was hardly unique to Christianity. In the *misogi* ritual, the *shugendo*, the mountain ascetics, would stand under a cold waterfall, before communing with the kami. And the Tendai Buddhists practiced *kanjo*, the sprinkling of water on the head as part of the ordination of a monk.

Yajiro couldn't help but wonder whether it was possible to reconcile Christanity with Buddhism, even as Buddhism and Shintoism had been reconciled.

"David Date," as he would now be known, boarded Yamaguchi's ship. Since Yamaguchi didn't have a cabin of his own, the captain lent him his own for the final ceremony. David made confession, and Yamaguchi gave him wheat *mochi* and grape wine. Then he made the sign of the cross on David's forehead, anointed him with oil, and slapped him on the right cheek. Date Munesane was now a *kirishitan*.

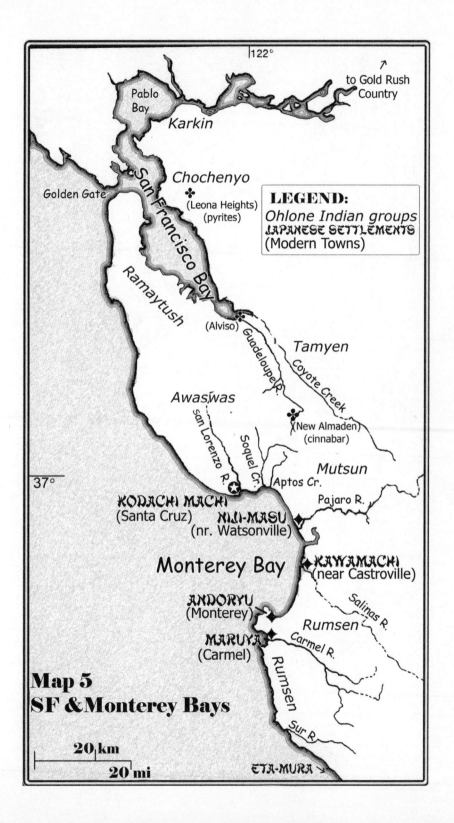

122°

to Gold Rush
Country

Pablo
Bay

Karkin

Chochenyo

Golden Gate

❀
(Leona Heights)
(pyrites)

San Francisco Bay

LEGEND:
Ohlone Indian groups
𝕁𝔸ℙ𝔸ℕ𝔼𝕊𝔼 𝕊𝔼𝕋𝕋𝕃𝔼𝕄𝔼ℕ𝕋𝕊
(Modern Towns)

Ramaytush

(Alviso)

Tamyen

Guadeloupe R.

Coyote Creek

Awaswas

San Lorenzo R.

Soquel Cr.

❀(New Almaden)
(cinnabar)

Mutsun

37°

Aptos Cr.

Pajaro R.

⭐

KODACHI MACHI
(Santa Cruz)

NIJI-MASU
(nr. Watsonville)

◆

Monterey Bay

◆ KAWAMACHI
(near Castroville)

ANDORYU
(Monterey)

◆

Salinas R.

Rumsen

MARUYA
(Carmel)

◆

Carmel R.

Rumsen

**Map 5
SF &Monterey Bays**

Sur R.

20 km

20 mi

ETA-MURA

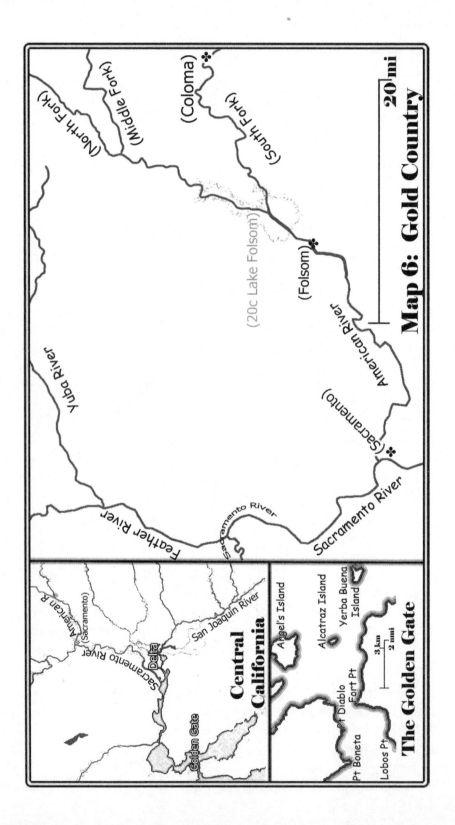

Map 6: Gold Country

20 mi

(North Fork)

(Middle Fork)

(Coloma)

(South Fork)

(20c Lake Folsom)

(Folsom)

American River

Yuba River

(Sacramento)

Sacramento River

Feather River

Sacramento River

Central California

American R

(Sacramento)

Sacramento River

San Joaquin River

Delta

Golden Gate

The Golden Gate

Angel's Island

Alcatraz Island

Yerba Buena Island

Pt Diablo

Fort Pt

Pt Boneta

Lobos Pt

3 km
2 nmi

Wild Geese

September 1634 to Fall 1635

A line of calligraphy:
wild geese above the foothills—
and a red moon for the seal.
—Taniguchi Buson (1716–1783)[3]

Early September 1634

Like a dog waiting impatiently for scraps from the master's table, Lord Matsudaira Tadateru's ship, the *Sado Maru*, marked time in central California waters, waiting for the heavy fog that blanketed the coast to dissipate.

For the moment, Tadateru had company in his misery. The First Fleet, carrying the first wave of Japanese Christians to California, had passed between Point Reyes and the Farralones, and descended to a little below thirty-eight degrees north. It then headed east, hoping to at least catch a glimpse of the Golden Gate, the narrow opening to San Francisco Bay. Lord Matsudaira

---

3   Translation by Robert Sund, from *Poems from Ish River Country, Selected Poems and Translations,* by Robert Sund, published by Shoemaker & Hoard, copyright © 2004 by Poet's House Trust and used by permission of the Trust.

Tadateru expected to do more than that; he thought of it as his gateway to restored honor and fortune.

The weather, however, had been disappointing. For several days, the First Fleet had languished in the waters between the Farallones and the presumed location of the Golden Gate, without ever sighting the latter. The east was a featureless gray mass.

Tadateru reached up and, self-consciously, fingered his topknot, one of the marks of his samurai status. When he was disgraced and forced to become a Buddhist monk, his old one had been cut off and thrown onto a fire. When Tadateru accepted the shogun's invitation to sail for the Golden Gate, and seek out the gold fields of California, he was given permission to grow it back. The shortness of his topknot was indicative of how recently he had been rehabilitated.

While Tadateru insisted on being addressed as "Lord Matsudaira," he was unpleasantly aware of the emptiness of the title. He had been "provisionally" awarded a ten-thousand-*koku* fief, the minimum for daimyo status. However, the fief had been depopulated when its Christians came out of hiding and accepted exile to America. Hence, at least in the short term, it was virtually worthless.

It was quite a come down for a man who had once held a fief that annually produced over four hundred fifty thousand *koku*.

But it was better than being a monk. And at least his wife, Iroha-hime, was with him once more.

Belowdecks, in Iroha's cabin, the floor was covered with clamshells. One hundred and eighty pairs take up a fair amount of room.

Iroha, sitting *seiza* style—buttocks on heels, knees together—had her eyes half-closed. She opened them, reached forward, and turned over two of the shells, a left and a right. Her action revealed that the insides of both were painted with the same image: Prince Genji visiting the holy man in his cave.

"*Awase!*" she called out. Match!

Iroha and her maid Koya were playing *Kai-awase*, a game centuries old. The set had been part of her trousseau.

Iroha put the matched pair in her pile. It was much larger than Koya's.

"I think you never forget a shell, Iroha-hime," Koya said ruefully.

"Winning is all about remembering. And I don't like to lose," said Iroha. "Your turn."

Koya gave her a sly look. "Do you think the real Prince Genji looked much like his picture, mistress?"

"Oh, yes. Almost as handsome as my husband."

Iroha was just two years younger than Tadateru. Their marriage was, of course, political. Tadateru was the sixth son of Tokugawa Ieyasu, the then-ruler of Japan, and Iroha the eldest daughter of Date Masamune, one of the most powerful daimyo, who had sworn allegiance to Ieyasu after the Battle of Sekigahara in 1600.

Iroha smiled as she remembered how, shortly before their wedding, Tadateru had shyly handed her a letter, which she had tucked into a fold of her kimono, and opened as soon as she had a moment's privacy.

It read: "My esteemed father has written, 'patience is the source of eternal peace, treat anger as an enemy.' Unfortunately, my temper is easily aroused, and this has gotten me into trouble on several occasions. I can assure you that my anger is usually a fleeting thing and I am almost always sorry afterward.

"I promise not to scold you without just cause. If I violate this promise, please show me this letter."

Iroha still had the letter, despite all that had happened since. During the years of their marriage, he did get angry with her from time to time—once he had even thrown a sake cup at her—but he had always apologized. Sometimes just minutes later.

In 1612, she and her husband had met Luis Sotelo, the Franciscan, who was then living in Sendai under her father's protection. Christianity had already been banned in the Tokugawa domains, but not in the rest of Japan. He had secretly converted them both to the Catholic faith. This forged another bond between them.

All was well until the spring of 1615, when Tadateru was summoned to lead his troops to war, the final struggle between the Tokugawa and the Toyotomi for control of Japan.

She shuddered involuntarily, as she remembered what followed.

"Iroha-hime, are you all right?" Koya said anxiously.

"So, sorry, Koya, I am tired all of a sudden. I think I will rest now. Please put the game away."

At last, Date Masamune, the grand governor of "New Nippon," decided that the First Fleet couldn't linger any longer; it would have to leave Lord Matsudaira Tadateru, and the "Golden Gate," behind. Iroha came to Masamune's flagship to say goodbye.

As he watched her boat approach, Date Masamune brooded over her future. As a wedding gift, the shogun had given Tadateru the rich fief of Takada. But then he had squandered his good fortune by acting quite imprudently. In 1613, he was implicated in the Okubo conspiracy, to overthrow the shogun with Christian assistance. In 1615, during the summer campaign against the Toyotomi, he permitted Sanada Yokimura to retreat into Osaka Castle. The final straw was when he refused to join his older brother Hidetada on a visit to the imperial palace, pleading illness, and went hunting instead.

Tadateru had been forced to shave his head and become a Buddhist monk, exiled to the monastery at Kodasan. He had, under orders, divorced his wife Iroha. Rather than become a Buddhist nun, or commit *jigai*—cutting her own throat—she had endured the ultimate embarrassment for a woman of the samurai class: returning to her father's home. And she had refused to even consider the possibility of remarriage.

Iroha had been overjoyed to hear of Tadateru's "rehabilitation," however provisional, and eagerly agreed to join him for the journey to the New World, even though they had not lived as husband and wife for nearly two decades. They had set sail for California less than a month after their reunion.

Date Masamune respected Iroha's sense of duty. But he couldn't help but think that her obligations to Tadateru were severed long ago, and were best left that way. Was he coming to the New World so that he and Iroha could enjoy life together? So that they could worship the Christian God?

No! Lord Matsudaira was here to restore his honor. That was fine...commendable...for him. But it was doubtful, very doubtful, that he saw Iroha's presence as more than evidence that his shame was finally expiated.

Date Masamune resolved to make one more attempt to dissuade her from continuing on a course that he was sure would lead to more suffering.

Fathers have duties, too.

"Iroha-chan, life will be difficult enough for you in a colony of several thousand Nihonjin." Date Masamune grimaced. "But assuming that Tadateru finds this Golden Gate, and enters San Francisco Bay, to remain in his company you will eventually have to trust yourself to a small boat making its way up the American River. You and your maid would be the only women on board, and you wouldn't have private quarters. Even in the captain's launch, his largest boat."

"I am prepared for the... inconvenience."

"It is not mere inconvenience that you face. Please, Daughter, look here." He gestured at a map that was fastened to the wall of his cabin. "You will be traveling through San Francisco Bay, San Pablo Bay, the Carquinez Strait, and Suisun Bay, just to reach the Delta where the Sacramento and San Joaquin rivers meet. Then you must go about seventy miles upriver to the vicinity of the up-time town of Sacramento, and look for the mouth of the American River.

"And then Tadateru has no clear idea where to go! The river labeled as the American River is this one." Her father pointed to the North Fork of the American. "But the encyclopedia said that Sutter's mill, where the gold was found, was at Coloma." His finger moved down two rivers, to the South Fork of the American. "Which is the unnamed river over here.

"And if that isn't bad enough, the economic map in that same encyclopedia says that the nearest gold and silver is up here." Masamune pointed to the California-Nevada border, near Reno. "In the high mountains."

"Neither Tadateru nor any of his companions have any knowledge of the rivers, or of the savages that live on their banks. And none of you has experience in looking for gold, so it may be many months, or even years, before he finds what he is looking for."

"My husband was given miners from Sado to help him." Sado was the fabulous Japanese gold and silver mine that had been discovered in 1601.

"My advisers tell me that the gold of Sado is in hard rock, in quartz veins, while the Sutter's Mill gold is probably *kawakin*." Placer gold, the gold found in rivers and streams. "The encyclopedia says that it was found in a river, while building a sawmill. And those miners from Sado were extracting ore from a known vein, not looking for gold in the wilderness."

"It doesn't matter. I am his wife and it is my duty to follow him," said Iroha.

"He did not take you with him to war, when he marched to Osaka, and neither should he take you with him on this chancy voyage of exploration."

"If it is chancy," Iroha said, "then that is all the more reason for me to come with him, as it may be my last chance on earth to see him."

Masamune's lips tightened. "If he truly cared for your well-being he would order you to remain with me."

"It is because he cares for me so much that he permits me to come. And he knows that I do not care to live if he is dead."

Masamune studied her expression. His own became stern. He was prepared to cause her a little pain now, if it would save her great hardship later. "You are not his wife. You were divorced by orders of the shogun."

Iroha fought back tears, and Masamune in turn fought to remain impassive. She retorted, "The shogun had no power to divorce us. We were secretly baptized, and as secretly given the sacrament of matrimony according to the Holy Catholic Church."

Masamune had long suspected this. Why else would she not have committed suicide? But in the Japan of Hidetada and Iemitsu, he had not dared to ask her, even in private. *Walls have ears, and stones tell tales*, his grandmother had told him.

"The shogun could break the bond formed by the public ceremony, the Buddhist one," Iroha admitted. "But not the Christian one. We were not, we are not, divorced in the eyes of God, or in our hearts.

"Please, Father. When you gave him my hand in marriage, it became my duty under Japanese law to follow him, even if it meant disobeying you. But while I do not need your permission to go, I would like your blessing."

"A blessing from a pagan?"

Iroha smiled faintly.

Masamune smiled briefly in turn. "I do not know whether you are in fact his wife, but you are most certainly my daughter. Stubbornness is what our family is known for. Yes, you have my blessing."

"Thank you, Father. And I have a long day ahead of me, so please have me returned to my ship. And to my husband."

Despite her brave words, Iroha was worried. She and Tadateru had lived apart for longer than they had lived together. At their reunion, Tadateru had been ebullient. But in the days that followed, as they made their preparations for departure, and then in the long sea voyage, she had caught unsettling glimpses of changes in him. The moments of happiness were fewer and shorter; those of anger or despair were more common and longer, than in the days before the siege of Osaka. Clearly, his long exile had darkened his soul. He seemed more, more—she searched for the word. Brittle.

Had it been up to her, they would just have declared themselves to be Christian, and accepted exile to New Nippon. Made a new life there, one free of the demands of rank.

But Tadateru had refused. For him, he said, it would just be another kind of exile. It would not erase the stain on his honor. Only his discovery of the gold fields, and his appointment as, oh, "Daimyo of Sacramento-han," would do that.

Iroha had accepted his decision, of course. Her tutors had drummed into her, "be loyal to your husband, be brave in defense of his honor."

But she worried that his decision might have repercussions, not just for her and Tadateru, but for her family. Her father had told her earlier in the voyage, "Iemitsu could have ordered *me* to go to San Francisco Bay. Or sent a faithful Tokugawa retainer. Why send Tadateru?" The likeliest explanation, in his opinion, was founded on Tadateru having one foot in the Tokugawa family, by blood, and the other amidst the Date, by marriage—the latter association being renewed now that Iroha had returned to him. Her father had concluded, "Clearly, if Tadateru succeeded, it would be proclaimed a Tokugawa success. And if he failed, it would be portrayed as a Date failure."

Imachizuki, the Sleeping and Waiting Moon (Three Days After Full)

One day, at last, in the mid-afternoon, the fog began to lift, but there was no sign of any break in the coastline. The Japanese didn't realize it, but the outline of the Berkeley Hills, on the opposite side of the Bay, and of Angel Island, merged into those of the northern and southern headlands framing the Golden Gate, thus concealing the presence of the Bay.

"May the makers of the American encyclopedia burn in Avichi, the lowest of the Hells, if they misdrew this San Francisco Bay," Lord Matsudaira shouted, at no one in particular. The captain nodded in polite agreement.

Still, Lord Matsudaira had come too far to just give up. He ordered the captain to trust to the up-time map, and the captain's latitude calculations, and take the ship closer to shore. The fog vanished, but it was not until they were perhaps six miles from the Golden Gate that they could see the water between the headlands.

"That's it?" asked Lord Matsudaira.

"It must be," said the captain.

"I thought it was a bay large enough to hold all the ships in the world. I can barely see any water at all."

"It's like the gate of a castle, my lord," said Daidoji Shigehisa, Lord Matsudaira's lieutenant. He had been masterless, a ronin, during Lord Matsudaira's exile, but had returned to his service when Lord Matsudaira accepted Iemitsu's offer and was given permission to recruit warriors. "We can only see a bit of the courtyard now."

The captain inclined his head. "If you're in doubt, Lord Matsudaira, we can zigzag a bit, so you can see more of the bay."

Lord Matsudaira thought about this for a moment, then shook his head. "No, take us straight in, before the damned fog returns."

The captain ordered the *Sado Maru* forward, but under courses, its lower sails, only. The Japanese sailors, accustomed to the battened sail of the Asian junk, had taken several weeks to learn how to set and unset the European style sails of the Dutch-designed *Sado Maru*, but after crossing the Pacific with them, it had become second nature.

Leadsmen called out the soundings as they inched forward. Almost immediately, they reported that the water was rapidly getting shallower. They were clearly coming over some kind of shoal.

"Can't we go faster, Captain?"

"We can, but we don't know this harbor at all. If we go too fast, we could find ourselves run aground on rocks. We have to go slowly enough so that if the bottom reaches up for us, we can steer clear."

"I suppose you know your own business," said Lord Matsudaira. His tone suggested that he was still reserving judgment, even though the captain had gotten them across the Pacific.

The shallowest parts of the shoal were revealed by the breaking of the waves, and the ship picked out a safe path. It was slow-going, however, and Lord Matsudaira was practically dancing with impatience by the time they made it into deeper water beyond.

The ship was now feeling the beginning of the ebb tide. Under gravitational orders from the moon and sun, over half a trillion gallons of water were streaming out of San Francisco Bay, and on the double. Their only way out was through the Golden Gate, barely a mile wide.

As the *Sado Maru* approached the Golden Gate, the wind continued to fall off, while the ebb tide became even more energetic, running perhaps five knots. Whereas before the *Sado Maru* was deliberately creeping forward, so it could avoid any dangerous rocks, now it was fighting for every yard made good, even though it had raised its topsails to capture more wind.

"Is it my imagination or are we fucking moving backward?" snapped Lord Matsudaira.

"I am sorry, my lord, the outgoing current is very strong. But I am sure it will abate in an hour or two."

"Do you notice how low the sun is in the sky? By that time it will have set."

The captain quickly glanced west. "Yes, you're right, my lord. We need the light in order to see our way clear of hazard, so I recommend we turn around now, and try again tomorrow."

Lord Matsudaira glared at him. "Turn back now? After we have waited a week—a week—for the fog to lift? And with the Golden Gate almost in our grasp? I'll have your head." The hilt of his katana, visible above the line of his shoulder, reminded the captain that this was not an idle threat. "Can you guarantee that the fog won't be back tomorrow?"

"It's a pity, I'm really very sorry—"

Lord Matsudaira pressed him further. "Can this tub go any faster? So we can get into the bay before sunset?"

"We can add bonnet and drabbler to the courses, to catch more wind." This was European terminology; courses were the lowest sails, and bonnets and drabblers were extra pieces of canvas that were laced onto them. "But the ship will be harder to control, and the channel looks dangerous.... Rocks on either side of us..."

Lord Matsudaira interrupted the captain's warnings: "Those who cling to life, die, and those who defy death, live." He was quoting the daimyo Uesugi Kenshin, the "Dragon of Echigo," who had died, in bed, almost half a century earlier. "Full speed ahead, and damn the rocks! Keep your eyes forward!"

The captain ordered that the extra canvas be added. And added a quick prayer, barely audible, to Kwannon the Merciful. The *Sado Maru* picked up a little speed, and Lord Matsudaira noted this with a smile of approval. The Golden Gate proper, the narrowest part of the strait, was getting ever nearer.

Offshore, the swells, like the wind, had come from the northwest. However, as they passed Point Boneta, the inshore edge was slowed by the shallows, causing the waves to sweep around and approach the Golden Gate from the west.

As the tide swept outward, it collided with the wind-driven waves heading eastward, the two crashing together like great armies meeting on some battlefield. The incoming waves were squeezed together and steepened. The *Sado Maru* bucked, like a horse trying to unseat its rider.

The helmsman of the *Sado Maru* stood on the quarterdeck, his hands on the whipstaff and his eyes on the compass. The whipstaff, a European innovation, was a long lever, hitched belowdecks to the tiller, so that the helmsman on a large ship could steer and also see where the ship was going. Or at least see the feet of the sails. The whipstaff could only move the tiller a little bit and some steering had to be done by appropriately setting the sails.

The whipstaff vibrated violently. "Someone, help me!" cried the helmsman. Another sailor ran over, and grabbed the whipstaff from the other side. Together, they brought the rudder under control. But only for a time.

The seas were at their most vigorous and confused in the narrow throat of the Gate, between Lime Point and Fort Point. It was there that the first disaster struck. They were heading east-northeast, and they buried their bow into the wave before them. The sails were braced to take best advantage of the northwest wind, and that meant that the wind not only pushed the ship forward, it also tried to force it leeward. This side force was normally resisted by the keel. With the bow buried, the resistance was greater forward than aft, and the stern surfed, pivoting the ship around to face northeast. The wind was now striking the sails more obliquely, enough to shiver the sails but not fill them. The ship was rapidly losing headway, and that in turn was making it more difficult to steer.

"All hands to braces!" the captain yelled. The braces were the lines that turned the yards, the horizontal spars that carried the sails. "Slack Windward Brace and Sheet! Haul Lee Brace and Sheet! Make All!" The captain was trying to regain control of the ship, by turning the yards to face the wind more directly.

But the Sea Hag of the Golden Gate still had the *Sado Maru* in its talons. Like a cat batting a mouse to-and-fro for its amusement, the waves buffeted the ship, which the swerve had left at a forty-five-degree angle to the waves. When the bow was on a crest and the stern in a trough, the ship turned to port. When the crest came amidships, it turned back to starboard. The first movement was stronger, so the ship progressively turned more and more counterclockwise. This brought the bow closer and closer to the wind.

Like a piece of driftwood, the ship gradually turned until its keel was parallel to the incoming waves. With its bow pointed northward, it was too close to the wind for the sails, even with the yards turned as far as the standing rigging would allow, to be effectual.

The waves were now violently rocking the *Sado Maru*. Belowdecks, Iroha-hime's maid, Koya, was whimpering in terror.

Iroha-hime wrapped her arms around her. "Easy, Koya. Don't be afraid. Join me, we will pray to Deusu." Koya nodded, tears streaking her face. "Repeat after me. Eternal and Almighty God, creator of the heavens, the earth and the sea, have mercy upon us. Be our Pilot in this, our time of need. Subdue the waves and the winds..."

They finished the prayer that Iroha-hime had composed. "Feel better, Koya?"

She nodded. At that moment they were thrown by a sudden movement against the side of their cabin.

When they recovered their footing. Iroha pointed upward. "Come with me." She didn't explain, but she had decided that if she were to die, she would rather be flung off the deck, than drowned like a rat in the darkness below.

When they came above, the second mate saw them. He hurried over, cursing, and quickly had them sit down on the deck. "It will be wetter, but you are less likely to be washed away." He lashed them to a deck projection, but left their hands free so they could hold on as well. "Do you have knives?" he asked.

Iroha nodded.

"Good. Then you can cut yourself free if you must. I must get back to my men."

The next big wave broke over the *Sado Maru*'s beam, and tilted the ship to port until its deck was nearly vertical. The men on deck screamed and grabbed for whatever hold they could.

With an awful cracking sound, much of the port bulwark was carried away by the weight of the water. And several sailors, who had grabbed it for safety, were carried away with it, howling in terror as they tumbled into the churning sea.

However, the loss of the bulwark allowed the water on deck to escape, and the ship ever so slowly righted itself. But not back to an upright position; it had a pronounced list to port. The helmsman fought to bring the ship back to a safer heading, without success; the tilt kept the rudder from biting properly, and the loss of forward movement meant that the rudder, even if fully immersed, couldn't turn the ship.

"Why are we still leaning?" Lord Matsudaira yelled to whoever could and would answer.

"Cargo or ballast shifted," one of the sailors called out. "Need to throw the deck cargo overboard, or—"

He didn't get to finish his explanation. Another wave struck the broached ship and hammered it back onto its side. The rest of the port bulwark vanished, along with Lord Matsudaira's informant. The heel-over was more pronounced, this time. The violent movements had parted some of the standing rigging, and as a result the affected masts were apt to fail if the ship were righted, and its sails exposed to the wind, without first replacing the missing lines.

The men still alive were hanging from the starboard bulwark, or from the base of a mast, or some chance protrusion from the deck. They were in no position to fiddle with the rigging or the cargo at this point.

The *Sado Maru* was well within the grip of the tidal current, which was still running west south-west, if not as rapidly as before, carrying it away from the Golden Gate and toward the open sea. However, the wind was also pressing on the great exposed part of the hull, pushing the hulk southeast. This first took the *Sado Maru* out of the strongest part of the tidal current, and then into an eddy that carried it in a counter-clockwise arc until it was heading east. At last, it ran aground on Baker Beach between Mile Rocks and Fort Point, dismasting itself in the process.

Soon thereafter, the moon, a few days past full, rose above

the Berkeley Hills and glinted down at the exhausted survivors. They had mustered barely enough energy to crawl above the high-water mark.

In the morning sun, the *Sado Maru* lay in uneasy repose between the high and low water marks. It was completely dismasted, and, driven against the rocks at the shoreline, there were great gashes across its bottom, like the claw marks of some prehistoric sea monster. Fortunately, those same rocks pinned it in the shallows, and it couldn't sink farther than it already had. Until, at least, the waves broke it completely to pieces.

"So how soon will you have her afloat?" Lord Matsudaira asked the captain.

The captain stood gape-jawed. He finally managed to say, "Afloat? Even with a shipyard close at hand, it would be difficult to make her seaworthy again. Here in the wilderness, it's impossible."

"I will not accept defeat," Lord Matsudaira announced flatly. "If you cannot get me to the other shore, I will appoint a captain who will."

Guard Commander Shigehisa coughed. "Milord, can we not walk around the Bay?"

"Let me see our maps." The maps, fortunately, had been rolled up inside bamboo tubes, plugged at both ends with tar, and thus were still dry.

Lord Matsudaira laid a string as best he could around the outline of the South Bay, then compared it to the scale. "I make it out to be a hundred miles. We will have only the provisions that we can carry, so we will have to hunt or fish periodically. On foot, we might make five miles a day. Certainly not more than ten. And we will encounter Indians along the way that we would avoid if we went by water."

Shigehisa was also looking at the map. "It's a pity; the northern route is shorter. By as much as two-thirds."

Lord Matsudaira's laugh was abrupt and bitter, a bark. "But we would have to cross the furious waters of the Golden Gate to get there."

The captain had also been studying the map. "Lord Matsudaira, two of the ship's boats survived the shipwreck, so perhaps we can row across. We can look on the bay side of this peninsula for a safe launching spot." He traced a path with his forefinger.

"Here—between the map's 'San Francisco' and its 'Oakland'—the crossing is less than three miles. Closer to two, in fact. Even rowing we could do it in an hour. And there's this Yerba Buena Island here, at the halfway point, if we run into trouble."

Lord Matsudaira raised his eyebrows. "Won't the Bay be too dangerous for small boats? Look what it did to the *Sado Maru*."

"The ebb current was very strong in the Golden Gate, because there was so much water rushing through so narrow an opening. The San Francisco-Oakland gap is perhaps three times as wide, and only the waters of the South Bay will ebb through it. Anyway, we can observe the tides for several days and launch when the waters are slack."

Lord Matsudaira rolled up the map, and placed it back in its storage cylinder. "So. We have two choices. Start walking, but if we do, we must walk the whole way, mining gear and all. Or trust ourselves to the water once again."

"Yes, my lord."

Lord Matsudaira turned to his lieutenant. "Do you have a recommendation?"

"My lord, I do. Let us remember that it does us no good to reach the gold fields, and dig up a bag full of nuggets, if we cannot bring word of our victory back to the shogun. For that we need a ship that can cross the Pacific, and I doubt that this boat the captain has in mind will do. Will it?" The captain waved his hand in front of his face, a sign of negation.

"What I propose is that we send a party overland to Monterey—"

"Enough! I will not go begging to my father-in-law to come and rescue me. That would be a most ignominious end to this adventure; I would sooner commit seppuku here and now!"

The lieutenant kowtowed. "Forgive me for being unclear. I meant that we should split our forces. The miners should be sent by water to the gold fields, as the boat will make it easier to transport the equipment there and the gold back. In the meantime, a land party should be sent to the colony at Monterey, to demand that a new ship be put at your disposal. Didn't your nephew, the shogun, decree that the grand governor was to give you his full cooperation? You are not begging, you are merely receiving your due."

"Well." Lord Matsudaira paused. "Since you put it that way.... Yes, that's reasonable. It will save time if the new ship can be summoned while the miners are en route. How long do you think it will take for the land party to reach Monterey?"

Shigehisa shrugged. "A month? Two months? Three?"

"My lord," said the captain, "we need to act quickly if we are to salvage as much of the ship's cargo and timber as we can."

"Yes, yes, proceed." The captain hurried off to give orders to the remaining sailors, and Shigehisa summoned the samurai to help with the task.

Lord Matsudaira watched them go. He then went looking for his wife.

"Iroha-hime, we must talk."

Iroha and Koya were above the high water mark, collecting wood that was dry enough to burn for the campfires. Some distance above them, two samurai stood guard. So far, no native had been sighted.

"Of course, Husband. How are you feeling? Have you rested at all?"

"My feelings are what you might expect, and I will rest when there is time to do so. Leave us, Koya." The maid hurried downslope.

"Our party is splitting up. Some to go north to seek out the gold for the shogun, and my true redemption, and some to go south, to Monterey.

"When I invited you to join me on this voyage, I thought that you would have the comforts, albeit limited, of our ship at least until we reached the mouth of the Sacramento, and most likely to where it meets the American River. But now we have no ship, and our largest boat was crushed beyond repair by a falling spar.

"All that the party going to the gold field will have are two small boats. Not even a captain's launch. There will be no privacy worth mentioning. It is unthinkable for me to permit a woman of your station to travel that way—and my promise to the shogun requires me to lead the party going upriver."

"But...But Tadateru... We were separated so long. Are we to be forced apart again? Surely, we have sailcloth to spare; a curtain can be rigged to give Koya and myself what little privacy we need."

"Privacy is not the only issue..." He closed his eyes for a moment. "I am well aware that your father considers my mission to be a challenge to his own authority in New Nippon. I am not confident that your father will send a ship to aid us if you are not present to insist he does. So you must go to Monterey."

Iroha stood in silence, head downcast. "If I must..."

"Iroha-hime, I know I have not always chosen wisely. But a man does not find a place in history by being cautious.

"The wind and wave were not mine to command, and so matters cannot be as either of us would have liked. As your husband, and the commander of this expedition, I could insist you go, but I prefer that you go willingly."

"I will go. Not willingly, but the padres have taught us that some things are destined to be."

Iroha waited until Matsuoka Nagatoki was alone. "Matsuoka-san, may we speak in private, please?"

Iroha had two personal guardsmen; Nagatoki was the older of the two, and thirty years her senior. Seventy years old, he was a veteran of the Wars of Unification. His family had long served the Date clan. When Iroha married Matsudaira Tadateru, he joined that lord's service. And when Tadateru was disgraced, Nagatoki returned to Date Masamune. He on board the *Sado Maru* by Date Masamune's command.

"I am just a poor woman, unschooled in matters of command, but I wonder how, without any beasts of burden, we are to carry all that we will need to reach Monterey safely. Food, water, clothing, weapons, ammunition, and many things I am sure I have not thought of."

Nagatoki glanced quickly at the dismembered carcass of the *Sado Maru*, then met her gaze. "I do wish we had horses aboard, it would make everything much easier now. But in a ship as small as the *Sado Maru*, it was not possible. And we'd probably have lost them in the shipwreck, anyway.

"Fortunately, this seems to be a bountiful land, and it is not yet winter. With weapons, we can catch fish, and birds, and beasts. And thanks to the advice of our Dutch friends, we have glass beads. They are light and small, and can be traded to the Indians for food.

"But I confess that I am worried about how you and your maid will fare on the journey that faces us. I think we should find a place near here to set up a permanent camp, and just send messengers to Monterey. Perhaps a samurai and a sailor by the coastal route, and two samurai inland."

Iroha's eyes widened slightly. "But that would mean splitting our forces further, when we are already weak!"

"Ah, Iroha-hime, you are truly your father's daughter. Your husband has assigned four of his samurai to stay with us, for your protection; that brings our core fighting force to six. Sending out the messengers would cut our samurai contingent in half. But what else is to be done?"

Iroha brushed back an errant strand of hair. "You know, when I was first married, Lord Matsudaira was named the daimyo of Takada, in Echigo. From time to time, we would visit Niigata, the home of our neighors to the north, the Mizoguchi clan. There, on the great river Shinano, I saw lumbermen steering rafts downstream."

"I remember the rafts, Iroha-hime."

"Nagatoki-san, there is plenty of lumber here, at the wreck. Could we build rafts, and pole, or row, or sail them down to the place the map called 'Alviso,' at the south end of this San Francisco Bay? It would be warmer there, the messengers going the inland route would only have to travel half as far to reach Monterey, and it would still be accessible by sea. Surely it would be a better place for a permanent camp."

"That's . . . that's an interesting idea. But it was tricky enough getting a small boat around Fort Point. A raft, I fear, would be very difficult to control; even at slack water there could be strong eddies."

"But if my husband would delay his departure a few days, his boats could be used to ferry the timber and other goods to the shelving beach on the far side of Fort Point, and we could build the rafts there. It is a short distance, perhaps two-tenths of a mile."

"Yes, I think that's a good idea. With rafts, we could transport more food, and more goods that could be used for trade, and we would be less tired, too. You should speak to Lord Matsudaira."

"I was hoping that you would do that. I think he is more likely to accept advice from a warrior of your experience."

Yerba Buena Cove,
San Francisco Peninsula

Iroha waved goodbye until the two boats carrying Lord Matsudaira Tadateru, his lieutenant Daidoji Shigehisa, Tadateru's remaining samurai guardsmen, the captain and the first mate of the *Sado*

Maru, several sailors, and the miners into the haze that concealed the far shore. Buena Vista Island was visible, at least, and they would keep it on their left side if they could.

She would have been happier if her husband had left her party one of the two surviving ship's boats. However, he would need to ascend the Sacramento and American rivers to reach the gold fields, and having two boats instead of one might mean the difference between life and death. At least he had allowed those two boats to spend a week ferrying timber and supplies around Fort Point, for use by Iroha's party, despite his eagerness to head north.

Tadateru had promised to leave a cairn on the Oakland side, to make it clear that he had made the crossing safely. There were several other "checkpoints" where he agreed to leave additional markers, to show his progress. Unless he left a message to the contrary at these sites, Iroha was to ask her father to have a ship waiting for Tadateru at modern Antioch, on Suisun Bay, next summer.

Iroha worried about him. Not just about his body, but his soul. She had heard about his threat to decapitate the captain on the very deck of his ship. And she had seen and heard him threaten others in the days since the shipwreck. A samurai had the right to kill a commoner, of course, but the right was not exercised often.

Iroha had hoped that once they arrived in the New World, the psychic scars of his exile would heal, like a pond thawing out in the spring after being frozen all winter. But now, it seemed that the damage was irreversible, like the charring of a stick of firewood. Iroha prayed that Deusu would relieve his troubled spirit, since he was now beyond Iroha's reach.

At last, Nagatoki spoke. "I am very sorry, Iroha-hime, but it is time we boarded the rafts."

South Bay, near modern Alviso, California

There had only been two Dutch-made spyglasses on the *Sado Maru*, Lord Matsudaira's, and the captain's. Since the captain had gone with Lord Matsudaira northward, he had—rather grudgingly—given his scope to Hachizaemon, the leader of the sailors who had remained with Iroha-hime.

In due course, Hachizaemon made a discovery. "Matsuoka-san, I think I can see the end of the bay. And there's an Indian on the shore."

"Just one?"

"Yes, sir."

"Armed?"

"He has some kind of bow. But he appears to be watching something. He is not looking our way."

"He is a hunter perhaps," Matsuoka suggested. "He waits for some animal to emerge from its burrow. Or to return to it."

"I will question him!" one of the samurai, Sanada Saburo, announced. "He can tell us where to find food and water."

How? Hachizaemon thought. *It's not as though the Indians speak Japanese.* But since he also thought his head belonged on his shoulders, and not bobbing about in the South Bay, he kept this opinion to himself.

Saburo stepped off the raft and onto what looked like land. It wasn't land, it wasn't water; it was something in-between, a mud flat. There were mud flats along much of the shore of San Francisco Bay, but they were especially extensive here. Indeed, the tide was at slack low water, so the real shore was quite far off.

Matsuoka ordered the rafts to hold their position until the samurai reported. Seeing one Indian didn't mean that in fact there was only one Indian, he told Iroha.

Saburo had made it halfway to shore when he ran into real difficulty. He stepped on a softer patch and suddenly sank several feet. The mud was at waist level and he started flailing about, trying to climb out of this unexpected hole.

That was a bad idea. He found himself several inches deeper in the mud than he had been previously. The mud, in fact, was doing a good imitation of quicksand. The quick movements of his legs and arms created a vacuum in the viscous mud, and the vacuum sucked him down.

Hachizaemon ordered his men to pole the lead raft forward, but they couldn't move it far enough to reach the encumbered samurai; after a point, given how low the tide was currently, there wasn't enough water to float the raft.

When the tide rose, that would change, but that would create its own problems. Like drowning Saburo.

From time to time, Hachizaemon looked through his spyglass

at the same rocks and trees. Yes, he thought, the water was rising. The question was now whether that rising water would carry the raft within rescue range before it drowned the samurai.

"What is that Indian doing now?" asked Iroha. "Is it some kind of dance?"

Hachizaemon trained the telescope on the native. "I don't know. He points toward us, he points toward himself, he throws himself flat on his back, and then he moves his arms and legs very slowly."

"Could he be telling Saburo-san how to save himself from the mud?" She started shouting instructions to the endangered samurai. Whether because her voice was too soft, or because he didn't trust survival advice from a woman, he ignored her. And sank a few more inches.

Matsuoka had been thinking about Iroha-hime's interpretation of the Indian's actions, and at last he decided that she was right. He repeated her advice, but as an order. A stentorian one.

Saburo obeyed, and stopped sinking. Soon, the lead raft was able to draw up to him, and he was pulled on board by his older brother, Jiro.

The sailors, being commoners, did their best to look everywhere except at the bedraggled Saburo. Saburo's fellow samurai felt no such compunction, and started joking about catching the largest mudfish they had ever seen, a five footer at least.

Oakland, California, and Points North

The crossing of the Bay was uneventful, but when Lord Matsudaira's party reached the opposite shore, by modern Oakland, they found a vast marsh. They had to proceed some distance inland to find rocks for building the message cairn.

Making their way northward also had its difficulties. Each of the boats carried a single sail, but with the wind coming mostly from the northwest, raising it was fruitless. They had to paddle, and the paddling had to be timed for slack water, or when the tidal currents were in their favor.

Once they entered San Pablo Bay, the northern extension of San Francisco Bay, they turned eastward, and with relief they laid their paddles aside and let the wind carry them. And it was by wind power that they passed through the Carquinez Strait

and into Suisun Bay. The Delta, where the Sacramento and San
Joaquin Rivers came together, lay ahead of them.

They spent several days scouting the delta, and then threaded
through it, after a few false turns, to the main channel of the
Sacramento.

Their progress was now hindered by the river current. With
the wind once again powerless to aid them, it was "five steps
forward, four steps backward."

It was with great relief that they found the place where, they
thought, the American River fed into the Sacramento. They made
camp below a lone oak.

That night, as Lord Matsudaira lay back on his sleeping mat, he
saw a meteor cross over Heaven's River, the Milky Way. He took
it to be a favorable omen. Didn't gold glitter like the stars in the
sky? A meteor, a fallen star, was a promise of treasure to come.

There was a grinding sound, and the *Ichi-Ban*, the "Number
One" boat, shook.

"Back water, back water!" the former captain of the *Sado Maru*
shouted.

The *Ichi-Ban* held for a moment, then the riverbed released
it, and the boat was back in deeper water. The "Number Two
Boat," the *Ni-Ban*, came up close behind, so that its prow almost
touched the *Ichi-Ban*'s stern.

"Find a deeper channel," Lord Matsudaira ordered.

The captain bowed his head deeply. "Forgive me, my lord, but
I think this *is* the deepest channel. The river is just too low, even
for a ship-boat."

Lord Matsudaira stared for a time at the water. "If I recall
correctly, the encyclopedia said that the gold was discovered
while a sawmill was built on the American River. According to
the Dutch barbarians, a sawmill requires several feet of water for
operation. So how can this be the American River?"

Shigehisa thought about this. "If this is the American River,
then according to the map, Folsom Lake should be about ten
miles upriver. A pair of samurai could run that far in a day."

"Pick our best runners," said the Lord Matsudaira.

The two samurai returned four days later. They bowed deeply.
"We are very sorry, my lord, we went two days travel upriver—at

least twenty miles—and did not find a lake of any kind. The river did fork, however."

"Ah! I was right! This is not the American River! The captain has failed me again! I should take off his head right now!" The captain's face blanched, but it was impossible for him to flee.

"Please refrain, milord," Shigehisa whispered urgently. "We need him to handle the boat if we are to search further up the Sacramento."

"Very well. We need him. At least until we find this confounded American River. But there will be a reckoning..."

The next day, they were once again fighting the strong currents of the Sacramento, and moving farther and farther away from, not closer to, the mouth of the American River. None of the Japanese knew that "Folsom Lake" had been created by the Folsom Dam, built in 1955, and thus not in fact part of the California landscape in 1634.

South Bay, near Alviso, California

"Welcome to 'Sadomaru Palace,'" said Iroja-hime. "Please come in and dine with me."

The palace in question was a lean-to, made of salvaged ship timbers and sailcloth. It was, perhaps, the nicest lean-to that the shipwrecked Japanese had made on the site of Alviso, but it was still merely a lean-to. Dinner, however, was more promising, as the South Bay was rich in fish, shellfish and waterfowl.

"To what do I owe the honor of this invitation?" Matsuoka asked gravely.

"To my being bored out of my mind," she replied archly. "Have you been able to make contact with the Indians?"

"I'm afraid not," the elderly samurai admitted. "They see us, and if we approach closer than half a *li*, they flee. If we had horses, we could overtake them, but on foot, pursuing them in their own lands is hopeless... even dangerous."

"What does Hachizaemon think?"

"Hachizaemon?" His tone suggested that he was at a loss to come up with any reason that the second mate could possibly provide useful advice on any nonnautical matter.

"He told me that he had sailed once on a Red Seal ship to

Manila and other exotic ports. So he has, perhaps, traded with people that didn't speak Japanese."

Matsuoka called for Hachizaemon.

"Yes, Matsuoka-san, how may I help you?"

Matsuoka explained.

"Well, I haven't done it myself. But I have heard that the Spanish in Manila have a 'silent trade' with the Apoyno of Luzon."

"Silent trade?"

"Yes, you leave goods out, and withdraw, and make a smoke signal or a drum beat or something of the sort. And then the second side comes and puts down something in exchange. And if the first side thinks this a good offer, they take it away, and leave their goods behind. And if they don't, they wait for the second side to either add to what they put down, or take away what they last offered and thus end the bargaining."

Matsuoka stroked his chin. "Now that you mention it, I think I have heard that the Ainu do such a thing with the even more savage barbarians of the islands to their north. But the problem is, we have no way to tell the Indians what we are interested in. They could put something out that is of great value to them, but worthless to us."

"Forgive my impertinence in making this suggestion," said Iroha, "but perhaps it doesn't really matter what we receive, if we just set out a few goods that even we can spare. What we are really bargaining for is their trust."

Matsuoka gave his final instructions to the chosen messengers, Saburo and his older brother, Jiro. "A great valley extends southeastward from the Bay. You should come, eventually, to a stream that flows from the northeast to the southwest. Or perhaps, you will find just a dry river bed, I can't say for sure." The stream that he had in mind was what the eighteenth-century Spanish called the San Benito River.

"It is perhaps eighty miles from where we stand. Count your paces." Samurai were expected to be able to estimate marching distances.

"Turn down that river, it should pass through a low spot in the hills, and join another river." That was the Pajaro. "Head southwest until you reach the sea.

"You should be on a great ocean bay, between two rocky points.

Search between them until you find the Japanese colony. Then ask for the grand governor, Date Masamune."

Hachizaemon gave them the spare ship's compass. "You'll have more use for this than we will."

Matsuoka had some parting advice. "Oh, and Saburo-san—stay out of the mud, if you can."

Late September 1634,
Monterey Bay, California

Monterey Bay is in the shape of a fishhook. The eye is at the northern end, at Point Año Nuevo, where elephant seals bellow at their rivals during the mating season. The Santa Cruz Mountains are the shank, their slopes a home for fog-loving redwoods. A nearly continuous stretch of white sandy beach forms the broad bend, with the mouth of the Salinas near the middle, and the rockier shore from the old time line city of Monterey to Point Piños, where the pine trees stand guard, is the barb.

A fair wind, blowing from the northwest, allowed the First Fleet, the motley collection of Dutch, Japanese and even hired Chinese ships carrying Japanese Christians into exile, to run almost downwind toward Monterey. The wary skippers gave a wide berth to the rocks of Point Piños, and slowly entered the bay.

Abel Tasman, commanding the Dutch *jacht Mocha*, was in the lead. When the waters shallowed out to thirty fathoms, the First Fleet naval commander ordered the fleet to reduce sail to just enough for headway, and Tasman was instructed to choose the anchorage.

When Tasman's ship came within half a mile or so of the base of the barb, where it was partially sheltered by both Point Piños and Point Cabrillo, the wind slackened and the swell of the sea was broken. He sampled the bottom, finding it to be sand and yellowish mud, and likely to be good holding ground. He anchored in seven fathoms, and signaled for the fleet to join him.

Several parties of samurai were landed on the flat ground behind the anchorage. One went west, toward a hill covered by pine and oak. A second went southeast, finding an estuary fed by streams. The third stayed behind, to make sure that loose-fingered natives didn't liberate the boats.

In the evening, their commander reported to Date Masamune.

"Our priorities are clear," he said. "Fresh water. Food. Shelter. Not just from the elements, but also from unfriendly Indians. What have you found so far?"

"There is no good site for a fortress here," said the scout leader. "The land near the anchorage is too low and flat. As for the hill to the west, it will take much time and labor to clear away the forest, and there is no good flat land at the top so we would have to build a foundation, too."

"Nonetheless, we must have some kind of fort to protect the anchorage. Captain Tasman says that the rest of the bay is completely exposed. Tell me more about this estuary."

The scout leader shrugged. "There is not much more to tell. It is shaped like the head and horns of a water buffalo—" he drew a "U" in the air—"with the horns pointing away from the sea. Streams run into each horn. The base is separated from the sea by very low ground, and at high tide the sea comes in."

"And what is the ground like between those horns?"

"There is something of a rise."

Masamune decided that he would establish a lightly fortified fishing village within the horns of the lake, which would serve as a moat on three sides. The walls and watchtower of the village in turn would provide some protection for the anchorage. The fisherman would use the anchorage for their boats, and they could start bring in fresh fish for the colonists. It would be several months before the farmers could harvest a crop.

One of Masamune's scholars coughed.

"You have a suggestion?"

"Yes, my lord. Depending on the height of the water at high tide, we could perhaps dam the lower edge of the estuary so the saltwater can't come in any more. It will then become a freshwater lake."

"Speak to the masons, and see if they agree that it is possible with the earth and rock available nearby."

He told the scout leader to take several Japanese woodsmen and Dutch artillerists with him to the hill to the west, and try to find a place where a battery that commanded both the harbor and the ridges near the estuary might be constructed without too much trouble.

Some of the fishing folk among the colonists were disembarked, and their new village was given the name of Andoryu, after Saint Andrew the Apostle, the patron saint of fishermen.

Date Masamune summoned his herald, and handed him a scroll. "Read it so all may hear and obey."

The *obugyô* cleared his throat. "Black Seal Edict, given under the hand of the shogun of Nippon, Tokugawa Iemitsu, court noble of the upper first rank.

"(1) It shall be unlawful for barbarians, or people from outside provinces, to enter or exit New Nippon to trade with the Indians without the consent of the taishu of New Nippon, or the shogun.

"(2) Within the province of New Nippon, freedom of worship is permitted, provided that it does not disturb public harmony.

"(3) It shall be unlawful for residents of New Nippon who are of the Christian faith to return to their former provinces without the consent of the shogun or his duly appointed representatives.

"(4) It is strictly prohibited to inflict injustices or crimes upon the Indians of New Nippon."

The herald paused for effect. "This edict is to be rigorously enforced by the authorities in New Nippon." The edict was similar to the one given a few decades earlier to the Matsumae clan, which held the monopoly on trade with the Ainu, the aborigines of Hokkaido.

Date Masamune ordered that this black seal edict was to be read aloud at every later settlement, too.

October 1634

The First Fleet worked its way up the coast to the mouth of the Salinas. More precisely, where the mouth of the Salinas was supposed to be. From the crow's nest of the *Date Maru*, they could see some kind of body of water behind the beach. Beyond that, there was a low hill, and far in the distance, a mountain range.

A launch was lowered into the water, and the sailors rowed a party of samurai to the beach. They spread out into a V-formation and moved cautiously east.

The body of water turned out to be a part of a river. The Salinas, without a doubt. However, the river mouth wasn't here.

Rather, a short distance south of the hill, the river made a sharp turn northward, and the area around the bend was fairly marshy.

South of the marsh, running parallel to the shore, there was long line of mammoth sand dunes. This was a mixed blessing; it screened that part of the beach from any Indians further inland, but it also meant that Indians could be close by yet undetected.

A second party of samurai was sent out to climb the dunes. This was not a terrain they were accustomed to; there were dunes near Tottori, on the west coast of Honshu, and also in Hamamatsu on the east coast, but none worth mentioning in Date Masamune's fief of Rikuzen. With every step, sand was dislodged, increasing the effort required to make progress upward. Lizards scurried out of their way.

As they neared the crest of the dunes, they crouched, and at last they crawled to the top. From this excellent vantage point, they could see that the Salinas wound its way through a great valley stretching out to the southeast. They didn't see any Indians, or even any habitations.

The question, then, was whether to land the colonists here—based on the map in the encyclopedia—or to head north, to the present mouth of the Salinas. However far north that might lie.

Tasman was sent northward, to see if the mouth could be spotted from the sea, and in due course he returned with the report that it was perhaps four miles up the coast...and that the land around the mouth was completely flat, and equally marshy.

Masamune decided that the southern site, with that hill, was marginally more defensible, and so the second settlement was made there. The "all clear" signal was given and the second contingent of colonists was brought ashore. Boats shuttled between the ships to the beach, disgorging men and women, as well as supplies, and returning for more. Haste was called for, because this site was unprotected from the wind.

A crude field fortification was erected on the low but steep-sided hill the scouts had spotted. By odd coincidence, this was Mulligan Hill, where, in the old time line, the Portola expedition of 1769 first sighted Monterey Bay. The new settlement was named *Kawa Machi*—"River City."

The samurai's horses were landed, and a dozen of the samurai swung themselves into the saddle and headed upriver.

✧   ✧   ✧

Spirits are everywhere, according to the Ohlone Indians. The greater spirits are those of the sun, the moon, the sky, the sea, the mountains. But there are spirits in every bird, every mammal, every fish. Each of these spirits can help or harm.

And then there are the spirits of the dead. They may not be the most powerful of spirits, but they know our strengths and weaknesses. When they leave the body, they flee west, following the Path of the Wind to the Village of the Dead, across the sea. But they will return, and trouble the living, if they are not properly propitiated.

When a man of the Ohlone, the people living on Monterey Bay, died, he was buried that very day, and most of his belongings were buried with him. His widow cut off her hair, and smeared her face with ashes or asphalt. His name would not be spoken until it was formally given to one of his descendants, after the mourning ceremony, lest he be summoned back inadvertently.

If the death was of an unmarried man, or of a woman, her nearest female kin would perform the widow's duties.

Each year, the mourning ceremony was held. The whole village gathered in the ceremonial house. It stood upon a rise in the land, and the area around it had been cleared with brush. In this way, if an enemy chose to take advantage of the distracting nature of the ritual, and attack at that time, they would see their foes approach.

As the sun set on the first day of the mourning ceremony for 1634, the leaders of the mourners, seated on the west side, the spirit side, began to wail. The village chief slowly circled the central fire, chanting.

> "Don't fail to hear me!
> "Don't fail to hear me!
> "Make ready for the mourning.
>
> "Make ready your offerings,
> "Your offerings to the dead.
> "Be generous, be generous,
> "So the dead need not return to beg;
> "So the dead need not trouble the living."

The fire flickered, and the smoke rising from it seemed, now and then, to form the faces of the departed.

The leaders rose and followed the chief, and they were now followed by other women, perhaps half a dozen. Around and around they went. Sometimes the chief gave an order, and they faced in one direction and gesticulated, or turned about and circled in the opposite direction.

But they never rested.

Occasionally, one of the onlookers would scuttle forward and cast an offering into the fire.

At last, three more women, each with blackened faces, came out of the darkness of the spectator circle, and each grabbed one of the walkers. Each pair sat, holding each other's shoulders, at the foot of one of the roof posts, and swayed back and forth, crying as they did so.

At last, the remaining marchers retreated into the outer circle, leaving only the chief as the center of attention. He spoke of the history of their tribelet, its triumphs and tragedies, and at last he sat down himself.

The next night, the mourning ceremony continued. Old men and women partnered up and cried together, then danced one by one about the fire. They were followed by the three widows, each of whom did the same and then was led away, crying, by another woman.

On the morning of the third day, the chief harangued the mourners before sunrise, and then some of the women filled a basket with water. They fished hot stones out of the fire and tossed them into the water. The chief and the eldest of the woman, each holding a cloth, sat facing each other, on either side of the basket.

The three widows were led up to them. The first woman leaned over, and waited expectantly. The two cloth-holders dipped their cloths in the hot water and wiped her face, taking care that the water would drip only outside the basket. She was now free of mourning restrictions.

The next woman came up, but her lean was perfunctory. She quickly straightened and backed away. This was expected, her husband had died only a moon before. She would mourn until the "cry" of the next year.

The third woman, First-to-Dance, came up. She leaned and waited. The washers exchanged troubled glances. This woman had been a widow for only three moons. It was a little too soon for her to be at liberty. But the choice was not theirs to make.

With slow, reluctant movements, they cleaned her face. If they were rougher than usual, to show their irritation, it didn't provoke any complaint on her part. The onlookers murmured. Only time would tell whether they would tolerate her infraction, or ostracize her for it.

Minutes later, a villager started screaming. "The dead! The dead have returned from the sea! We are doomed!"

There was a mass exodus from the place of assembly, and all eyes were turned west. There, the men and women of the First Fleet were being disgorged, and the masts of more than a score of ships were dark against the morning sky.

The vessels used by the Indians of Central California were little rafts woven of tule reeds. A few had seen the plank canoes of the Chumash of the Santa Barbara Islands, farther south, but you might as well compare a minnow to a whale. The great ships of the First Fleet were beyond their experience.

One Indian pointed at the ships. "Those—those are the very islands of the dead, with dead trees standing upon them," he urged, his voice quavering.

First-to-Dance's expression was more curious than frightened. "They wear clothes that are nothing like ours, so how can they be our dead?" she asked.

"Who knows what the dead choose to wear, fool woman!" said one of her tribesmen.

The chief was anxious for the well-being of his people, and very conscious of their inability to fight so many strangers—be they living or undead. He welcomed the opportunity to act. "This is your fault, First-to-Dance! You dishonored the dead!" And he struck her senseless.

The Indians looked at each other, and voiced the thought that had come to all of them.

"Run!" They fled upriver, leaving First-to-Dance behind them.

"So how is our patient?" asked Date Masamune.

"Alive, at least. Her pupils are the same size, so she is not concussed. She will have an extremely picturesque bruise for several weeks, I am sure. She has been able to take water, and I am switching her to soup, soon. I think the brown seaweed will be the most efficacious, but—"

"But you can spare me the medical details, just do what you think best. And have me informed once she is speaking."

First-to-Dance had been awake for several hours. As soon as she was awake enough to appreciate the alien character of the words spoken in her presence, she had schooled herself to remain still. When the voices receded, she had ever so slightly opened her eyes, hoping that her long eyelashes would hide them.

It was annoying not be able to move her head, but her only advantage right now was that her ... rescuers? captors? ... didn't know that she was awake. Alone among enemies, she must be as brave as Duck Huck, the monster-killer, and as clever as Coyote his grandfather.

She couldn't help but wonder whether they were in fact the Dead returned, as her fellow tribesmen had assumed. They certainly were not dressed like the People. At this time of year, Ohlone men would be naked, and women would just wear an apron, unless there was bad weather, or a ceremonial need for extra garments. Was it cold in the Land of the Dead? Well, cold breezes came off the sea, so perhaps that explained it.

One of the men spoke. Of course, she had no idea what he was saying, but the speaker made it clear that he knew she was feigning sleep: He put his forefingers on his own eyelids, and lifted them up.

First-to-Dance opened her eyes and tried to sit up. She immediately felt light-headed. The man was beside her in an instant and steadied her. He spoke again in his incomprehensible language.

First-to-Dance had no idea why she couldn't understand him. Wouldn't the Dead still remember the speech of the People? She didn't resist, what was the point? Dead or alive, he was stronger than her, and she didn't know where she was, how many friends he had, or where her tribesmen had fled.

They were in a hut of some kind, made of an unfamiliar wood. It didn't seem to have any openings, but then he slid away a part of a wall and stepped out, beckoning to her to follow.

She blinked her eyes as they emerged into the daylight. They were on a high place, looking down at the bay. There were giant huts, with trees growing out of them, floating on the water.

So it was true! The Dead had returned!

With great daring, First-to-Dance asked, "Who were you in

life? How long ago did you die? Why have you returned? Were our offerings too small?" In a smaller voice, she added, "Is my dead husband among you?"

The man spread his hands, bowed to her, and left the room.

The third colony site for the passengers of the First Fleet was at the mouth of the Pajaro River, not far from the twentieth-century town of Watsonville. Perhaps a mile from the coast, and a third of a mile from the near bank of the Pajaro, the Japanese found a large hill, perhaps a quarter mile square, with good defensive potential. It had steep sides, and it was connected to the next hill by a narrow ridge that could easily be blocked. A castle might one day be built here, overlooking the village at the riverside. For the moment, though, the settlement was just as crude as the others.

The colonists of the Pajaro River settlement were primarily farmers, but they found themselves doing a lot of fishing. The steelhead trout were running that month, and the colonists were quick to improvise nets and string them across the river.

The colonists had been astonished and pleased to see the steel-heads, because they looked almost identical to a fish found in some rivers back home: the *Niji Masu*. The colonists decided to name their settlement after the fish. It sounded better, at least, than the first name that Date Masamune's explorers had come up with: *sawa-be*, the edge of a swamp.

"We weren't sure that we should disturb you, milord—" The speaker was the headman for the final Japanese settlement, by the San Lorenzo River, near modern Santa Cruz.

Date Masamune took a deep breath. "Be at ease. You did the right thing."

"Should we—"

"Please. I thank you, but I would prefer to contemplate this sight in silence."

The headman bowed, and backed away.

Date Masamune walked forward slowly, like a man in a trance. He turned to the scholar that accompanied him.

"Do you remember your first moon-viewing, Shigetsuna? Your first tea-ceremony? That is how I feel today. Call back the headman."

The headman returned. "How may I help you, my lord?"

"Summon the colonists." With a fearful glance over his shoulder at the Taishu, the grand governor of New Nippon, the headman hurried off.

Date Masamune gazed solemnly at his subjects. "In our ancient homeland, we have many beautiful or useful trees. The mulberry and the fig; the paper and lacquer trees; the cherry and the plum; the pine and the cedar. But the trees that stand across the river, ah, they put all the trees of Nippon to shame."

Masamune, whose city of Sendai became known in Japan as the City of Trees because of the plantings he encouraged, had seen his first grove of redwood.

"Henceforth, this village is to be known as Kodachi Machi." This mouthful meant, "Tree Grove City." Masamune slowly turned his head, staring at each of the colonists. "I will appoint a forest officer, as I did for Rikuzen. No tree is to be cut except with his permission, and without planting a new tree in its stead."

He motioned to the headman, who yelled, "Dismissed!"

Masamune turned to Shigetsuna. "I think we will also do as we did in Sendai; set up tree nurseries, for both the trees from home and the new ones we find here."

"We have already done so in Andoryu, with the seeds, cuttings and tub trees we took across the sea."

"I want it done in all of the settlements of New Nippon. Who knows where, in this strange land, a Japanese tree will grow well? Consider which useful trees we still need seeds or cuttings for, and send for them. They may be brought over by the Second Fleet."

The ships returned to the anchorage of Monterey/Andoryu, where they were best protected from the vagaries of the weather. They would wait there until the sailors were fully recovered from their voyaging, and then return to Japan. Some, no doubt, would be part of the Second Fleet, carrying the next batch of *kirishitan* to the New World, in 1635.

The *Ieyasu Maru* had worked its way south down the Pacific Northwest Coast, making note of the lay of the coast; in particular, possible harbors for future settlements. It had not made any further native contacts, but that didn't mean that the Indians hadn't been watching.

Under what western sailors called a "mackerel sky," but the

Japanese termed *iwaishigimu*—sardine clouds—the *Ieyasu Maru* rounded Point Año Nuevo. The rocks at the northern end of Monterey Bay had been so named by Sebastian Vizcaino in 1603, as it had been spotted on New Year's Day.

As Monterey Bay opened up before it, a guard ship ventured out from Kodachi Machi to greet it. Despite the *Ieyasu Maru*'s European lines, its "rising sun" emblem left no doubt as to its origin.

What did surprise the guardsmen was that the *Ieyasu Maru* was not a straggler from the First Fleet, but rather had voyaged across the Pacific independently.

"Where do you come from?" their commander asked.

"Japan," answered Captain Haruno.

"Where have you been?"

"Many places."

"Who are the natives I see on board your ship?"

"Indians."

It soon became apparent to the guards that Captain Haruno was not going to regale them with an epic story. Indeed, after a few more polite deflections, he insisted that a messenger be sent to the grand governor, and he didn't even allow his people to spend the night in the village.

The next morning, a small squadron of samurai rode up, and Captain Haruno and the rest of his company were guided to Date Masamune's present camp. The grand governor greeted them warmly, then had them divided up to be debriefed by various advisors.

Katakura Shigetsuna, the grand governor's chief advisor, did spare a moment to promise Haruno and Tokubei that the grand governor would honor them for their rescue of the castaways, and the discovery of iron on Texada. Indeed, he assured them that the grand governor would mention their discovery prominently in his report to the shogun. But he also warned them to be patient; there were many more immediate demands on the grand governor's attention. "Rest while you can," he added.

Captain Tasman was amazed by how quickly the village of Monterey/Andoryu was assembled. Assembled, not built; many of the *kirishitan* had simply packed up their homes, which were made of cedar or pine, and shipped them to the New World. Katakura

Shigetsuna had told the captain that back in Japan, whole towns had been disassembled and reassembled in a new location.

Likewise, some of the *kirishitan* fishermen had taken their boats along. Masamune had encouraged this; the sooner the boats were in the water, catching fish, the sooner the colonists could stop living off the dried provisions they had taken along for the voyage. The waters of Monterey Bay proved to be extremely rich, although all the Japanese colonists, even the fishermen, were looking forward to their first rice harvest. Rice, however, was planted in the spring. What they could plant now was *mugi*: wheat, barley and rye.

Masamune had started across the Pacific with two thousand colonists and five hundred retainers. One in ten of the colonists, and one in twenty of the better-nourished retainers, had died at sea. The remainder was still a good many mouths to feed.

The rest of First-to-Dance's tribelet, the Kalenta Ruk, had fled upriver, and no other Indians had yet been encountered by the Japanese of the "River City" settlement.

Date Masamune met there with his advisers. "That the natives avoided us was convenient when we were most vulnerable, while we were landing and before we had built up defenses. But now it would be good to speak to them, have them tell us what is good to eat and what isn't."

The Japanese had been mainly eating fish since landing. The farmers were planting wheat on the high ground, but it would be awhile before it could be harvested, and they were none too sure how well their wheat would do in this soil and climate.

"I am sure that girl we picked up could tell us, if only we could speak to her," said his son, the newly christened David Date.

Several of the Japanese had attempted to communicate with First-to-Dance, both by sign language and by trying to teach her Japanese and learn her own language. Progress was slow. Hold up a finger, and say a word. Do you mean "finger"? "One"? The direction "up"? It took time for each side to see what the different things that a particular word applied to had in common.

One word that they were quite interested in learning the name for was the one for the creature from which First-to-Dance's robe was made. This robe was the skin of a sea otter. When the physician had first examined her, he had commented on how marvelous the material was, warm and waterproof. He was from the *yukiguni*, the "snow country" of Japan, and he was sure that this might be something that could be sold back home. Masamune had emphasized the importance of finding such products, to assure that the motherland would continue to supply them with the goods they couldn't make themselves.

"Let's put her on a looser leash," said Masamune. "Let her wander around a bit, observe what she eats and drinks. Perhaps she would be more comfortable with some female company?"

Masamune decided that escorting First-to-Dance was exactly what was needed to distract Chiyo from archery practice.

Instead, of course, Chiyo insisted that her brother teach First-to-Dance, too.

First-to-Dance was somewhat nonplused by this development. Her people used the bow-and-arrow, but hunting was a male occupation. She absolutely refused to handle the bow, but was willing to watch Chiyo. And David Date, his aide Nobuyasu, and their friends.

In turn, Chiyo and Mika watched First-to-Dance. They discovered that she was perfectly happy to eat not only the fish caught by the Japanese fishermen, but also grasshoppers, caterpillars, and lizards. Frogs and toads, she ignored.

First-to-Dance collected acorns, too, knocking them from the limbs of the oaks that grew here and there, and putting them in the bag Chiyo had given her. She gave them to Chiyo, who had absolutely no idea what to do with them. Even after First-to-Dance engaged in an elaborate pantomime.

It was Mika, Chiyo's maid, who discovered the answer. She had, apparently, found that stories about the Indian woman were in great demand among the Japanese. One night, she described First-to-Dance's antics to a family that came from the Goto Islands.

"Acorns? I love acorns," said the mother. "We ground them up and put them in a pot, and boiled them until the water turned brown. Then we threw out the brown water and did it again and again, until the water was clear." That was done, she explained, to remove whatever gave raw acorns a bitter taste.

"Oh! That's what First-to-Dance was doing! Or something like it, at least." The word was spread and the Japanese colonists began gathering acorns in earnest. Fortunately, the acorn crop was bountiful in 1634.

Sacramento River Valley

Lord Matsudaira's party turned onto the Feather River, hoping that it was the American. The water level, at least, was much greater, a better fit for Matsudaira's preconception of what the American River should look like. Shigehisa had his doubts, however. The map showed the American meeting the Sacramento River from the east, whereas this tributary came in from the north. When Shigehisa pointed this out to Lord Matsudaira, he dismissed it abruptly.

"So? I wouldn't expect the map to show every little twist and turn. It will turn east eventually."

But days passed, and by Shigehisa's reckoning, they were still heading north as they progressed slowly upriver. It wasn't until they reached the confluence of the Feather and the Yuba that Shigehisa decided that he had to speak up again. By his recollection, the up-time map hadn't shown any significant branching of the American until above Folsom Lake.

"Lord Matsudaira, may I please see the American map again?"

The map was a copy, of course, of the one in the American encyclopedia, but the Japanese artist who prepared it had duplicated every stroke. A short line was drawn, perpendicular to the river, immediately below "Folsom Lake." This, according to the map's translator, was a *seki*: a dam.

The Japanese had dug ditches and dammed rivers for irrigation purposes for centuries, perhaps millenia. Neither Matsudaira nor the shogunate officials who had sent him had thought to question the presence of a dam, in California. Even the red-haired barbarians, the Dutch, had said they had dams, after all, so why not the California Indians?

But the Japanese had seen no trace of native agriculture. And if there was no agriculture, there would be no need for irrigation . . . or for dams. Shigehisa hurriedly explained his reasoning to Lord Matsudaira.

Lord Matsudaira tried to stand, lost his balance, and nearly fell out of the boat. When he regained his seating, and his dignity, he stated the logical implication: "And so the lake doesn't exist either. We were on the American River after all, and we didn't realize it!"

His expression changed from thunderous to uncertain. "But wait. What about the water level for Sutter's sawmill?"

Shigehisa shrugged. "Perhaps it is still the dry season for this region."

"All right. First thing tomorrow morning, we head back downstream. At least it should be easier paddling back down the Sacramento than paddling up."

Lower American River

What wasn't easier than before was paddling *up* the *American River*; the water levels were still low. Only the seagulls, walking along the edges of the gravel bars, were happy; the salmon had spawned and lay dying, practically at their feet.

Lord Matsudaira looked like he had swallowed something unpleasant, but was too polite to spit it out. "Shigehisa! What is your advice?"

"Let's leave the boats under guard here, and escort the miners upstream until they find the gold. When the water level rises we can bring up the boats."

Lord Matsudaira agreed, and assigned Shigehisa to command the boat guard—the captain, the first mate, the sailors, and another samurai. Lord Matsudaira and the remaining four samurai left with the miners the next day.

Kiyoshi, the foreman of Lord Matsudaira's miners, wondered once again what horrible crime he could have committed in his last incarnation in order to find himself on the American River, looking for gold.

Kiyoshi and his crew came from the great gold and silver mine at Aikawa, on the western coast of Sado Island, which lay off the coast of the province of Echigo. The gold was discovered in 1601 by a local merchant. The miners of Aikiwa were accustomed to digging through andesite tuff with chisels and hammers, following the great Torigoye vein several hundred feet underground.

Confronted with the American River, meandering across its flood plain, they had not the slightest idea where to start looking for gold.

But having observed how Lord Matsudaira treated the captain, Kiyoshi was quite certain it would not be wise to admit this.

Monterey Bay

At Masamune's request, several boats of fishermen had gone looking for sea otters. They found them, floating on their backs in the waters off Kodachi Machi/Santa Cruz, and also on the wild side of the Monterey Peninsula between Monterey and Carmel.

At first, the Japanese fishermen hunted the sea otters more or less the way they hunted dolphins back home; their boats spread out in an arc and drove them, with nets strung between the boats, toward the shore. This didn't work quite as well with sea otters as it did with dolphins, because sea otters could run away on land. Hence, they found it was necessary to first set some men down on the beach, armed with spears and clubs, before starting the otter drive.

Only a few hunts were carried out, because the Japanese had no special fondness for otter meat, and they had no idea how well the furs would sell in China or Japan. Some sample furs would be sent back home, and, well, the Second Fleet would come in 1635 and tell the colonists whether to harvest more.

"Next," said Inawashiro Yoshimichi. He took a moment to smooth out his formal *kami-shimo*.

One of the *kirishitan* waiting patiently in line came forward.

"Name?"

"Yamaguchi Takuma."

"Can you write?"

"Yes, sir."

Inawashiro handed him three sheets of mulberry bark paper, a brush, a pot of ink, and an ink-stone.

"Write your letters to home today, the ships are leaving this week. Tell your *kirishitan* relatives and acquaintances how wonderful it is to be a *kirishitan* in New Nippon. It is wonderful, neh?"

"Yes, but—"

"Next!"

November 1634,
Monterey Bay

Winter had come, and with it, increased fog and rain. The rains swelled the Salinas, and at last the river broke through the sand bar that had puzzled Masamune's advisers, forming the southern mouth of the river. They knew from the encyclopedia entry on California that summers would be dry; they surmised that in the summer, the ocean would reform the sand bar.

They had asked First-to-Dance about the river, and she had told them "water come, water go." At first, they thought that she meant that the river was a place of flowing water. But now, they feared that she meant that the river actually dried up during the summer. That didn't happen in Japan, but the scholars knew that it was a problem in western China.

Orders were given for irrigation ditches to be dug, and streamlets dammed to catch the rain and hold it for future use.

Between modern Gilroy and Hollister

"I think that's the river channel we want," said Saburo.

"You said that the last two times, too," said Jiro. "They were both dead ends."

"Well, I have to be right sooner or later. If only I could see through the mountains, right to the sea."

Jiro looked at Saburo. "The mountains, younger brother, are a manifestation of the Illusion we call the World. To see through it, you must—fuck!" Jiro had just tripped over Saburo's outstretched foot.

"The foot, elder brother, is also Illusion," Saburo said airily. "Perhaps we can pretend that the mountains are at least as real as my foot?"

Jiro and Saburo had gained some hope when the channel they were following joined another, larger one. Still, they had yet to see Monterey Bay. It was already late in the day, so they started to make camp.

"Jiro, wait, I think I saw a horseman crest that hill."

"That's preposterous—Hey, I saw him, too!"

"Indians?"

With the air of superiority that is genetically incorporated into older brothers, Jiro told Saburo, "The Indians don't have horses."

"So those must be Japanese! Fellow samurai!"

"Or Spanish," Jiro cautioned.

But Saburo was already running forward, shouting and gesticulating.

Jiro ran after him.

The party of horsemen spotted them, and headed their way. It was soon apparent that they were, indeed, Japanese. When they came within hailing distance, Jiro and Saburo discovered that they were Date Masamune's men, exploring the upper reaches of the Pajaro River. The Japanese settlement of Niji Masu/Watsonville was only a dozen miles away, downriver. Jiro and Saburo doubled up behind two of the riders, and the scouting party took them home.

The following morning, Jiro and Saburo were loaned horses by the commander at Niji Masu. They rode south along the coast, and by dinner time they were in the presence of Date Masamune at Kawa Machi/Salinas.

They were the first to carry word to the grand governor of the debacle at the Golden Gate; the other pair of messengers, the ones who were to follow the coast to Monterey, hadn't made it. They were presumed dead.

Captain Haruno and "Tenjiko" Tokubei, still recuperating from their exploration of the Vancouver area, received an urgent summons to Date Masamnune's still ramshackle fort.

"Success brings rewards, but also punishments," he told them.

They smiled uncertainly.

"Those who achieve great things are expected to move on to even greater accomplishments," he explained.

That sounded even more ominous.

"In this case, I need you to sail at once to San Francisco Bay. You are to go first to the south end, where my daughter Irohahime and her companions are encamped. They were shipwrecked by the Golden Gate last September. You will then head north, exploring as you think best, but you must be at the mouth of the Sacramento River by July, to meet her husband, Lord Matsudaira

Tadateru. If he does not show up by the end of August, you will return here. Iroha-hime is to come back here with you, with or without him. Even if she protests."

Tokubei and Haruno exchanged glances.

"Great Lord," Haruno replied, "we will of course act as best serves you and your daughter's interests. However, it will not help your daughter if we are lost at sea. The encyclopedia revealed that in northern California, the rainy season is October to April.

"And it is not just the rainy season, it is the season of great storms, with high winds and therefore powerful waves. As we experienced on our passage south to Monterey. Hence, I would recommend that we not leave until April or even May."

"That's a long time to wait," said Masamune. "Is it truly hopeless to leave any sooner?"

"Hopeless, no," said Haruno. "Dangerous, yes. And with the First Fleet departed, this is the only ship you have. If it's lost, you will have to wait until the Second Fleet comes, next fall, to have another chance."

"I think it is perhaps a mistake to place too much faith in what the encyclopedia says. For all we know, the climate has changed over the years. Please take your ship up to the Golden Gate this month. Judge firsthand whether it is safe to proceed through the strait. If it isn't, return and try again in April.

"I must trust your judgment, as you have already proven your ability by your exploration of the northlands." He paused. "But if you succeed in passing the Golden Gate this year, you may expect additional rewards, befitting the risks you have taken."

After Haruno and Tokubei left, Masamune summoned Jiro and Saburo.

"The rescue mission is being prepared. Missions, I should say. I am so sorry, but I must split you up. Jiro-san, you will go by sea, with Captain Haruno and Tokubei-san, as soon as their ship is refitted.

"Saburo-san, you will go by land, and you will leave this week. You will guide a troop of samurai, and they will bring extra horses, enough for all of Iroha-hime's party.

Each of you may wait up to a week for the other to arrive, but no more. Iroha-hime's safety is paramount."

South Bay, near Alviso, California

The local Indians had become friendly with Iroha's party, and had brought them food: acorn mush, berries, fish, and so forth. However, she had been running out of small gifts to reward them with, and she and Matsuoka were worried as to what would happen once they were no longer able to reciprocate. There were hundreds, if not thousands, of Indians in the area. If they became hostile, they could make short shrift of the small Japanese party, despite the superior skills and equipment of the two Japanese samurai who had remained with her. Quantity has a quality all its own.

Banks of the American River

"Dispose of the body," said Lord Matsudaira, who then cleaned and sheathed his katana. He walked away from the corpse without a backward glance.

The victim of the samurai lord's rage was not the former captain of the *Sado Maru*, but one of the miners. The unfortunate man had been executed for insolence. His crime had been to say that their search for gold was a waste of time just as Lord Matsudaira passed within earshot.

Kiyoshi reflected that if the man had only had the wits to hold his tongue, he would probably have lived longer in America than if he had remained in Japan. He was not a real miner; he was a convict who had been sentenced to a life term working in the mine, draining the lowest levels one bucket at a time.

His death presented Kiyoshi with a problem. That being, what to do about the body? In Japan, in the Shinto religion, contact with the dead was ritually polluting, and was left to the eta, the Japanese "untouchables." But there were no eta on the *Sado Maru*. Nor were Japanese Christians any more enthusiastic about handling the dead, as their European instructors considered gravedigging to be a dishonorable occupation. If Kiyoshi could speak to the local Indians, he could perhaps persuade them to deal with the body, but they had seen no Indians recently. In any event, they didn't know their language.

Kiyoshi picked out the two lowest-ranking of the remaining miners and ordered them to bury the corpse. After much argument, they did so.

Kiyoshi rose groggily. The sun had only just cleared the horizon, and scattered trees cast long shadows that in his half-awake state led Kiyoshi to imagine them the fingers of *oni*, Japanese demons.

He quickly made a Christian sign of aversion, followed by a Buddhist one, just to be safe.

As his head cleared, he became more and more sure that something was wrong. But what? Then he realized the answer: two men were missing from the mining camp. The very men who had conducted the burial the day before.

He shivered involuntarily. Had their state of impurity rendered them vulnerable to some *American* demon?

He called out, but they didn't answer.

Kiyoshi quickly woke the others. They grabbed weapons and searched the area, spiraling outward.

They didn't find the two missing men. But they did find footprints leading to the water, and then disappearing in the muck.

With some reluctance—as headman he could be held accountable for the actions of his men—he informed the samurai on duty that the men were missing. A samurai joined the search, to no avail.

Kiyoshi suggested that the men had been taken by the Indians, or perhaps by some water beast.

The samurai was skeptical. "I see no sign of a struggle.... And didn't you have a man posted on guard? Why didn't he call out?"

"The man who disappeared was the watchman on the last shift. He was taken by surprise, perhaps while relieving himself," Kiyoshi suggested.

The samurai snorted. "There aren't enough of us to conduct a proper search, especially since we don't have horses. But I will have to report this to Lord Matsudaira."

Kiyoshi shivered once again. There were more fearful beings than hypothetical American demons.

The samurai returned, this time with several of his fellows. "By order of Lord Matsudaira, we are taking over the night watches. And you and your men are to be roped together, night and day. So there are no more mysterious disappearances."

December 1634,
Off the Coast of California

It had taken several weeks to refit the *Ieyasu Maru* to return to sea, and Captain Haruno had practically danced with impatience until they pulled out of the little harbor at Andoryu/Monterey.

To reach the Golden Gate, the *Ieyasu Maru* found it expedient to take a circuitous route. Monterey Bay lay to the south, but the prevailing winds of the California coast come from the northwest, and the California current sets south along the shore.

The rescue ship sailed directly away from land until it crossed the 125th meridian. It then encountered more variable winds, and made northing whenever it could. Eventually, it clawed its way up to the 38th parallel, and turned eastward. This process took perhaps two weeks, even though, when it had come south from British Columbia, the passage from the 38th parallel to that of Monterey had taken a single day.

South Bay, near modern Alviso, California

Led by Saburo, the samurai scout troop at long last reached Iroha-hime's refuge. Each scout had an extra horse on a lead, so all of Iroha's party would be able to ride back. Saburo proudly advised Iroha that he had come to rescue her, and that soon she would be safe with her father in the Monterey Bay colony. She had thanked him, and neither agreed nor disagreed with his statement that she would need to be ready to leave in a week's time.

The week passed.

"I am sorry, Saburo, but I cannot go with you," said Iroha. "I will wait for Captain Haruno to arrive, and go with him to rescue my husband. Then, and only then, will I go to Monterey Bay."

"But ... But, Iroha-hime, your father was most insistent that we wait no more than a week for Captain Haruno, and if he had not arrived by then, we were to take you with us."

"My husband commanded me to remain here, and of course his authority overrides that of my father."

"Actually," said Matsuoka, "his command was that you go to your father in Monterey."

"Yes, but that was because he thought that I might need to plead with my father in person to assist Lord Matsudaira. But Captain Haruno was sent to aid him, not just to rescue me, yes?"

Saburo admitted that this was the case.

"So there is no immediate need for my presence in Monterey, after all. Indeed, it would be best that we can report to my father that Captain Haruno has succeeded in entering the Bay. Otherwise a third ship will need to be sent out, to look for him, too."

Saburo looked at the troop commander, who looked at Matsuoka.

"All right, one more week," said Matsuoka. "But after that, if there's no sign of the *Ieyasu Maru*, you will ride with us to Monterey if I have to tie you onto the saddle."

Near the Farallone Islands, outside San Francisco Bay

"What great luck, Captain Haruno!" Jiro exclaimed. "No fog today!" He paused. "Why are we slowing down? Shouldn't we hurry through while we can?"

"We must check for hidden dangers, honorable samurai. I am lowering a boat to take soundings, I don't like the look of the water ahead. If you want a better view of what it's doing, you may go forward."

When Jiro walked out of earshot, Haruno snorted, and whispered to Tokubei, "The grand governor expects us to be bold. He does not desire that we be stupid."

Kinzo, the *Ieyasu Maru*'s coxwain, reported back a few hours later. "There seems to be a very large bar in the shape of a folding fan, in front of the strait. I wouldn't want to cross it during a storm, but it won't be a problem with the seas as they are now."

"What was the current like?" asked Haruno.

"When I started, the waters were a bit confused; the swells were from the northwest, and they seemed to be meeting a tidal ebb. But I think the tide has nearly slacked off by now."

"We'll go a bit deeper in, and anchor," Haruno announced, "and then you'll take the boat in all the way in and find an anchorage. I'll not trust my ship to the word of a landsman as to where we can pass the night safely."

Kinzo and his men raised a sail and, under both sail and oar, steered their longboat toward the mouth of San Francisco Bay. Jiro had insisted on joining them, saying, "For the honor of Lord Matsudaira, at least one member of his party should be on the boat that is the first to enter San Francisco Bay by the sea." Apparently, he felt that the shuttling of supplies around Fort Point by the surviving boats of the *Sado Maru* was best left out of the chronicles.

They rounded Fort Point and continued east, passing cautiously between Clark's Point and Yerba Buena Island. The peninsular coast pulled inward here, forming a cove overlooked by Telegraph Hill.

This seemed an eminently satisfactory anchorage, and they tried to return to the *Ieyasu Maru*. That proved easier said than done. The tide had turned, and the waters of the Pacific were now pouring into the Bay.

With the wind against them, and the current too strong to fight with oar power, they returned to the cove and beached their boat.

In the meantime, the *Ieyasu Maru* was having trouble holding its position. The wind had picked up, and the inward tidal current had strengthened. Its anchor lost its grip on the bottom and the *Ieyasu Maru* lurched forward.

"Up anchor!" Captain Haruno ordered. "Make sail!" His junior officers shouted out the step-by-step instructions to get the ship under way.

"Better to go in now, under control, then be carried willy-nilly by wind and tide," he told Tokubei.

Riding the flood tide, and with the wind at their back, the *Ieyasu Maru* sped eastward, like a traveler running to reach the gate of a city before it closed for the night. Iwakashu's miners were stationed all along the railing, as extra lookouts. Iwakashu, at least, was glad to be on this rescue mission to San Francisco Bay. Which, he hoped, would give him the opportunity to see the fabled American River—and perhaps its gold.

✧   ✧   ✧

At last, the *Ieyasu Maru* passed between Lime Point and Fort Point. For the first time in history, a sailing ship had entered San Francisco Bay.

Off to port, Haruno could see Horseshoe Bay, and beyond it, the stretch of open water leading to Angel Island. Richardson Bay and Raccoon Strait were hidden by the northern headlands, but shown on his copy of the encyclopedia map of San Francisco.

Alcatraz Island was directly ahead, and, on starboard, the coast of what would become the modern city of San Francisco. It didn't look much like what was shown on the map.

Studying the color of the water, and the behavior of the waves, Haruno was leery of the narrow passage between Alcatraz Island and the San Francisco peninsula. "Reduce sail!" he ordered. He wanted more time to decide how to proceed.

"Any sign of the longboat?" he called up to the lookout in the crow's nest.

"No sign, Captain!"

Tokubei tapped his shoulder, and pointed at Richardson Bay, which had come into view on the port side.

"Looks lovely," Haruno acknowledged, "but I can't sail closely enough into the wind to take advantage of it."

"We could set out the other boat and warp ourselves in," Tokubei suggested.

"True. But unless you see our longboat hiding there, I think it best to look for an anchorage downwind. We have to head southeast to rescue Iroha-hime, anyway."

The captain ordered a course set to take them between Angel Island and Alcatraz. This required that they sail close-hauled, but they were still enjoying the assist of the flood tide.

As they sailed deeper into the Bay, Captain Haruno ordered that the ship be brought around, first to an easterly heading, then southeast, then south. It was now the *Ieyasu's Maru's* turn to pass between Yerba Buena and Clark's Point, and when they did so, a cry went up. "The boat, the boat!"

"A fair anchorage," said Tokubei.

Captain Haruno nodded. "We'll pass the night here, and greet her ladyship tomorrow."

The next day, they were ready to sail out of Yerba Buena cove and proceed south. Unfortunately, Susanoo the Wind God had other ideas. Over the course of the night, the wind had veered, from northwest to northeast to southeast. It was impossible to sail out of their anchorage.

Kinzo and Jiro requested permission to take the longboat south, to bring word to Iroha-Hime that help was on the way. The longboat, after all, could be rowed.

Captain Haruno refused. "I need the longboat to scout ahead and take soundings."

In the evening, the wind died down altogether, but by the second day after their entry into the Bay, it had picked up again, and blew once more from the northwest. By noon, they were at the southern tip, and the longboat was winding its way through the sloughs toward Iroha-Hime's camp.

South Bay

Much to both Iroha and Matsuoka's relief, the *Ieyasu Maru* had sailed into sight before the deadline Matsuoka had set had passed.

But its arrival sparked a new debate. Who was to board the *Ieyasu Maru*, and who would be escorted back by the land route? Iroha of course wanted to rejoin her husband, and she pointed out that the *Ieyasu Maru* could afford her and her maid the privacy she would have lacked on Tadateru's little boats. Matsuoka thought that she would be safer on the *Ieyasu Maru*, than on an overland route exposed to Indian attack, and hence was no longer willing to insist on her immediate return. Of course, if she went, so would he, and her other personal guardsman.

Jiro and Saburo, reunited, thought that it might be their duty to their lord to rejoin him, even though they would much rather be on horseback than on a ship again. Matsuoka sensed their discomfort, and eased their conscience by ordering them back to Monterey.

Hachizaemon was anxious to be back on a ship again, even with a strange new captain. The other shipwrecked sailors had decided that San Francisco Bay was unlucky, and they wanted no more of it.... Even if the alternative was getting on top of a horse.

Hence, it was just Iroha, Koya, Matsuoka, his junior samurai, and Hachizaemon who boarded the *Ieyasu Maru*, and the rest rode, whether happily or painfully, for Monterey Bay. They would bring word to Date Masamune that his daughter was safe on board the *Ieyasu Maru.*

Near modern Oakland, California

Captain Haruno lowered his spyglass. "I saw no sign of this supposed cairn."

"It isn't easy to find stones to pile up if you land on a marsh," Tokubei pointed out. "And even if you find them, the pile would probably sink."

"I suppose we had best send out search parties," said Haruno. "We want to make sure that Lord Matsudaira made a successful crossing."

"If he didn't he might be stranded on Angel Island. Or even on Alcatraz."

"That is so. Tokubei, you take one boat; have Hachizaemon take another. Explore a half-day's march inland, and return. In the meantime, I will take the *Ieyasu Maru* around Angel Island and see if any stranded Nihonjin put in an appearance."

"You are sure you want to split our forces in three?"

"I think it is an acceptable risk. The Monterey Bay colony has not had any violent confrontations with the local Indians, and Iroha-hime found the South Bay Indians to be helpful. In any event, we aren't moving far apart. If you need help, fire a gun. The sound should carry well enough over the water."

Each of the two search parties included several of the *Ieyasu Maru's* miners; Haruno had figured that since they had to search the countryside anyway, they might as well keep their eyes open for something useful. Iwakashu was with Tokubei's contingent. Tokubei had allowed his men to spread out, provided they stayed within hailing distance.

After about an hour of wandering, Iwakashu approached Tokubei. "Sir, you need to see this."

Tokubei followed the mining engineer, who led him to a large patch of exposed rock.

"What am I looking at?"

"The cap of Daikoku," said Iwakashu mysteriously. Daikoku was, Tokubei knew, a Buddhist God of Wealth. He was usually depicted as a fat, happy man with a sack of treasure slung over one shoulder, and holding a magic mallet aloft with his free hand.

"Please, explain what you mean. I don't see any gold here..."

"Gold? No, not likely. Possible, but not likely. But this is a place strong in yin, where treasures are hidden beneath the surface.

"This rock is well weathered. Here is *sekitekkou*, the red earth of iron, and there is *kattekkou*, the brown earth of the same metal." A modern geologist would call them hematite and limonite. "You see how different they are from the dull rock nearby?

"I call them the caps of Daikoku, because they often lie above a deposit of metal ore. Most often, *outtekou* or *oudoukou*." Those were pyrite and chalcopyrite. "What miners call 'fool's gold.'"

"Okay, you've had your little joke," said Tokubei. "Let's go back now."

"You don't understand, do you?" said the miner.

"Understand what?"

"That we can make sulfur from them. The Chinese roast *outtekou* over charcoal; the breath of Huchi, the goddess of the volcano, emerges from it, and cools to make sulfur."

Sulfur. Tokubei knew that to Lord Masamune, sulfur might be more valuable than gold. The shogunate restricted the supply of gunpowder to the colonists, perhaps fearing that they would one day try to force their way back into Japan. The Dutch would sell more, but they tried to "catch a sea bream with a shrimp"; charge a lot for a small amount.

Gunpowder had three ingredients; charcoal, saltpeter, and sulfur. Charcoal was easy, in Japan it was made by charring a hardwood, *hannoki*. There were surely American woods that would work well enough. Saltpeter could be collected in certain desert regions, or made from night soil.

But sulfur, Tokubei had thought, was only available as the yellow crystals found near certain hot springs. Hot springs the Japanese explorers had yet to find in America, although some of the mountains Tokubei had seen in his journey down the coast were surely volcanoes, and where there were volcanoes one might hope to find hot springs.

"Say nothing of this to anyone, and I will make it worth your while."

✧   ✧   ✧

Four men met that night in the captain's cabin of the *Ieyasu Maru*, with a guard posted outside the door.

"So, this sulfur you speak of will enable the grand governor to make his own gunpowder," said Hosoya Yoritaki. He was the commander of the *Ieyasu Maru*'s samurai marines. "I think that he will find that a most attractive prospect. It is best that we not be dependent on gunpowder from home. It is merely a matter of prudence; we don't know when we might need it to fend off the Indians, the Spanish, or even the Dutch, and our supply line is very long and frail."

"I am a big believer in prudence," said Tokubei. "It is interesting, is it not, that this sulfur deposit is not shown in our maps from Grantville?"

"Most interesting," Iwakashu agreed. "The up-timers do not know everything. Do you think that the grand governor will communicate this discovery to the shogun?"

There was a silence.

"I think...I think," said Yoritaki, "that the grand governor will be of the opinion that the shogun's interest is primarily in precious metals, as evidenced by Lord Matsudaira's mission. There is no lack of sulfur in Nippon, the Land of Fire. There will, I daresay, be no need to speak of so inconsequential a matter."

"And surely," said Iwakashu, "if the presence of pyrites in California was information that the shogun should be aware of, the buddhas and kamis would have seen to it that they were shown on those very maps that he was given by the Dutch barbarians."

A rather foxy expression passed briefly over his face. "So we are, perhaps, obligated by the mandate of Heaven to maintain secrecy, lest this information become known in Japan before the buddhas and kamis are ready to reveal it."

"If we leave the miners here, the sailors will talk about it once we return to Monterey," said Captain Haruno. "Even if they don't realize that we are mining sulfur, or iron, they will think that we are mining gold. And that will attract undesirable attention to this place."

Tokubei shrugged. "What of it? The colonists of Monterey are *kirishitan*, they are forbidden to return to Japan."

"But our sailors are not *kirishitan*," said Yoritaki, "and they can speak of our find once we sail back to Sendai. And the shogun has spies in Sendai, of that I can assure you. For that matter, there is probably at least one spy among our sailors, since they have license to return.

"So we need an excuse for leaving the miners and some samurai here. An excuse that will not excite undue curiosity."

The others fidgeted.

At last, Iwakashu made a proposal. "In Go, it is wise to sacrifice the smaller group to save the greater one. Let us say that we have found **copper**. It may even be true, as *oudoukou* is a copper ore. Copper is valuable enough that we would want to mine it, but it is not worth shipping back to Japan, where it is plentiful. And it is not a metal that the shogun would mind us controlling. By the time his spies report otherwise, New Nippon will be able to survive on its own."

"We hope," Yoritaki muttered.

Lower American River

Kiyoshi, as foreman, did not suffer the indignity of being roped, and hence could scout ahead. He was walking on a large sand bar on the south bank of the American River, near the site of the modern town of Folsom, when he tripped. He started to lever himself up, and then stopped suddenly—he had caught sight of an intriguing glint from a rock a few yards away. He approached it, half-crouched, and, grunting, turned it to better expose the surface of interest. He saw what appeared to be small gold scales.

He proudly showed his discovery to Lord Matsudaira.

Lord Matsudaira, of course, was overjoyed, and insisted that Kiyoshi accept, as a gift, the Lord's own smoking pipe. It had a bamboo shaft, and a silver mouthpiece and bowl, the latter engraved with the Matsudaira *mon*—three hollyhock leaves in a circle, the same as that of the Tokugawa.

It might have been more useful if they still had any tobacco left, but Kiyoshi appreciated the gesture.

He requested permission to have the miners untied so that they could better search for more gold, and Lord Matsudaira agreed, provided they were tied up again each night.

As Kiyoshi assigned his men to work different sections of the sand bar, he gestured with his new pipe, as if it was a scepter.

❖   ❖   ❖

After a week of searching, Kiyoshi's men had found a few more gold flecks and, in a crevice, a small gold nugget. Unfortunately, as lode mining men, they knew nothing of panning for gold. That was something done in Japan, not by honest miners, but by *yamashi*. Literally, it meant "mountain expert," but in common usage, a *yamashi* could be a "prospector" or a "swindler."

Still, Kiyoshi wished he had some *yamashi* with him. But at least Lord Matsudaira was in good humor... at least for the moment.

"Hatomoto Shigehisa."

"My lord, how may I serve you?"

"Walk with me." They walked out of sight and hearing of the crewmen of the *Sado Maru*.

"Look at this!" Lord Matsudaira held out his hand, the nugget resting on his outstretched palm.

Shigehisa bowed. "I am overwhelmed, my lord. You have found the gold field."

Lord Matsudaira lifted his hand in thanks. "Your words are most welcome. But the real gold field must lie further upstream. Above the fork our scouts found previously, the streams run through gorges. The real gold mines must be there, I think, where we can see the very bones of the earth."

"Will you be taking a boat, milord? The river is at least a foot higher than it was when we first came here."

"No, I think not. There are two rapids just in the stretch of water we have been working, and I expect that once we enter the gorges, we will find much whitewater. A boat will be too much trouble."

"Is there room to walk beside the river? Or is the gorge too steep-walled?"

"At least on the lower stretch we have spied out, there is room. Further up, who knows? But I have tired of sitting in camp watching the miners turn over rocks and sift their fingers through the sand and gravel."

"May I accompany you, my lord?"

"No, I need you to hold this nugget for me. It would not be good if I tumbled into the water, and lost it."

"It will be my honor and pleasure, Lord Matsudaira."

Modern weather forecasters call it a "Pineapple Express." The Polar jet stream forks, and the southern branch guides a tropical

air mass northward and eastward, bringing warm air and tor-
rential rainfall to the western coast of North America.

On the shores of San Francisco Bay, there was a bit of flooding, but this only inconvenienced the passengers and crew of the
Ieyasu Maru. The miners sought temporary refuge on board the
ship, and the ship took shelter from the wind on the lee side of
Angel's Island.

The rain was heavy at times, leading Iroha-hime to compare the
Ieyasu Maru to Noah's Ark. Tokubei, from the time he spent on
Dutch ships, understood the reference, and expressed his earnest
hope that the rain would not last forty days and forty nights.

In the Central Valley to the north, a much more dangerous
situation developed. The waters of the Sacramento rose, then
subsided a little as the storm system continued eastward.

But it was a temporary reprieve. The storm bombarded the Sierras with warm rain. The rain permeated the snowpack. Within a
matter of hours, it had melted much of the snow at intermediate
elevations. The melt water hurtled down the narrow canyons of the
upper reaches of the Feather and American Rivers, turning them
into maelstroms of white water. The flood front descended to what
was normally the more placid lower sections of these rivers. Here,
the water rapidly overflowed the banks, and spread out, forming a
temporary lake that stretched out as far as the eye could see.

Storms of this nature struck the Central Valley at least once
a generation, perhaps more often, and the elders of the Indian
tribes were quick to spot the signs and chivvy their people to
safe ground. The two Japanese deserters, who had taken refuge
with those Indians, followed their lead.

The Japanese strung along the American River were caught
by surprise.

"I've never seen anything like it," said Captain Haruno.

"Nor I," Tokubei agreed.

"What is the matter?" asked Commander Yoritaki.

"The tide... It's been a full day and it hasn't changed direction," said Haruno.

Iroha and Senior Guardsman Matsuoka Nagatoki stood nearby,
and they overheard this exchange. "Excuse me, Captain Haruno,
what do you mean?" she asked.

"Usually, the tide comes in and out twice each day. But we

have been fighting a nonstop ebb tide since we left our harbor yesterday morning. We've barely made any northing at all."

"If we hadn't had the benefit of a southwest wind, we'd have been moving *backward*," Tokubei added.

Iroha pondered this for a while. "The Almighty acts in mysterious ways. Excuse me, please." She went below, calling for her maid, with Nagatoki leading the way as a bodyguard should.

Tokubei looked at Captain Haruno. "Her Almighty has apparently dumped a heck of a lot of water on the lands to the north, and it's running south now. Enough to overwhelm the normal tides. That's the only explanation I can come up with."

"Well, it's better than that the Dragon God has misplaced his magic tide-flow jewel."

North Fork, American River

"Milord, I don't like how fast the water is rising," said one of the two samurai accompanying Lord Matsudaira's samurai.

"Neither do I," said Lord Matsudaira. "But we can't climb these cliffs. At least, not quickly enough to save ourselves. Our only hope is to get back out of the gorge, to where the slope is gentler, and then climb to high ground."

Naturally, they were scrambling downstream as they spoke. The gap between the river's edge and the gorge wall had been narrow when they began their exploration, and now it was getting ever narrower.

It was not flat land, but scree; broken rocks that had tumbled downhill. It was difficult terrain to cross both safely and quickly, but speed was of the essence.

One of the samurai took an incautious step, lost his balance, and fell into the water.

"He's down!" yelled another samurai. "No, his head's above water." He passed out of sight as the river curved.

"We must catch up to him!" Lord Matsudaira commanded.

They found that the fallen samurai had managed to swim to the water on the inside of the bend, where the current was slower, but seemed to be unable to free himself completely from the water's grip.

"Hold my swords," said Lord Matsudaira.

The samurai took them, protesting, "My lord, you cannot risk yourself, we are sworn to protect you."

"And two of you can protect me better than one, neh?" he said as he stripped down to his loincloth. "I am a master of *suei-jutsu*." That was swimming as a martial art. "Can you say the same?"

The samurai could only bow his head. He could hardly claim to be superior to his lord in that skill, after such a boast.

Lord Matsudaira jumped into the water. It was bitter cold, draining away his life-force. He had to force his limbs to move; his arms and legs were as stiff as the puppets of *ningyo-joruri*. At last, he reached his target, and took hold of the fallen samurai. Slowly, very slowly, they inched toward the bank.

"My lord, watch out!" The samurai that Lord Matsudaira had left on dry land was pointing upstream, his features contorted.

A fallen tree swept down the river, and it spun in the eddy of the inside bend, striking Lord Matsudaira in the head. He went under, as did the man he had been trying to save.

The remaining samurai then dived in after them.

Lower American River

Downstream, where the miners were active, the rise of the river was more gradual, but the samurai guard refused to untie the men, or let them leave the riverbank, without orders.

Kiyoshi bowed. "Then run down to Shigehisa-san, ask him to bring up the boats."

"My orders say that I am to stay here."

"Then let me go!"

"My orders say that you are to remain here and supervise the miners."

"Supervise them doing what? Drowning?"

"Orders are to be obeyed, not questioned."

Kiyoshi bowed even more deeply. "You are right, of course, I will go back to mining."

The samurai didn't answer.

Kiyoshi picked up his shovel. "Cave in!" he shouted.

The samurai looked at him, perplexed.

The miners, still roped together, ran up the bank, toward

Kiyoshi. The rope, strung taut, caught the samurai's legs behind the knees, and he fell backwards into the water.

Kiyoshi slammed the shovel down upon him.

The samurai fumbled for his katana, but it was trapped underneath.

Kiyoshi struck again. The samurai was dead.

The miners stood silent.

"He fell in the water. He was dashed against the rocks."

The miners nodded.

Kiyoshi pushed the dead samurai's body into the river. The miners had pulled out their belt knives and were already cutting themselves free.

By now, the water had lapped over the riverbank, and was swirling about their ankles.

Kiyoshi pointed northward. "Run for the hills!" They ran.

Unfortunately, they were still far from high ground. When the water came up to their calves they despaired of reaching it in time, instead seeking out the nearest of the oak trees that dotted the lowland. Soon, they were huddled precariously in the branches.

And then, one by one, the trees toppled into the water.

"Row, damn you, row!" yelled Shigehisa. The sailors labored at the oars of the *Ni-Ban*, the first mate handling the tiller. Even Shigehisa was rowing. "Our comrades are depending on you!"

The captain, in the *Ichi-Ban*, didn't bother appealing to the crew's finer sentiments. "You sluggards! You good-for-nothings! Put your backs to it, you cockroaches!"

But neither approach was particularly successful. The American River had, within hours, gone from a trickle to a torrent, and they couldn't make any headway against it.

At last, exhausted, they turned the boats westward and let the current carry them back downstream.

January 1635,
Carquinez Strait

"You are the only survivors?" Iroha's voice was matter-of-fact, but her gaze seemed haunted.

"Yes, milady," said Shigehisa. "Only those of us who were in the boats, or very close to them, at the time of the flood. The others wrestled with the *kappa*...and lost." *Kappa* were the malicious river-spirits of Shinto mythology, who often drowned travelers attempting to cross the swift, dangerous mountain streams of Japan.

Iroha-hime frowned at the pagan reference but didn't object to it directly. "I will pray to São Vicente for my lord's soul." Saint Vincent of Saragossa was the patron saint of Lisbon, and the Romans had thrown his body into the sea.

"After the disaster," Shigehisa continued, "I thought it best that we make our way down to the South Bay, to reinforce you. But of course you intercepted us here, while we were still on our way."

Shigehisa lowered his voice. "There is one more thing, Iroha-hime. He gave this to me." He handed her the nugget.

"Why haven't you shown this to Captain Haruno, or Commander Yoritaki, or Mr. Tokubei?"

He looked away from her. "Because they are in the service of your father, the Grand Governor Date Masamune, and your husband was in that of the shogun, Tokugawa Iemitsu."

"And you weren't sure that the two were, ah, quite the same thing?"

"I thought that perhaps it was best that you decide who should know about this discovery."

"Thank you, Shigehisa-san. What will you do now?"

"Now? I am masterless, a ronin, once more. An old ronin. Perhaps I should join my lord in death."

"Serve me instead, and live."

"You? Forgive me, but women have not commanded men since the time of Sengoku, and then only rarely."

"My father has only one son, and two daughters, in this land. I do not think he can afford to treat us like ornamental plants for his garden. And even if it has not been 'official,' in the Time of Troubles, a wife sometimes had to hold a castle against an enemy while her lord was in the field.

"I intend to suggest to my father that I lead settlers from the Second Fleet back to the South Bay. I already know the Indians to be friendly, after all. Why lose the benefit of the work I have done with them already?"

"I will think upon it."

✧   ✧   ✧

Iroha held the gold nugget up. It sparkled in the sunlight. It had a cold beauty, she thought, a beauty without mercy, a beauty that had brought her husband to his death.

Once he had found the nugget, he had accomplished the task set by the shogun: He had found the gold fields. He could have rejoined her, and together they could have journeyed to Monterey.

Instead, he stayed. Why? What allure did the gold possess, that she did not?

If her husband had been less concerned with status and wealth, and more with love and faith, he would still be alive.

Had he ever cared for her? As Iroha? Or only as the daughter of the great and powerful Date Masamune? Would he have invited her to rejoin him if her father did not command the First Fleet?

She knew that as a samurai woman, she should not care. Marriage was an alliance between families, it had nothing to do with love.

But she cared.

And she cared about the colonists, too. Once the shogun was given tangible proof that the gold of California was not a fantasy, he might think twice about allowing the *kirishitan* to live there. The Tokugawa had taken control of all the gold mines throughout Japan, heedless of the claims of the local daimyos.

The Dutch were allies now, but they were also a potential threat. Japan didn't have enough ships to transport all the *kirishitan* by the shogun's deadline without their aid. And if the Japanese sent a large number of miners to the Bay, the Dutch might well learn of it. If they knew that those miners knew exactly where to go to find gold, the Dutch would be sorely tempted to wrest San Francisco Bay, and perhaps all California, away from the Japanese. And the Japanese in California were still too few to stop them.

A seagull swooped low across the water, and rose with a small fish gleaming in its mouth. The bird, at least, had no fears as to the consequences of finding a treasure.

Iroha tossed the nugget into the still-muddy waters of the Carquinez Strait. It made a soft "plop," as if a frog had jumped in.

February 1635,
Kodachi Machi/Santa Cruz

"Sanada Jiro and Sanada Saburo, please come forward," said Date Masamune.

The two samurai, wearing their formal attire, complied, then bowed deeply.

"Your feat in crossing the wilds of California, first to bring word of the plight of Iroha-hime and her party, and then to lead a rescue party to her, reminds me of the deeds of Hi no Omi no Mikoto the days of the Emperor Jimmu. It was that great samurai that led the imperial party to Yamato, earning himself the epithet, Michi no Omi, the Opener of the Way. You have opened the land road to San Francisco Bay.

"Since your service to Lord Matsudaira Tadateru was released by his death, you are offered positions as members of the grand governor's personal guard, with suitable stipends."

Saburo and Jiro exchanged quick glances, and bowed again.

"My brother and I thank you deeply," said Jiro. "May we respectfully request that we be assigned to the protection of Iroha-hime?"

"That is indeed her wish, and I am pleased to make it my command."

"Next. Captain Haruno. Please rise."

The captain did so haltingly.

"It would be remiss of me not to assure that you did not suffer an economic loss as a result of your spending your time on missions of exploration and rescue rather than trade. So, besides the payments you have already received from me, I have decided to give you the exclusive right to sell sea otter pelts in Japan. You will pay our house the standard commission. This exclusivity will last for two years, after which we will review how well you have done."

"I do not know the words to thank you, my lord."

"Thank me through more fine deeds, Captain. And Captain—I think the time will come when we will need you to captain a warship, not a merchant ship. So learn what you can of such matters from our Dutch allies."

"Last but not least, Mr. Tokubei."

"Y-yes, my lord?"

"You go by the nickame 'Tenjiku,' do you not? Because you once visited the fabled land of India, where the Buddha was born?"

"Yes, Grand Governor."

"Well then, I give you the right to use Tenjiku as your *kamei*." The *kamei* was the house name, and only a samurai could have one. "You have a *wakizashi* already, but you must now have a katana. Now, where will we find one in this wild land of California?"

Masamune snapped his fingers. "Hosoya Yoritaki!"

The commander of the *Ieyasu Maru*'s samurai came to attention. "Sir!"

"My daughter Iroha-hime has requested that her husband's katana be given to Daidoji Shigehisa, his lieutenant, and he in turn has asked me to offer his own long sword to you, in gratitude for your own role in the rescue of Iroha-hime and his party. Is that agreeable to you?"

"Of course, my lord," said Yoritaki.

"And would you be willing to give your katana, in turn, to your comrade at arms Tenjiku Tokubei?"

Yoritaki nodded. "With great pride." The exchanges had, of course, already been proposed and agreed to in private. The only one to whom it came as a suprise was Date Masamune's newest samurai, Tenjiku Tokubei.

Spring 1635,
Kawa Machi/Salinas

It had become quite apparent to First-to-Dance that, despite initial impressions, the visitors were *not* her ancestral dead. They acted as if they were alive; eating, drinking, pissing, shitting, and fornicating. Her people had never been very clear as to exactly what happened in the Land of the Dead and she supposed that it was possible that the dead mimicked the living. But if that were the case, wouldn't they also speak the language and preserve the dress and customs of the People?

The Japanese had made clear to her from their gestures that they came from across the sea. And she had seen their ships, floating in the water. Her own people weren't seafarers; they built little rafts of *tule*, the marsh reeds, and they used them only in quiet waters. But she couldn't deny the evidence of her own eyes;

the Japanese had come over the Great Water. So she supposed that the Land of the Dead was simply farther away.

Even if the visitors were living folk, they were nonetheless very powerful. So powerful that she had sometimes wondered whether she would be better off joining their community than remaining with her own people. She had been quick to notice that there were more men than women among the Japanese. Well, that was something she didn't have to decide right now. Especially since they were shooing her off. Date Masamune had decided that there was more to be gained by returning First-to-Dance to her people than by keeping her in Chiyo's company. She was to be given presents and sent on her way.

First-to-Dance resolved that she would find her tribesmen and then, somehow, turn the arrival of the Japanese to her advantage...

The Ohlone people did not live in just one place. Each tribelet, consisting of a couple hundred Indians, had a reasonably permanent winter settlement, and several summer camps. And every once in a while, they would decide that a particular site was unprofitable, or unlucky, and replace it with a new one.

Still, First-to-Dance had a fairly good idea of where her people would have gone after abandoning the coast to the Japanese.

When she strode into the clearing, conversation stopped abruptly. She understood why; to them she was one who had been touched by the spirits, and survived. The supernatural was now wreathed about her like the fog that waxed and waned along the California coast.

"You're in big trouble," she announced. "You have made them angry."

"Who?" asked the chief, his voice quavering. "The Dead?"

First-to-Dance had already considered and rejected the idea of insisting that the Japanese were ancestral ghosts. Close and prolonged observation would reveal otherwise.

"Worse than that," she said, her voice a stage whisper. "They are the Guardians of the Lands of the Dead. They are alive, but they have great power. They decide whether the dead are treated well or poorly in that land. And our people have failed to make any offerings to them, all these years. So they will punish us, unless..."

"Unless what?"

"Unless someone persuades them that we didn't know any better, and are ready to make amends."

"I will send our speaker to them." The speaker was second-in-rank to the chief, and had served as an envoy to other Ohlone tribelets.

"But... Ah, well. He is already an old man, with few summers left to him. He has little to lose..."

"What do you mean by that?" asked the speaker, somewhat sharply.

"The Guardians are so very angry. They might kill our envoy...."

The speaker's wife gave the speaker a nudge. "Send her in your place. They have already let her live once."

The speaker cleared his throat. "Since First-to-Dance has already, um, begun negotiations, perhaps it is best that she should continue..."

The chief grunted. "Where's the shaman? Let's find out what he thinks...." The shaman's nephew was sent to look for him, and the chief stalked into his hut. Hence, he didn't see First-to-Dance run after the boy.

The chief frowned. He didn't much like First-to-Dance. She had been married when she reached puberty to his uncle, and he was pretty sure she had cheated on him. She certainly hadn't shown him the respect that he deserved. He had been a great warrior in his youth...

A high-pitched voice intruded on his thoughts. It was the boy he had sent out earlier that day. "The shaman has come."

The chief emerged from his hut, and greeted the shaman. First-to-Dance stood a little behind him.

The shaman spoke up. "You will all recall that I spoke of a dream which foretold that this would happen."

"I don't remember..." said the chief, rather doubtfully.

"Oh, I do," said First-to-Dance brightly. "We are fortunate to have so farseeing a medicine man."

The chief had the feeling he was being conned. And that somehow, that little minx First-to-Dance had managed to form an alliance with his shaman. But he remembered how frightening the samurai on their horses seemed at the Time of Mourning. Even now, he wasn't convinced that they were entirely human. Perhaps they *were* the Guardians of the Land of the Dead. And if not, well, First-to-Dance would regret that she had trifled with him.

"All right, First-to-Dance, tell us exactly what these Guardians want from us...."

She did. And she also told them what they needed to do for her, so that she could properly serve as their speaker to the guardians.

Niji Masu (Watsonville)

Konishi Hyonai had been an important man in his village before he confessed to being a *kirishitan*. His grandfather had been a *ji-samurai*, who farmed in times of peace and fought in times of war. In 1591, then-Shogun Hideyoshi issued the Edict on Changing Status, which forced the "country samurai" to choose whether to forfeit samurai privileges and give up their weapons and other special privileges, or to become full-time retainers and live in castle towns. Hyonai's grandfather was one of the many who decided to surrender the sword and pick up a hoe.

Still, his fellow villagers did not forget his former status, and at village gatherings he was always given the seat of honor. Naturally, he was chosen as the village headman, the *shoya*, the only villager who could legally present a petition to the daimyo's district officer, the *daikan*. When he died, his son took his place, and in his turn, Hyonai did the same.

Since many of the farmers of Niji Masu came from his district, Hyonai found himself chosen as the headman of the new colony. And as headman, he found himself forced to deal with the farmers' outrage when they were told that they would be planting vegetables, not rice, in the spring.

Hyonai walked slowly toward the quarters of Moniwa Motonori, Date Masamune's *daikan* for Niji Masu. As he walked, he turned over in his mind the words that he must speak, polishing them until they were as smooth as the pebbles in the bed of a swift mountain stream.

"A thousand pardons for this intrusion on your time, *daikan*."
"Ah, Hyonai. Your family is well?"
"Quite well. *Daikan*, the farmers of this village are very grateful that by the grace of our shogun, Lord Iemitsu, and his grand governor, Masamune of the Date, their miserable lives were spared, and they were permitted to practice the Christian religion in this new land.

"Honorable *daikan*, I am sure you are familiar with the age-old saying, 'who can ever weary of moonlit nights and well-cooked rice?' The moon rises and falls just as often as it did in the old country. But what of rice? We took rice across the Great Ocean with us, and we eat it when we are homesick. Every week, we have less of it than we did before. If we are not allowed to plant it here, then one day soon, we will run out. We did not mind planting wheat and barley last autumn, those are winter crops. But it is now spring, and if we cannot see the cherry trees blossom, or hear the skylark sing, then at least let us prepare the paddies and sow the uneaten rice. Until we eat rice that we have grown in this land, we cannot call it New Nippon, we cannot call it home."

"Hyonai, I thank you for sharing your concerns with me. Our lord's scholars knew about this land before we boarded a single ship. They told him that this would be a great place for growing vegetables, but that they were doubtful that rice would grow here. You must trust to their judgment."

"Most worthy *daikan*, I have another saying to remind you of: 'You will never behold the rising sun by looking toward the west.' We will of course grow vegetables as the lord commands. Last month, we sowed maize and beans, and in summer, we will plant the sweet potatoes and the onions. But if we do not plant any rice, how will we know for sure that rice cannot grow here? Here in Niji Masu, it rains more than in Andoryu, but less than in the mountains that loom over Kodachi Machi. Walk around this land, and it is colder in some places, warmer in others. Perhaps we can find a good place for a rice paddy."

Moniwa Motonori bowed respectfully to the grand governor's chief advisor, Katakura Shigetsuna. The latter gestured for him to sit. Motonori gracefully knelt, folding his legs beneath him. He waited in silence for Shigetsuna to speak.

"My lord has instructed me to explain our agricultural policy to you, that you may better reassure the farmers under your jurisdiction that their petition has received a fair hearing." Shigetsuna paused a moment to collect his thoughts. "As perhaps you know, by act of Heaven"—he declined to specify whether this was the Buddhist, Shinto or Christian Heaven—"a town of the future was brought into our world. This town, Grantville, was part of a great kingdom that stretched from this coast to the one far to our east. The town had books of great learning, called 'encyclopedias,' and several of these were delivered as gifts to the shogun. These books provided information on how hot and how rainy this land, which they call California, is. And they provided similar information for Japan. Even though we do not know how they measure 'temperature' and 'precipitation,' we can compare the numbers for California to those for Japan. It was clear that this 'Monterey Bay' that we have colonized is much drier than Japan, save for eastern Ezochi, and also has cooler summers."

Motonori was no farmer, but he knew the rhythms of rural life, and understood the significance of these teachings. Rice was called "the child of Water." If the land around Monterey Bay was dry, then it would have to be irrigated in order for a rice crop to be possible. But that wasn't all. Even in Japan, the rice crop would fail if the summer was too cool. That was why there had been little effort to grow rice in Ezochi, the land of the Ainu.

"So, will rice become something that is just remembered and not eaten?"

"No, no," said Shigetsuna. "At worst, we can pay for Japanese or Chinese rice with goods from New Nippon. But we know rice was grown in Grantville's California, in the valleys of the Sacramento and San Joaquin rivers."

"So why did we come to Monterey Bay?"

"Military considerations. The rice growing areas are well inland, we would have to deal with more Indian tribes. And those lands have gold, and thus will soon attract the Spanish."

"Ah. I must bow in reverence to your superior knowledge of this land. However... I do know a bit about how our peasants think.... Could we perhaps authorize them to construct a small rice paddy? One near a river or marsh, so irrigating it is not a lot of work? 'Experience is the best teacher.'"

The adviser snorted. "'Experience is a comb which nature gives to men when they are bald,'" he quoted. "But I will pass on your suggestion."

May 1635,
Kawa Machi/Salinas

"One should never ponder the purpose of an order," said Hosoya Jinbei, "merely obey." He was one of the older samurai in the settlement, and had once guarded Date Chiyo-Hime and her wet nurse. He had fought at Sekigahara.

Watari Yoshitsune, a samarai of the younger generation, scowled. "But this order... It is one thing to order us to attack an enemy, even if it means certain death. It is another to treat us as if we were commoners." The samurai in Salinas had been ordered to help with the wheat harvest.

"Requiring us to help with the farming isn't treating us as commoners. *Ji-samurai* did it, in the old days."

"These are not the days of our grandfathers."

"Happy are the samurai who have long been in service to a lord," said Toshiro Kanesada. "In time of peace, they can study the classics and practice in the *dojo*. If you were a ronin, as I was until this voyage, you could have found yourself a body-guard to a fat merchant, or worse. I have known ronin who worked as carpenters or plasterers, ronin who made lanterns and umbrellas. Even ronin who were merely bandits. A ronin would not be so quick to complain about fishing or farming... especially in a foreign land where one may be attacked at any time."

"But if we help the farmers, when will we have time to practice our martial arts? When I practice *iaijutsu*, I make a thousand draws in a single session," Yoshitsune protested.

"Enough talk," said Jinbei. "It is time to help with the harvest. Yoshitsune-san, as you swing your scythe, pretend that you are cleaving a foe. Or several foes at once, if you like."

But Hosoya Jinbei was himself more troubled than he let on. He was a senior retainer, and despite what he had said to the others, he had questioned Date Masamune about the orders.

Respecting Jinbei's many years of faithful service, Masamune had explained his reasoning. In Japan, one in twenty Japanese was samurai. Here, in New Nippon, thanks to Date Masamune's contingent of retainers, it was about one in five.

The colonists and the retainers had brought food with them, of course, but they had used up several months worth while on board the ships, and more after arrival. They had started fish-ing, hunting, and gathering of fruits, berries and nuts, soon after coming ashore, but farming was a more drawn-out process. They were still eating more than they were producing... And as far as food was concerned, the samurai weren't producing at all. Date

Masamune had finally decided that they had to pitch in more than just shooting the occasional deer.

Jinbei had expressed his appreciation for Date Masamune's wisdom. But he objected to the shattering of social order. First, Masamune had decided to train a militia, to let peasants parade as if they were warriors. And now he was forcing samurai to work in the fields, as if they were peasants. Under these circumstances, Jinbei warned, how long would it be before the peasants decided that they didn't need samurai at all?

Masamune had smiled and reminded him that during the sixteenth century, the Age of War, many peasants had become ashigaru, infantrymen, and yet samurai still ruled Japan. And that in the same period, *ji-samurai* had done exactly what Masamune was asking his retainers to do now. He thanked Jinbei for his advice.

So Jinbei understood his lord's reasoning. Still, understanding a decision and accepting its consequences were two different things.

Niji Masu/Watsonville

Churoku's eyes widened in amazement, then narrowed with anger. "Murata! Togu! What do you think you're doing?"

His fellow farmers Murata and Togu were carrying a stone statue down the hill from their house. "What does it look like we're doing?" said Murata. "We're carrying the *ta no kami* to the paddy, so he can become the *yama no kami*." In Shinto belief, the *ta no kami* was the spirit of the field, and the *yama no kami*, the spirit of the wild lands, the wooded slope above the village. "Otherwise, the rice will not grow. Now, step off the path, so we can get by."

"The Forest god? The Field god? There is only one God, the Christian God. How can you call yourselves *kirishitan* and curry the favor of demons?"

Murata's face reddened, and it was the red of anger, not exertion. "Demons? The kami aren't demons. They are angels. Please do not insult me, I am no demon worshiper."

"Or perhaps the kami are avatars of the Christian God," said Togu. "Does not the *Tenchi*, the Tale of the Creation, say that *Deusu* has forty-two forms?"

"That is nonsense. You must not do this." Churoku set himself squarely in their path, and crossed his arms to form an "X." The gesture meant "closed" or "forbidden."

He glared at the two brothers. "It was one thing to carry out these pagan rituals when we were still in Old Nippon, and were compelled to do so lest we be revealed as *kirishitan*. It is quite another to do so here, in New Nippon, where we may openly follow the Faith."

Murata eased down his end of the idol, and Togu followed suit. Both grunted with relief at the easing of their load. "You have your opinion, and we have ours," said Murata, his voice rising. "Now, let us pass!"

"I'm telling you, Murata, this is a Christian paddy. I'll not have you desecrate it by erecting the image of a false god! If you want to grow rice the heathen way, then make your own paddy somewhere else!"

"You're not our padre or our lord, Churoku! I helped dig the ditches to water the seedlings, and this is my paddy as much as yours. This is your last chance."

Churoku waved his hand back and forth in front of his face. And then stuck out his tongue at them.

They charged him. It was two-against-one, but Churoku was a precocious member of the new militia, and he had his walking stick. He sliced at Murata's feet, forcing him to leap backward, then jabbed Togu in the belly. "For the Holy Spirit!" Churoku shouted. Togu bent over, holding his tummy, and groaning loudly.

Murata advanced, and Churoku feinted at his face, then rapped him on the knees. "And the Holy Christian Church!" Murata fell, but Togu was now back on his feet and ready for a second round.

By now the commotion had attracted attention. Other villagers had rushed outside. Some just gaped at the fight; others laughed and placed bets. Finally, two of the samurai assigned to Niji Masu appeared on the scene.

The senior samurai commanded them to stop fighting. "Churoku! Murata! Togu! On your knees, this instant, or your heads will roll." The three commoners quickly complied. "Hands behind your backs." The junior samurai tied them up. They were chivvied down the path, and confined in a hut.

"The magistrate will deal with you in the morning," the senior samurai said. "In the meantime, enjoy the view."

"And the company," added the other samurai. He laughed.

The next day, the three men were brought before the *daikan* Moniwa Motonori in his capacity as magistrate of Niji Masu/ Watsonville. Motonori heard their stories, and wrinkled his nose. "To cultivate rice, we must work together. But the three of you have disturbed the harmony of this village.

"You are each sentenced to one hundred lashes."

Once they were led away, he had Hyonai summoned.

"Hyonai, Hyonai. I am sure you have heard about the quarrel yesterday. I thought that by permitting your farmers to plant rice, it would lead to an increase in harmony, not in discord."

Hyonai kowtowed. "I apologize, on behalf of all of the farmers, and not just those three fools, for the disturbance."

"So what do you suggest I do, Hyonai? Forbid the rice cultivation after all? Allow it, but without the old rite? Require that tradition be followed, too? Divide the paddy lands in two, Christian and non-Christian?"

Hyonai pondered the question. "The culture of Japan is a culture of rice," he said, his words as slow as a river in summer. "We do not merely eat the grains, we make clothing out of the *wara*, the dried straw of the rice plant. The rice is our mother and our father. We celebrate the first work in the rice field, the sowing, the planting-out, and the harvesting.

"The people know, deep in their hearts, that as *kirishitan*, they should not continue the old rituals, but they need new ones to take their place. Otherwise they will lapse into bad habits.

"Let those who best know the words of the Lord In Heaven devise new rituals, rituals that are similar, where possible, to those we have done since time out of mind, yet pleasing to Deusu."

And so Imamiro Yojiro, who, as a lay catechist, was the First Fleet's highest-ranking religious leader, found himself at a field altar near the mouth of the Pajaro River, asking that Saint Isidore the Farmer, canonized in 1622, bless the rice paddy of Niji Masu.

There was, of course, no *torii*, the red-painted gate that marked a Shinto shrine. But Yojiro thought it most convenient that the kanji character "ta," meaning a rice paddy, was a square divided by a cross in the middle. He had a sign erected with the cross painted in red and the square in black. The spectators could see "ta," or just the cross, as they pleased.

Girls carried the seedlings from the nearby nursery to the paddy, for transplanting. They were dressed in special costumes: red pants, green shirts, and hats festooned with greenery and flowers. They walked clockwise around the paddy, singing the rice-planting song, as their fathers and brothers played flutes, beat on drums, rang bells, or banged wooden blocks together. They were followed by the samurai, dressed in full armor.

At the end of his prayer, Yojiro thanked "God in Heaven, He Who Blesses the Growing Rice." The words "growing rice," in Japanese, were *ine-nari*. Yojiro was well aware that this would evoke remembrance of *Inari*, the Great Kami of Fertility.

Kawa Machi/Salinas, Summer 1635

David Date coughed to get his sister's attention, and pointed down, toward the outer gate of the little castle of Kawa Machi. "Well, it appears that your Indian friend First-to-Dance has come up in the world."

Date Chiyo-Hime saw that the figure down below was indeed First-to-Dance. Chiyo summoned Mito and they walked briskly— running would have been undignified—down to the gate to greet her.

As before, First-to-Dance was wearing a double apron, braided tule in front, buckskin in back. The same otter skin robe she had before covered her shoulders, but it was only loosely clasped, allowing glimpses as she walked of the large, ornate necklace she now wore. The sunlight glinted off her new earrings. The two men following her were carrying baskets, and their manner was ever-so-slighty subservient.

Date Masamune had been surprised to learn that among First-to-Dance's people, a woman could be a chief. It wasn't common, because the office usually passed from father to son, but if no son were available, the old chief's sister or daughter was considered the next best choice. Likewise, a woman could serve as a "speaker," dealing with neighboring tribes.

Before, First-to-Dance was of interest primarily as a source of information, and, secondarily, as an intriguing companion who might distract Chiyo-Hime from other mischief.

Now, she was a diplomatic envoy of a tribelet of perhaps a hundred people. While her people were certainly no match for the Japanese militarily, Masamune was anxious to avoid unnecessary conflicts. There was no telling when a Spanish ship would spot the Japanese settlements.

First-to-Dance bowed in the manner that Chiyo-Hime had taught her. "Noble Guardian, I offer the greetings of my people to yours. I bring you gifts." These included tobacco, shell beads, feather headdresses, and strips of rabbit skin. Masamune didn't know it, but these were all traditional offerings to the spirits. There were also a few small stone mortars, containing red and white pigments.

"And I have gifts for you," Masamune said. These included a steel knife, a bolt of silk, and a mirror. The mirror had a bronze back, with a chrysanthemum blossom design upon it, and a reflective surface that was a tin-mercury amalgam.

"My people hope that you have enjoyed your visit." First-to-Dance's clear implication was, *and they are looking forward to your departure.* "We wish you a safe return to the Island of the Uttermost West." In case he had missed the implication.

"Alas, those who are still here cannot return. But we look forward to helping the Ohlone, our younger brothers." There were, in fact, some among the Ohlone who could pass, appearance-wise, for Japanese.

"Will you help us kill our enemies?" asked First-to-Dance. The Indians of central California were not especially warlike, but they did have disputes over access to hunting and fishing grounds, and there were tit-for-tat killings, too.

"If you are attacked without provocation on your part," Masamune replied, "we will come to your aid. But if you make unprovoked war on others, we will be very angry. But have no fear, our thunder sticks will frighten away your enemies."

First-to-Dance was silent for a time. Then she said, "Will you teach us how to make the trees that run on water?"

Masamune waved his hand in front of his nose, as if he was trying to waft away an unpleasant odor. "The time for that will come." The Japanese ships gave them the advantage of interior lines if any of the coastal settlements were attacked by the Indians. Masamune was in no hurry to make it possible for the local Indians to conduct raids by sea. It was bad enough that the Chumash to the south and the warlike tribes of the Pacific Northwest had canoes. "But we will be happy to share with you the fish of the deep waters. And the fruits of our fields."

"The Ohlone come to the Great Sea each year to collect mussels, abalone and snails, and fish for surfperch, and rockfish and cabezon." She used the Indian names for these, of course; she had taught the words to Chiyo-Hime and Masamune's scholars. "But they have not been able to do so for many moons, as they are afraid of offending the Guardians."

"They are welcome to come; there are enough for all. Let them come to the beaches and rocks in good spirit. But they should come in twos and threes, lest they frighten away the fish and offend Ebisu, the God—excuse me, the Patron Saint—of Fishermen." Masamune didn't want large groups of Indians near the Japanese settlements.

First-to-Dance inclined her head. "And we will show you the hidden woods, where acorns are bounteous. And you may come there to collect them. In twos and threes, so as not to displease the Spirit of the Forest."

Fall 1635,
Niji Masu/Watsonville

The wheat and the barley, the rye and the millet, all had grown well. The rice, well, that was another matter. The milder summer of Monterey Bay had seemed a blessing, at first; it meant that the rice plants didn't drink as greedily as they did back home. Which was just as well, as it barely rained during the summer. They irrigated the paddies with water ponded during the wet season, but that wasn't enough; they had to mix in some of the bay water.

There was much argument as to the reason for the failure. Some blamed the saltiness of the bay water. Others complained that it never became hot enough for the grain to ripen properly. Hyonai, in fact, feared that this was the case. Feared it because, while the peasants could find more fresh water in the mountains, and build aqueducts to carry the water to the field, they couldn't make the sun any warmer.

There were also arguments of a more theological nature. Some loudly and repeatedly insisted that it was a mistake to deviate in the slightest from the old Shinto rituals. Perhaps, they said, Deusu delegated rice growing to the kami. If Deusu minded the *kirishitan* following tradition during the decades of hiding, why wouldn't he have blighted their crop, again and again, until they learned their lesson?

Others decried every one Yojiro's ritual concessions. They thought that the villagers should have asked for the blessing of the saint and left it at that.

The only point on which everyone agreed was that they were unhappy not to have any New Nippon-grown rice.

Kawa Machi/Salinas

The morning sun had not yet dried out the blood when Date Masamune came over to inspect the body. Hosoya Jinbei still gripped, even in death, the *kozuka*, the disemboweling blade.

Seppuku—ritual suicide—could be committed for many reasons. *Jun-shi* was following one's lord into death; it was forbidden by law but still happened from time to time. *Gisei-shi* was self-sacrifice, perhaps a defeated lord killing himself as part of a peace settlement. *Sokotsu-shi* was to win forgiveness for a mistake. *Fun-shi* was a general expression of indignation with the vagaries of fate. *Kan-shi* was more specific; it was to reprove one's lord.

Another samurai, young Watari Yoshitsune, sat quietly beside Hosoya's corpse. After a moment of quietly studying the grim tableaux, Date Masamune spoke to him.

"You were his *kaikatsu*?" The *kaikatsu* was the "second," who delivered the killing stroke that put the principal out of his misery. It was in theory an honor to be named as *kaikatsu*, but samurai were not eager for this honor. Not out of squeamishness, but because if they botched the beheading stroke, it was extremely embarrassing.

"Yes. I was privileged to be a student at Muso Shinden-ryu." That was the school, founded by Hayashizaki Jinsuke Shigenobu, at which *iaijitsu*, the art of sword-drawing, was taught.

"Thank you for serving him so well," said Masamune. The praise was honest; Yoshitsune had halted the beheading stroke just short of completion; the strip of skin tethered Jinbei's head to his body, keeping it from flying off and rolling about in an unseemly manner.

Masamune picked up Jinbei's *jisei*, his death poem, which lay beside his last cup of sake.

> Old warriors dream
> of battles of youth.
> Grasses sway
> over comrades' graves.
> The winds still.

Jinbei had also left behind a letter, which revealed Jinbei's purpose in committing suicide. It was not *kan-shi*, because Jinbei acknowledged the logic of Masamune's orders. It was *fun-shi*; Jinbei's resolution of his unhappiness over what he saw as the unavoidable degradation of the samurai by common labor. The last straw was the failure of the rice harvests at both Niji Masu and Salinas; to him, it meant that the sacrifice they had made was purposeless.

Masamune folded the two papers into a fold of his hakama. "Kindly summon all of the samurai at this settlement. I wish to address them about Jinbei's death."

Date Masamune didn't seem to be shouting, but his voice could be heard across the assembly ground. "Jinbei was like a forest giant, whose great canopy long sheltered the Date clan. But what happens to a forest giant when the typhoon blows? Its virtue becomes a vice, as its many leaves and branches catch and multiply the force of the wind. The tree tries to stand fast against the onslaught. It stands unbending, because the girth of its trunk gives it no other choice. When the sky clears, either the tree still stands, or it lies on the ground, dead.

"New Nippon is a new land, and in it we must emulate the saplings, not the ancients. We must bend with the wind when the alternative is ruin."

Chiyo told First-to-Dance about the ritual suicide of Hosoya Jinbei, whom she had known since she was a little child.

"But why would he kill himself?" asked First-to-Dance.

"The way of the samurai is found in death," Chiyo told her.

First-to-Dance would have questioned her further, but they were interrupted by a summons from Chiyo's father.

As they walked to his receiving room, First-to-Dance thought about what Chiyo had said. *The way of the samurai is found in death.* First-to-Dance had told her people that the Japanese were the Guardians of the Land of the Dead to serve her own purposes, not because she had believed it herself. But perhaps the spirits had spoken through her, and revealed a truth. Perhaps the samurai, the bearers of the two swords, were indeed the Guardians.

A week later, Masamune addressed his samurai once again. "I have thought about the duties of retainers to their lord, and of the lord to his retainers. To prosper in this new land we must change some of our ways, but perhaps I tried to change too many ways too quickly.

"So, for the time being, my samurai are not required to help with the farming and fishing. However..." He let them wait for the completion of his thought.

"However, only those samurai who volunteer to help in that way will be permitted to join in the expeditions I will be sending out. Perhaps to enjoy the glory of finding a place where rice will flourish.

"Dismissed."

The guardsman standing on the watchtower at the Kawa Machi castlelet saw smoke rising from Point Piños. It faded, then a second column rose into the sky. This was clearly a signal, from a lookout on the point, and not a forest fire.

The Kawa Machi soldier grabbed the conch shell that hung nearby, and blew. An officer clambered up the ladder to see for himself. He looked, and said, "Beat the Great Gong."

By the third beat, samurai were already pouring out of the barracks, bows or arquebuses in hand, and swords in their scabbards.

By the time they had reached the battlements, Kawa Machi had sent up a smoke signal of its own. Soon, there were black clouds of warning above Andoryu/Monterey, and Niji Masu/Watsonville, and Kodachi Machi/Santa Cruz, too. Signal guns boomed repeatedly.

The alarm subsided when the ships came at last into view. While some were of barbarian design, others were clearly junks, and all were flying a flag with a red sun disk, the *hinomaru*, on a field of white.

The Second Fleet had arrived.

First-to-Dance had persuaded some of her kinfolk to come to Kawa Machi for a Japanese celebration. It began with the Lord's Prayer, led by Imamiro Yojiro and David Date, and joined in by all of the *kirishitan* of Kawa Machi, both the old California hands who had arrived a year earlier, and those who had just arrived on the Second Fleet.

Flanking the Christian altar, there were two daises, the *kamiza* for the Shinto deities, and the *goza* for the emperor of Japan. Date Masamune, in his capacity as a court noble of the Upper First Rank, made obeisance to the kami on the emperor's behalf, arranging an offering of sake, rice porridge and steamed rice on a reed mat. The rice, of course, had come from the stores of the Second Fleet. Some of the newcomers looked unhappy about the coupling of this pagan ritual with the Christian rite, but they didn't object openly.

The fact that the spectators nearest the front were all pagan samurai, several hundred of them, and of course wearing their swords, probably had something to do with this reticence.

"Please translate what I say for your friends," Chiyo told First-to-Dance. "This ceremony is *Niinamesai*," she told them. "Back home, we would celebrate this on the Day of the Rabbit of the Eleventh Month, the Dutch December. But here we have decided to hold it in the month that we arrived in Monterey Bay and met your people.

"The name means, 'new-taste-ritual.' Today we offer a taste of the harvest to Heaven, to thank it for providing the rain and sun so that our crops will grow, and protecting the crops from vermin of all kinds."

In California, only the Indians of the southeast grew crops. First-to-Dance told her tribesmen that the Japanese had made a powerful magic which caused plants to multiply.

"We are sad that our favorite plants, our rice, would not grow here. But our kinfolk on the ships that have just arrived have brought rice to share with us, and in turn we are giving them, and you, fresh vegetables and fruit."

There was sweet potato and white potato, brought to Japan by the Portuguese in the sixteenth century, and initially deprecated as *bareisho*—"horse fodder." They were grown in the uplands. There were artichokes, cucumbers, and melons, sown in the summer. There were deer, brought down by samurai archers, and rabbits, caught in farmers' snares. There were wild birds, too. And fish of course.

The *kirishitan* of the Second Fleet tore greedily into this repast, such a refreshing change from their shipboard diet. And the Indians were amazed by all the strange new foods—but this didn't stop them from eating them.

And so the Ohlone Indians of California enjoyed their first Japanese thanksgiving.

Autumn Wind

September to October 1635

The autumn wind:
for me there are no gods;
there are no buddhas.
—Masaoka Shiki (1867–1902)[4]

Late September 1635,
Andoryu (Monterey), California

"Red flag! Red flag!" Marina shouted. "Are you all blind, and deaf to boot?"

Her fellow *kirishitan* were neither, but those in her immediate vicinity were engrossed in a gambling game. She got the gamblers' attention by kicking sand over the dice.

"Hey, what do you think—"

"Red flag, you fools!"

The gamblers stifled their protest, and looked up toward the lookout tower, perched precariously on the pine-covered point marking the southern end of Monterey Bay. There, two watchers were posted, and one of them was indeed was waving two red flags over his head.

---

4 Translation by Harold G. Henderson, *An Introduction to Haiku*, 164 (Doubleday & Co., Inc., 1958)

Another was sending smoke signals into the air.

It was now the gamblers' turn to yell. "Red flag!"

Hearing the commotion, and then seeing the red flags for himself, Sakai Kuroemon, the samurai in charge of the small battery that guarded Andoryu, ordered an *ozutsu*, a Japanese-made swivel gun, to be fired off.

On the beach to the east of Andoryu, First-to-Dance turned to her companion, the grand governor's daughter, Chiyo-hime. "Are we under attack by the Southern Barbarians you told me about?"

Chiyo-hime stifled a laugh. She couldn't help but wonder what the Spanish reaction would be if they knew that a scantily clothed and illiterate Ohlone Indian had characterized them as "barbarians." She had never met a Spaniard herself—the Spanish had been banned from entering Japan in 1624, and she had not met any of the missionaries who sneaked in afterward—but Chinese traders had commented on the hauteur of the hidalgos in Manila.

"No, no. The signal gun would have been fired more than once if ships had been sighted. Even friendly ships. They must have sighted a school of sardines."

It was true. A school of sardines could be as many as ten million fish. The sardines jerked and splashed about in a way that set up characteristic ripples, evident to a trained observer. In shallow water, the school disturbed the bottom, giving the water a pinkish tint. And the sky above the school held its own clues; seabirds and dolphins treated the horde of sardines as if it were a parade of Osaka street vendors at festival time, selling sushi from their carts.

Three boats had put out to sea. Two were net-boats, *amibune*, and the giant sardine net, over a hundred fathoms long, was suspended between them. It was heavy, and fifteen men were needed on each *amibune* to handle it and to maneuver the boat.

The two senior fishermen on the third boat, the *tebune*, were monitoring the movements of the school and giving orders to the *amibune*. Once the latter were together, behind the school, the fishermen grunted and heaved.

"There goes Uncle Long Sardine Net," Marina said to no one in particular. "We'll eat well tonight."

With the net cast in the water, the *amibune* separated, drawing the net into an arc facing the beach.

On the beach, the local headman was leading a prayer to the Virgin Mary, and "the Angel Ebisu." Herded by the *amibune*, the sardines continued to head toward the beach, so apparently the Shinto God of Fishermen did not object to his transfer to the Christian Heaven. The prayer thanked the heavenly powers that the waters of Monterey Bay, for most of the year, was well endowed with sardines, and that near their homes there was a beach, with a shallow, smooth sea floor beyond, on which they could operate their beach nets.

As soon as the *amibune* reached water shallow enough to stand in, the villagers waiting on the beach ran out to them, and the ropes were passed on to their willing hands. All of the residents of Andoryu helped pull the net to the shore, even children, and women with babies tied to their backs. Caught up in the excitement of the moment, First-to-Dance ran to help, leaving a bemused Chiyo-hime and her samurai guard behind.

With the net ropes safely handed over, some of the *amibune* crew jumped off to help with the hauling, while the rest maneuvered their boats back behind the seine, and beat the water with bamboo poles.

One of them, a young man named Yakichi, grabbed the same rope that First-to-Dance was holding. "Take a step back, now," he cried. "Keep the tension steady, don't jerk the line! Step back again, that's good!"

The villagers whooped when, at last, the vast haul of sardines was safely deposited on the beach, above the high water line. First-to-Dance let go of the rope with a sigh of relief.

"I guess we'll be having sardines for the evening meal," Chiyo said to her guard.

"For the next few weeks at least."

The Second Fleet had arrived a week earlier, and the tired and hungry passengers, at least, would appreciate the fresh catch.

However, the grand governor, Date Masamune, had no intention of permitting all of the new batch of colonists to settle at Monterey Bay. The fledgling settlements, at modern Monterey, Salinas, Watsonville and Santa Cruz, could absorb only so many new people at a time. The rest would have to move on.

He gave the necessary orders.

✧   ✧   ✧

Yakichi bowed politely to Sakai Kuroemon. "You called for me, sir?"

"Yes. You are a younger son. Your brother will one day own your family's fishing boat, you will at best be one of his crew."

"I suppose..."

"But your headman speaks well of you, and there's an opportunity. We have a new batch of colonists, who have no knowledge of California. If you would be willing to go with the ones we are sending around the Monterey peninsula, to the place the lord's scholars call 'Carmel,' and teach them how to fish these waters, we can give you some special privileges..."

"Please explain, I am quite interested."

The samurai did so.

"I'm your man," Yakichi said.

Carmel Bay, California

The ship bearing Yakichi and a contingent of the Second Fleet's colonists rounded the Point of Pines, and continued around the Monterey peninsula. Its destination was the mouth of the Carmel River, where it would be establishing a *han-no han-gyo*, a half-farming, half-fishing village.

If Monterey Bay was a fishhook, Carmel Bay was a trident, with the center tine broken off near its base. The center tine was Carmel Point, and was flanked by sandy beaches. But most of the coast, from Cypress Point in the north to Lobos Point in the south, was rocky.

Carmel Point hooked southward, giving some protection to Carmel Beach where the river mingled with the sea. Nonetheless, the skipper hurried the passengers off his ship; the anchorage had a rocky bottom that he didn't like at all.

The passengers decided to lay out their village, which they named "Maruya" after the Virgin, on a low rise that overlooked the last bend in the Carmel River, a bit over half a mile from the shoreline. As a symbol of their thanks to God for their safe voyage, on the bank of the Carmel they erected a giant cross, twenty feet high, made of native pine.

Maruya/Carmel

The fishermen and samurai of Maruya milled about the Cross of Thanksgiving, erected when the colony was founded a week earlier. An early bird among them had been heading down to where his boat had been left the day before when he noticed something odd about the cross. He walked over for a closer look, then ran back to the village to report.

They had yet to see a single Indian. But there were arrows planted in a circle around the cross, and strings of shells hung on the arms. Were the arrows a challenge, a warning to stay where they were, or a sign of peace, being directed into the ground?

A messenger was sent over the hill country to Andoryu, and from there to the little castle at Kawa Machi/Salinas.

Date Masamune asked First-to-Dance, who had spent the previous winter with the Japanese, and was now the "speaker" for her tribelet, to go to Maruya and advise what the Japanese should do next.

October 1635,
Kodachi Machi/Santa Cruz

The overseer scowled at the new colonists. "You've gawked and lazed around long enough, it's time for you to get to work.

"If you knew how to fish, you'd be down here." He gestured south, toward the water. "And if you knew how to farm, you'd be out there." He gestured east. "Jesu help me, you're a bunch of peddlers and shopkeepers and artisans from Nagasaki and other towns, with no useful skills. Not useful here yet, at any rate."

He spat. "So permit me to introduce you to your new friends, Father Axe and his brother, Uncle Shovel."

Yamaguchi Takuma's fingers flew, shifting the beads on his abacus, calculating the supplies they would be needing the next day. Occasionally, he glanced at the perspiring laborers. Preparing the ground for a *yamashiro*, a mountain fortress, in the hills above Santa Cruz, was hard work, and he was glad that he had a skill that freed him from the obligation of manual labor.

One of Date Masamune's advisors, the old battle-horse Katakura

Shigetsuna, had picked the site. It was a long ridge, partially protected by creek gorges. The laborers would clear off the trees and
level the ridge; the timber and earth would be used to construct
a palisade and rampart.

Takuma had sat in on one meeting in which Shigetsuna
explained the project to his foremen and Kodachi Machi's guard
commander, Kanno Shigenari. The site included a small spring,
and the water supply could be augmented by building cisterns
or digging wells. It was more than a mile from the coast;
that distance, plus the elevation, meant that it was safe from
bombardment by Spanish warships. The Spanish could drag the
guns into firing range, but it would take time, and the Japanese
would express their disapproval with their own weapons: cannon, handguns, bows, and even ballistas and catapults. They, at
least, didn't require precious gunpowder.

Given time, the Japanese would strengthen the defenses: add
lookout towers, top the walls with thatch or shingles to protect
them from the weather; dig trenches for rolling stones down upon
the enemy; and turn neighboring hilltops into additional baileys.

Takuma thought it sad to think that the Spanish, who had
helped introduce the Christian faith to Japan, might attack the
kirishitan of Kodachi Machi. He had, very politely, suggested to
Shigetsuna that a large cross be erected on the watch tower, so
that if the Spanish came by, they would know that the town was
Christian and not shoot at them. Shigetsuna had thanked Takuma
for his suggestion, and asked him whether Buddhists ever made
war on fellow Buddhists. Takuma had to admit that they did.

But he still thought it might cause the Spanish to hesitate. So
why not?

Date Masamune's Yashiki (Fortified House), Kawa Machi/Salinas

First-to-Dance was studying her appearance in the mirror that
Chiyo had lent her. She wanted to look her best before she met
the messenger from Maruya/Carmel. First impressions mattered.

"This is foolish," said Swims-Like-Seal. He was one of First-
to-Dance's tribesmen, and had been one of the Indian guests at
the feast welcoming the Second Fleet.

"Why do you say that?"

"You should be here, with the leader of these strangers—"

"The Guardians of the Dead," First-to-Dance reminded him.

"If you say so." Swims-Like-Seal was one of the tribal skeptics, which was probably one of the reasons he had been sent. There was a faction within the tribe that didn't much like First-to-Dance. "But my point is that you should be with their big chief, the One Eye, bargaining for concessions for our people. Not gallivanting around looking for the people of the south."

"You don't understand. I help him, he helps me."

"Well, don't be away so long that he forgets that you're out there helping him."

First-to-Dance hadn't yet learned how to ride a horse. The only horses in America were those brought by the Europeans, or now, by the Japanese. She would have been happy to walk to Maruya/ Carmel but her escort insisted that this wasn't dignified enough for one traveling in an official capacity, she must either ride a horse or be carried by bearers in a palanquin.

"Please...wait...a moment...First-to-Dance!" It was Shigetsuna, huffing and puffing.

She stopped what she was doing, and bowed. Both the Indians and the Japanese agreed on the importance of showing respect for one's elders.

"How may I help you, Wise One?"

"One of the presents you gave to us upon your return was a red face pigment. Where does that come from?"

"It's a soft red rock, it comes from a ridge that lies halfway between here and the Sea of Tule." Tule was the bullrush that grew in the swampland of the southern end of San Francisco Bay. "We trade for it, or sometimes our people go there to collect it ourselves."

"I see," said Shigetsuna. "And which tribe controls it?"

"Controls? I don't understand...."

"In which tribe's land does it lie?"

"It moves."

"Moves? The land moves?"

She pursed her lips. "So sorry, I am not clear. The red-earth-place doesn't move. Sometimes it is part of the land of the Awaswas, sometimes of the Mutsun, sometimes of the Tamyen."

"Ah, I understand. It lies between their villages. And can you draw me a picture in the sand that shows the way?"

"I can't, but Swims-Like-Seal has been there." She spoke with him rapidly. "Yes, he can draw you a picture."

"I would like that. In fact, it would be even better if he could lead some of our samurai there. He would be well rewarded."

There was a quick negotiation, with First-to-Dance interpreting, and Swims-Like-Seal agreed to the terms.

First-to-Dance's escort helped Shigetsuna mount his horse, and then Swims-Like-Seal got up behind him. This was possible only because the horse was one of the European horses that the Dutch-Japanese invasion force had captured from the Spanish in Manila. The Japanese captors preferred the smaller Japanese breed they were accustomed to, and so Date Masamune had acquired European horses at a bargain price.

"Forget the palanquin," said First-to-Dance to her escort, eyeing his waist. "I'll double up with you."

Kodachi Machi/Santa Cruz

"Hiraki, where is your grandfather?" asked Yamaguchi Takuma. "It's almost time to eat."

The nine-year-old looked up. "He went off looking for herbs."

"Yesterday," his mother Mizuki volunteered, "he was chortling about some plant he found in the scrubland out to the west. You know, that field that was partially cleared last year. I bet he's out there again."

"Should I send Hiraki to fetch him?"

"Let him enjoy himself; he's retired after all. I'll give him some rice-gruel when he comes in."

Maruya/Carmel

"So, you are our native expert," said Toshiro Kanesada. He put a slight stress on the word "native" that First-to-Dance didn't like. It was a pity, because otherwise First-to-Dance thought that there was plenty to like about him. He was well-muscled without overdoing it, and taller than most of the Japanese. And he moved like a mountain cat.

"I think we can handle the matter on our own."

Chiyo had warned First-to-Dance that Kanesada might be a bit resentful of her presence. Kanesada had once been an up-and-coming member of the guard of Honda Masazumi, the lord of Utsunomiya. But in 1622, Masazumi rebuilt a castle without the shogun's permission. He lost his fief and was sent into exile, and of course all his samurai, including Kanesada, became ronin. It was very difficult for a ronin to become a retainer once more, but the assembly of the First Fleet had created that opportunity.

Kanesada had recently transferred to the small garrison at Maruya/Carmel, becoming its commander. He had put in for the transfer after the ritual suicide of his friend, Hosoya Jinbei.

"I am just here to help prevent misunderstandings," said First-to-Dance. "The grand governor told me, when I last dined with him, that he has great faith in your abilities." Thus simultaneously buttering Kanesada up, and putting him in his place.

First-to-Dance carefully inspected the Indian artifacts that had been placed in the vicinity of the Maruyans' cross. She jiggled the shells, and felt the feathers on the arrow shafts. The Maruyan headman and Lieutenant Kanesada watched her.

"Is this going to take all day?" Kanesada asked.

She ignored him. At last she announced, "this is mostly a peaceful offering, made by the Ixchenta. They live on the other side of this river, near the mouth."

"Why do you say, 'mostly'?"

She frowned. "Putting an arrow into the ground is a sign of peaceful intent. But using so many arrows seems to me to also be a veiled threat, 'we are many, we have arrows to spare, so don't mess with us.'"

"What do you think we should do next?" asked the headman.

"Set out gifts for them."

Kanesada agreed. Without discussing it with First-to-Dance, he also placed a samurai in hiding, to spy on the Indians when they came and report back how many there were, their weapons, their state of health, and so on.

One day, the gifts vanished.

The samurai watchman never saw the Indians, coming or going.

Kodachi Machi/Santa Cruz

Yamaguchi Takuma stood outside his home, and greeted his guest. His guest, in turn, bowed and handed over a present, medicine in a clamshell.

"What an honor!" cried Takuma. "I could hardly believe it when I saw you come off the ship. Up to now, we have only had a *doshiki*, and a few confraternity leaders like myself, to serve the religious needs of a community of over a thousand Christians. But now we have you, a Franciscan brother! Trained in a seminary in Manila, no less!"

Friar Franciscus Tanaka put a finger to his lips. "I would prefer that you say nothing of the matter until the ships leave..."

"I don't understand..."

"Don't you?" The friar stared at him. "Haven't you wondered why there are no priests among you, or among us new arrivals?"

"I assumed that it was because none of the Japanese-born priests had come out of hiding yet."

"No, no, there was one; from Nagasaki. And was he sent to Monterey Bay, with the other *kirishitan* from Nagasaki? No. He wasn't even placed on the same ship. His ship parted from us early, going somewhere far to the north.

"Plainly, this grand governor doesn't want the *kirishitan* of Monterey Bay to have a priest. And if gambling weren't sinful, I would wager that if I had let the inspectors know that I was consecrated as a friar, I bet I would be shivering somewhere up north, too. Because the grand governor doesn't want us 'corrupting' his precious samurai."

At least the grand governor's samurai aren't hanging us upside-down in a pit of shit, thought Takuma. But rather than say so, he bowed deeply and ushered Friar Franciscus Tanaka into the *zashiki*, the most formal room of the house. It was the only room whose floor was completely covered with *tatami* mats, no doubt brought to California from Japan. Their presence marked the Yamaguchi family as being one of quite prosperous commoners before their journey into exile; even a century ago, only samurai dwellings would have had them.

✧   ✧   ✧

In the *zashiki*, the friar was invited to sit with his back to the *tokonoma*. This was the *kamiza*, the "top seat." It would, after all, be gauche to force the guest of honor to view the contents of that alcove: a picture scroll from home, and a bouquet of native flowers.

Franciscus started to murmur some obligatory words of gratitude for the honor bestowed upon him, when the words caught in his throat. An unmistakable *butsudan*—a Buddhist altar—sat on a cabinet on one side of the room. The doors were closed, but Franciscus knew what would be inside.

No doubt it was necessary to have a *butsudan* back in Nippon, during the decades of persecution. The authorities might at any time search a home for signs of christian worship, and, failing to find such, still find it suspicious if there were no signs of proper obeisance to the buddhas and kamis. But why would it be brought here, where Christianity was legal?

He sniffed the air. No...yes.... There was a taint of incense. Incense sticks had been burned here, probably this very day. Probably in front of an *ihai*, a spirit tablet, now safely stored in the butsudan.

"Is something wrong, Brother Franciscus?" asked Takuma.

Franciscus wanted to rail at him and his wife, but this was not the time. Not when he was a guest at their home. But it horrified him to find a a *butsudan* in the home of a *mizukata*, an elected baptizer for a Christian community.

His gaze rose to scrutinize the ceiling, especially above the doors to adjoining rooms. Well, at least they hadn't compounded their heresies by putting a *kamidama*, a Shinto shrine, between the crossbeams.

He breathed in and out slowly. "No," said Franciscus, "nothing is wrong."

Maruya/Carmel

The first arrow lodged in the straw canopy that shaded the fishing boat.

"Did you hear something?" Yakichi said sharply to his companion, Sakuzo. Thanks to his deal with the authorities, Yakichi had been able to borrow the money for a part-share in Sakuzo's boat, brought over from Japan.

The second arrow just missed Sakuzo's head, and only because he happened to lean over the gunwale to look for fish at the key moment.

"Fuck! We're being shot at!" Yakichi shouted. "Keep down," he added, and took his own advice.

They were, at the time, about a mile north of the mouth of the Carmel River, about two hundred yards away from Carmel Beach.

They hastily turned the boat toward the open sea, which both made the boat a smaller target, and also allowed them to quickly open up the range. After some frantic paddling, they turned once more to parallel the shore. Very cautiously they made for the river mouth.

As soon as they saw the village women standing in the shallows of the river, washing clothes by kicking them about with their feet, they started yelling for them to run to the fort and alert the soldiers.

"Where is First-to-Dance?" Kanesada demanded.

The sentry gawked at him. "I think . . . I think she said she was going off to gather berries, sir."

"We can't wait for her. Sound assembly! For both the guard and the militia!"

"The militia is responsible for village defense, I am leaving four guardsmen on foot to assist them. The rest of us will ride a sweep to the north, to where the shooting occurred."

Kanesada swung himself into the saddle, and his fellow patrollers followed suit. They rode perhaps two miles, through meadows and open woods, without spotting any Indians.

This is a waste of time, Kanesada decided. *By now, they are back in their village, congratulating themselves on giving us a scare. Well, I'll give them a scare.*

"Back the way we came!"

They rode back, and this time, they crossed the Carmel River. It was still low water; the winter rains hadn't yet begun. He knew, from conversations with First-to-Dance, where the Indian camp was mostly likely to be; it would be positioned near a place convenient for catching the salmon running down the Carmel.

The Indians weren't accustomed to horses, and therefore they reacted by fleeing or hiding, rather than fighting. Hiding, however, was not a good idea, as the Indians didn't have time for stealth, or for hiding the signs of their passage. Two women and a child were taken prisoner, and brought back, tied to spare ponies, to serve as hostages.

As he and his men rode back through the gate of the Maruya fort, Kanesada felt quite pleased with himself.

"Are you sure that these are the same Indians that attacked your fishermen?" First-to-Dance demanded.

"Not these individuals, of course, but their tribe," said Kanesada. "Their camp was only a few miles away from where the shooting occurred, so who else could it be? And we hold the entire tribe responsible for the actions of any of its members." Japanese law included the principle of collective responsibility.

"May I see the arrows that were fired at the fishermen, please?"

Fortunately, the fishermen had pulled them out of their boat and brought them to the fort, as proof that they had been attacked, and weren't malingering. First-to-Dance studied them carefully, her brows narrowing as she did so.

"What happened to the arrows that were left in the ground by our Cross?"

"The headman has them. He kept them as souvenirs."

"Please have him bring them here."

In due course, she laid them out, one next to the other, on the floor. She set the two new arrows a foot or so away from the old ones, close enough to make comparisons, far enough away to avoid accidentally mixing the two groups.

She looked up at Kanesada. "As I feared, they are not from the same tribe."

"How do you know?"

"The way they are painted is different."

"Wouldn't that just mean that they were made by different Indians of the same tribe? So they'd know who made a kill?"

"Yes and no. The old ones were made by three different makers, and the new ones by two others. But on the butt ends, the old ones all use two colors, and new ones just one. That tells me that the new ones are from a smaller tribe than the old ones; they needed fewer colors to tell whose was whose.

"And look at the patterns. All of the old ones have eight painted short bands and then a long one, in alternating colors. The new ones both have two long bands, with an unpainted gap in-between."

Kanesada took a deep breath, then slowly exhaled. "All right, I'll have you question the hostages. See what they say about these arrows."

The hostages were a disconsolate heap of misery on the floor of the gathering hall of the Japanese village, their hands and feet tied, a guard watching their every move. Not that they could move much. Their eyes were downcast, but they looked up when First-to-Dance spoke to them, and showed them the arrows.

First-to-Dance translated. "They say that their people, the Ixchenta, had nothing to do with this attack. They say that the arrows are made by the Achista, who live to the north, and are their enemies.

"Why, they say, have you attacked them? Did they not welcome you? Have they not let you catch salmon in the river that their grandfather's grandfather fished in?"

Kanesada stared at her, then dropped his gaze. "I have failed my lord. I have made enemies of our friends, and our real enemies are laughing at us. I must make amends."

He gave orders for finer food and drink to be brought for the hostages, and presents too, from his own belongings.

"Tell them that I apologize for my mistake, and that I will set them free as soon as I have given them gifts to make up for the deed." First-to-Dance did so.

"No," said Kanesada, "that's not enough. I must atone... personally."

First-to-Dance looked at him, in horrified surmise. "Please, no, Kanesada-san!" First-to-Dance had seen Jinbei's body, shortly after his ritual suicide, and Chiyo-hime had described to her, in morbid detail, what was involved. "Lord Masamune has absolutely forbidden *seppuku* without his prior written permission!"

Kanesada's shoulder slumped. "So I must endure the shame."

"Is there nothing else you can do, to satisfy your honor, that is less... permanent?"

Kanesada looked at the headman, who had been a silent witness of the conversation with the Ichxenta Indians. "Do you have a *muchi*?" The headman nodded uncertainly. The *muchi* was a scourge, a piece of bamboo to which barbed thongs were attached. "Please bring it to me," Kanesada ordered.

As he waited for the headman to return, Kanesada laid down his swords, and undid the top half of his *hitatare*, letting it hang down from his obi-sash. First-to-Dance couldn't help but admire the view.

Kanesada swung the wicked looking *muchi* back over his shoulder, whipping those barbs deep into his flesh. First-to-Dance flinched.

After giving himself twenty lashes, Kanesada handed the *muchi* back to the headman, bowed to the Indians, and said, "tell them they are free to go." He gathered up his swords and left the room, upper body still bare.

Kodachi Machi/Santa Cruz

Hiraki bowed to his parents. "Will grandfather be all right?"

Takuma and Mizuki exchanged glances. "The headman has sent a mounted messenger to Kawa Machi, to ask that Ihaku-sama come and see him," Takuma told him. "He is a very great physician from Kyoto. He treated the big merchants, and the samurai, and even the cloud-dwellers." The last was the poetic name given to the *kuge*, the court nobles. They didn't pay well, but the prestige of administering to the court did attract a snobbish clientele that had money.

"Once, he was permitted to reach between curtains and touch the emperor's toe!" Mizuki added. That was, of course, the emperor Go-Mizunoo, who renounced the throne in 1629, as part of the political fallout from the "Purple Clothes Incident" two years earlier. "And yet, after the 'America' Edict, he revealed himself to be a *kirishitan*. Think of what he has sacrificed for the faith. How can he fail, being so knowledgeable and yet so holy?"

At last, Ihaku arrived, together with his apprentice. At the entrance, he carefully set down the katana that, as a doctor, he was permitted to carry.

Mizuki greeted them and led them to her father-in-law's bedside.

"Daizo, tell me about your illness." Daizo mumbled something, eyes closed. "Daizo?"

Ihaku turned to Mizuki. "When did he first become sick?"

"About three days ago he complained of a headache," said Mizuki. "I felt his forehead and it was hot to the touch. Yesterday he was nauseous, his tummy hurt, and he vomited several times that night. Today he was listless, and I noticed that he had a rash on his palms, wrists, soles and ankles. He says his calves are aching, too."

Ihaku felt old Daizo's forehead, and motioned for his apprentice to do the same. Ihaku looked at him. "What is your diagnosis?"

"Mine?"

"Is there another apprentice in the room?"

"There is excess of both dampness and heat." Meaning, diarrhea and fever.

"And what is the proper treatment?"

"We must cool the blood with *Qin-Wen-Bai-Du*, and dry the digestion with *Huo Xiang Zheng Qi Wan*. As for the head and muscle aches, moxibustion would be best." That involved applying mugwort to a patient's skin, near appropriate acupuncture points, and burning it. "But I think we have run out, Ihaku-sensei."

"Mugwort?" asked Mizuki. "Daizo-san said he found some, or at least a plant like it. I'll fetch it." She came back with some California mugwort. "He found it a week or two ago."

Ihaku rubbed it on his own skin, then sniffed it. "I think this will do.

"I am getting too old for this traipsing about, especially in this alien land," he told his apprentice. "Perhaps you should stay here and be their resident physician."

"I am not worthy."

"When I am dead, you will have to be worthy."

Maruya/Carmel

"I think I must tender my resignation as commander," said Kanesada.

"Don't be foolish," First-to-Dance replied; "that was a stroke of genius."

"What, attacking the wrong Indians?"

"No, *that* was stupid. I meant, scourging yourself."

"I did it because it's what the Christians do as penance for sins."

"Well, that sort of 'self-sacrifice' is what *shamans* do. The Indians went home thinking that you are a powerful medicine man. They will go out of their way to please you, I think."

Kanesada's eyebrows twitched, ever so slightly. And then he smiled, so evanescently that First-to-Dance wondered whether she had imagined it. "I suppose I can wait and see how matters unfold. I can always resign next month, if need be."

First-to-Dance wondered what she might do to persuade Kanesada to smile some more.

Kodachi Machi/Santa Cruz

Hiraki suddenly poked his head through the sliding door. "Grandfather wants you, Poppa."

Takuma walked, first quickly and then slowly, to Daizo's sickroom.

He was astonished to find his grandfather chanting "Namu Amida Butsu." This was the the *nembutsu*, the ticket to Amida's Western Paradise for the followers of "Pure Land" Buddhism.

"Father! Have you forsaken Our Lord Jesu?"

"Oh no," said Daizo weakly. "Look!" He held out his rosary beads. "I prayed in the Christian manner first. But what if Deusu refuses to have mercy on my soul? For more than half my life, I was proud, and greedy, and lustful. I pray to Amida Buddha so I can go to the Pure Land if I am not found worthy of Heaven."

Takuma couldn't help himself. He laughed. "Always trying to hedge your bets, Father."

"It's good business sense. Hmm. While you're at it, make sure to have an *ihai* made for me."

The *ihai* was a memorial tablet; the family would pray before it during the Forty-Nine Days of Judgment, in which the fate of the new soul was decided. That is, which heaven, if any, it would go to, and if it were sent to *jigoku*—the Buddhist hell—how many millennia it would remain there. Pure Land Buddhists didn't rely on *ihai*; they thought that faith in Amida Buddha was sufficient for them to be reborn directly to Paradise.

The early Christian converts burnt their family *ihai*, but this was construed as evidence that the Christian church did not believe in filial piety, leading to official displeasure. The Jesuits decided to tolerate ancestor veneration as a secular practice; the Franciscans, Dominicans, and Augustinians, whose missionaries began coming to Japan in 1602, vehemently disagreed. For the *kirishitan*, it had all been very confusing.

"My illness has reminded me of how close I am to passage to the other side," said Daizo.

"Don't speak that way, Father. Your fever has gone down; soon you'll feel yourself again."

"Maybe, maybe not. But the next time, Death may take me suddenly by the throat, and deny me the opportunity to say what I must. We need to talk about the division of my property, and the future of our family."

And so they spoke. Then Daizo said, "My throat is dry, bring me some sake."

"The doctor said, 'no strong drink.'"

"And if I die tomorrow, nonetheless, would you want your memory burdened by the thought that you had denied me one last pleasure?"

Takuma brought him the sake.

But the fever returned, and the rash continued to spread, until it covered his entire body. Each day, Daizo seemed less and less aware of his surroundings. He also complained about there being too much light in sick room. Three days after Ihaku's visit, Daizo took a sharp turn for the worse. He was short of breath all day, and awoke several times that night, gasping for air. In the morning, Takuma couldn't help but notice how swollen Daizo's legs and abdomen had become. Takuma sent for Dr. Ihaku once more.

Ihaku returned, and then motioned Takuma out of the sickroom. He slid the door shut and whispered, "I am sorry. He has less than one chance in ten thousand of living." The physician's shoulders slumped, ever so slightly. "There is nothing I can do, other than join you in prayer."

The next day, Daizo was dead.

The *ojiyaku* had arrived at the cemetery. His title literally meant "the grandfather official," he was the leader of the local chapter of the Sodality of the Blessed Virgin Mary, a Jesuit confraternity. As such, he outranked Takuma, who was merely a *mizukata*, a baptizer.

The *ojiyaku* held up a candle and slowly and reverently drew two strokes in the air with it, one vertical, the other horizontal. Then he lit it and blew it out, three times in succession, and each time cried, "The way is open!" He lit it a fourth time and placed it down beside the corpse of Daizo, the revered father of Yamaguchi Takuma. Hiraki held his mother's hand.

He very carefully took out of a bag a small porcelain flask, kissed it, and removed the stopper. Inside was a small quantity of holy water. It was an extremely precious commodity in California. Since there were no priests to bless water locally, it had to be blessed by the imprisoned missionaries back home, and then shipped across the Pacific. The shogunate charged dearly for it. The First Fleet had nearly run out of its entire supply, but fortunately more had been brought over by the Second Fleet.

The *ojiyaku* dipped a piece of bamboo into the flask and then used it to sprinkle a few drops over the deceased. The mourners then joined him in prayer. They prayed that the man's soul would go to heaven, and they prayed that the deceased's ghost would not wander during the first forty-nine days after death, when it was most dangerous to the living.

At last, came the final "Amen!" The *ojiyaku* put an *omaburi*, a paper cross, into the deceased's right ear, and then motioned for the coffin to be closed. There was, of course, a cross incised into the lid. Several strong men grabbed hold of the coffin handles and delicately lowered it into the grave.

The *ojiyaku* was handed a shovel, and he thrust its blade into the earth. He lifted, and upended the first, ceremonial dirtful onto the coffin. Then he handed the shovel to one of the younger men, and the grave was soon filled in.

Ninth Month, 13th day (October 23, 1635)

There was a long, slow procession to the cemetery outside the town. The colonists placed flowers and lit candles on the graves, and then sat down on the grass nearby and opened their picnic baskets. They spent most of the day "visiting" with (and sometimes toasting) the dead.

Their serenity was disturbed by the arrival of Franciscus and his followers, some of whom looked as though they had been doing some drinking of their own.

"Are you good Christians?" he asked the mourners. "It is good to pray, in church, for the reduction of the departed's time in Purgatory. But I think that some of you have gone beyond that. How many of you keep *ihai* in your homes? Do you burn incense and kowtow to them, as if their souls were enshrined in them? Do you pray to your ancestors, asking them to aid you, as if they were the demons who masquerade back in Nippon as buddhas and kamis? Do you have *butsudan* or *kamidana* in your homes?

"If you have done any of those things, then you are not Christians at all, you are apostates. You should be denied all communions of the Church and when you die, you will go to Hell for all eternity."

There was a stunned silence. It was *Otomurai*, the day for remembering those recently dead, and praying that if they were in purgatory, that their souls would quickly pass into heaven. Before Christianity was banned in Japan, there would have been a mass in church, at least in those towns that had a church. But a mass could only be celebrated with a priest. Now, the *kirishitan* had to make do with *Otomurai*, itself a fractured memory of the Catholic All Souls' Day. To the mourners, there was nothing un-Christian about what they were doing.

Yamaguchi Takuma tried to intercede. "Please, Brother Franciscus, you are disturbing the harmony of the occasion. Let us have the leaders of the confraternities meet with you to discuss your concerns, and we—"

"Why should I consult with you? Are you my equals in Christian learning? I studied the faith in a seminary in Manila. You had what, ten days instruction in the catechisms, spread over as many years?

"And as for you, Takuma, you are one of the big offenders! You have a *butsudan*, wreathed in incense. Why, I think your father's death is divine punishment for your family's sins!"

Takuma's eyes widened. "How dare you!"

"To Takuma's house," Franciscus shouted. "Smash the *butsudan*, burn the *ihai*! Set an example for the community; no backsliding is to be tolerated."

Takuma tried to block them, but was knocked down. But Franciscus and his followers didn't get very far, as Takuma's friends slammed into them.

Some minutes later, the brawl still going strong, the samurai arrived, and trussed up everyone still standing. Katakura Shigetsuna and David Date came and questioned everyone; Takuma and his friends were released, with warnings and fines, and Franciscus and his supporters were sent to Date Masamune for judgment.

Date Masamune cleared his throat. "Ahem. Herald, please remind everyone present of the text of clause five of the Edict of Kan'ei 11 concerning the *kirishitan*."

The obugyô bowed, took a deep breath, and began reciting it from memory: "'In order to be permitted to go to New Nippon, they must take oath, on pain of eternal punishment by the Father, Son and Holy Ghost, as well as by Saint Mary and all Angels and Saints—'"

"Skip to part (c), please," Masamune interjected.

"Ahem, '(c) they will not oppress the worshipers of the buddhas and kamis, or the followers of Confucius, in that land, or prevent any Christian from renouncing that faith and returning to any of the traditional religions of Nippon.'"

Masamune stared at each of the prisoners in turn. "You took that oath?"

They inclined their heads.

"Say 'yes' or 'no,' please; you were quick enough to speak earlier."

"Yes, milord," they chorused. Franciscus tried to justify his actions, but didn't get far. "But—" A guardsman silenced him with a heavy slap against the side of his head. Blood trickled from the corner of his mouth.

"And, Herald, what says clause two of the Black Seal Edict concerning New Nippon?"

"'Within the province of New Nippon, freedom of worship is permitted, provided that it does not disturb public harmony.'"

Masamune said nothing for a whole minute. Naturally, no one else dared break the silence. Finally, he pronounced his judgment. "Prisoners, you are oath-breakers and law-breakers. I could have you beheaded here and now. I could crucify you, or burn you at the stake. I could have you bound and thrown into the sea, or left as chew toys in front of a bear den. Moreover, under the doctrine of collective responsibility, I could punish every member of your families, to the same or a lesser degree.

"However, I have decided that the most appropriate punishment for you is internal exile. Our Indian friends have shown our scholars the rock from which they make their red body paint. It's *tansha*, which our Dutch call cinnabar. The Dutch are willing to pay handsomely for it, our Indians are going to lead us to the site, and you are going to do the mining."

The cinnabar deposit he had in mind was New Almaden, in modern Santa Clara County, named by the Spanish colonists of the old time line California after the Almaden mine in Spain. One of the Spanish missionaries that once came to Japan could have warned the prisoners that this sentence wasn't much of an improvement on beheading. The mine of *old* Almaden doubled as a penal institution, and one out of four of its prisoners died of mercury poisoning before their scheduled release dates.

"Assuming you cooperate with the soldiers and overseers I send along, I will permit you to worship there as you think best.

"And may your God have mercy upon you."

Maruya/Carmel

"Well, Kanesada-dear, I have good news and bad news," said First-to-Dance. "Which do you want first?"

He didn't object to the familiar use of his first name. They were in private, and, the day before, he had joined First-to-Dance on one of her berry-picking expeditions. Just the two of them.

"The good news, I guess."

"Relations with the Ixchenta couldn't be better. They appreciated your pushing back the Achista to the far end of the cape, and they are still talking about what a powerful magician you are.

"In fact, I just found out that only a week after your scourging, a whale was stranded on the coast near their main village, and many of the Ixchenta are sure that it was the result of your magic. They called the ship that you and your colonists came in 'the whale with wings,' and they say 'the blood of the Great Witch Doctor of the Waters calls to the creatures of the sea.'"

"What's the bad news?"

"They've finished eating the carcass and they want you to do it again."

The Night Heron's Scream

November 1635 to Fall 1636

A lightning gleam:
into darkness travels
a night heron's scream.
—Matsuo Basho[5]

Castle of Date Masamune, grand governor of New Nippon,
Kodachi Machi (Santa Cruz, California),
November 1635

"Then Mitsumori stabbed me," gasped Date Masamune.

Date Chiyo-hime's *nohkan* shrilled in alarm.

"And cut off my head," Masamune added.

His son Munesane, recently baptized as David Date, beat out a rapid tattoo on the *taiko*, and his daughter Chiyo lowered her flute.

"My body is now but dust. My soul has suffered two hundred forty years in Warrior Hell. Pray for me." Masamune dropped to the floor.

Masamune rose slowly and removed his mask. "I hope that wasn't too painful to watch."

---

5   Translation by Harold G. Henderson, *An Introduction to Haiku*, 50 (Doubleday & Co., Inc., 1958)

"It was splendid," said Date Iroha-hime, his eldest daughter, the Audience.

Her family had just finished performing one of the great Noh dramas, *The Warrior Sanemori*. The ghost of Sanemori, who died at Shinowara, had appeared to a traveling priest, played by Masamune's advisor, Katakura Shigetsuna, and was urged to make confession in order to progress. He did so, and then disappeared.

"I am sure it is the best Noh performance ever seen in California," said Masamune drily.

Amateur theatricals were not the norm in samurai households until the middle of the eighteenth century, but the Japanese in California had been forced to improvise their own entertainments.

"So, Daughter, should I dye my hair, too?"

Sanemori had been seventy-two years old, and he had concealed his age so that the enemy champions would not decline a challenge to single combat. Date Masamune was sixty-eight, as the Japanese counted age.

"Only if you must seek death in battle to expiate some great shame, like Sanemori's," Iroha-hime answered, with some asperity. "But that can never be."

Something in her father's expression caught her attention. "Honorable Father, it is time you told us what has been troubling you since the coming and going of the Second Fleet."

Date Masamune and Shigetsuna exchanged lightning glances; the advisor shrugged minutely.

"Yes, please tell them, Father," said David Date.

Chiyo's head snapped around. "You knew something and didn't tell me?"

Date Masamune's eyelids flickered slightly. "Oh, very well. Munesane was never good at keeping a secret from you... Once you knew that there was a secret to pry out of him."

He sighed. "The Second Fleet brought me a letter... from the *bakufu*." The government.

"Oh dear, what did it say?"

"Nothing good. The words are fixed into my memory, as if they were branded on the skin of a criminal. 'Concern has been expressed that the cost of maintaining the colony of New Nippon has been high and that you have sent back little in the way of goods to justify this expenditure. Some have suggested that this California is not a suitable place for settlement and that the support of the colony should cease. Of course, the ban on the practice of the evil religion in the homeland would still apply.'"

Iroha's nostrils flared. "So they would leave the *kirishitan* in exile, to survive or starve, whatever the case may be. What would happen to the *kirishitan* still in Japan?"

"I assume that they would either be shipped off to Macao, or executed outright, if they refused to recant. But please, there's more: 'Others suggest that it was unjust to impose so formidable a task as governing a new colony on so accomplished a personage, when he is at an age that merits the comforts of retirement.'"

Masamune snorted. "They want to put me out to pasture, neh? But I digress. 'It is difficult to form a well-considered opinion from so great a distance. Hence, you are hereby advised that in one year's time, commissioners will be sent to study the colony and its management. By order of the Council of Elders.'"

Chiyo frowned. "Then we have until next September or October, whenever the Third Fleet arrives, to either be producing enough of a surplus so that future immigrants will not need to carry more food than what is required for the voyage itself, or to be have some valuable commodity we can ship home to pay for our keep."

"An excellent summation," Shigetsuna acknowledged.

"So . . . Father . . . do I need to reveal my secret?" asked Iroha. Her secret, known to this circle and few others, was that her deceased husband's expedition had succeeded in finding gold on the American River, although most of his party had paid for this achievement with their lives.

Date Masamune wrapped his Noh mask in silk and placed it in a storage box. "Only as a last resort. Gold is too valuable; the commissioners might decide that the governorship should be transferred to a Tokugawa crony." Masamune forebore to point out that her husband, the shogun's uncle, could have been considered such.

"What about the iron ore the *Ieyasu Maru* found on Texada?" asked his son.

"We don't know if we can rely on it," said Shigetsuna. "No iron ore has been shipped here. We don't even know if the colony was established successfully. And even if it was . . . will the shogun let us mine it?"

"What about the local redwood timber?" asked David.

"Not valuable enough, at least for shipping across an ocean. But I suppose it helps a little. Better than dried fish, at least."

Date Masamune snorted. "You sound like the stepmother in the story of the 'Old Woman's Skin.' This rice is too soft. This rice is too hard."

"I tell you exactly what I think, my lord."

"I know, and I value your polite candor. For now, I think our best hope is the cinnabar." Cinnabar, an ore of mercury, was used in the red lacquer of samurai armor, and in the red paint of major shrines. A little was mined in Japan, but it was mostly imported from China.

"Could we enter the *sho-za*?" asked David Date. In 1609, Odagiri Sukeshiro of Sakai had been given a monopoly on the cinnabar trade, the *sho-za*, most likely as a reward for espionage activity on behalf of Tokugawa Ieyasu, the present shogun's grandfather.

The monopoly is only on the cinnabar itself, not the ink," Masamune reminded him. "So at worst, we make the ink here. Or we sell the cinnabar to the Dutch, and send Dutch goods back home. We might even get a better price that way." Recently, Date Masamune and his advisors had learned from the Dutch that the cinnabar could be roasted to liberate quicksilver, and that this could be used in the isolation of gold dust.

"Perhaps we should sell licenses to the Dutch to pan for gold, and sell them the cinnabar, too."

"One day, I think we shall," said Masamune. "And of course they know about the California Gold Rush. Thus far, their interest in the California gold country has only been mild, because it's so hard to get to, and they figure it would take months if not years to actually find the gold. They have, I think, better prospects closer to home."

"Remember that words, once let loose, cannot be retrieved even by a team of four galloping horses. Once we tell them that we actually found the gold, and where to look, they will certainly come. And if we aren't strong enough by then, they will just take the land from us."

New Almaden, California

The arrow struck Brother Franciscus in the back as he fled. His companions paused, grabbed him under his arms, and half-carried, half-dragged him to safety. As they hid behind some rocks, they could hear the samurai lieutenant shouting orders, and the neighs of the horses as the samurai set out in pursuit of the Indians that had attacked the mining party.

The Ohlone woman First-to-Dance had told the Japanese about the Indians' cinnabar mine in New Almaden, near the south end of San Francisco Bay. So Date Masamune had sent both soldiers and laborers there, to take control of it.

Before the coming of the Japanese, Indians traveled hundreds of miles to visit the mine and collect cinnabar for making face paint. To gain access, they had to first give presents to one of the nearby tribal groups, the Awaswas, Mutsun, or Tamyen. Now all three of those groups were shut out. And they weren't happy about it.

Two samurai walked into the guard barracks beside the cinnabar mine; they had just come off watch. "There's no getting around it," said the junior soldier, Hasunuma Masayuki. "We need more leather armor. For the workmen, that is." The Japanese had once used leather plates as part of their armor, but when firearms came into common use, they were mostly replaced with iron ones.

"The militia want it too," his senior, Saito Nagato, reminded him. "And they have priority over miners." The Dutch had told the Japanese about the Spanish *soldados de cuera*, the leather jacketed dragoons who defended New Spain's Indian frontier. While the militia couldn't hope to be given horses to ride—that was still a samurai prerogative—the *cuera* was a reasonable demand.

Leather was cheap in cattle-rich New Spain. But there were no cows in California, because they weren't native, and the Japanese only brought a few breeding pairs. Their *wagyu* were used as beasts of burden, not as sources of milk or meat.

Hasunuma shrugged. "Well, then we are going to lose miners."

"There's nothing that can be done," Saito told him. "It's going to be almost a year before the Third Fleet arrives. That's the soonest we can ask for more from home. And haven't you read the new standing orders?"

"'Economize!'"

Saito smiled. "That sums it up. Pass me the oil, please." Saito carefully applied a few drops to a cloth, then commenced cleaning the blade of his katana.

"Here you go," said Hasunuma. "Seriously, the Indian attacks are getting more frequent. It's going to hurt cinnabar production." The Indians were adept at crawling into bow range, and ambushing the workers. They had also stolen some of the samurai guards' precious horses.

"I know." Saito wiped the blade with a cloth, and held it up, letting the light glance off it. Satisfied, he sheathed it. "I will put in the request. Just don't get your hopes up."

Kodachi Machi (Santa Cruz)

Clickety-clack. Kobayashi Benzo froze.

The lieutenant coughed. "I believe you dropped these." He held in his hand the three dice that had just slipped out of the sleeve of Benzo's *kataginu.*

"Gambling again, Benzo?"

"Certainly not, Lieutenant."

Then why were these dice in your possession?

"Those aren't for gambling! They are for divination."

"Oh, how does that work?"

"I roll the three dice. Odds count as three, evens as two. So the totals are six, seven, eight or nine, which of course are old yin, young yang, young yin, or old yang. I do it six times, and that gives me the hexagram of the I Ching."

"Fascinating. I am quite a fortune-teller myself, in a small way. I hereby predict that you are going to go on a long journey, to a place you don't want to go, but you will go without complaining, because otherwise something worse will happen...."

Eta Village,
Estero Bluffs, Morro Bay,
Early Spring 1636

Benzo hopped off the boat. "Aren't you coming?" he said to the fishermen who had given him passage down to Morro Bay.

"No thank you. We will camp here on the beach." Clearly, they were intent on minimizing their exposure to the wretches who lived here.

Benzo trudged up the trail. After rounding a sharp turn, he came face-to-face with an old man. The latter quickly prostrated himself. He was clearly an eta, an outcast, as his hair wasn't gathered into a queue.

"Tell the headman I have a message from the *daikan* Inawashiro Yoshimichi-sama. He is to come here to meet me, I do not wish to be defiled with the dust of your hovels."

The old eta's head quivered slightly. Clearly, he didn't want to risk raising himself up to nod his head more clearly.

"I am turning my back now, so I don't need to see you. Go!"

The old man hobbled off, and a moment later, Benzo turned back, and settled into a sitting position.

After a time, he heard rustling sounds, and stood. Benzo was not about to allow his head to be lower than of an eta, even for a moment.

A man appeared, and bowed respectfully to Benzo. "Most honorable samurai, I am Danzaemon, the headman of the *kawata*." The word meant "leather worker." The eta didn't use the word "eta," which meant "much filth," to refer to themselves.

The eta were those who dealt, like their ancestors, with dead bodies, human or animal. They might be executioners, undertakers, or leather workers. In the native Shinto religion, they were considered to be defiled by this exposure. The introduction of Buddhism didn't improve their position; the killing and eating of animals was forbidden. Before the coming of Christianity, almost all of the eta were followers of Pure Land Buddhism, as it was the only Buddhist sect that would admit them. However, in Nagasaki, the Christian missionaries had once sought to convert the eta, and there were thus still some Christian etas when Iemitsu had announced that the *kirishitan* could practice their religion in the new California colony.

There was more rustling, and a second, younger man appeared.

"Ah, and this is Kenji, my assistant. You must be cold after your voyage, are you sure we can't bring you a cup of sake?" It was a barbed offer; Benzo would have to purify himself after such contact.

Benzo shook his head curtly. "I am here to inform you that production of leather *manchira* must be doubled." The *manchira* was an armored vest. "And we also need more *haidate*." Those were the thigh guards for samurai cavalrymen.

"Doubled?" cried Danzaemon. "Do you think you can get cotton from a stone?"

Benzo considered cutting Danzaemon down for his insolence. It would add a pleasant fillip to a sour day, but it would make for much trouble in the long run. Slaying an ordinary eta was one thing, but a headman's death would necessitate paperwork. Worse, a new headman would have to be appointed, which would mean that a senior samurai, a *hatomoto*, would have to come to the *eta-mura*. He would not be happy with Benzo for making this necessary.

"What's the problem?" Benzo gritted out.

"The problem, oh master of warfare, is that you can't make leather without skins to tan. If we kill the *wagyu* we have left, our breeding pairs, we won't have any next year."

"What about deer? There surely are deer in the woods."

"Indeed there are, and we have deer skins drying even as we speak. Unfortunately, the deer have proven to be quite reluctant to donate their skins to the glory of New Nippon. It takes much time to hunt them down.

"Worse, these woods are rife with great bears, who are equally interested in the deer, and not inclined to share."

"So kill the bears!"

"It takes many arrows. A bear pierced by just one or two is an Annoyed Bear, not a Dead Bear, and an Annoyed Bear is worse than a shortage of deer."

The assistant headman coughed. "An Annoyed Governor might be worse, in the long run, than an Annoyed Bear."

"Ah, very true," said Danzaemon. "So, to avoid annoyance on both counts, give us guns and powder, and we will get rid of the bears. And then the deer, and deerskins, will multiply."

Kodachi Machi (Santa Cruz)

Shigetsuna looked up from the scroll he was reading. "Guns?"

"Guns." Inawashiro Yoshimichi, the *daikun* responsible for relations with the eta, grimaced. "I'd prefer to just send a party of samurai to clean out these bears, and then move on. Nothing good can come of giving guns to eta. And the samurai on garrison duty here would normally enjoy a bit of action."

He spat. "But the samurai would have to spend weeks in the vicinity of the *eta-mura*. The pollution would weigh heavily upon them."

Shigetsuna shrugged. "'Fifty steps, one hundred steps.' I suppose giving the eta a few guns would be the least evil choice. Of course, they will be too defiled by the usage for a samurai to ever hold them again. Have the triggers painted white, as a warning." White was the color of death and the supernatural.

Morro Bay,
Late Spring 1636

"Have you ever see a gun so old?" The eta huntsman held up the arquebus.

"Perhaps it belonged to Oda Nobunaga's father." Oda Nobunaga was the first of the Great Unifiers of Japan; his father died in 1551. The Portuguse had introduced firearms to Japan in 1542.

"It's a very pretty club."

"Enough joking around. Let's see if it can still shoot."

It did. Surprisingly well, in fact.

Gorosaku pointed at the trunk of a nearby cypress tree. There was bear hair on it, white-tipped. A grizzly had given itself a back scratch here.

Hikobei nodded, then crouched. A moment later, he found a bear print at the base of the tree. It was still fresh, perhaps hours old. He looked up at Gorosaku. "Let's get the others."

The local Chumash Indians ate acorns, roots, berries, elk, deer and fish. So did the grizzlies. If Indian women went out to gather acorns, they would set pickets, just as rabbits might have one of their number scanning the sky for hawks. If the men went fishing, they would avoid the spots that the bears favored.

It was rare for the Chumash to hunt grizzlies. They were brave, not suicidal.

But occasionally, the grizzlies hunted them.

"I am a deer," White Cloud reminded himself. He wore a deer head mask, and was crouched down. He used his left hand to drag himself forward, his right carried his bow and a few arrows.

The herd noticed him, and recoiled. From a safer distance, they stopped to watch him.

White Cloud had also stopped, and watched them. "I am a deer, I am one of you."

After a time, he resumed his movement toward the herd.

They reacted again, but this time they didn't flee quite as far, they weren't so sure he was a threat. "I look like a deer, sound like a deer, smell like a deer."

At last, they let him move among them, their thoughts focused on finding the tenderest shoots.

Another hunter was present, watching the herd, picking out the weakest member. White Cloud. "He looks like a deer, sounds like a deer, smells like a deer. I think he would taste like a deer," the grizzly perhaps thought to himself. Or perhaps the grizzly, who was well past his prime, thought that White Cloud would be easier to catch.

The wind shifted, and the herd caught the scent of grizzly. It stampeded, leaving White Cloud in its dust. A moment later and he smelled the grizzly, too, and joined them in flight.

But a grizzly can run twenty-five miles an hour for two miles without faltering.

"What the hell is that?" said Gorosaku, hearing the sound of breaking branches.

The first deer ran past them before the Japanese could react. They put an arrow into the second, however.

They gawked at White Cloud as he ran toward them. An Indian wearing a deer's head was quite outside their experience.

Then they heard the roar of the pursuing grizzly.

Three bowmen fired, all at once, as if the arrows were released from the giant bow of some celestial warrior. The grizzly snarled, but kept coming.

Gorosaku fired his arquebus. The range was less than optimal, but the ball struck the bear in the shoulder, and checked the bear momentarily. The bowmen fired again. Gorosaku fell back to reload; the rate of fire on a muzzle loader was nothing to brag about.

Hikobei waited. The grizzly stopped for a moment, pawing in irritation at the shafts of the arrows still stuck in it, trying to dislodge them.

A third round of arrows flew through the air. One was an Indian arrow; White Cloud had turned to help his unexpected allies. Both the Japanese and Indian arrows just annoyed the beast, but its reaction bought time for the gunmen.

Hikobei still waited. The grizzly came forward, but more slowly. Twenty yards. Fifteen. Ten.

And then Hikobei fired, his shot striking the grizzly in the forehead, a bit below between the eyes. It dropped.

Gorosaku put another ball into it, for good luck.

White Cloud walked slowly toward Hikobei, hands raised. The Japanese hunters allowed this, but they kept their hands near their knife hilts, just in case.

White Cloud stood within hand's reach of Hikobei; the Indian was a head taller. "Greetings, 'Little Giant.' Thank you for saving me from the bear."

This was mostly lost on Hikobei at the time, he didn't know the language of what scholars would call the Obispeno Chumash. But he could guess that White Cloud was happy not to be in a grizzly's tummy, and Hikobei bowed.

White Cloud presented him with a little deer bone whistle.

Hikobei studied it, then gave it a tentative blow. White Cloud smiled again.

In the meantime, several of the Japanese had rigged up a branch so that they could carry the bear carcass back to the *eta-mura*.

"Let's get this food back to the village," said Gorasaku. "Those deer are thoroughly spooked, there's no point in hunting them right now."

Hikobei nodded, and motioned for White Cloud to follow them. Hesitantly, he did so.

The Japanese eta village stood on Estero Bluffs. Indians had once lived there; the Japanese had found their grinding holes. The Japanese had known that there was still an Indian village on the far side of Morro Bay, but had carefully avoided it. And as far as they knew, the Indians had avoided them, too.

One of First-to-Dance's tribesmen, Talks-While-Walking, had been assigned to the eta to serve as their translator in dealings with other Indians. All of the Japanese settlements now had such translators, personally selected by First-to-Dance. The gifts given to these translators, while modest by Japanese standards, were of great value to the Indians. This, of course, created obligations on their part to First-to-Dance, their patroness.

This was Talks-While-Walking's first opportunity to translate since they left the Monterey Bay area, and he addressed White Cloud with great formality.

Unfortunately, White Cloud had no idea what Talks-While-Walking was saying. And vice versa. The Ohlone language was of the Penutian language family, while Northern Chumash was Hokan. However, White Cloud could tell, from the other Indian's body language, that he was receiving a polite greeting. That was good enough. It was hard for him to give Talks-While-Walking his full attention, anyway, when the exotic Japanese were around.

White Cloud was given a tour of the village, the Japanese goods were even stranger than the Japanese themselves. Finally, he worked up the courage to ask, by gesture, whether he could touch Hikobei's arquebus. Hikobei held it out, two handed, for White Cloud to inspect. White Cloud reached out a finger, and held it just above the barrel, as if it were a cooking pot and he wanted to make sure it wasn't too hot to touch. At last, he touched it, and ran his finger lightly down to the muzzle. "Boom!" he said.

That didn't require translation.

Neither did White Cloud's smile.

On the beach near the Japanese village, White Cloud pointed first to himself, and then across Morro Bay.

"He says that he is from the other side," Talks-While-Walking explained.

White Cloud pointed at Hikobei and Gorasaku, then, with three fingers, toward the Sun.

"In three days, come visit him at his village."

There was, of course, much discussion of the matter. Should Hikobei and Gorasaku go? Should they be accompanied by others, besides of course Talks-While-Walking? Should they go by land or by sea? And most important, should they bring firearms?

The firearms, of course, might create awe, causing the locals to treat the Japanese with great respect, even subservience. Or they might excite the Indians' greed, enough so the Indians would be willing to steal, even kill, to acquire them.

Danzaemon finally decided that Hikobei and Gorasaku, and their translator, would go by boat, without the arquebuses. However, they would take with them the bear's claws and teeth, to serve as both presents and as reminders of the fighting prowess of the Japanese.

✧   ✧   ✧

Hikobei and Gorasaku beached their rowboat on what a modern Californian would call Morro Strand State Beach. As they pulled the boat up to high ground, a peregrine falcon screeched at them, then sped toward its nest on nearby Morro Rock.

White Cloud stood on the beach to greet them. He and Talks-While-Walking exchanged signs. While the Indians of California didn't have a universal or comprehensive sign language, like the one that would develop on the Great Plains, some simple, concrete concepts could be communicated to other tribes. Indeed, even the few Spanish visitors to California, like Cabrillo in 1542, had been signed to.

Hikobei was surprised to find another wooden planked boat on the beach. The Indians of Monterey Bay only paddled about, close to shore, in little tule rafts. This Chumash boat was made of pine, without any internal ribs, and painted red. The planks seemed to be tied together with plant fibers, and the seams were caulked with a strange black material. Later, he learned that the boat belonged to a visitor, one of the Island Chumash of the south, and the local Chumash themselves only had tule boats.

White Cloud ceremoniously led them back to his village, which was located a short distance inland, near a small creek. As they approached the village, a dog darted out, and started barking at them. This caught the attention of White Cloud's tribesmen, several of whom came out, weapons in hand. After a sharp exchange with White Cloud, they lowered them, and smiled at the Japanese visitors.

They were introduced to the chief. He had done much traveling in his youth, indeed, he had been to Monterey Bay, and even as far as the cinnabar mine, and he still remembered a little of Talks-While-Walking's tongue.

This didn't come as a complete surprise to Hikobei, since he had known that in Talks-While-Walking's tribe, there were those who could speak the language of a neighboring tribe.

What did come as a surprise was that one of the Chumash knew a few Japanese words. At first, Hikobei thought that one of the kirishitan fishermen might have been shipwrecked here. But no, the Indians of Monterey Bay had learned a little Japanese, and as they traded with their neighbors, the new words had passed along with the goods. So the Salinans learned Japanese from the Costanoans, and the Chumash from the Salinans. Given that

California Indian languages were so diverse, Hikobei couldn't help but wonder whether Japanese might soon become the trade language for the central California coast.

The chief welcomed them. Indeed, he told them that they could stay as long as they wish. "Only, please kill more bears."

Maruya (Carmel, California), Summer 1636

The eta were supposed to deliver their leather goods to a storehouse constructed near Maruya. They would lock them up, and then hoist a flag to let the *kirishitan* in Maruya know that they had made a delivery. The eta would be allowed time to withdraw to a camp down-shore, and the Maruyans would come pick up the leather, and leave supplies for the eta. The eta would return for these, then sail home.

This time, matters were different. What the Maruyans found in the storehouse wasn't leather, but a note. The note demanded that the eta be given the same rights as other Japanese: to dress as they did, to live in the towns, to serve in the militia, to attend prayer services, and so forth. It was signed by the "*Shin-Heimin*"—the "new commoners."

Kodachi Machi (Santa Cruz)

"We have a problem," Shigetsuna announced. "The eta have staged a *chosan ikki*." It was a time-honored tactic for farmers at odds with their daimyo. They would harvest their crops, pack their things, and cross the border into the next han. Their lord, of course, could not lead soldiers into another daimyo's domain without permission, not only from that daimyo, but from the central government. From this temporary safe haven, the farmers would send petitions to the latter, asking for it to intercede. If the dispute could not be settled quickly, the new daimyo might let them stay permanently, or the central government might get fed up with the old daimyo and dispossess him on grounds of mismanagement.

"But what lord could they take refuge with?" demanded Date Masamune. "There are no other daimyo, no other *han* here."

Shigetsuna bowed. "But there are many Indian tribes. They have taken refuge, it seems, with the Chumash. According to the encyclopedia, the Chumash live on the coast from San Luis Obispo to Malibu, and on the Channel Islands, and inland as far as the western edge of San Joaquin Valley. Just the coastal section alone is, as I best I can figure it, two hundred miles long."

"So ... They can hide from us easily."

"Unless you are willing to force the Chumash to give them up."

"Is that what you advise?"

"We must resolve this crisis, peacefully or otherwise, before the commissioners arrive. Failing to keep the eta under control could be considered 'mismanagement.' And anyway we need the leather."

"I don't understand," said First-to-Dance. "What's wrong with skinning animals? All women of the People must do it."

"I understand, but your people don't follow the way of the kamis and the buddhas," said Chiyo.

"That's fine for you and your father. But your brother, David, and most of your people, they are following the Way of the Christ. Does the Christ say that it's bad to skin animals?"

Chiyo thought about this. "Not so far as I know. Let's go ask my brother."

They found him studying an *ikebana*, a flower arrangement, and put the question to him.

"No-o-o ..." he admitted. "But the *kirishitan*, they learned the new religion from the Jesuits and the Franciscans, and in the countries they came from, butchers and tanners were considered to be dishonorable occupations. So the padres wouldn't have challenged the status of the eta."

"But why did the Christians think it dishonorable?"

David Date shrugged. "Because of the contact with blood?"

"So, just like Shinto!" said Chiyo.

David reached out, repositioning one of the flowers in the vase. "Fish cannot climb trees."

"It's too bad, then, that these eta are Japanese, not Indian, since then you wouldn't care if they skinned animals or not," said First-to-Dance.

The two women were about to leave, when suddenly Chiyo stopped short. First-to-Dance almost collided into her. "Wait a moment," said Chiyo. "Why must the eta remain Japanese?"

"You can be adopted into a new tribe," said First-to-Dance. "Then you no longer belong to your old tribe."

The young samurai thought about this. "I think I heard that a few years ago, a hundred *kirishitan* lepers were exiled to Luzon so that samurai swords would not be defiled with their blood. I am not sure whether, once in exile, they could still be considered Japanese.

"And I have heard that the Chinese Emperor has ruled that those Chinese that choose to live in foreign lands are no longer Chinese. That's why he ignored the massacre of the Chinese in Luzon some years back."

"You see!"

"Well, I make no promises, but I'll see what Father thinks."

"I must confess that David's proposal bothers me," said Shigetsuna. "The young of frogs should be frogs, and the children of eta should be eta."

Date Masamune clapped him on the back. "Poor Shigetsuna. You live in interesting times. As my son said to me, when there's need, fish must learn to climb trees."

Eta Village,
Morro Bay

The eta gathered together around Danzaemon.

"Well, what did the message say?" asked Hinkebei.

"The message enclosed a draft proclamation. The Grand Governor Date Masamune will make it public only if he is assured that we will accept it.

"The grand governor says that he does not have the authority to alter the terms under which those Japanese who are eta must live. However, if we are adopted into an Indian tribe, we are no longer Japanese, and hence we cannot be regarded as eta."

The crowd murmured. Danzaemon motioned for them to quiet down.

"The grand governor will give us permission to be so adopted only if we agree to meeting certain continuing obligations concerning the supply of leather to New Nippon, and that under no circumstances will we take up arms against New Nippon, even if our new tribe is at war with them."

Danzaemon raised his arms. "My friends, I believe we can consider this a victory!"

They cheered.

"Hikobei, you must find out whether the Chumash are willing to adopt all of us on such terms."

Date Masamune passed the reply to Shigetsuna. "See? Problem solved. Issue the proclamation that the residents of 'Kawata Mura' have renounced Japanese citizenship and are now to be treated as Chumash Indians."

"I doubt that our people remember to treat them as Indians and not as eta. As the saying goes, 'Sparrows, though they live to be a hundred, do not forget their dance.'"

"Write to this Danzaemon, remind him that his folk should dress as do the Chumash when they come among us. That will help. If that is not enough, well, the whip improves a faulty memory."

Yamaguchi Takuma deftly pushed down the five earth beads on the third rod, away from the reckoning bar, and moved a heavenly bead down toward it. The *soroban* that Shigetsuna-sama had lent to him had twenty-seven rods, each with two earth beads and two heavenly beads. Not, of course, that Takuma had much occasion to express a number with that many digits—the councilor had never asked him to count the number of grains of sand on the beach!—but the extra rods made it convenient to work with several different numbers at the same time. To multiply, for example.

The *soroban* made arithmetic so easy, he found it hard to believe that in his grandfather's day, merchants still used calculating rods. Of course, not every merchant was as adept as Takuma; he could even divide one number into another.

This magnificent *soroban*, of course, was not intended for a crass commercial use. Rather, it was for managing the accounts of a great estate. Takuma was proud to be considered worthy to help Shigetsuna-tono with those of New Nippon itself. Unfortunately, there weren't enough hours in the day to do all of the calculations himself, together with all the other tasks he had been assigned.

"Gombei!"

That was his assistant, who hurried in. He had been engaged in what he thought was brilliant conversation with the daughter of the family who lived next door.

"Sir!"

"I need these calculations done by sunset. Remember, they are for the grand governor, so all the multiplications and divisions must be done twice, and make sure you get the same result each time."

"Yes sir. Uh, what if a pair of calculations disagree?"

"Then redo them until you get the same number three times in a row!"

Mathematics was not Gombei's strong point. Especially when he could hear Shima singing a risque folk song as she went about her chores.

"Oh! my darling boy!" she sang. "Though first we slept a *hiro* apart, by rolling we came together..."

Gombei's only chaperone was Takuma's son, Hiraku. He was playing with toys in a corner.

Shima was still singing: "Yes, we slowly came together..."

Gombei stuck his head out the door. "Hey, Shima, the acoustics are better in here. Why don't you come in and keep me company?"

"Perhaps another time, Gombei dear," said Shima. "Hurry up, and you can take a walk with me." She paused. "If, that is, you can finish before the hour of the Ape." That was late afternoon.

Gombei was hurrying, all right. But the saying was, "he who chases two hares will not even catch one." Trying to do the arithmetic faster just led to more mistakes, and thus more rechecks.

Finally, Shima strode in. "How much longer are you going to be, Gombei?" No "dear" this time.

"I'll be out as soon as these fucking beads give me the same answer three times in a row for 256 times 3473."

"Don't look at me," said Shima, "I've never touched a *soroban* in my life."

"It's 889,008," said Hiraku, the forgotten boy in the corner.

"Really?" said Gombei. "I got that the first time. But then I got 888,548."

"Oh. Then you did the last part on the wrong rod," Hiraku explained. The last part, by the Japanese method, being the multiplication of the leftmost digit of the 256 and the rightmost of the 3473.

"Hiraku, how did you know the correct number?" asked Shima. "You weren't even looking at the *soroban*, let alone moving the beads."

"I just picture the beads in my head."

✧   ✧   ✧

Shima mentioned Hiraku's mathematical ability to her mother, who told Hiraku's mother, who told his father. Takuma had not, it turned out, taught Hiraku how to use the *soroban*. He had apparently learned by watching and listening to the lessons that Takuma had given to the apprentice.

Takuma was shocked and pleased to discover that Hiraku was not only adept at addition, subtraction and even multiplication, but that he had figured out for himself that the *soroban* could be used to calculate in hexadecimal as well as in decimal. It had this ability because the *soroban* was copied from the Chinese *Suan Pan*, and in China there were sixteen *liang*-ounces to the *jin*-pound, and sixteen *dou* of grain to the *yu*.

The following week, Katakura Shigetsuna invited Takuma to the castle. It was a mark of approval, especially since the invitation included Takuma's family.

"Your calculations have been of great assistance in the construction of the castle in a timely and accurate manner, Takuma. I am promoting you, effective immediately."

Takuma thanked him profusely.

"Keep up the good work. Now, who's the little fellow hiding behind you? And has he any skills yet?"

"My son. He is very skilled in mathematics."

"Oh?"

Takuma had Hiraku do some mental calculations for the councillor's entertainment.

"I have a copy of *Jinko-ki* I can lend you," Shigetsuna declared. "Why don't you help Hiraku study it? A talent like his should be nurtured, for the good of the realm." *Jinko* meant "small-large," and *ki* was a treatise, so the manuscript was a study of numbers, from smallest to largest. It was written by Yoshida Shichibei Koyu in 1627, and it taught, among other things, how to extract square and cube roots using the *soroban*.

Date Masamune and his son stood on a tower, watching the moon rise over the Sierras.

"It's easy enough to say politics is politics," Masamune grumbled, "but it's still painful to contemplate being relieved of my grand governorship. I defy any of my peers to have done better, under such circumstances. A virtually unknown domain, populated by savages who don't speak our language. Fractious colonists, from every part of Japan, thrown together and forced to form a community. Religious differences between the colonists and the samurai who protect them."

"Surely your governorship is safe now," said David Date. "The *kirishitan* troublemakers are mining cinnabar, God help them. First-to-Dance negotiated a truce with one of the tribes attacking our miners, and we trounced another, so cinnabar production is up. The eta, excuse me, the "Chumash" *kawata*, are working again, so we have leather."

"True. But our hold on the mine remains tenuous. By the time the commissioners arrive, the truce could break down, and then matters could be . . . uncomfortable. Nor am I sure that the commissioners will place their seal of approval on the eta solution. It was . . . unorthodox."

Maruya

Yoshimichi had a strong sense of duty. That sense extended, however reluctantly, to keeping up with paperwork. He was now down to the letter he had put off for last, as it came from Danzaemon. Having to deal with the eta—ex-eta, he reminded himself—was, he was sure, punishment for the sins committed in his last incarnation.

The letter, of course, was written on recycled paper. Back home, there were people who made a living collecting paper trash and selling it to used paper warehouses. From there, it went to the paper mill to be reduced to pulp and reborn, a little grayer and coarser, as a blank sheet of paper. Here in California, recycling was even more important, but of course it was practiced on a smaller and more informal scale.

Before he broke the seal, Yoshimichi noted that it wasn't made of wax, but rather of a strange black material. It was the first time he had ever seen petroleum tar.

The letter was addressed to "the Honorable ex-*Daikan* for the ex-*Eta*." Yoshimichi snorted.

"As you see, we are now above quota for leather hides," Danzaemon had written. "Most are deer skin, but there are a few bear skins. There are plenty more bears where those come from; please send more powder and shot. Some more guns would be nice, too; the damn things take too long to reload.

"It would be very nice if the Dutch could be persuaded to bring us cattle; I think cattle would do well here. At least our cattle would, and I imagine the Dutch beasts aren't that much different.

"I enclose a present for you, it's a drill used to make holes in shells. The Chumash hang the shells on strings and use them as money, or trade them to the inland tribes. I think you will find the present most interesting."

The letter was signed by the "Master" of the "Brotherhood of the Hide." Later, Yoshimichi would learn that this was done in mimicry of the most important of the Chumash craft guilds, the "Brotherhood of the Canoe."

The *daikan* grumbled. "Powder? Shot? Guns? Not a chance. I am not going to set a cat to guard dried bonito. Not twice, at least." He called for his assistant.

"We will have an archery and gunnery competition for the samurai." As he spoke, he unwrapped the present from Danzaemon. "The six best will have the honor of conducting a bear hunt for—" He stopped speaking, staring at the drill bit.

"Sir?"

"A hunt for the benefit of our Chumash friends. Which I will attend personally. Free my calendar."

Morro Bay

Yoshimichi crossed his arms. "All right, Danzaemon, you got my attention."

"Would you like some shells, Inawashiro-sama?"

"Don't trifle with me. I am not that idiot Benzo. The drill bit was made of jade. Is there jade in Chumash territory?"

"Not as far as I know. The fellow I got the drill from, he said that he got in trade from the Tsetacol. That's the next little tribe north of here, along the coast, around the place marked as Cambria on our map. My village sometimes trades with them, sometimes fights with them. I can find you someone who has been there before.

"Now, I hope that in view of the value of this information I have provided, that you will reconsider our request for more gunpowder..."

North Along the Coast

Inawashiro Yoshimichi and his six samurai worked their way north by sea, in the large fishing boat that had brought them to Morro Bay. They were accompanied by one of the Chumash, who had shown much curiosity about their vessel. His name, if they could trust their translator, was Keeps-Canoe-Off-Rocks. It sounded like a good omen, if nothing else.

The Indians of Tsetacol greeted them. More precisely, they greeted the Japanese warmly, and Keeps-Canoe-Off-Rocks and their Ohlone translator with considerably more reserve.

As Yoshimichi walked through the village, it was apparent that he was among a different group of Indians. For one thing, their huts were rectangular, while those of the Chumash were round. For another, when one of the samurai spotted a condor and aimed his bow at it, the Tsetacol tribesmen became extremely agitated, enough so that Yoshimichi ordered the bowman to stand down. Yet, in the Chumash village at Morro Bay, Yoshimichi had seen a condor sacrificed by a shaman. A twentieth-century anthropologist would have labeled the Tsetacol as Salinan.

Keeps-Canoe-Off-Rocks spoke some Salinan, which would have been more useful if Yoshimichi's translator knew more Chumash. However, Yoshimichi felt fairly confident that the Tsetacol didn't have any more jade, and that they got it by trading with villages farther north.

Beyond the Tsetacol were the Chaal, who lived between Cambria and San Simeon. When the Japanese boat approached the shore, the Chaal shot at them. The samurai were eager to shoot back, but Yoshimichi ordered them to hold their fire. A second and then a third volley of arrows came their way, and one struck a crewman.

"Return fire," Yoshimichi ordered. The samurai were happy to oblige him.

They heard an Indian cry out, and Yoshimichi ordered "Desist!" His immediate purpose wasn't to massacre the Indians, just to make sure they didn't think the Japanese were patsies.

They tried to make contact again the next day. This time, they landed unopposed. However, when they cautiously ventured inland, they found that the Chaal had hastily abandoned their fishing camp. Clearly, if the Chaal had jade, Yoshimichi wasn't going to find it this time around.

He decided that pursuing the Chaal with so small a force was a really bad idea, and the Japanese returned to their boat.

A turn of the weather brought fog to the coast, and they had to give a wide berth to Ragged Point, which lay a few miles north of San Simeon.

Not far north of Ragged Point, the terrain changed. The Santa Lucia Range marched beside the sea. There was mile after mile of sea cliffs, against which the waves beat furiously.

They would have to wait for better weather to make landings here, even if they were lucky enough to find a sandy cove.

Yoshimichi reluctantly gave the order to sail to Maruya. Perhaps First-to-Dance, who had been off on a mission to the Ixchenta when he had gotten Danzaemon's message, could provide some guidance. Jade didn't have the mystique in Japan that it had in China, but it was still valuable.

"I think this is made of the same material as your drill bit." First-to-Dance handed over a green stone.

Yoshimichi pulled out a knife, and tried to scratch it. The knife had no effect; a good thing, since jade is harder than steel.

"Well, is it jade, Yoshimichi-san?" she demanded.

"Come outside with me." He studied it in the harsh light of the afternoon sun, tilting it this way and that. "It is like the ocean, it has translucency, depth. I would swear that it is jade. Where did you find it?"

"One of the Ixchenta had it. They call this a warming stone; it is placed in the campfire, to heat it up, and then it's carried along when you must go somewhere that's cold."

"Is it found on Ixchenta land?"

"I don't think so. At least, this one came in trade from the Esselen. The Ixchenta say that the Esselen live on the cliffs of the coast to the south."

"Great. I can go up and down this coast, year after year, until I am old and my teeth fall out. Unless you can show me on a map where the Esselen live."

First-to-Dance wasn't sure of the exact location—her tribe didn't trade with the Esselen directly—but she thought it was the Big Sur country, somewhere between the mouth of the Carmel and the up-time town of Lucia. That narrowed the search area down a bit.

Yoshimichi swore. "All that time with the Tsetacol and the Chaal wasted."

"I am sorry to add to your troubles, but you need to know about the Esselen. They are very shy, they are hard to find, and their language is difficult to learn."

Yoshimichi swore again.

With some trepidation, Yoshimichi reported to Shigetsuna. The latter, fortunately for Yoshimichi, was willing to be philosophical about it: "If there's a jade drill bit among the Chumash, and a jade warming stone among the Ixchenta, there's certainly more jade in the Big Sur country, waiting for us to find it."

When he in turn, reported to Date Masamune, they agreed that the best strategy was to show the finds to the commissioners and to be cautiously optimistic about the chances of finding the source.

"Emphasize that finding the jade without Indian assistance would be like trying to find a needle at the bottom of a lake," said Masamune. "And that we have already invested two years in gaining the trust of the local Indians, and if we are persistent they will eventually lead us to the jade. Do not volunteer that our local Indians are of the wrong tribe."

Fall 1636,
Kodachi Machi, Santa Cruz

"My lord, a messenger has come from the pilot-major of the Third Fleet, informing us that the lord commissioners will disembark as soon as appropriate preparations are in place to receive them."

Date Masamune raised his head. "Yes, yes, we will—what was that phrase the Dutch told us?"

"Roll out the red carpet," said Shigetsuna. Coincidentally, red was an auspicious color in Japan, associated with protection against the demons of disease.

"Did the message inform us of the names of the lord commissioners?"

"Yes. The good news is, one's a Sakai." In other words, a relation of Sakai Tadakatsu, the senior councillor who had persuaded

Iemitsu to issue the New Nippon Edict. "Sakai Tadayoshi, to be specific. I don't know him personally, however.

"Then there's a Hotta." Shigetsuna made a face. Hotta Masamori was a leader of the anti-Christian faction. It was a foregone conclusion that *any* Lord Hotta was here to do mischief.

"Last but definitely not least, there's Matsudaira Nobotsuna." The first Tokugawa shogun had formerly been known as Matsudaira Motoyasu. The shogun's heir received the surname Tokugawa; all of his other sons took Matsudaira. Unlike the other two men, Nobotsuna was himself a senior councillor. Masamune recalled hearing the Dutch speak warmly about him. But even if he weren't hostile to Christians, he could be expected to be wary of the possibility that New Nippon could be a springboard for a challenge to the supremacy of the Tokugawa clan. In other words, while Masamune needed to impress Lord Sakai with the potential of California, he couldn't afford to be too persuasive. At least not in Matsudaira's hearing.

The Tokugawa were great believers in hammering down nails that stuck out too much.

Shigetsuna took the distinguished visitors to the shores of the Monterey Bay. Shigetsuna pointed out a particular stretch of water; there, several dozen sea otters floated on their backs, holding paws so they didn't drift apart.

Japan had started exporting sea otter fur to China back in 1483. The sea otters didn't live in Japanese waters; the Matsumae clan bought the skins from the Ainu of Ezochi (Hokkaido), to the north of Japan. Most of the skins came from still farther north, from the Ainu of the Kuril Islands.

"So many," said Lord Sakai.

Shigetsuna shook his head. "I have seen a 'raft' of two hundred of the beasts."

"I am surprised that you haven't killed them off already."

"We limit our hunting in this area, for the sake of good relations with the natives. We have wooden boats, and can go further afield, they can't."

"What do they use?"

"It's like the tub boats of Sado Island, but made from tule reeds. It can only be paddled with the current."

"Why haven't you shipped these furs back home?"

Shigetsuna looked at him with amazement. "We have! A shipment went home with the Second Fleet."

"Hmm. My clerk reviewed the manifests from all the ships of the Second Fleet. He said nothing about furs."

"It would no doubt be interesting to compare our copies with those your clerk saw."

Lord Sakai nodded. They both knew that the customs inspectors in Nagasaki could be persuaded to ignore errors or omissions in manifests, for a suitable inducement. "Have your man Takuma speak to mine."

The show-and-tell continued. "Now, here we have a treat for you," said Shigetsuna. He pointed out a small fishing boat, with one man on board. "Watch!"

Perhaps a minute later, the fisherman picked up a long bamboo pole and thrust it into water. A young woman, wearing just a loincloth, climbed up this impromptu ladder and pulled herself into the boat.

"Watching her is indeed a treat," said Lord Sakai with a smirk, shading his eyes so he could see her better.

"I had a different treat in mind. Can you make out what she is carrying?"

"Why—abalone!" Abalone was a luxury food in Tokugawa Japan. Only a few privileged daimyo could buy fresh abalone.

"Do you have anyone who knows how to make *hoshi-awabe*?" Lord Sakai asked eagerly.

That was dried abalone, which was exported to China.

"We do." He and Lord Matsudaira exchanged looks. Lord Hotta contrived to look bored.

The party rode next to see the "Fathers of Trees," as Shigetsuna called them: the great redwoods.

"They are most impressive," said Lord Matsudaira.

"Lord Date comes here, when his work permits, to meditate. He values the shade of a big tree."

Lord Matsudaira raised an eyebrow. Taking shelter in the shade of a big tree was proverbial, it meant to attach one's self to a great house. The implication was that Date Masamune was so attached, and the implication was that he served the Tokugawa.

"Furs, and shellfish, and wood are all very well, but where's the famous gold of California?" said Lord Hotta, lip curled.

Shigetsuna sighed. "In another few years, when our numbers

and resources are greater, we will be ready to make another attempt on the gold fields."

"No need," said Lord Matsudaira, "other arrangements have been made."

"Arrangements?"

"Yes. It seems that our Dutch friends have suffered setbacks lately. The barbarians of France, England and Spain have leagued against them, and destroyed much of their fleet." This had happened in August 1633, but it took quite a few months for the news to reach East Asia. "Early this year, they petitioned the shogun for permission to found a settlement of their own in California. And to look for gold. Since your son-in-law was unsuccessful, the shogun thought that they should be given the opportunity."

"And where is this settlement of theirs going to be?"

"It is in the place that the up-timers call San Francisco. Their colony ship accompanied the Third Fleet across the Pacific, much as Lord Tadateru's did your own. My consolations to his widow, by the way."

It was, of course, almost exactly the situation that Date Masamune had been trying to avoid: the Dutch deciding who could sail into San Francisco Bay. His only consolation was that since Iroha and her samurai had opened the overland route from Monterey to the South Bay, he could leapfrog the Dutch and send colonists to occupy the Sacramento-San Joaquin River delta. Not just to control access to the gold fields, but also because his advisors thought that it might be possible to grow rice there.

"Of course, the grand governor will be responsible for making sure that they account to the shogun for his share of any gold they collect."

Lord Hotta and Councillor Shigetsuna stood in a high place, watching the moon set. When it at last vanished from sight, Lord Hotta spoke. "I will be very blunt, Councillor Shigetsuna. If it were up to me, the *kirishitan* would not have been allowed to found a colony at all. They believe that the obligation to obey this Jesu of theirs is higher than the one they owe to the grand governor, and through him to the shogun. They believe, I warn you, that since the grand governor is not a Christian, that they can pick a new ruler who is...like the king of Spain."

Shigetsuna spread his hands. "The grand governor has addressed this problem already, Lord Hotta. His son Munesane has been baptized, as 'David Date,' and thus is a Christian ruler, as much as the king of Spain."

"Your lord is clever. Perhaps too clever for his own good. Some of the *kirishitan* will see this as a subterfuge, at least so long as Date Masamune remains in California. They will deem the son to be merely a figurehead, and the father to be the true ruler. Does Date Masamune intend to convert?"

"No, he does not. But the reality is that he is old, and once he dies, David Date's position as a true Christian ruler will be indisputable."

"The other problem that I see, Councillor Shigetsuna, is that the province of New Nippon is very large. Larger, indeed than the homeland itself. To give so great a province into the rule of one person, old or young, seems... imprudent."

"It is great in area, and perhaps in potential, but for now, its population and productivity are small, and so they will remain for many years to come."

"Perhaps. I am willing to defer to my colleagues and support the continuation of the *kirishitan* emigration, and of Date Masamune's governorship—on two conditions."

Shigetsuna stared at Lord Hotta. "And what might those be?"

"First, I understand that you have plans to mine iron on this Texada Island. I want that island to be settled, and the iron controlled, by Buddhists of my choosing. That way, if worst comes to worst, the king of Spain does not gain an iron mine."

"Your Buddhists, but still under the governorship of Date Masamune? I suppose my lord might accept that. Although I cannot make a commitment without discussing the issue with him. And provision would have to be made for any *kirishitan* already on Texada. What is your second condition?"

"Half the jade you find is consigned for sale to the trading house I select."

Date Masamune eyed her speculatively. "First-to-Dance, you have been your tribe's emissary to New Nippon for some months now. It is perhaps time to take your role as emissary to the next level."

She cocked her head. "What does that mean, exactly?"

"The shogun, the ruler of Japan, wants to meet an Indian. Two Indians, a male and a female, actually. Think about whether you would like to be the female."

✧   ✧   ✧

Chiyo bowed to the lord commissioners, seated on the dais beside her father, and recited a *tanka* composed by Princess Nukata a thousand years earlier. When she finished, she bowed again, and they clapped politely.

"Next," said Shigetsuna, "we have a Young Arithmetical Sage to amaze us."

Hiraku stood up. And froze.

Shigetsuna rescued him. "If I may ask each of our esteemed guests to name a three digit number..." They did so. "Young Hiraku, what is their sum?"

He answered.

The demonstration proceeded from there to multiplication, division, and extraction of roots.

Finally, Shigetsuna called for a table to be brought out, and on it an assistant laid out a counting board, essentially a rectangular grid. Beside it, the assistant placed a bag of sangi, the red-positive and black-negative counting rods.

Shigetsuna posed this problem to Hiraku: "Suppose five large containers and one small container together hold three koku of rice, while one of the large and five of the small containers together hold only two koku. Show me what is the capacity of the large and small containers."

It was one of the classic problems from the ninth chapter of the *Chiu-Chang Suan Chu*, written during the Han dynasty. Hiraku could not read Chinese, of course, but Shigetsuna had personally taught Hiraku the method.

Hiraku arranged the *sangi* on the board: one and five, five and one, and two and three. He then multiplied and subtracted several times. When he was done, he had zero and one hundred twenty, twenty-four and zero, seven and sixty-five.

"The small container holds seven twenty-fourths of a koku, and the large one, thirteen twenty-fourths."

Shigetsuna cleared his throat. "The answer is...Correct! Thank you, Hiraku."

"And now Date Iroha-hime will play for us on the *koto*."

Lord Commissioner Sakai coughed. "That merchant's boy— Hirako, is it?"

Date Masamune reluctantly corrected him. "Hiraku."

"He is quite bright. A crane in a flock of fowls, neh?"

"I am not so sure," said Masamune. "His father has a head for numbers, too."

A servant shuffled by. "Some wine, my lords?" The Japanese of California didn't have sake, because of the problems they had experienced cultivating rice, but they did have wine made from the wild grape of California.

After his cup was refilled, the lord commissioner pressed his point. "Large fish should not live in a small pond. The boy should be in Japan, where he can sit at the feet of the greatest of scholars."

"Perhaps. But how is that possible? He is the son of a merchant, and he is a *kirishitan*."

"Easily solved. I will adopt him into my own family! He will then be a samurai, and of of course he will become a Buddhist and thus can reenter Japan."

Date Masamune, a father himself, was silent for a moment. "You do him a great honor. But please, do not speak of this publicly yet, I must make proper investigation of the boy's genealogy, and whether he was born under auspicious stars. My astrologer will need your birth sign, too, to make sure you're compatible."

Lord Sakai guffawed. "You sound like an old go-between, warning the family elders that they need to find out more about the bride they've been offered. But do what you think necessary."

A messenger brought Lord Sakai's offer to Hiraku's parents, and Takuma and Mizuchi stared at each other.

"What do we do now?" Mizuchi asked, wringing her hands. "He's only nine years old. If we hadn't left Nagasaki, it would be another year or two before he would start an apprenticeship."

"We must admit that is a far better opportunity then any possible apprenticeship. And if he did start an apprenticeship, you know that he wouldn't be allowed to visit home for five years."

"Yes, but we could come to see him. And when his apprenticeship was done, he could return home and help you." She held her hand to her mouth. "You realize...you realize that we would never see him again! We are exiles, remember."

Takuma pondered this. "I want...we want...what's best for Hiraku, but to never see him again, yes that would be hard to bear. But couldn't he come to see us?"

Mizuchi picked at her kimono. "I suppose. But the journey across the Great Sea is dangerous. And would he be allowed to return here for good? To see him for a few months, a decade from now—I think it would break my heart."

"And then there's the religious issue," Takuma reminded her.

"Yes, in Lord Sakai's house, he could not be a Christian. And if he does not remain in the Faith, he is damned."

"So...we refuse?" she asked hopefully. "With extreme apologies, of course?"

Takuma fidgeted. "I wish I was sure the decision is ours alone. If we displease Lord Sakai, what will happen to us? Not just our family, but to all of us?" Takuma was now a respected if junior member of Shigetsuna's staff; he had heard the rumors that the lord commissioners had power to cut off the colonists' umbilical cord back to the motherland. What would the grand governor do if Lord Sakai was angry? Hiraku might be taken from them, even without their consent. The three of them might be sent off to the cinnabar mine, or forced to leave and live, if they could, with the wilderness Indians. And their friends could be made to suffer on account of their refusal.

They talked about it for hours. If only they had not lost Takuma's father. They needed his counsel now. They opened the *butsudan*, and burned incense before it. Even as they prayed for his guidance, they despaired. More than forty-nine days had passed, and so he was no longer merely a spirit of the dead, a *shrei*, he was a *niisenzo*, a new ancestor. But it would be thirty-three years before he was a full ancestral spirit, a *sorei*.

They could, in theory, pray to the *sorei* of earlier generations. But they were Buddhists; only Takama's father had been a *kirishitan*, and thus likely to be sympathetic to their plight.

They prayed, also, for the intercession of *Maruya-sama*, the Virgin Mary. She had refused to marry the king of Roson, according to the stories they had heard; perhaps she would reveal to the Yamaguchis how they could safely refuse the commissioner's offer to adopt Hiraku.

The next morning, Mizuchi told her husband, "*Maruya-sama* came to me in a vision, she said to speak to Iroha-hime, the grand governor's daughter."

Iroha heard them out, then gave them her opinion. "I will not say whether this adoption is a good thing or a bad one, only how it might be prevented without dangerous repercussions.

"By itself, the fact that your son has been raised as a Christian is not likely to be considered a strong enough objection."

"To take him out of the Church will doom him to hell!"

Iroha-hime sighed. "That's not how the lord commissioner will see it. You know the proverb; 'there are many paths up the Mountain, but the view of the Moon from the top is the same.' Lord Sakai thus would not think it consequential to ask Hiraku to change from one Buddhist sect to another. And considering that Christianity is now labeled 'the evil religion,' he may think he is doing your son a favor to lead him back to Buddhism, whichever temple he chooses.

"But I think it helpful that you are not a mere Christian follower, you are a baptizer. A member of the ecclesiastical hierarchy, neh? And so we can remind the lord commissioner that many of the Shinto priestly posts are hereditary."

"What of it? I am not a priest! And the Christian priesthood is not hereditary. Why, the priests don't even marry!"

"Those are details we need not trouble the lord commissioner with. And besides, from what I have heard, it is not unusual among the European nobility for the second son of each generation to enter the priesthood. That makes it hereditary in a practical sense, I think.

"Anyway, he cannot interfere with the normal inheritance of priestly positions without the approval of the commissioner of Temples and Shrines. Who is, alas, an ocean away."

Takuma and Mizuki relaxed, ever so slightly.

"And I think there is a second string we can fit to this bow. There is the matter of filial piety. He is your only child, who else is there to care for you in your old age?

"Let me speak with your son; I must coach him as to exactly what to say."

Hiraku bowed deeply. "Most Honorable Lord Commissioner," he piped. "I have spent hours in prayer and meditation, seeking to understand whether it is the will of Heaven that I accompany you back to Japan." He declined to mention whether he had the Christian or Buddhist Heaven in mind.

"I must consider, not only what is best for me, but what is best for my family and my community."

The lord commissioner nodded in approval.

"Greatly though I would value the opportunity to accompany you across the Great Ocean, I must remember the teachings of Confucius: 'If your parents are living, don't go on a long trip.'

"Also, eager though I am to sit at the feet of the great mathematicians of the realm, I must consider it my duty to put my poor skills at work where they are most needed, in this New Nippon, an island in a sea of, of..."

Iroha mouthed the word he was looking for.

"...barbarism. Not only as a mathematician, but also as a keeper of the sacred water, like my father before me." Shinto also had water purification rituals, and this, Iroha-hime knew, would logically call to the lord commissioner's mind the practices of Shintoism, including priestly inheritance.

Hiraku took a breath. "Moreover, I have not accomplished any great feats of mathematics yet; I am still unworthy to be adopted by so great a lord. Instead, I ask that I be permitted the honor of incorporating a single *kanji* of your name into my own." This was common enough, actually. Japanese changed their names on certain occasions; for example, when a samurai child became an adult, usually at age fifteen, he would take an adult name, which included a character from the name of his father or godfather.

Hiraku bowed again.

"Well, that was well spoken," the lord commissioner said. "If that is truly what you want..."

First-to-Dance reached for another mallard feather. She hummed as she carefully inserted the feather between the stitches of the basket she was finishing. It had to stick out enough so that the colors could be seen, but not so much that it would tear out easily.

She had no need to make baskets, of course; her Japanese connections had assured her access to premium trade goods, and by Ohlone standards she was extremely prosperous. She had even been courted by the eldest son of a chief of the Uypi, who lived on Soquel Creek, near Kodachi Machi/Santa Cruz. But unfortunately for him, her aspirations had changed.

So. Japan. Should she go? The sea journey would be long and frightening, of that she was certain. But Lord Commissioner Sakai, the friendly one, had promised that if she came, he would look after her as if she were his own daughter.

Chiyo had told her that she had been described to the lord

commissioner as being an "Indian princess," and to say nothing to contradict that. The higher her assumed status, the better she would be treated.

Was it worth it? It would bring her to the very center of power, Edo Castle itself. The contacts she would make! The advantages it would give her people! The profits it could bring her! It made her head spin, just thinking about it.

But wait a minute. She knew from discussions with Chiyo and her other Japanese female friends that Japanese women were expected to be seen but not heard. In public, at least. That would make it rather difficult for her to make any deals.

Unless... Unless she picked the male Indian. One who was impressive to look at, easy to push around, and spoke no Japanese whatsoever. Or at least willing to pretend that he didn't. So she would be his "translator." She smiled. He would babble something, and she would say whatever needed to be said.

She would miss Toshiro Kanesada, of course. But it wasn't as though there weren't plenty of samurai in Japan!

Chiyo had warned her to expect to be exhibited to the shogun's other guests as an exotic discovery. She didn't mind that, either, within reason. As long as the shogun didn't decide to make her a permanent part of his menagerie. Chiyo's father would, of course, obliquely and delicately remind the shogun's councillors of the diplomatic importance of permitting her to return, but the shogun's whim was still law. So there was an irreducible risk.

Still, life was full of risks.

First-to-Dance looked at her basket. It was made in the traditional way, from woven shoots and roots, dyed in vegetable colors, but it showed a grizzly snarling at a dragon, the latter copied from one of Chiyo's sake cups. The grizzly was brave and powerful, but she had no doubt that the dragon would prevail if the grizzly insisted on fighting.

"I will go to Japan," she announced. "If I may choose my companion, that is."

The lord commissioners were seated on a dais, with their herald on a mat nearby.

Date Masamune was on a second, smaller dais, facing them, with his son and Shigetsuna flanking him. His daughters, Iroha and Chiyo, were nearby, hidden beyond a screen. Other high-ranking samurai of the New Nippon colony sat in ranks behind Date Masamune, and servants stood just outside the audience room, ready to enter if summoned.

"At least I am not on the white sand," Masamune whispered to Shigetsuna. This was a reference to the place where prisoners and witnesses knelt before a magistrate.

The commissioners' herald rose. "Date Masamune, Echizen no Kami, Mutsu no Kami." Those were Masamune's formal titles, normally used only when he was presented at court.

"Grand Governor of New Nippon."

"On behalf of the mighty shogun of Japan, Iemitsu-sama of the Tokugawa, the lord commissioners Matsudaira-sama, Sakai-sama and Hotta-sama, as faithful servants of the shogun, have reviewed your governance of New Nippon.

"Hark now to their words." The herald bowed to the grand governor, and knelt gracefully in the formal *seiza* position, his buttocks resting on his heels.

Lord Matsudaira's gaze swept the room. "According to the records provided to us, some six thousand Nihonjin, of whom five thousand were *kirishitan*, left Japan with the First or Second Fleet. Of these, perhaps nine in ten survived the journey. Of those, about eight in ten are still alive.

"Before leaving Nippon, we consulted with the Red Hairs as to what losses might reasonably be expected in establishing an overseas colony. Based on what we were told, you have done well in minimizing loss of life."

Lord Matsudaira took a sip of tea from the cup placed beside him. "Questioning has revealed that there have been some religious disturbances, resulting in the internal exile of certain intransigent Christians. We expect you to remind the *kirishitan* that their religion was banned in the homeland because of such intransigence and that intolerance will not, ah, be tolerated. The treatment accorded to the *kirishitan* awaiting transport, and the continued support of this colony, depend on obedience to the Edict of Exile!

"We are pleased to note that besides extensive fishing, you have been able to plant and harvest several crops since the formation of the colony, thus reducing the amount of supplies that the colonists of the Third Fleet have had to bring with them.

"However, the failure to raise rice remains a concern."

Masamune coughed.

"You have a comment, Governor?"

Masamune nodded. "Last year we explored the delta of the Sacramanto and San Joaquin Rivers. The ground appears suitable for rice cultivation, and according to the Indians there, the Karkin, the summers are warmer than here. My intent is to send some of the *kirishitan* of the Third Fleet there as soon as they fully recover from the rigors of the sea passage."

"I will pray to Inari for your success," said Lord Sakai.

"But will Inari care what happens to a pack of *kirishitan*?" Lord Hotta muttered. "In my—"

"I commend you," said Lord Matsudaira. "This delta is far away, is it not?"

"It is some days' journey by land. Once we have more horses—which of course we can breed, so we don't have to keep bringing them across the sea much longer—the journey will be easier."

Lord Matsudaira spread his hands. "I confess that until I sailed down the coast, I had no real conception of just how large this America is. Now I do.

"Masamune-san, while we may disagree with some of your decisions, we do not doubt your loyalty to the shogun, or that the colony of New Nippon has prospered under your leadership.

"But we do question whether so large a realm, with so few Nihonjin amidst many savages, can truly be governed by a single man. You are confirmed as grand governor of the province of New Nippon, but we must insist that the province itself be divided into two or more domains. We decree that the Monterey Bay area shall be one *han*, and we appoint your son, Date Munesane, as its daimyo. Since he is now a Christian we think this is logical.

"We leave it to your discretion to appoint a second daimyo, for the *han* of San Francisco Bay. This, I assume, will include the Indian's cinnabar mine, your fishing village on the South Bay, the new Dutch settlement at San Francisco, the new copper mine near 'Oakland,' and the rice paddies you plan for the Sacramento-San Joaquin Delta. And the gold fields of the American River, once they are definitively located."

Date Masamune heard a faint sound from behind the screen.

"The third han would be 'Thousand Islands' and would include Vancouver Island, Texada Island, and any other nearby island or coastline worth taking. Please remember our understanding that Texada Island is to be occupied by Buddhists. We will make the arrangements for suitable colonists to be sent out with the Fourth Fleet."

"And you better start sending us iron," added Lord Hotta.

Lord Matsudaira held up his hand. "Our information is that the Indians of the region are of a warlike nature. We think that a military commander of your experience belongs there, not here in California. Unless, of course, there is an imminent threat from the Spanish in New Spain."

"We expect you to develop a proposal for the administration of settlements between San Francisco and Vancouver," Lord Sakai added. "But for the moment there aren't enough Nihonjin there to matter."

Lord Matsudaira stood, followed an instant later by his colleagues. "Congratulations, and good luck, Grand Governor."

"I envy you, Masamune-dono," Lord Sakai added. "I know you would prefer not to spend the remainder of your life in idleness, and die in bed."

"May the buddhas and kamis watch over you," said Lord Hotta.

The lord commissioners walked out and returned to their suite.

"The world is dark, yet can I see to walk, the silver moon illuminating my path," Date Masamune murmured.

𝔖tretching 𝔒ut
ℭast of ℭharacters

Story Abbreviations

AMAZ: Amazon Adventure
2STARTS: Second Starts
MARMISS: Maria's Mission
BEYOND: Beyond the Line

TIGER: Riding the Tiger
KING: King of the Jungle
SUNMOON: Tears of the Sun,
Milk of the Moon

Abbreviations

OTL: Original time line
NTL: New time line
HDT: Historical down-timer

A few characters are omitted. A complete cast of characters, with additional details for some characters, will be available online (see Afterword).

Adrienszoon, Dirck: Captain of the *Eikhoorn*, later commandant of Fort Lincoln, guarding approaches to Gustavus (Paramaribo). (**TIGER, SUNMOON**)

Afia: Young Ashanti woman. (**SUNMOON**)

Aka: Ndongo warrior. (**KING**)

Ama: Ashanti woman, Chief Antoa's wife. (**SUNMOON**)

Antoa: Coromantee (Ashanti), leader of the Ashanti rescued by the Gustavans. (**KING, SUNMOON**)

Aossey, Leila "Lolly": Middle school science teacher, girl scout leader, gardener. Friend and landlady of Maria Vorst. (**2STARTS**, mentioned in **MARMISS, TIGER, SUNMOON**)

Bartley, David: Precocious financier. (**2STARTS**)

Baum, Lorenz: Master carpenter, Gustavus colony, in early 1636. Not to be confused with the sawyer, Denys Zager. (**SUNMOON**)

Borguri: Imbangala leader. (**KING**)

Bender, Heinrich: Gustavus colonist from Heidelberg, blacksmith, later bauxite miner and member of colonial militia. (**MARMISS, TIGER, KING, SUNMOON**)

Berry, Edna: One of the "Plant Ladies." (**2STARTS**, mentioned in **MARMISS**)

Blauveldt [Blauvelt, Bluefields], Abraham (HDT, d 1663?): Privateer and explorer, associated with Old Providence Island colony and exploration of coastal Honduras and Nicaragua. (**BEYOND**)

Claus, Carsten: Organizer for Committees of Correspondence, assigned to the USE's Suriname colony founded in early 1634 at Paramaribo. Later, the acting governor. (**MARMISS, TIGER, KING, SUNMOON**)

Coqui ("Frog"): Manao Indian, Kasiri's brother. (**AMAZ, TIGER, KING, SUNMOON**)

Cornelis: Lower steersman (second mate) of the Walvis. (**BEYOND**)

da Costa, Henrique Pereira: Portuguese criollo (born in Brazil but of European descent), orphan, Marrano (secret Jew), da Costa family factor in Belém do Pará, Estado do Maranhão (northern Brazil) and one of its first residents (which implies that he came there in 1616 or soon thereafter), backwoodsman, started first Hevea rubber tapping operation of NTL. (**AMAZ, TIGER, KING, SUNMOON**)

Dreeson, Elva: Middle school art teacher. (**2STARTS**)

Faye: Leader of the Mandinka rescued by the Gustavans. (**KING**)

Gentileschi, Prudentia [Prudenzia] (HDT): Daughter of Artemisia Gentileschi and Pierantonio Stiattesi, friend of Maria Vorst, sent to Grantville in August 1632, became part-time assistant in middle school and high-school art classes in Grantville. (**2STARTS, MARMISS**)

Gribbleflotz, Dr. Phillip Theophrastus: Alchemist and astrologer; searches for the "perfect aluminum pyramid…" (**2STARTS**)

van der Goes, Jan Adriaanszoon (HDT): Commander of Fort Kykoveral on the Essequibo. (**AMAZ, TIGER**)

Heesters, Kaspar: DeVries's "facilitator" in Grantville. (**2STARTS**)

Jenkins, Phil: Son of Walt Jenkins, in canoe competition. Has interest in "forestry and forest management," which leads to him working with Maria Vorst. (**2STARTS, MARMISS, BEYOND**)

Kasiri ("Moon"): Manao Indian. (**AMAZ, TIGER, SUNMOON**)

Kojo: Ashanti tribesman. (**KING, SUNMOON**)

Krueger, Michael: Gustavus colonist. (**TIGER, KING**)

Lawler, Irma: One of the "Plant Ladies." (**2STARTS**, mentioned in **MARMISS**)

de Liefde, Heyndrick (HDT): David de Vries' cousin. (**2STARTS, MARMISS, TIGER, KING, SUNMOON**)

Lowe, Hugh: In 1633, the former president of the Grantville Chamber of Commerce, and MC for the Grantville Investment Roundtable. (**2STARTS**)

Lucala: Leader of the Ndongo rescued by the Gustavans. (**KING**)

Marshall, Captain _____ (HDT): Leader of the 1630 English Puritan settlement at Marshall's Creek, Suriname. (**MARMISS, TIGER**; mentioned in **BEYOND**)

Maurício: Henrique's servant, African descent, son of one of Sergio da Costa's housemaids, born into slavery, trained as an interpreter, manumitted by Henrique. (**AMAZ, TIGER, KING, SUNMOON**)

Mueller, Johann: Journeyman glassmaker from Lauschasent to Gustavus (Paramaribo, Suriname) colony. (**MARMISS, TIGER, KING, SUNMOON**)

Neilsen, Captain _____: Captain, Danish airship *Sandterne*. (**SUNMOON**)

Parente, Bento Maciel (the Younger) (HDT): Slaver-explorer, son of the Capitan General of Pará. (**AMAZ, SUNMOON**)

van Rijn, Dirck: Gustavus colonist. (**SUNMOON**)

Rishworth, Samuel (HDT): Minister to Old Providence Island colony, early European opponent of African slavery. To learn more about him, see Kupperman, *Providence Island, 1630–1641: The Other Puritan Colony* (1995). (**BEYOND**)

Schellinger, Jan Tiepkesz(oon): Captain of the yacht *Eikhoorn* in NTL December 1632. In OTL, commanded the *Rensselaerwyck* on its voyage from Amsterdam to New Netherland, September 25, 1636–April 7, 1637. (**2STARTS**)

Schooneman, Jakob: Captain of *Koninck David*. (**BEYOND**)

Scott, Francis: Captain Marshall's second in command. (**MARMISS**)

Smoot, Jan: Gustavus colonist. Some kind of shopowner. (**SUNMOON**)

Soares, Captain Diogo: Captain of the garrison of Belém do Pará. (**AMAZ**)

von Sommersburg, Count August: Count (Graf) of Sommersburg county, an imaginary geographical entity, essentially Soemmerda and other territory north of Erfurt. USE Secretary of Transportation in 1633. (**2STARTS**)

de Sousa [Souza], Francisco: President of the Municipal Chamber of Belém. (**AMAZ**)

Stein, Erasmus: Bauxite miner in Gustavus, 1636. (**SUNMOON**)

Stull, Joseph: In 1633, managing transportation matters for NUS. (**2STARTS**)

Temakwei: Lenape Indian. (**2STARTS**)

Tetube: Woman from an Arawak-speaking tribe in northern Suriname. (**KING, SUNMOON**)

Vijch, Marinus: Captain of yacht *Hoop*. (**BEYOND**)

Vorst, Adolph [Vorstius, Adolphus] (HDT, OTL 1597–1663): Maria's brother, son of Aelius Vorstius. (**2STARTS**)

Vorst, Maria: In 1632 she arrived in Grantville, a widow (husband lost at sea somewhere in Asia) and amateur artist with a botanical bent. (**2STARTS, MARMISS, TIGER, KING, SUNMOON**)

de Vries, Captain David Pieterszoon (HDT, c1593–OTL 1662): Sea captain, explorer, founder of the "Gustavus" (Paramaribo) colony in Suriname. (**2STARTS, MARMISS, BEYOND, KING, SUNMOON**; mentioned in **TIGER**)

Yost, Andrew: Manager of Grantville Freedom Arches, leader of local Committee of Correspondence. (**2STARTS**)

Zager, Denys: Master sawyer for Gustavus colony. (**MARMISS, TIGER, KING**)

Rising Sun
Cast of Characters

Story Abbreviations

CUCKOO: Where the Cuckoo Flies
LEAVES: Fallen Leaves

GEESE: Wild Geese
WIND: Autumn Wind
SCREAM: Night Heron's Scream

Abbreviations

OTL: Original time line
NTL: New time line
HDT: Historical down-timer

Japanese honorifics

In conversation, honorific suffixes are attached; -sama for a superior, -sensei for a teacher, -san for an equal, -dono for an equal of high rank, -hime for a lady of samurai or noble rank. I also used the endearment -chan ("dear") for females. The "-san" evolved from "-sama." The honorific can be attached to a title, a family name, or a given name, the last being less formal.

Cross-References

All main entries are given last name first, which is the traditional order for Japanese names. Because of this, I have also included cross-references by first name.

Benzo, see KOBAYASHI
Chiyo, see DATE
Haru, see TERASAKA
Haruno, see YAMADA
Hiraku, see YAMAGUCHI
Hyonai, see KONISHI
Iemitsu, see TOKAGAWA
Iroha, see DATE
Isamu, see OYAMADA
Jacob, see de VEER
Jinbei, see HOSOYA
Jiro, see SANADA
Kanesada, see TOSHIRO
Kanzaburo, see NAKUMURA
Katsuo, see KATSUO
Kuroemon, see SAKAI
Masamune, see DATE
Masayuki, see HASUNUMA
Mizuki, see YAMAGUCHI
Motonori, see MONIWA
Munesane, see DATE

Nagato, see SAITO
Nagatoki, see MATSUOKA
Nobotsuna, see MATSUDAIRA
Nobuyasu, see RUSU
Pieter, see van SANTEN
Saburo, see SANADA
Sadamitsu, see HASEGAWA
Shigehisa, see DAIDOJI
Shigenari, see KANNO
Shigetsuna, see KATAKURA
Tadaaki, see ABE
Takuma, see YAMAGUCHI
Tadakatsu, see SAKAI
Tadateru, see MATSUDAIRA
Tadayoshi, see SAKAI,
Takara, see NAKAMURA
Tomomochi, see SUMITOMO
Yajiro, see IMAMURA
Yoshitsune, see WATARI
Yoritaki, see HOSOYA

❖   ❖   ❖

Abe Tadaaki (HDT, 1602–OTL 1671): Senior councillor to the shogun. (**CUCKOO**)

Campen: Captain of the Dutch ship *Blauwe Draeck*. (**LEAVES**)

Churoku: Peasant farmer in Niji Masu. Militiaman. (**WIND, GEESE**)

Daidoji Shigehisa (HDT): A samurai in Matsudaira Tadateru's household before Tadateru's disgrace. In story, Lord Matsudaira's lieutenant and "guard commander." (**GEESE**)

Danzaemon: "Official" name for headman of the eta of Morro Bay. (**SCREAM**)

Date Chiyo-hime: Date Masamune's daughter, born later than 1613, possibly to a favored concubine. (**LEAVES, WIND, SCREAM**)

Date Iroha-hime (HDT, 1594–OTL 1661): Eldest daughter of Date Masamune, divorced wife of the disgraced Matsudaira Tadateru, reunited with him upon his NTL rehabilitation. (**GEESE, SCREAM**)

Date Masamune (HDT, 1567–OTL 1636): Nicknamed "One-Eyed Dragon." Daimyo of Rikuzen (Sendai). Renowned military commander. In new time line 1634, appointed grand governor of New Nippon (California). (**LEAVES, GEESE, WIND, SCREAM**)

Date Munesane, baptized **"David"** (HDT, OTL 1613–1665): Masamune's sixth son. (**LEAVES, WIND, SCREAM**)

First-to-Dance: Ohlone Indian, emissary to the Japanese. (**LEAVES, WIND, SCREAM**)

Franciscus, Tanaka: Japanese born Franciscan brother (irmao). (**WIND, SCREAM**)

Gombei: Takuma's assistant in Monterey Bay colony. (**SCREAM**)

Gorosaku: Eta and hunter. (**SCREAM**)

Hachizaemon: One of the mates on the *Sado Maru*. (**GEESE**)

Hanako: Wandering nun affiliated with nunnery at Kamakura. (**CUCKOO**)

Hasegawa Sadamitsu: Officer in the service of the Lord of Beppo, in charge of Japanese Christian prisoners. (**CUCKOO, LEAVES**)

Hasunuma Masayuki: Junior samurai stationed at cinnabar mine in 1636. (**SCREAM**)

Heishiro: Japanese captain of shipwrecked merchant ship *Yahiko Maru*. (**LEAVES**)

Hikobei: Eta hunter. Nicknamed "Little Giant" by the Chumash. (**SCREAM**)

Hosoya Jinbei: Senior retainer of Date family, older samurai at Kawa Machi/Salinas. (**GEESE, WIND**)

Hosoya Yoritaki: Commander of the *Ieyasu Maru*'s samurai marines. (**LEAVES, GEESE**)

Hotta, Lord: Commissioner sent in 1636 to evaluate Date Masamune's rule. (**SCREAM**)

Hotta Masamori (HDT, 1606–OTL 1651): Junior councillor, OTL 1633, senior councillor, OTL 1635. (**CUCKOO**, Mentioned in **SCREAM**)

Ihaku (HDT): Physician. (**WIND**)

Imamura Yajiro: Supposedly, a Japanese Christian dojiko (lay catechist). In fact, a Tokuguawa onmitsu (spy and agent provocateur). (**LEAVES, WIND**)

Inawashiro Yoshimichi: Daikan responsible for Eta Village on Morro Bay, but based at Santa Cruz. (**GEESE, SCREAM**)

Inoue Masashige (HDT, 1585–OTL 1662): A chief inspector for the shogunate. (**CUCKOO**)

Iwakashu, "Singer-to-Rocks": Pseudonym of mining engineer and prospector in Date Masamune's employ. (**GEESE**)

Kanno Shigenari (HDT, 1596–OTL 1636): Date Masamune's close retainer and formerly the personal loader of his matchlock gun. Guard Commander of Kodachi Machi. (**WIND**)

Katakura Shigetsuna (HDT, 1585–OTL 1659): Chief councillor to Date Masamune in New Nippon.

Keeps-Canoe-off-Rocks: Chumash Indian, acts as guide to Inawashiro Yoshimichi on his jade hunt. (**SCREAM**)

Kenji: Assistant headman of the eta settled at Morro Bay. (**SCREAM**)

Kinzo: Coxswain of *Ieyasu Maru*. (**LEAVES, GEESE**)

Kiyoshi: Foreman of Matsudaira Tadateru's miners. (**GEESE**)

Kobayashi Benzo: Samurai stationed at Kodachi Machi (Santa Cruz) in 1636. (**SCREAM**)

Kodama Katsuo: A ronin in Edo. (**CUCKOO**)

Konishi Hyonai: Village headman of Niji Masu/Pajaro. Grandson of a ji-samurai. (**WIND, GEESE**)

Koya: Maid to Date Iroha-hime. (**GEESE**)

Little Otter: Alsea Indian, younger son of Standing-on-Robe. (**LEAVES**)

Magome Joseph "Anjin" (HDT): Hatomoto in the service of the shogun. Half-Japanese son of William Adams, English pilot. Recruited to assist in translation of up-time English texts given to the shogun. (**CUCKOO**)

Marina: Christian fisherwoman, settled in Andoryu. (**WIND**)

(Deguchi) Masaru: Samurai under Yoritaki. (**LEAVES**)

Matsudaira Nobotsuna (HDT, 1596–OTL 1662): NTL commissioner sent in 1636 to evaluate Date Masamune's rule. (**SCREAM**)

Matsudaira Tadateru (HDT, 1592–OTL 1683): Sixth son of Tokugawa Ieyasu, and uncle to Shogun Tokugawa Iemitsu. Married Date Iroha-hime. Disgraced in 1615–19 and forced to divorce Iroha and become a Buddhist monk. In story, provisionally rehabilitated and given command of an expedition to San Francisco Bay and the Gold Rush country. (**GEESE, Mentioned in SCREAM**)

Matsumoto: Matmaker in Nagasaki and neighbor of Takuma. (CUCKOO)

Matsuoka Nagatoki (HDT, 1564–OTL 1644): The senior of Date Iroha-hime's two personal guardsmen on the *Sado Maru*. (GEESE)

Mika: Date Chiyo-hime's maid. (LEAVES, WIND)

Moniwa Motonori: Daikan of Niji Masu/Pajaro. (GEESE, WIND)

Murata: Peasant farmer in Niji Masu/Pajaro. (GEESE, WIND)

Nakamura Takara: A physician in Osaka, on pilgrimage. (CUCKOO)

Oyamada Isamu: Samurai with naginata, under Yoritaki. (LEAVES)

Rusu Nobuyasu: Aide to Date Munesane. (WIND)

Saito Nagato: Senior samurai stationed at cinnabar mine in 1636. (SCREAM)

Sakai Tadayoshi: Commissioner sent in 1636 to evaluate Date Masamune's rule. (SCREAM)

Sakai Kuroemon: Samurai in charge of the small battery guarding Andoryu. (WIND)

Sakai Tadakatsu (HDT, 1587–OTL 1662): Senior councillor (*roju*) 1624–OTL 1638. Tairo ("Great Elder"), OTL 1638. (CUCKOO, LEAVES)

Sakuzo: Japanese Christian fisherman living in Maruya/Carmel. (WIND)

Sanada Saburo: Samurai in Matsudaira Tadateru's service. (GEESE)

Sanada Jiro: Samurai in Matsudaira Tadateru's service. Saburo's older brother. (GEESE)

van Santen, Pieter (HDT): Chief Dutch factor in Japan in OTL January 31 to September 6, 1633. (CUCKOO)

Shima: Young woman, Takuma's neighbor in Monterey Bay colony. (SCREAM)

Standing-on-Robe: Alsea Indian. (LEAVES)

Sumitomo Tomomochi (HDT, 1607–OTL 1662): Coppersmith, on pilgrimage. (CUCKOO)

Swims-Like-Seal: Member of same tribelet as First-to-Dance. (WIND)

Talks-While-Walking: Ohlone Indian, assigned to act as translator for the eta. (SCREAM)

Tasman, Abel Janszoon (HDT, 1603–OTL 1659): Dutch captain. (LEAVES, WIND)

Terasaka Haru: Samurai under Yoritaki. (LEAVES)

Togu: Peasant farmer in Niji Masu/Pajaro. (GEESE, WIND)

Tokagawa Iemitsu (HDT, 1604–OTL 1651): Shogun of Japan (the third Tokugawa shogun). (**CUCKOO, LEAVES**)

Tokubei, "Tenjiku" (HDT, 1612–OTL c1692): Upper steersman (first mate) and supercargo of Japanese ship *Ieyasu Maru*. (**LEAVES, GEESE**)

Toshiro Kanesada: Former ronin, now in service to Date Masamune. (**GEESE, WIND, SCREAM**)

de Veer, Jacob: Upper steersman (first mate) of the Dutch ship *Blauwe Draeck*, and past visitor to Hirado, Japan. (**LEAVES**)

Watari Yoshitsune: Young samurai in Date service, at Salinas. (**GEESE, WIND**)

White Cloud: Northern (Obispeno) Chumash Indian. (**SCREAM**)

Yamada Haruno: Captain of Japanese ship *Ieyasu Maru*. (**LEAVES, GEESE**)

Yamaguchi Daizo: Takuma's father, retired. The Yamaguchis are commoners so this is not a true surname, but most likely an indication of geographic origin. The modern city of Yamaguchi didn't exist yet but the name literally means the "mouth of a mountain," i.e., a mountain pass. (**WIND**)

Yamaguchi Takuma: Merchant. Japanese Christian from Nagasaki (on Kyushu). Mizukata (baptizer) of his group of hidden Christians. (**CUCKOO, LEAVES, WIND, SCREAM**)

Yamaguchi Mizuki: Wife of Takuma. (**CUCKOO, LEAVES, WIND, SCREAM**)

Yamaguchi Hiraku: Son of Takuma, Official age of seven as of efumi ritual conducted on February 14, 1633. (**CUCKOO, LEAVES, WIND, SCREAM**)

Yakichi: Christian fisherman, younger son, initially settled in Andoryu/Monterey, became mentor to Christians in Maruya/Carmel. (**WIND**)

Yells-at-Bears: Woman of the Snuneymuxw (Coast Salish) Indians. (**LEAVES**)

Zhang: Chinese doctor, visitor to Japan. (**LEAVES**)

Afterword

For those readers who want to know more about my source
material, and why I used it the way I did, I am making detailed
author's notes available at www.1632.org in the "Gazette Extras"
section. So if you want to know, say, the real-life inspiration for
my account of the capture of the slave ship in "Riding the Tiger,"
or why I thought that the anti-Christian shogun Iemitsu could
plausibly agree to ship the *kirishitan* into exile, that's where to look.

By presenting them online, I can make them more detailed
than if I included them here, and I can also update them in
response to questions (or new research).